The Afflicted

A Novel

Andy Strutt

ArrowGate

Published by Arrow Gate Publishing Ltd
London
14 13 12 11 10 9 8 7 6 5
Copyright © Andy Strutt 2013

Arrow Gate Publishing's titles may be purchased in bulk for educa-
tional, business, fund-raising, or sales promotional use. For information, please email arrowgatepublishing@ymail.com

Arrow Gate Publishing Ltd Reg. No. 8376606

A CIP catalogue record for this book is available from the British
Library

ISBN 978-0-9575930-7-7

www.arrowgatepublishing.com

Arrow Gate Publishing Ltd's policy is to use papers that are natural,
renewable and recyclable products and made from wood grown in
sustainable forests. The logging and manufacturing processes are
expected to conform to the environmental regulations of the country
of origin

Printed in the United Kingdom

To my wife Narissa without whose help and support I would never have finished this novel

"Live as if you were to die tomorrow. Learn as if you were to live forever."

– Mahatma Gandhi

One

Gleaming amongst the run-down prefabricated industrial units stood the ultra-modern Swiftgene genetics research facility. It was the jewel in the crown of the small Hove community, nestled right on the outskirts of Brighton city centre providing much needed employment in the area during the worst global recession in decades.

The building was impressive, a testament to architectural ingenuity; a piece of modern art made from concrete, steel and glass. The grounds outside were professionally landscaped and the entire perimeter was surrounded by a plethora of mature trees flown in from all over the world with no expense spared. The block parking spaces were marked with bricks of different shades rather than the usual tarmac and white paint. The interior décor was no different. As with many of today's corporate giants, its walls were a mixture of classical and modern art, and on first impression it did not lend itself to being a futuristic, cutting-edge genetic research facility. There were dozens of laboratories all stocked with the latest scientific gadgetry, everything you could possibly need to manipulate the genome and push back the frontiers of science.

A tall, athletically built man stood in the far corner of one of these laboratories dressed in threadbare trousers and a stained, crumpled shirt, looking strangely out of place amongst the modern surroundings. In his hands, he held a stack of printouts from one of the nearby machines and he scratched his head unconsciously as he attempted to review several days' worth of analytical data.

Despite appearances, John Simmons was definitely not out of place in the lab. He was in fact one of the world leaders in the field of genetic engineering, even though his bedraggled appearance suggested otherwise. In the years he had spent at Swiftgene, he had been personally responsible for decoding and reporting the gene sequences for several of the world's most potent diseases as well as designing a plethora of new genetic strains of animals and plants. It was very different from his early career teaching molecular genetics at Cambridge University, where he had utilised his access to their well-funded labs to begin a distinguished career in research. He had enjoyed the position tremendously and had only relinquished it following a long and painful divorce, escaping to West Sussex with little more than the clothes on his back and an old Honda Civic. He often reminisced about the good times he had spent expanding the minds of young students eager to learn the craft.

Unnoticed behind him, a bearded man dressed in an expensive designer suit had made his way over and was waiting patiently for the preoccupied scientist to notice him. Richard Jennings was the managing director of the Swiftgene facility at Hove, a hard taskmaster and extremely unpopular amongst all levels of staff. What made it worse to most of them was the fact that he was a mediocre research scientist who understood very little of what they did. Like many people in his position, he had crawled his way up the slippery management slope by proving to be a cold, calculated sycophant who knew the right people to please and by standing on the shoulders of other, more talented, scientists.

John had, however, sensed his presence and decided to ignore him, even though Richard stood almost directly behind John, tapping his foot impatiently. Richard was annoyed by his subordinate's lack of respect, something that made John a bit of a hero amongst the other staff. Finally, Richard's patience wore thin and he cleared his throat in an exaggerated manner, forcing John to acknowledge him, albeit with a disgruntled look on his face, barely disguising his contempt for the older man.

"Morning Richard, what can I do for you?" he asked, forcing himself to use a pleasant tone of voice whilst putting on a strained smile.

"You promised me an update on the gene sequence separation two days ago. Have you managed to isolate the correct fragments from the test cultures yet?" Richard asked rudely, skipping any pleasantries as was his manner.

"I haven't provided you with an update because I've not finished growing the cultures. I can't isolate what I don't have, can I?"

John replied, this time not even attempting to hide his annoyance.

Richard's face showed no recognition for John's tone of voice and continued to harass him.

"You told me you would have this done by now. We need to move this forward as soon as possible," he said crisply, ignoring the scientist's sarcasm.

"Richard, it doesn't matter how much pressure you put on me. I can't make the cultures grow any quicker and I can't separate the correct vectors until the bacteria have finished multiplying. If I'd started the separation, we wouldn't have enough material for the trials," John tried to explain, his irritation growing every time the man opened his mouth.

The Afflicted

The Escherichia Coli he was currently attempting to ferment was a common species of bacterium found everywhere in nature and was a favourite test subject of the geneticist because of its ease of use. The public, however, shied away from it because of its association with several cases of food poisoning caused by the consumption of raw or undercooked beef. The batch he was working with had been cultured and was now growing quite happily in the sample ovens under optimum reproductive conditions, but as he had told Richard on several occasions, the process was still very slow when large amounts of material were required.

Richard, noticeably oblivious to the feelings of others, had started to discern the other man's growing anger and knew that if he pushed too hard, John would just become more obstructive. To prevent the discussion from declining any further, he decided to take a different approach and chose to appeal to John's scientific vanity instead.

"Look, I'm sorry. I didn't mean to sound so pushy. It's just that we're all very excited by your preliminary report. The company is trying to secure more private sector funding and based on your early results, we've invited potential investors to visit sometime this month, on a date still to be arranged. It would be to everyone's benefit if we had managed to isolate enough material to begin testing by then. These types of people are difficult to please and the fact that they're keen to get on board tells you that they believe in the potential of your work, but if we have already begun trials, then they are more likely to agree to part with cold hard cash," Richard said smoothly, making sure he complemented the man's scientific prowess.

John appeared to relax a little, but he still wanted to make sure Richard had no illusions as to the position of his work. He was a perfectionist and preferred to take the time to do something correctly rather than rush it for the benefit of others.

"Richard, I appreciate your enthusiasm but these are the first large scale cultures we've attempted. If we want to start the first phase of testing, we must have plenty of starting material to harvest enough of the appropriate DNA vectors. The good news is, once the fermentation is complete, it won't take me very long to have the first batch of serum ready," John said, gesturing to the rows of large glass bioreactors bubbling away in the sterile incubators.

John sympathised with the management for the bureaucracy they faced and understood that his work was only possible with the correct financial backing, but he personally did not have time for internal politics. He loved to do a pristine job, because doing a rushed job would inevitably lead to mistakes and occasionally even the death of test subjects.

"No problem, I understand, but can you at least give me an approximate timeline and an explanation of where you are? Then I can give them an update to keep them happy. For starters, what are you doing to remove the target genes from the bacterial cells?" he asked, attempting to compromise with the reluctant scientist.

John was about to reply when he noticed Richard's attention unexpectedly drawn elsewhere. He was now peering with interest at a young woman who had just entered the lab. She was smartly dressed in a short business skirt and flatteringly cut blouse, although her bland white protective footwear spoilt the overall effect. She spotted them and began to walk over, pulling on a lab coat as she approached and beaming broadly at the pair of them.

She was slim and exceptionally attractive, one of the reasons John had noticed her around the building, but no one had introduced them. Richard was also smiling, obviously pleased to see her and rapidly losing interest in the conversation with John.

A little perturbed by the interruption, John continued with his explanation regardless, tapping on Richard's shoulder to regain his attention as the newcomer strode confidently across the lab and joined them, leaning against a nearby bench so she could eavesdrop on their discussion, all the time smiling sweetly.

"As you may be aware, all bacteria are prokaryotic and therefore have the ability to divide into two identical daughter cells that are exact duplicates of the original. They can repeat this process indefinitely, barring accident or foul play, as long as the correct nutrients are present, in effect making them immortal. Eukaryotic organisms, such as us, have cells that are only able to divide a finite number of times before transcription errors, mutation, or death of the cell occurs. Bacteria don't experience this as they have an array of mechanisms responsible for repairing cellular and DNA damage. I've identified the genes responsible for those processes and then isolated them from the first test cultures. When those cultures were allowed to reproduce, the cells only managed to divide a certain number of times before the damage made them non-viable and they died. In effect, I gave them the ability to age the same way as our cells can," he explained.

Looking at Richard's blank expression, John realised his boss didn't have the slightest clue about cellular division. A minor oversight when you manage a genetic engineering firm. The woman, however, had been listening with interest and had no problem comprehending the theory.

"Really! You managed to halt the repair processes during binary division? So any replication damage to the DNA is transmitted to the daughter cells and therefore prevents the expression of certain proteins?" she asked, tucking her long flowing blonde hair into a hair band as she spoke, revealing a long slender neck with perfectly smooth, slightly tanned skin.

Since no one had formally introduced them, John stared at her suspiciously, wondering what her interest was in his work. Given her well turned out appearance, he had wrongly assumed that she was in management, or possibly administration. A little confused he answered, wondering exactly what her profession was,

"In theory yes, this means that I've isolated the genes responsible, at least in part, for the aging process."

Richard was now well out of his depth and used the opportunity to interrupt the conversation. He had no interest in the actual mechanics of the process. He just needed to know enough to attract the investors, as they themselves were only financiers concerned with the product and its potential for profit.

"Sorry John, I wasn't sure if you'd met; this is Dr Guinevere Taylor, another of our resident molecular geneticists. She works in the Genetic Reconstruction Department," Richard said, finally introducing the newcomer.

A look of awkward realisation spread across John's face; he had heard the name banded around his section. He considered it office rumour and had paid little attention; however, the rumours had spread through the entire company like wildfire. Dr Taylor was an up and coming star, a leader in the field of reverse DNA replication and as a company, Swiftgene was exceptionally fortunate to have enlisted someone so talented. The problem was, if the rumours were true, she was supposedly dating Richard, a fact that had already made her very unpopular.

Not a man to prejudge someone, and knowing he had seemed a little rude, John offered the attractive woman his hand.

"No, we haven't met, but I'm familiar with her work," John answered. "Dr Taylor I make a point of reading as much published work within the field as I can, and your theories are some of the most advanced I've read for a long time. If I'm not mistaken, you're attempting to reverse engineer therapod dinosaur DNA from a modern avian species?" he asked politely, his interest piqued.

She was tall and slim with long flowing blonde hair, stunningly attractive and had a figure many women half her age would kill for. She shook his outstretched hand gently and her delicate fingers felt cool and soft against his. Smiling, she nodded politely in acknowledgement. Guinevere looked him straight in the eyes holding his gaze, and he noticed that she had the most striking blue eyes he had ever seen.

They seemed to twinkle mischievously under the bright fluorescent lighting.

"I am extremely flattered you are aware of my work. Unfortunately, most geneticists regard me as a pariah as there isn't much credibility associated with my line of research thanks to the Jurassic Park films. You are, however, correct and we intend to create an actual, viable embryo in the future and maybe even take it to full term," she said modestly, shaking his hand enthusiastically and allowing her hand to linger in his.

The extended contact suddenly made him feel a little uncomfortable and John withdrew his hand gently but firmly.

He moved back a little, staring at her.

"Don't be so modest, the scientific community may not agree with your choice of subject, but I assure you the techniques you've developed are cutting edge and respected by many, myself included," he answered, his flattery entirely sincere.

"Thank you," she said, blushing slightly, "and I'm thoroughly familiar with your earlier work on the mapping of bacterial and viral genomes. That somehow pales when compared to your current project though. I can't believe how far you've progressed from the preliminary findings in such a short time. Can you clarify one point that I was a little unsure about?" she asked, her professional interest in his work apparent.

11

Andy Strutt

"Of course, it's always good to meet someone who shares a common interest in the mysteries of DNA," said John smiling. He was already beginning to find her quite charming, a trait not always found in people as attractive and intelligent as her.

"Am I correct in assuming you are going to attempt to splice the prokaryotic gene sequences you isolated directly into a eukaryotic genome? Because if you do that successfully, you would potentially have discovered a cure for aging, a modern day fountain of youth," she inquired excitedly, understanding perfectly the potential implications to the future of medicine.

For the briefest of moments John wondered if the young woman was purely mocking his outrageous intentions and he found himself trying to read her tone of voice. She looked at him expectantly and her facial expression definitely suggested fascination and sincerity, so he decided to give her the benefit of the doubt. He was not in the habit of making enemies unnecessarily and even if the rumours were true, it served no benefit to alienate her before knowing her better.

"That is the extreme version of the theory, yes. After all, there are many factors associated with the aging process. What I'm more interested in is the cellular repair mechanisms and their use in treating genetic disorders. As you know, there is a small question surrounding the division of the nucleus; unlike eukaryotic cells, prokaryotes don't have them and that could be a problem. It may well be that the new genes may not work if a nucleus is involved," he replied, "if so the project would be dead right there and then."

She nodded to show her understanding, but still found the whole possibility intriguing, grasping concepts in seconds that older and more experienced scientists would never understand, Richard being one of them.

"Of course, that's a good point, but surely it depends on the delivery method. How are you intending to introduce the DNA vectors through the cell membranes, and once there how will they target the correct position in the genome?" she asked, articulating with her hands excitedly in an attempt to emphasise her meaning.

John was definitely impressed. Gwen had an excellent professional reputation and he was beginning to realize that it was well earned.

Against his better judgement, he found himself warming to her. It was nice to talk to someone without having to 'dumb down' the conversation. Relishing her fascination, he continued with the explanation.

"Firstly, I have converted the fragments into their equivalent messenger RNA counterparts, enabling me to assimilate them into a sterilised flu virus from which I have removed the ability to reproduce. Then I packaged the newly constructed RNA strand into a modified bacteriophage casing designed to target specific sites on eukaryotic cells instead of their usual bacterial hosts. When infection occurs and the genome is injected through the cell membrane, the viral enzymes convert the RNA back to DNA before finally inserting into the targeted gene sequences. If successful, this will transfer the required codes to produce the proteins responsible for cellular repair directly to the host cell," he explained, the tone of his voice growing in pitch as his enthusiasm began to show through. He could tell she was thoroughly excited about the potential for his work unlike Richard, who at this point in the conversation did not understand a single word and was beginning to look a little awkward.

"Look, you two, can you save the technical talk for some other time? John, what I want to know at this moment is when do you think you will have enough material to begin the first phase of primary testing? I need a reliable estimate to satisfy the investors... Can you provide one?" Richard asked rather abruptly, interrupting the discussion.

Annoyed again by his rudeness, John turned to face Richard and despite his irritation, managed to keep his temper in check. It was becoming a habit to have to hide his obvious contempt for the man's complete inability to grasp the most fundamental aspects of genetic manipulation, despite being in charge of a company specialising in it. John picked up his tattered leather bound notebook and began to flick through the pages. The book was his lifeline where he kept all his ponderings and personal observations, stuff that would never see the pages of an official report. He found the page he was searching for. Marking the position with his finger and staring into the distance, he began his calculation.

"The cultures will be finished later today. I'll separate the bacterial samples out tomorrow then extract the DNA vectors and convert them to RNA by Friday. The fragments will have to be multiplied using the PCR equipment and reconstituted, so they will be ready no earlier than Wednesday next week. However, you must understand the complexity of the process, so it's only an educated guess," John said, offering no assurances.

"I suppose we'll have to live with that then, but keep me informed if anything changes," Richard said quietly. He was a lot happier now he had the information he needed and turned to leave without saying another word, scribbling something into his Filofax as he strode away. Gwen, however, had not finished grilling John and stayed to finish their discussion, fascinated by his theories.

"Dr Simmons, I am extremely interested in how you intend to target the correct sequences in the genome to insert your fragments into, let me guess you're..." she started to ask, but Richard interrupted from the other side of the lab.

"Dr Taylor, have you got a moment? I would like to catch up on your research, if you please?" Richard's tone of voice hinted that it was not a suggestion but a command.

Richard had expected Gwen to follow him on his way out and was a little envious at the way the pair seemed to have bonded in such a short time, their interest in genetics uniting them. When he had first met her it had been much more difficult for him to gain her attention. She had shown very little interest in him, forcing him to go the extra mile to gain her attention. Richard also hated the way other men constantly stared at her, and being an intensely jealous man, Gwen's eye-catching appearance and pleasant disposition was a constant challenge to his ego.

Gwen's reaction to Richard caused John to smile; she had rolled her eyes in exasperation, suggesting that she found his manners, or lack of them, to be an annoyance. John found this little observation of great interest; romance held little room for irritation, especially this early in a relationship. Ignoring Richard momentarily, she once again offered her outstretched hand to John.

"Dr Simmons, it really has been a pleasure and I look forward to finishing our little discussion at some point. I'm going to enjoy finding out more about your work," she said politely, smiling as she shook John's hand.

She turned and walked over to Richard and John could tell by her body language that she was very angry. He chuckled to himself as Gwen's slightly raised voice as she approached Richard indicated her displeasure. They disappeared through the double glass doors of the lab.

What a strange couple, John thought. She must be at least ten years younger than Richard and probably twenty times brighter. What he did notice, however, was the hypnotic sway of her perfect hourglass figure as she walked. She moved with all the grace of a catwalk model, even wearing flat-soled safety shoes and a lab coat. Seeing her so well dressed and looking smart made him feel a little self-conscious about his ancient bedraggled clothing, something that did not usually concern him. He returned to his notes smiling thoughtfully; he could certainly appreciate the attraction from Richard's point of view, but John could not fathom her interest in him.

Andy Strutt

Two

John checked the cultures at the end of the day and although the results were good, he decided to leave the bioreactors running overnight as a precaution. In the field of genetic research one usually had so little material to work with that the larger the sample of material to extract from, the greater the chance of success.

Finished for the day, he trudged across the dimly lit company car park. As usual, he had stayed far longer than he had intended, and a good portion of the evening was now gone. John often lost track of time since the divorce, having nothing to rush home to other than hours of mindless drivel on the television. He had recently obtained a large digital flat screen and satellite dish, so at least now he could watch it in crystal clarity, but sadly it did not improve the content.

As he approached his battered red Honda Civic, he smiled affectionately. She was twenty years old and he could barely keep her running, but she held fond memories for him. Regrettably, however, he doubted if she would pass the upcoming MOT test, forcing him to invest in a new car. He climbed into the ancient vehicle, the rusty door creaking loudly in protest as he pulled it closed. Crossing his fingers, he turned the ignition key, hoping the car would start at least once more and smiled thankfully as the engine coughed and spluttered to life.

The drive home was relatively uneventful and fifteen minutes later, he pulled up outside the dingy one bedroom flat he called home. Without getting out, he stared at the dirty windows feeling a little depressed, unwilling to face another night of soap operas and film repeats. He glanced in the opposite direction towards The Black Dog pub, deciding instead to partake in one of his favourite pastimes, the consumption of large volumes of alcohol.

The Black Dog was like many small village pubs, a fire burning in the hearth, piebald seats and garish horse brasses hanging from the ancient wooden beams, but it was close to home and the staff were always friendly. He glanced around as he entered and, as usual, the place was virtually empty. In one corner, an old man nursed his pint of ale as he watched a young couple holding hands near the ancient slot machine. Emma, the rather buxom landlady, was leaning against the inside of the bar, her auburn hair a warning of her occasional fiery temper, the effects of which he had been unlucky enough to witness a couple of months ago when a loud-mouthed youth had become a little brash with her. John cringed in horror just thinking about the dressing down the young man had received, much to the amusement of his mates.

"Usual, Dr Simmons?" she asked in her usual welcoming tone, smiling as he joined her leaning on the bar.

"Please, Emma. And for the last time my name is John," he replied, resting his foot on the base of a barstool and glancing around once more.

"Whatever you say Dr Simmons," she replied, pulling on the pump handle and smiling, refusing as always to comply.

Emma was old fashioned. She thought anybody who had worked hard enough to earn the title ought to take pride in it, as she had reminded him on several occasions. He smiled wryly as he waited for his beer, handing over the exact change in exchange for his drink. He carried his drink over to his regular table in the corner, not interested in any conversation and sat down, deep in contemplation. Today was the anniversary of his son's death five years ago. His life had been so much different then; he had a beautiful wife, a lively but sweet seven-year-old boy, a large house and a prestigious job lecturing at Cambridge University.

Mark, his son, had been plagued with an extreme case of asthma from birth. Routinely taken to hospital with severe attacks, added to the fact that he had enough allergies to have a journal named after him, the boy certainly did not have the greatest start in life. However, he and his wife, Brenda, had been so proud of the boy; the way he managed his condition independently, refusing to let it get him down, astounded them.

He was full of life and got annoyed at his parents whenever they tried to molly-coddle him.

John remembered those good old days fondly - his life was a picture of perfection and apart from his son's occasional attacks, he had had everything he ever wanted. Then the outbreak began; swine flu, a terribly infectious disease that spread in weeks to every corner of the globe, infecting hundreds of thousands before it had run its course.

The first recorded case in the UK had been a couple returning from their honeymoon in Mexico. Next, an old man who had arrived on the same plane, and then it seemed that every day after that, more cases emerged until finally world leaders had declared a global pandemic. Swine flu had jumped the Atlantic Ocean, hitchhiking on the unsuspecting holidaymakers and was now spreading through the country like wildfire.

The government did everything it could but simply could not produce the inoculations fast enough, even after implementing a scheme to capture the more vulnerable members of society preferentially. The government selected Mark due to his illness, and he had been due to receive his injection the following afternoon when the worse that could happen, did happened.

He contracted the disease. Mark didn't stand a chance, even though they rushed him to hospital and the doctors placed him in intensive care immediately. Despite round the clock professional care, he grew weaker and weaker by the day and all they could do was watch him slipping away slowly. Unable to do anything more, the hospital had made the little boy as comfortable as possible, allowing him to spend his last few hours in a drug induced coma.

John had learnt from this experience, as only a parent could, the meaning of true loss. He was devastated but Brenda was inconsolable, lashing out at everyone and everything and almost losing her mind to grief. She had searched for someone to blame and John had been the easiest target. People like him were responsible for diseases like swine flu, she had accused. She had refused to understand why, with all of his training, he had been unable to lift a finger to help, on several occasions blaming him directly in public. He had been too upset to fight back, realizing that there was no point arguing, and quickly the perfect marriage had dissolved away into nothing. Her bitterness drove a wedge between them and the relationship became irreparably damaged. She had punished him further by taking everything, leaving him nothing but the clothes on his back, a few photos and the Honda Civic his father had given him.

John had not argued. He later learned to accept that it was not his fault, but at the time he had agreed with her. He had played out a hundred scenarios in his head, wondering if there was something else he could have done. Since signing the divorce papers, they had never spoken. The last thing he remembered as he walked away was her reprimanding stare. The hardest thing was that he knew as time passed she must have realised her mistake, but she had never sought him out or attempted to contact him.

He thought back fondly to the time they had spent with their son and smiled. The reason he had kept the car for so long was partially because his father had given it to him, but mostly because he and Mark had gone everywhere in it. John couldn't leave the house without Mark tagging along, something that had driven Brenda mad at the time. Now as he sat in the pub drinking one beer after another, the pain began to fade and he remembered the good times; the times which they had spent laughing and, little by little, the bitterness began to subside.

By closing time, he was completely drunk, barely able to stand and very fortunate that he lived just across the road. Despite that fact, the walk home still took him several minutes as he navigated the various hazards such as the curb, a parked car that appeared to match his every move no matter how hard he tried to avoid it and his house key with a life of its own, hiding in one of his pockets. He managed to get the decrepit front door open, knocking a great deal of the peeling paint onto his hallway floor in the process.

Slamming the door shut behind him, he staggered haphazardly through the flat, bumping into furniture as he went and knocking a dinner plate from the coffee table in the living room as he passed. He finally managed to find the bedroom and sat down heavily on the edge of the bed, picking up a photo from the bedside cabinet in shaky hands, studying it. Brenda's smiling face was a painful reminder of the past, Mark's boyish grin tugged at his heart, and John looked relaxed and even handsome. They took the picture in Bristol. John gently stroked the faces of his wife and son, bursting into tears as the grief came rushing back with the force of a storm. It was the same every year since it happened; he allowed himself this one night to remember them before forcing back the pain and going about his daily routine, throwing himself into the only thing left that mattered to him: his work.

John flopped back on the bed clutching the photo. Still sobbing, he lay there for a while staring at the ceiling before the effects of alcohol finally helped him fall into unconscious oblivion. Still clothed, he slept, his conscious mind no longer plagued by the demons of his past.

***

The week went quickly as John worked on the preparation of his new serum and very soon, it was Wednesday, the day he had predicted to Richard that the work could be finished. He arrived early in the morning, excited after leaving the DNA solution chromatographically separating overnight.

If everything had worked, the required samples would be ready for phase one of testing.

He darted briefly into his office only to dump his battered leather jacket and grab his old stained lab coat, which he pulled on as he headed for the lab. He pushed both swing doors open at once, banging them against the rubber stops in his eagerness and rushing past rows of complex looking analytical equipment covered in flashing lights and brightly lit LCD displays.

Along the entire backbench were a series of glass columns, each filled almost to the brim with a white crystalline solid designed to help separate the individual components of the samples he had diligently prepared. If he had done his homework, each of the individual components of the serum would be attracted by differing amounts, allowing the equipment to separate and purify them.

John spotted Brian, the student laboratory technician, and approached him eagerly to check on the progress. Brian was a twenty year old undergraduate on his year's industrial placement as part of his biochemistry degree and, like most students, lacked enthusiasm for early morning starts. As John approached, he was leaning back in a chair with his feet on the bench reading a heavy metal magazine.

"Brian, any problems overnight?" John asked as he loomed over him.

Shocked by the sudden appearance of his placement manager Brian jumped, almost falling out of his seat in the process. He hurriedly tucked his magazine into the nearest drawer and jumped to his feet.

"Bloody hell Doc! Don't creep up on me like that, I almost had a coronary," he said, placing his hand on his chest directly over his heart. He then stood looking expectantly at John, having not heard the original question.

"I asked if there have been any problems overnight. Did all the separations work okay?" John repeated, examining the remnants of the overnight experiment.

"Yes, everything went fine. All the cultures ran through the ion filtration media as expected and the automatic samplers collected fraction Number 20, except for this one," he said, leading him to one of the columns.

"What happened?" John asked.

"When I came in this morning the solvent pump had stopped for some reason, so the fractions did not separate correctly." He lifted the pump by its cable to show John, but it appeared normal and it still worked when he activated the switch.

"Not to worry, we still have twenty-nine pure samples which should give us enough material for hundreds of test subjects to begin with. Where have you put them? They still need to be kept secure," asked John, stressing the importance.

At this stage of the project, even the tiniest amount of manufactured product could be worth millions of pounds to a competitor.

There were no cases of proven industrial espionage in the pharmaceutical genetics sector but John did not intend to be the first victim.

"I put them all in the sample fridge," Brian answered, pointing to a row of tall silver glass fronted cabinets along the far wall. "I capped them all, then marked them up with a sample number and product name as you instructed. By the way, if you don't mind me asking, what does 'Methuselah' mean?" he asked curiously.

John smiled ironically, "I don't know if you're familiar with the bible Brian, but in the Old Testament there are several references to men who lived to be hundreds of years old. The most ancient of these was Methuselah who was reputed to have lived to the ripe old age of nine hundred and sixty-nine years old, if you believe in that sort of thing. We chose the name as a joke because of the theoretical effect on the aging process," he explained.

Brian looked at him bewildered and John let him return to his magazine, carefully moving the samples to the secure refrigerator in his own laboratory. Each of the senior researchers had one with keys held only by the owner, and Richard Jennings for security purposes. In John's mind they were essential; there were many inexperienced or student technicians in the building and it would be an expensive mistake if critical samples were to go missing or be damaged this late in the process. His own samples were the result of months of careful experimentation and preparation.

Satisfied that they were safely stored, John headed towards to the testing facility to check that the rats he had procured had been delivered and were settled in. He strode along with a spring in his step, more so than he had for years, having anticipated this day all week. He had worked long hours checking all elements of the process, meticulously collecting and recording copious amounts of data at every stage in the synthesis to eliminate any potential errors. Finally, they were ready for possibly the most crucial and definitely the most nerve wracking stage, the first clinical trials.

The potential for his new drug was overwhelming. John knew that if the serum was successful it would render thousands of different treatments and medicines obsolete overnight. His name would be recorded in historical texts alongside the likes of Alexander Fleming, the discoverer of Penicillin. With a project this earth shattering, it was not too far-fetched to expect a Nobel Prize nomination.

It was a hive of activity at the trial facility when he arrived, as cages were being set up along the three central benches. As dictated by the Medicines and Healthcare products Regulatory Agency, the room was spotlessly clean and designed to be entirely sterile. The strict guidelines in place instructed to keep the animals used in trials in as stress free an environment as was humanly possible. Despite the precautions, John always thought these rooms smelled slightly of damp animal fur and faeces even though the air was specially processed through high efficiency particulate air filters. He had designed the first round of experiments to test the effects of the serum on a type of cancer known as Hodgkin's lymphoma, a form that attacks the lymphatic systems producing painful tumors in the lymph nodes of its victim. He would treat ten of the rats artificially infected with the disease with Methuselah to assess the drug's potential effectiveness against cancerous tumours. He would also use two control groups of healthy animals - one treated with Methuselah and the other with harmless saline solution.

John watched with interest as a technician carefully placed the rats into their individual cages, while another recorded details from the certificate of origin onto a mountain of paperwork. It was a long, painful process but necessary to ensure traceability. To help, the rats were also issued with a radio frequency tag, each one of them uniquely identifiable, eliminating any chance of a mix up. They were all docile creatures, bred for generations in captivity in carefully controlled conditions and were well used to being handled. Each was fitted with a temperature sensor and other analytical probes designed to monitor their physiological condition. It was expensive to use this equipment but John had insisted; he was meticulous when it came to trial data.

There had been many horror stories in the past of drugs not being checked correctly, one of the most famous being thalidomide whose optical isomer had turned out to be a teratogenic compound causing severe birth defects in human beings. Nothing would be released from any trial for which he was responsible until he was one hundred percent certain it was safe.

John heard someone else enter the lab behind him and was not surprised to see Richard walking towards him. Given that he was such a poor scientist, John was a little confused as to why Richard was so involved in the practical side of the trials. People like him were usually more interested in the results and the potential income of a project, none of which they would be able to guarantee for several months. Being in a relatively good mood, John chose to ignore the fact that the man was probably just checking up on him and turned round to face him.

"Ahh John, you're finally in! Is everything ready?" Richard asked, taking an unsubstantiated dig at John's time keeping. John was old school and always arrived early and left late, working far more hours than his contract stipulated.

Gauging his mood as confrontational, John braced himself for another round of interrogation. He did, however, have a secret weapon; whenever Richard began to bug him, he would revert to speaking in extraordinary levels of technical detail. He knew his superior did not understand a word and he took great pleasure in making the man uncomfortable.

"Yes, all the animals procured are here and have been logged. We have managed to collect enough serum to treat around two hundred and ninety specimens. I am hoping to be able to perform tests on several of the target diseases over the next few months if everything runs smoothly," John informed him.

"What about this trial, will you be ready today?" Richard asked impatiently.

"We should be ready to start this one in a couple of hours, I just need to double check everything as a precaution," John informed him, noticing Richard seemed uncharacteristically edgy, as if he wanted to tell him something but did not know where to start.

In John's experience, that usually meant bad news for him.

"That's great, but before you begin there has been a slight change of plan, I have been speaking to the potential investors and they're extremely excited about your new product. So much so that we have some very attractive offers on the table already. Because of that, I have decided that we need to commit extra resources to the project. I have decided to assign Dr Taylor to the project to work alongside you. Someone with her background and credentials would certainly add a lot of credibility to your work," said Richard hesitantly, braced for John's negative reaction.

Richard personally didn't care what John Simmons thought about his decision; his motive was purely ulterior. He hoped that inclusion into a high profile project like Methuselah would soften Gwen up to his advances. Since they had met, she had refused any form of physical intimacy, protesting that she wanted to take things slowly. Besides, he was painfully aware that there was no glory in her field of research given its controversial nature, even though she adamantly defended her work.

John's reaction was initially one of surprise but quickly changed to anger at the obvious interference. Blood rushed to his face causing his cheeks to turn purple, the vein in his temple began to throb noticeably, and he let Richard have it with both barrels.

"I have spent more than eighteen months on this project and you expect me to just sit back and share the credit with some newcomer just because you are..." he began to say, cutting off his sentence halfway through.

It took an enormous amount of self-control but he managed to calm down a little. Getting annoyed at the boss was one thing; voicing an unsubstantiated rumour involving the managing director and a female member of staff was another. Although he didn't voice the opinion, he did suspect a little more than your average nepotism at play. His brief respite allowed Richard to interrupt and attempt to explain his obviously biased decision.

"Now you look here, Gwen Taylor is one of the leading experts in the field of genetic engineering. She would bring a fresh perspective to the project and I'm sure the extra pair of hands would come in useful," Richard snapped back at him angrily.

Though he knew his own motives were less than ethical, Richard did not like his decisions being questioned by subordinates, especially snivelling scientists like John Simmons. Richard had always been a little jealous of the man's intelligence and knew that John took great pleasure in making him feel stupid whenever he could.

"I don't care what her credentials are; it's a complete travesty to bring in someone new at this stage. I've spent a lot of my own free time making sure this project stayed on schedule and I refuse to be pushed to one side to let someone else take the credit for my hard work!" John responded threateningly, standing face to face with Richard.

He now stood mere inches from him and being a lot taller and better built, Richard suddenly felt quite intimidated. John had a laid-back attitude, rarely even raising his voice, but Richard had managed to provoke him and now he made no effort to hide his complete disdain. Richard took a precautionary step back and lowered his voice by several decibels, painfully aware there were now other people in the lab taking an interest in the confrontation. Unlike him, John was very popular and dressing him down in front of them would certainly not gain him their respect.

"John, you have my personal guarantee that you will receive full credit for your efforts. Everyone here, Dr Taylor included, recognises the amount of time and hard work you've already put into the project. You have done a fantastic job as we have come to expect from you, but you must realise how much extra credibility an internationally renowned geneticist like Dr Taylor would add to the project, not to mention the additional funding she would attract if the two of you were involved. You have no idea how important Methuselah is to Swiftgene, and all I want to do is make sure I have my best people on it," Richard tried to explain in a much quieter voice, knowing he could not afford to alienate Dr Simmons at such a critical point in the project.

But John was not ready to step down yet and was determined to have his say.

"In the case of this product, it's the results that will do the talking and not the qualifications of those doing the work. And for the record, I don't need to rely on the credentials of a young upstart like Dr Taylor, my own are more than adequate," he hollered at his tormentor, before turning away and striding towards the door, indicating he had no intention of discussing the matter any further.

John removed his lab coat and threw it onto the bench before slamming the door shut behind him. Richard was stunned by John's volatile reaction. He peered around the lab and watched as the technicians hurriedly returned to their work, amused by his predicament but frightened of his disapproval. With a scowl on his face Richard left the lab, his ego severely dented.

Once in the corridor he picked up his pace and headed off to find Gwen. At least she should be happy with the news, he thought. They had been dating for several months now but she still showed no interest in making their relationship physical and he was hoping that would soon change.

Pleased with himself, he strode confidently with a new purpose, forgetting about John Simmons for the moment.

Gwen was beavering away in her office when Richard arrived and she seemed mildly irritated when he entered without knocking.

Richard found, much to his surprise, that her reaction was not as he had predicted after giving her the news, far from it in fact.

"Are you crazy? Please tell me you're joking!" she exclaimed, standing to face him, her features twisted in disbelief.

"I thought you would be happy, you were only complaining last weekend that you didn't get the recognition you deserved. Working on this project with John Simmons is ideal; there would be international acclaim for everyone involved if Methuselah works as projected," he said incredulously, taking a step back in shock from the angry young woman. Being a corporate climber himself, her negative reaction to his help surprised him.

"You never listen to a word I say, do you? Or are you just too stupid to understand? Of course I would like to have more recognition, but for my work, not by shining in someone else's reflected glory. All the way through my academic career, people have accused me of climbing due to my looks and not my intellect. Now you have just played straight into their hands," she growled angrily, frustrated by his complete misinterpretation of her previous comments.

She wondered what her colleagues would think of Richard's stupid action and her expression changed from one of anger to one of embarrassment. She had already caught wind of some of the things people had said behind her back and she certainly did not want

John to believe that any of them were true; she respected his opinion too much.

"Oh my God! What do you think John Simmons is going to say? There are already rumours flying about the place that I got the job because we were going out, even though that started afterwards. What do you think they're going to be saying behind my back now? I won't be able to show my face ever again. Everyone will think I'm trying to sleep my way to the top and it wasn't even my choice, you moron!" she said, expressing her distaste for him clearly.

Gwen could already picture the gossiping faces and the furtive glances she knew they would give her when the news spread. She looked at the expression on Richard's face and realised he had been expecting her gratitude.

"I'm sorry you feel that way, but there's a legitimate reason to put you on the team. John is the only one who fully understands the work, especially the technical aspects of the process. I can't afford to leave myself in such a precarious position where a disgruntled employee could hold the company to ransom. There is more than you can imagine riding on the success of his work so I can't allow him to walk off and leave everyone involved in the lurch," he said, trying to defend his actions.

"What exactly are you asking of me?" she queried angrily with arms akimbo.

"I want you to learn everything you can about his work so he can never put me in a position like that," he told her, trying to qualify his decision as legitimate.

Gwen, however, was very intuitive and had noticed Richard's nervousness. "What do you mean 'too much riding on this project'? What are you hiding from us? Is the company in trouble?" she asked curiously, closely examining his expression looking for more clues.

Richard swallowed hard and became very defensive, eager to be out of her office all of a sudden.

"Of course not... just forget I said anything. All I wanted to stress is that I need to get you involved, that's all. It's purely a matter of business continuity. Wrap up your work for the moment; your project is officially on hold as of now. John is due to start the first trial today so I suggest you go and see him as soon as possible. I have already told him you have been reassigned," he answered nervously.

"I'm sure you have," she murmured, still seething with anger.

Richard ignored her comment.

"Anyway, I'm busy this morning so I'll speak to you later," he stammered, before he hurried away without giving her a chance to continue her interrogation.

The Afflicted

Gwen watched him curiously as he disappeared. It was not the first time she had seen him behave in this manner. Richard was always very secretive when it came to company finances and she began to suspect that maybe there was something untoward going on at Swiftgene. She made a mental note to herself to question him further when the opportunity arose, but for now, she began scribbling down a series of instructions for her technicians, determined to continue with her own work in secret, regardless of his instructions. He may be forcing her onto the Methuselah project but she had worked far too hard to abandon her research just like that.

Three

Half an hour later, Gwen found herself nervously approaching John's office door. She could see through the window and watched him digging angrily through his desk drawers. There were piles of paper everywhere with books stacked on every available surface except the bookshelves themselves, a complete contrast to her obsessively tidy office. He did not look happy and she guessed her reception would be less than welcoming this time. She swallowed hard, forced a smile, and knocked on the office door timidly. She opened it and stepped in without waiting for a reply. Gwen did not want to give him the opportunity to ignore her while she had the self-confidence to face him.

John turned round and upon spying her, his expression quickly changed from frustration to one of annoyance, standing there staring expectantly at her, refusing to initiate the conversation himself. She swallowed again, building up her confidence and began to speak.

"Dr Simmons, I understand you must be angry, but I want you to know that I had nothing to do with Richard's decision to put me on your project. The first time I heard anything about it was when he came to see me half an hour ago, so I had no idea he was planning anything like this at all," she said nervously.

Prior to that time, John had actually taken a shine to this attractive young woman and had been looking forward to spending more time with her, discussing their shared interest in genetics. Following his discussion with Richard that morning, however, his opinion had changed drastically. As far as he was concerned, the rumours he had been purposefully ignoring appeared to be true. He was more annoyed by the fact that he considered her talented enough not to need the assistance of a sleaze bag like Richard Jennings to further her career.

"Dr Taylor, I'm not particularly interested in who is to blame for the current situation. The only thing I'm certain of is that I will not allow you to come in and wrestle my work away from me. I've invested far too much time and effort for that to happen and I told Richard as much," he replied icily, his eyes cold as he looked at her with distaste.

"Dr Simmons, I have no intention of taking over your project. As I said, it was just as much a shock to me as it was to you. Richard has even told me to suspend my own project, something you of all people must understand doesn't make me very happy at all. I tried to refuse and he told me in no uncertain terms that I had no choice," she stated, stressing how strongly she felt for her own work.

She was close to a breakthrough that in itself would be internationally noteworthy, although not on the scale of something like Methuselah. Her words had no effect on John as he looked at her in disgust, despite his usual amicable self.

"I wouldn't worry about your research, Dr Taylor, I'm sure Richard has other plans for you. I mean, he is right; you're one of the most prominent figures in your field. What would I do without someone of your superior credentials to validate my own work?" he asked, allowing sarcasm to creep into his voice.

He watched her physically wince; making it obvious, he had hurt her with that last comment.

Gwen could understand John's failure in believing her, but she was not going to stand there defenseless and allow him to blame her for someone else's actions. The line of her jaw hardened and she took a step closer before snapping back at him.

"How dare you? You seem to have already made up your mind about me, why I am here and what my motives are, but I would have thought an intelligent man like you would have known better than to prejudge other people. You might not believe me, but I swear I had nothing to do with any decision, and despite what several people here think, I'm not just some blonde bimbo. I have a doctorate in molecular genetics from Cambridge University and I don't need to sleep my way to a better job," she responded angrily, challenging him to say another word on the subject.

Her reaction took John by surprise and he realised with embarrassment that he had also jumped to conclusions. She was correct; he didn't know what she was like and her reaction was not that of someone who was guilty of using her body to climb the corporate ladder. Examining her a little closer, her posture and expression suggested that maybe she was just as annoyed by Richards's decision as he was. He broke eye contact, staring down at his own feet and suddenly felt mortified by his own behaviour.

"I'm sorry Dr Taylor, that was bang out of order. I suppose I have jumped to conclusions without speaking to you first. I'm usually a good judge of character and you've given me no reason to doubt what you've just told me. I apologise for my outburst. Please accept that the situation is a little frustrating for me. I'm sure you can appreciate how it looks from where I am standing," he said quietly.

"Apology accepted, and I have to be honest with you, I think you're right. Richard's motives are exactly as you have said. He thinks Methuselah will help me climb the greasy pole but I must reiterate the point, he did it entirely without my knowledge or collaboration," she explained, her tone softening, relieved that John could at least see her point of view.

"I'm afraid your reaction has made it entirely obvious; you must be more than a little annoyed if he has postponed your project," said John with understanding.

"You don't know the half of it, but in the spirit of honesty and cooperation I can tell you that he has other reasons for my inclusion," she told him.

John raised his eyebrows with interest, "And they are?"

"Currently you're the only person who knows all the technical details and he's very threatened by that. He told me in his own words that he expects me to shadow you closely and make sure that situation changes as soon as possible. That's the reason my work was cast aside without a second's thought," she informed him, alerting him to the real conspiracy.

Despite his little outburst, Gwen had a great deal of respect for John and hoped he would reciprocate if she was totally honest. John glanced at her curiously; he had not expected that little morsel of information and it moved him a giant leap towards trusting her.

She hadn't needed to tell him and could have easily continued with the charade, reporting to Richard in secret.

"You mean he actually expects you to spy on me, a work colleague?" he asked for clarification.

Having taken the first step to convince him of her sincerity, she decided if they were to work together, there must be no secrets between them.

"Not exactly spy on you, just learn enough to re-move your potential leverage. I think the company must be having some sort of financial trouble because he stressed just how important your work was to Swiftgene. He wouldn't answer any of my questions on the matter, but it certainly seemed odd to me," she ex-plained carefully.

Gwen was amazed at just how easy she found it to open up to him, especially as she was dating the man they were discussing.

Something about his openness and honesty made her very comfortable. Usually she found it difficult with men, given that most of them were interested in her for less than honourable reasons.

John began pacing up and down the office mutter-ing under his breath before turning to face her.

"That conniving little toad! I'm almost tempted to walk out right this second and leave him high and dry," he threatened.

"Look, I'm not happy about the situation either, but I give you my word that I will not play the political game and report back to him just to satisfy his paranoia. On the other hand, I don't see why we should suffer just because he has delusions of grandeur either. Besides, after what he has done to us I would personally be happy to watch him squirm," she reassured the slightly older man who was smiling knowingly.

John sat down thoughtfully, examining the beautiful young woman in front of him with a fresh perspective. She really was an interesting character and he hoped she was on the level, otherwise he would find himself in a compromised position. Trusting his better judgment, he decided she was being honest and came to a decision.

"Okay, it will be useful having someone with your background to help out or to bounce ideas off. I certainly can't do that with Richard; he doesn't know his prokaryote from his carrot stew," John said.

Gwen chuckled at the reference and nodded in agreement.

"However, I want your agreement that this is my project and I take the lead. You can help me publish when we're finished and you will get your fair share of recognition. Do we have a deal?" he asked optimistically, offering to shake her hand.

"Deal, but I am not going to be a glorified lab assistant either. I expect to work alongside you as an equal, and that you'll keep me in the loop at all times. If you agree to that, I'll be happy to follow your lead. We can jointly decide exactly how much information Richard needs to know, bearing in mind this was not my first choice either," she stated.

John nodded without hesitation.

Gwen reached forward and grasped his hand, shaking it vigorously.

She realised that despite the abysmal way Richard had handled the situation, she had just been handed the ideal opportunity to work with one of the most talented geneticists in the world.

The additional benefit of a prestigious project like this would certainly enhance her CV as Richard had suggested, but she felt a lot more comfortable with the support of John Simmons.

"Agreed, then we're off to a flying start. Can you see a tatty brown leather notebook anywhere? It has all my notes and calculations in it but I can't remember where I put it," he asked, smiling hopelessly.

With barely a glance round the office, she pointed to his right hand, which was resting on top of the filing cabinet. Under his palm was the missing book, which he picked up and grinned sheepishly, blood rushing to his cheeks.

In the testing facility, the rats had settled in and the initial data had all been recorded. Having spent their entire lives in captivity, they were used to being moved from place to place and sat passively in their cages. They barely noticed humans scurrying around and remained both unaware and unconcerned as to why they were there. The only thing they cared about was access to water, food and a dry, comfortable nest in which to sleep.

A series of capped syringes were being prepared. Filled with a pale yellow liquid, they were placed along the benches, one in front of each cage. The doses had to be exact and John had measured and weighed each one himself to eliminate any potential errors. As the clock approached midday, John made his final rounds, checking every individual piece of monitoring equipment before picking up his ancient Dictaphone.

"Methuselah trial zero, zero, one. The ten trial subjects and the ten control subjects are about to be injected with the Methuselah serum. A further ten control animals will receive equivalent amounts of sterile saline solution. Subjects are equipped with automated heart rate, temperature and blood pressure monitors. On top of this, blood samples will be taken twice daily to analyse for the protein markers identi-

fied in report Simmons 110423. Positive identification will verify successful gene insertion," he said, speaking into the tiny device as he held down the red record button.

He gave a signal and three laboratory assistants, one to each row of animals, began injecting the rats in turn with the appropriate syringe. The animals were so docile they didn't even react to the needle hanging limply in the technicians' hands. Inside their bodies, billions of invading bacteriophage particles suspended in saline squirted into their turbulent blood streams. Instantly these particles were caught in the flow and circulated throughout their tiny bodies, passing to all the internal organs, muscles and tissue, before beginning to attach to the individual cells. Target receptors on the cell membrane walls activated the bacteriophage causing the invading genome to be injected through the cell wall.

The virus particles were ideally constructed, designed to act as billions of tiny hypodermics and yet they were not a creation of man, originally evolving to attack bacterial species. All types of cells gradually became infected, from the nephrons in the kidneys to the neurons in the brain, the virus quickly proliferating through every biological system in the body.

The animals' automated replication systems, evolved over millions of years, fired into action. First, they sliced up the RNA strands then converted them to DNA fragments and finally inserted them into the host's own genome. Within minutes, the fragments had been adsorbed and were indistinguishable from the original DNA. Unable to differentiate, the cells began to manufacture the new proteins, releasing them into the cytoplasm to begin the repair processes and enhancing the host cells as they did so.

In the blood stream, a few errant particles remained. Although significantly different to Methuselah, they were targeted just as well. These invaders also experienced biological changes, but they were alien to the host. Evolved to attack the blood constituents they changed as ancient genes were reactivated. These unknown invaders found themselves attracted to specific receptors on the concave face of red blood cells and started to attack. On entry, they immediately cannibalised the cell, recycling the material to produce copies and manufacturing a few dozen before the cell began to die. Each of these copies, however, was slightly different from the original. Mutated by the new proteins Methuselah had created, they carried some of the enhancements, but not all.

As the blood cells died, the membrane began to warp as tiny new bacteriophage cases were manufactured before finally releasing the modified contagion back into the bloodstream to start the process all over again. This alien virus was very adaptable and made its way into other body fluids, ready to be transmitted at any opportunity. The rats' bodies were not without defences though, and to counteract the infection their bodies began to produce various immune factors, helping to keep the harmful invaders at bay. As the blood cells were attacked, the body began to find itself requiring replacements. The production of bone marrow increased, with the combined effect of ensuring that the impact of the unknown virus was momentarily kept in check.

"When do you think you'll start to see the first signs that the therapy has been successful? Presumably the blood test will show any changes before we see any physiological changes?" asked Gwen, reading the report John had dug out for her that identified the gene sequences he had targeted.

The theory was sound, but as all scientists know, theories do not always materialise in real life situations given the number of variables involved, especially in the complex biological structure of a mammal.

"The treatment should be very fast. I would expect the majority of the bacteriophage to have already attached and inserted the new RNA. After that, the speed will vary depending on the targeted cell. Cells like muscle should absorb the new vectors very quickly. However, fatty tissue should take significantly longer.

Then you have the rates of transcription and translation that also vary. It could happen in a few minutes or up to several hours, though I would be disappointed if we didn't see some evidence of the new proteins in this evening's blood sample," John explained hopefully, showing her his crossed fingers.

She smiled understandingly, "Well we can only hope that with a bit of luck, by this time next month, if your theory is right, you'll be a very famous man."

"Let's not count our chickens before they hatch; there are still so many variables that can affect the outcome. If we insert the genes in the wrong place we may deactivate critical genes in the host's DNA. The effects from that could be devastating to the animals, so I would prefer to wait and see," he cautioned.

He secretly shared her optimism. It had crossed his mind once or twice in the past few weeks what success would do to his career, but publicly he chose not to jump the gun.

She returned to the report, subconsciously brushing her hair back over her shoulder exposing the delicate curvature of her neck. He had deliberately tried not to focus on her appearance, but the more he got to know her, the more he found himself gazing in her direction. He would not have been human if he didn't appreciate her good looks but, considering he was not a lecherous man by nature, doing so made him feel a little uncomfortable. In order to distract himself he took the opportunity to find out a little bit more about her project.

"Speaking of counting chickens, I was reading through your latest paper last night. Fascinating stuff! I was astounded to see that you had identified the gene required to activate the growth of a reptilian tail in the embryo of a chicken!" he exclaimed.

Turning to face him, she smiled broadly, her eyes twinkling with excitement but correcting his mistake.

"No, the gene was already active to grow the tail, but in modern birds, a new gene is activated which causes its re-absorption during the embryonic stage. That was the gene I discovered and all I did was switch it off and the tail continued to grow. In theory we can leave the embryo to full term and it would hatch with a small but distinct dinosaur tail," she said, happy that someone was interested enough to read her work without derision.

They chatted for several hours, Gwen catching up on the basics of the project and John enquiring about the ins and outs of reverse replication of therapod dinosaurs. Being quite amused that she had refused to shut down her project when instructed, he decided to add insult to injury and help her with it. After all, they both knew it would annoy Richard should he find out. Knowing there was no point in scrutinising the animals at this stage, they decided to take a long lunch and left Brian the lab technician to overlook the progress.

Next to the animal holding facility was an observation room fitted with a one-way mirror. It was currently in darkness. A figure was sitting with his finger on the intercom button that enabled him to listen to the conversation in the adjoining room without anyone observing him. His paranoia growing, Richard scowled as he watched the pair beginning to bond.

He already disliked John immensely and his distaste grew as he listened to their little plot to ignore his direct instructions about Gwen's work. There was nothing he could do about it, and if he tried to discipline them he would lose all co-operation from within the Methuselah project, and that was something he could ill afford at the moment.

Richard had been sort of dating Gwen for a few months; she was the ideal trophy girlfriend, but she was still unwilling to advance any further than a goodnight's kiss, ostensibly withdrawn around him and his friends. It provoked him to see John and Gwen laughing and joking together as if they had known each other all their lives.

He rose disgruntled and after checking to make sure there was nobody in the corridor, he quickly darted out of the room and made his way to his office. There he relaxed back into the large, comfortable leather executive chair he had specially ordered at great expense to the company. He picked up the telephone and tapped in a number that was now very familiar to him. Waiting patiently, he listened to the ringing on the other end of the line until someone answered.

"Hello, it's Richard Jennings; I'm ringing to give you an update on Methuselah. The first trial has started on schedule as I promised it would and Dr Simmons has confirmed that we should start to see the first effects by the end of the day if everything has gone to plan," he told his secretive contact.

To that day he had no idea who the person was or who they worked for, but as long as the money was good he didn't care.

"Did you dope all the samples with our little additive as instructed?" his contact asked firmly.

Richard was not even able to hear their true voice as they used some form of electronic scrambling device. He could not identify the gender of his contact at that point in time, not that it would have made a difference to him.

"Yes, I removed an uncontaminated sample first and sabotaged the equipment to make it look like it had failed. Then I spiked all the other samples as you instructed before the laboratory technician came in this morning. He bottled them all up without suspecting a thing. Are you sure Dr Simmons' analysis will not detect the foreign substance?" he asked apprehensively.

Richard had arrived at three o'clock in the morning and met security guards on site. He used an international conference call to America as a plausible excuse for the odd time to occupy the building. The samples had been easy to dose and now there was an unknown vector mixed with John's wonder cure.

"If you provided us with the correct analytical method for the gel electrophoresis then our additive will not be retained, the test will detect only the new Methuselah proteins. As long as you were not detected, we're safe," the voice confirmed.

"Yes, I guarantee I wasn't. Out of interest, what was the substance I added? Is it something that will affect the results of the trial at the early stages? If it does, Dr Simmons may postpone any further testing," Richard asked nervously.

Although he had promised his contact exclusive rights to the product, the longer he played out the situation, the more money he could obtain from the legitimate investors as well.

"That's none of your concern. All I need to do is make it public knowledge that you've been misappropriating company funds to pay off your own private gambling debts and you're finished. You have no choice but to follow my instructions to the letter, and whilst you do, I'll continue to pay you handsomely. Look at it this way, when I'm finished, you'll be an exceptionally wealthy man," the voice stated, subtly threatening Richard.

Richard had been desperate when his supporter had first contacted him. He had spent a lot of time with his wealthy friends in the casinos and unlike them, could not afford the extravagant lifestyle. In one visit alone he had lost almost half a year's salary trying to impress them. Suddenly, he had two mortgages and owed tens of thousands on several credit cards with nowhere near the means to pay it back. Facing bankruptcy, he had started by signing a few cheques to a false business he had set up himself. Greed had set in and soon there were more, the figures growing larger each time and the overall amount becoming quite substantial. Still addicted to gambling with his friends, his debts had continued to grow despite the regular influx of illegal earnings.

His contact had somehow known about everything and Richard's first worry had been blackmail. Instead, they had offered him substantial amounts of money in exchange for information about the Methuselah project. Richard had no option but to accept and found himself trapped in the deal, unable to stop even when he had cleared his debts. He had considered disappearing with the excess cash he had accumulated, but he suspected these were not people who would allow him to just walk away, so he kept feeding them the information. He had also continued with his private company and was now comfortably well off; although, he couldn't afford the lifestyle to which he thought he was entitled.

"Yes I understand that, but I'm a little concerned that your addition may stop John's serum from working. If he is right, we'll stand to make billions from this new wonder drug. I just don't want to see its development stopped by unnecessary complications," Richard said feebly, knowing that, for now at least, he would have to comply with their demands.

"Richard, thanks to all the research data you've sent me, I'm perfectly aware of the serum's potential. The theoretical increases to longevity and the treatments for a wide range of genetic disorders alone are quite astounding. What you have not considered is that once treated, patients will not require subsequent doses as the changes are permanent. At first, this would be an enormous market and anyone with shares in the project would become very rich very quickly. However, once everyone has received it, the market for Methuselah would dry up, and not just that, but hundreds of other money making medicines would become obsolete. What we've introduced renders Methuselah inactive after a short period of time and therefore guarantees future sales. Now do you understand why I needed to step in and take control of this drug?" the electronic voice asked rhetorically.

A look of realisation spread across Richard's face. He had never considered the consequences of what was a panacea. If they cured everyone, then Swiftgene would essentially be putting themselves and the rest of the industry out of business. If he allowed Dr Simmons' drug onto the market in its current form, it would ruin many people's livelihood. Shrugging, he replied, satisfied that for now at least he was solvent and could expect more payments in the future.

"Okay, I understand. Have you couriered the money as we agreed, £250,000 delivered straight to me in an unmarked parcel?" he asked, his greed now taking precedent over caution.

"Your money will arrive around noon tomorrow, exactly as we agreed. What about your part of the deal? Have you sent me the pure uncontaminated sample? It's imperative that we retain a sample of it for control purposes," the voice asked, abnormally eager.

"No problem, I popped out myself and posted it with a same day delivery service this morning, so you should have it later today. I couldn't risk using our shipping department just in case it was ever traced back to me," Richard replied with confidence.

He had tried to query the courier on several occasions about the location of the drop, but the address was only a cover and the courier was intercepted on each occasion. His contact wished to remain anonymous at all costs.

"Okay, that's all for now, but remember, you are to send me copies of everything. All research, results and processes as they are developed. Also, record any conversations you have with the team. Sometimes the most critical information is passed by word of mouth. We want to be able to reproduce Dr Simmons' process at a later date, but he must remain completely unaware of what we're doing," ordered the voice. It was obvious to Richard that his contact would not tolerate any disasters, especially so close to the solution.

The phone went dead, leaving Richard listening to the disconnected tone without so much as a goodbye. Smiling, he dropped the handset back on its cradle and leant back in his chair, placing his hands on the back of his neck, his fingers intermeshed to support the weight of his head. Whether he went with the legitimate investors or with his undercover contact, he stood to make an absolute fortune.

His preference now was to go with both, accumulating a sizeable nest egg for his retirement. He knew that sooner or later his dodgy transactions would be noticed, so he had only a finite amount of time to squirrel enough away. If he pushed it too far and somebody un-covered his indiscretions, Richard would certainly be facing prison time, hence the plan to rush the project through as fast as he could. His contingency plan was a substantial villa somewhere in South America where the weather was warm and nobody asked too many questions. However, one thing he knew was essential: it was time he avoided those damn casinos!

Four

After a well-extended lunch break, John and Gwen returned to the lab to find that one of the technicians had returned the results of the first blood test. John made them the highest priority, knowing he would not sleep a wink that night if he didn't have some good news, no matter how small.

"Dr Simmons, look at this!" exclaimed Gwen, excitedly passing him the crumpled computer printout, her sparkling blue eyes wide with amazement.

"What is it?" he asked, snatching the paper from her, finding her exhilaration contagious.

"Every single protein marker you predicted has been detected in every treated rat. You know what that means don't you? Your experiment is a one hundred percent success," she replied, beaming from ear to ear.

Much as she respected his talents, even she had been dubious about his claims of DNA absorption times and she could see from the look on his face that he was thinking exactly the same thing. John examined the sheet of paper thoroughly, not believing the evidence as he checked every single trace individually.

"It's even better than I had hoped; not only are we detecting the proteins, but look at the levels. The genes are already highly active," John added, the tone of his voice rising with hopeful anticipation.

John noticed that Gwen's face was glowing as she also meticulously checked the results for errors. He realised how alive she looked and self-consciously began to wonder how she perceived his shabby appearance.

"You must be very proud! Imagine all twelve of the inserted DNA vectors beginning translation this quickly. You would have assumed that they would activate at different rates, but you haven't missed a single gene," she said, pointing to the array of traces on the electrophoresis plate.

"It certainly looks like it," John said reflectively, not really paying attention to her as he scanned the results several times, the sceptic in him looking for a flaw. A perfect result at the onset of a trial was very rare as there was always the chance that he had overlooked something.

"John, do you realize what this means? You're the first geneticist to actively target and insert an external gene into the mammalian genome in a live subject. That process on its own could win you the Nobel Prize even if the rest of the experiment fails to work," she said smiling.

"Maybe," he said, still not paying her his full attention.

"In fact, with these results alone and your earlier predictions, I'd bet that you'll be nominated several times," she said, jumping up and down jubilantly before throwing her arms around his neck and giving him a tight celebratory hug.

Taken completely by surprise he rested his arms gently on her shoulders and gave her a tentative pat on the back. John could not help but notice the pleasant sensation her firm young body aroused in him as she pressed against him. He had not experienced these sensations since the divorce. Hurriedly, he stepped back to make sure his own body's reactions did not give him away. He felt blood rushing to his cheeks as he examined her smiling face, looking for any hint that she had noticed. She either had not or couldn't be bothered in the excitement of the moment.

Richard strolled in unannounced, snooping around to see if there was any progress. He saw Gwen throwing herself into John's arms and his twisted mind could not help but writhe with jealousy. He didn't appreciate any girlfriend of his behaving affectionately towards another man, especially someone like John Simmons. Joining them, he forced himself to smile while discreetly placing himself between the two, facing John and with his back to Gwen.

"What's going on? Has it worked?" he asked, feigning interest. His presence dispelled any excitement in the room instantly.

"The preliminary stages are certainly pointing towards that, yes, but as you know this is the first day and we need to analyze all the results first," answered John, his voice suddenly becoming serious and professional in front of his line manager.

He had, however, noticed the look of distaste on Richard's face and took great pleasure in the man's obvious discomfort, despite his overreaction. Unfortunately, there was nothing for him to be jealous about.

Gwen, annoyed by Richard's obvious rudeness, shoved him to one side so she could speak to them both at once rather than the back of her boyfriend's head.

"I agree with Dr Simmons, we need to proceed with caution. This is only the first trial after all," she said indignantly, staring reproachfully at Richard as she spoke, not that he seemed to notice, which irritated her further.

John, sensing the awkwardness, returned to scanning the results in an attempt to avoid any further discourse with Richard. He began to regret he had when he spotted a flaw. Now it was a proper trial, he thought.

"Hold on a second, there is something else here. Look on the electrophoresis results. We have an additional trace between proteins seven and eight that should not be there. It's faint now, but it definitely shouldn't be there. There is nothing in the untreated specimens suggesting that it's caused by the treatment," he said worriedly, holding the two traces side by side for comparison.

"Perhaps it's a metabolite or one of the expected proteins that is being denatured?" Gwen suggested, peering over John's shoulder at the two sets of results.

"I suppose it could be a denatured protein, but it's far too heavy to be a metabolite. Smaller molecules would pass straight through the sample media without being detected with this test method," John answered, now holding the results up against the light, "the worrying possibility, however, is that we have inadvertently activated another gene somehow."

Richard's complete lack of genetic engineering knowledge left him reeling and he began to feel a little uncomfortable. He had an entirely different suggestion for why the additional trace was present and, unknown to the others, he was absolutely correct. Not knowing the identity of the contaminant, he began to worry that the new material was something they could use to discover that someone had tampered with the samples. Relying on the little knowledge he'd retained from his years at university, he attempted to divert their attention.

"How is that possible? I thought you'd targeted specific regions on the host genome. Surely it's impossible for you to insert them elsewhere?" he suggested nervously.

"I did, the RNA strand was cut into the required fragments during the process but there would have been inactive portions left over. If one of these fragments were to be inserted accidentally, then it's possible that the new gene sequence created could actually be viable," John answered defensively.

"And what if that's true? What difference would it make?" Richard queried.

"If that's the case, then the protein could be the result of a statistical long shot. Another active gene, especially one we're not familiar with, would force us to shut down the trials until we can identify it. You must realise that a rogue gene could prove fatal to the host," John explained.

Obviously flustered, John collected the pile of paperwork and grabbed his notebook before disappearing out of the lab, muttering under his breath as he went. Much to Richard's disgust, Gwen went running after him and he really started to feel intimidated by how eager she was to spend time with John. It didn't matter to him that she had a valid scientific reason; Richard's envy was illogical.

However, he pushed his jealousy aside for the moment; one thing that was more important to him than any woman was money. If the project was delayed in any way then his cash flow could alter dramatically. Even worse, if the two scientists couldn't find another explanation for the new trace, they would have to scrutinise the original serum in more detail and that would reveal the contaminant he'd added. He doubted the finger of blame would point in his direction, but there would be a major hold up and possibly an investigation, one that could deter the investors from providing funds so readily.

"Damn it!" he cursed under his breath and headed out of the lab.

There was no point standing around waiting; he could only hope the scientists would discover an alternate explanation.

Back in the office, John and Gwen meticulously went through every result, bouncing dozens of theories off one another as to the cause of the thirteenth peak. As they discussed the problem both of them became intensely aware of each other's talents. After all, they were both leaders in their respective fields.

Despite the seriousness of their predicament, John found himself staring at her without realising it. He was ardently admiring her shapely figure and graceful demeanour and had begun to regard her as more than a friend. For the first time in many years, he was noticing a member of the opposite sex for her feminine charms, a thought that made him feel a little awkward. He had always prided himself on treating women with respect, refusing to view them purely as sex objects even as a hormonal teenager, yet here he found himself doing just that. John realised that he was happy that Richard had seconded her to the project in spite of his original intentions. Shaking his head for clarity, John forced himself to concentrate on the problem at hand and not get distracted.

"It can't be a contaminant in the original messenger RNA sample, I've checked the genetic markers for all twelve vectors, and they're all correct. Besides, I ran the analysis myself and there was only one trace on the results," John said, again running through the possibilities.

"Unfortunately your suggestion that we have somehow activated or created a new gene does seem to be the most likely option, but the odds of that are astronomical. We would have to examine the original genome from one of the rats and compare it to the new and improved one. Then we may be able to trace back to the viral RNA from which the fragment must have been taken," she suggested, looking sympathetically at her partner.

"And we both know a detailed analysis like that would take several months," he agreed reluctantly. "Not to mention the time it would take to redesign the Methuselah genome!"

She knew how much this had meant to him and placed her hand on his to comfort him, giving it a reassuring squeeze. Even as he found himself beginning to accept the inevitable, John found time to enjoy the warmth of her touch.

"The problem we have is that the protein produced could be anything. It may be totally benign or it could act on one of the body's critical systems," he said, trying to think of a way of determining the function without starting again.

John was surprised as she suddenly snatched her hand back from his and sat upright in her chair. She began rummaging through the pile of reports he had given her covering the majority of his initial research. The excited look returned to her face as she finally retrieved the one she had been searching for and handed it to him. He looked at the report detailing the twelve expected fragments with a bewildered expression on his face.

"We know what the twelve vectors are, it's the thirteenth we can't identify!" he re-iterated.

"I know, but there is one thing that we've failed to consider. All mammals share a common ancestry as far back as single celled organisms don't they?"

"Yes, we know that, but how does it help?"

"As they evolve, thousands of these gene sequences have been added, changed or switched off," she replied with an exasperated look on her face.

Whatever she was trying to show him completely eluded John and he just stared at her expectantly.

"So what? I still don't see how it applies."

"Your Methuselah is designed to repair damage in DNA; it's possible that the bacterial DNA has repaired a dormant sequence, one that was already present but inactive," she told him.

A smile crossed her face as she saw the look of realisation begin to form.

"Of course, how could I not have spotted it myself?" he asked rhetorically.

"I'll bet my career on it that there'll be more proteins on the next test as more and more of the old genes are reactivated," she added happily.

She glared at him, challenging him to look for a flaw in her logic.

But she could see that he was totally engrossed by the idea. John slapped his own forehead in realisation, mentally berating himself for not seeing such an obvious solution.

"After billions of years of evolution there are hundreds of thousands of potential genes and we didn't take them into consideration at all," he said, jumping to his feet in excitement.

"That's good though, isn't it? Not only was your theory correct but it means that the protein is unlikely to be harmful to the body?" she asked hopefully.

He nodded but she could still detect a small element of reticence.

"Are you thinking the protein could still be dangerous?" she asked with disappointment.

"Yes, mammalian DNA has evolved through thousands of species. The last thing we want is for the rats to start growing flippers or gills," he cautioned.

He was, however, quite hopeful, sharing her optimism that the changes would be benign. There was also the option that the genes were duplicates of those already active in the body. They both laughed, relieved they had found the potential problem. All they had to do now was wait for the next sample to be analysed to prove their theory.

Hiding in the corridor just out of sight, Richard heaved a huge sigh of relief as he eavesdropped on their conversation. That was too close for comfort, he thought to himself. At least an alternative theorem would keep them off his trail for now. Checking to make sure there was nobody around, he disappeared into John's laboratory.

The lab was empty so he made his way over to the secure refrigerator and unlocked it with his master key. He removed one of the numbered Methuselah sample bottles and dropped it quickly into his pocket. To ensure that no one would miss it, he wrote a note onto the log sheet, 'Sample twenty-nine removed for secure storage in central archive' then signed and dated the entry.

He wanted an insurance policy should anything else go wrong. He needed evidence that someone had contaminated the sample in case his secret contact decided to set him up to take the blame.

Whistling confidently, he strode out of the laboratory and made his way back to his office as if he did not have a care in the world.

The laboratory was almost entirely in darkness, the only illumination provided by the flashing LEDs and control interfaces on the array of complex scientific equipment. Every so often, there would be a whirr as one of the pieces of automated equipment began a new analysis cycle shortly followed by the sound of results printing.

It was the early hours of the morning and the only human presence was the occasional silhouette of a passing security guard on the lab window in the corridor, shining his torch into the vacated lab every so often. They had strict instructions not to enter as the trial was confidential and the area had to be sterile.

The rats were sleeping and they appeared normal; nothing seemed to have changed. Internally, however, there was a different story unfolding. Their bodies were beginning to change in subtle ways. New alien proteins, unseen in a eukaryotic cell for millions of years, sprouted in their thousands, each one of them initiating repairs to the hundreds of microscopic impairments present in every multi-cellular creature on the planet. Impairments caused by the aging process, damage to the various cell components by toxins, free radicals and the accidental flaws caused during cell division.

Cell membranes began to grow thicker, skin grew more flexible yet tougher and the metabolism of the creatures increased dramatically, in effect, a sort of anti-aging process. Muscle cells began to multiply, the fibre density increasing three fold causing a change that would improve physical strength and speed. Brain cells that usually die throughout the course of every creature's lifetime began to repair themselves and re-align. Neuron density started to increase leading to enhanced IQ and reasoning capabilities. Their bodies' own immune systems and healing processes were being enhanced, aiding the fight against the mutated viral contaminant that was still targeting red blood cells. Modified T-cells, B-Cells, and a range of immuniglobins flooded into the blood stream to join the fight. Only time would tell which way the balance would fall and determine the outcome of the sabotaged experiment. For now, their body systems were winning, but the virus was far from defeated.

***

John arrived very early in the morning and was greatly surprised to find Gwen already there, checking on the animals. Smiling to himself, he hurriedly dropped his coat and briefcase in the office and grabbed his stained lab coat from behind the door. He paused for a second to examine his apparel and, for the first time in months, dropped the dirty one into the laundry basket in the corridor before retrieving a clean one from his locker. Eager to join his new colleague, he entered the lab pushing open both swinging doors at once before striding over to Gwen to see if there was any news.

"Dr Taylor, what are you doing here so early? It's barely six o'clock" he asked inquisitively.

"I could ask you the same question. Personally, I was so excited last night that I couldn't sleep. All I could think of were those results. I'm really keen to find out if we were right and there are more than thirteen traces when we check today," she answered.

Gwen turned and leant on the bench with her elbows, her chin resting on the palms of her hands, reading the physiological results taken overnight. John studied her. She had pulled her long blonde hair away from her face, holding it tightly in a ponytail. Her face was perfect; her skin had a slight olive brown tint and was perfectly unblemished. She was the sort of woman you saw on the television advertising expensive perfumes dressed in nothing but negligee. Her back curved down towards her perfectly formed bottom that pressed tightly against the fabric of her lab coat. She had a black skirt on underneath, short enough to reveal her smooth milky coloured thighs but long enough to give her an elegant appearance.

For the second time in two days, John found himself admiring her perfect figure with less than honourable intent, and berated himself for being so weak. She was dating their boss after all and women of her caliber and appearance don't look twice at scruffy scientific types like him, despite how friendly they may seem. He was concentrating so deeply on his internal dilemma that he didn't realise when she turned to face him.

"Is everything okay, Dr Simmons? You look lost in your own little world," she said innocently.

Blood rushed to his cheeks like an embarrassed student as he realised she had caught him staring at her. A thousand excuses popped into his head and he used the first one, which seemed slightly plausible.

"Sorry Dr Taylor, I was thinking about our conversation yesterday and the errant protein," he stammered before scurrying off, ashamed of his behaviour and hoping she had not realised what he was doing.

Gwen smiled knowingly.

She was no stranger to the admiring glances of men, although she found most of them offensive. Many would stare openly, undressing her with their eyes, but with John Simmons it had somehow seemed different. At least he had the good manners to appear embarrassed by his actions.

Instead, she found it strangely flattering and took the trouble to watch him walk away.

John was tall, about six foot, and it was obvious that he looked after himself physically. His shoulders were broad but seemed to slope forward as he moved and she sensed an aura of melancholy about him as if he was hiding a deep sadness.

It might explain why he took little pride in his appearance and wore the same style of threadbare clothing day in, day out. Richard did care about that; he took great pride in his appearance and constantly worried about how others perceived him. In fact, he spent more time getting ready in front of a mirror than most women.

Sighing, she returned to the pile of traces she was about to examine before John arrived. It only took a glance before she turned and shouted across the lab.

"Dr Simmons, we were correct; I re-ran the analysis this morning with fresh blood samples and there are now three more new traces. It looks like Methuselah is resurrecting more than one dormant gene!"

John rushed over and she handed him the pile of results. He held them up to the light one at a time, noticing where Gwen had circled the new traces in red pen. There was no way of identifying what the new material was or why it was being produced, but it confirmed their theory. They would now have to rely on the physiological monitoring to see what, if any, the effects were going to be.

"If these results continue to increase, I think we are going to see some significant physiological changes in the animals. Have the other tests turned out any unusual signs of activity?" he asked, looking at her expectantly.

"Yes, we're seeing elevated levels of white blood cells and other immune related vectors," she answered, passing him the haematology report.

"That's something I would expect from the cancerous rats, they will be producing elevated amounts due to damage in the lymphatic system," he explained, checking through the list of numbers.

Gwen shook her head and pointed to the animal numbers printed on the top of each sheet.

"No, we are seeing them in both groups of treated animals. The cancer free rats are also showing them. It appears the red blood cell count is also slightly low compared to yesterday," she countered.

He knew as well as she did that those figures suggested that there was an infectious agent present in the blood stream. John inspected the results himself and noticed that there was a definite trend starting to appear on the readings for each individual subject. It was small for now, but significant enough to show on all twenty treated animals.

"It may be an immune response to the bacteriophage delivery system we used initially. Once the target RNA is injected into the cell, the casing is left floating round the blood stream. If the body recognises them as alien, the immune system will attack them," he theorised.

Gwen considered this for a moment.

"Possibly, but If I remember correctly, the immune cascade would not affect the red blood cell count. Is it possible the blood cells themselves were targeted in high numbers by the initial treatment?" she suggested.

"No, the bacteriophage was not injected in high enough numbers to effect that many red blood cells and the target receptors are different on them. The invading virus prefers those found on other types of cell. Even if they did accidently attack in large numbers, the new genes were designed not to damage the host cells," he answered.

The evidence pointed to something else in the blood stream and, unfortunately for them, they were correct.

"Could some of the original flu virus be reproducing? The cells would be damaged as the new virus particles were released," she asked.

"No, that's impossible, the reproductive aspect of the viral RNA was deactivated and besides, the flu virus would not attack the blood stream, it would be found in the respiratory system," he said, scratching his head, perplexed.

"What about all the new proteins and precursors, is it possible that the immune system is targeting them?" she asked, clutching at straws.

"I don't think so; they're naturally produced by the body, but I suggest we sit and wait to see what happens. I am also intrigued to see how the cancer cells will respond to the gene therapy," he replied, "as you are aware, cancer is basically only a cell with damaged DNA."

"You're right, there's no point sitting here watching them. We need to keep an eye on the trend to see which way it goes. I think I'll catch up on a little reading if you don't mind," she told him.

"No problem, if anything changes I'll let you know."

Gwen headed towards her office, removing her lab coat as she walked across the lab. She was wearing a cream coloured blouse underneath with a rather revealing neckline that displayed her more than ample cleavage. The effect was tantalising and John found it difficult averting his gaze. He wondered if dressing this way came naturally to her, always revealing enough of her body to look sensual without ever appearing cheap. The problem was the whole effect was stunning and men did take notice of her everywhere she went. Unfortunately for her, the wrong sort of man always approached Gwen. The decent men who would appreciate her for her other qualities were always too polite or too shy.

She paused briefly in the doorway and glanced back.

"Speak to you soon?" she inquired demurely.

"Yeah ... I'll see you later," he stammered, once again embarrassed she'd caught him staring and hurriedly began rummaging through the results to hide his shame. Gwen smiled knowingly and left him to his work.

By now, the rats were beginning to sense that something inside them was changing. As their bodies adapted they began to feel an increasing level of hunger as the raised metabolic rate caused their bodies to require more energy to fuel the improvements brought on by Methuselah. Bones that had stopped growing as the rats approached adulthood were now beginning to expand once again, the dormant genes reactivated. Muscle mass was increasing steadily and soon even the humans would begin to detect the changes.

The host's DNA in the tumour cells seemed different and the mutations caused by the cancer cells appeared corrected. The lumps began to reduce in size, removing the painful pressure on the rats' lymphatic systems, slowly allowing them to begin working once again. Methuselah had also begun to affect other parts of the body, now the eyes, the ears, and many other smaller systems. As it started to work, these systems also began to show improvements as the new genes were inserted.

John was right. He had discovered the biological equivalent of the fountain of youth. The rats were actually beginning to show all the signs of a reduction in age. However, the contaminant virus was also beginning to take its toll. Even with red blood cell production at a maximum and the enhanced immune system to fight the infection, the virus was spreading. Each of their bodies were now craving the nutrients required for the production of more red blood cells, the proteins, fatty acids and most of all the iron needed to produce haemoglobin. Because their appetites had increased, the specially formulated dry food was no longer giving them what they needed and the hunger steadily grew.

John returned later that day and noticed Brian had performed weight checks on the trial animals. He quickly scanned down the list and immediately noticed that there was a definite trend appearing in the treated animals.

"Brian, are you sure these figures are right?" John asked, waving the shabby clipboard at his student technician.

"Yes Doc, I weighed them all myself," Brian replied, not even looking up from his magazine.

John looked in disgust as the boy nodded his head to music playing through the headphone in his left ear. No matter how hard he tried, he just couldn't seem to engage Brian's interest in a subject he himself found fascinating.

"Are you sure? Because group two, the cancer free rats, have increased in weight by an average of four percent overnight. I would expect a little variation but not all trending in the same direction. That's highly unlikely, statistically speaking," John stated, dubious of the results he was seeing.

Brian reluctantly put down his magazine and plucked the earphone from his ear, shoving it haphazardly back into his jeans pocket before joining John to examine the results.

"Look Doc, I did exactly what you said, I weighed them when you told me to. Maybe they have eaten a big lunch," he joked drily.

As a student earning considerably less than his boss, his work ethic and enthusiasm may have been very low but he prided himself on being efficient. He had followed John's instructions to the letter.

"Very funny, but I would have expected to see variations in weight going down as well as up. These results are very interesting," John commented.

He checked the equivalent figures for the tumour carrying rats and there was the same trend, if a little less pronounced. The weight of each animal had increased by almost the same amount in each case.

"No, you're right Brian; this group shows a pretty consistent rise as well, even if the figure is a little lower at two percent. Perhaps we are seeing a lower weight gain because the tumours are reducing in mass", he tried to explain, but he could already tell that Brian had lost interest.

"Don't ask me Doc, you're the brains of the operation, I just work here. All I can tell you is that I did exactly what you told me to do. I weighed the animals, the food, and the solid waste. I recorded the amount of water each of them had drunk and collected the urine from the catheters," he said, pointing to each set of results in turn.

John nodded. Brian was correct. Everything was consistent across each of the trial groups. Not only were the treated animals gaining weight but they were also eating considerably more than the control specimens, even the rats suffering from cancer, who would otherwise be expected to show a reduced appetite.

"The serum must have increased their metabolism, something we expected to see in the long term but nothing so pronounced in such a short space of time," he mused, more for his own benefit than the disinterested student.

"If you say so Doc!" answered Brian vaguely.

"I wonder if the aging part of the theory is also proving itself to be correct." John said, growing a little more excited.

"You mean they're getting younger?" asked Brian, surprised by his boss's comments.

"Possibly, but we won't know for sure for a few days yet. One last thing, have you noticed any reduction in the size of the tumours?" John asked.

"I haven't noticed anything so far, but it's difficult to tell. Can I make a suggestion, although it may sound a little stupid?" asked Brian.

"No of course, go ahead."

"I saw a program on spider bites and the doctor drew a circle around the affected area. If you do that round the tumours you should immediately spot any changes," Brian said hesitantly.

"Actually Brian, I think that's an excellent idea. In fact can you go and do that right away, using a black marker will be easier to see against the skin," John instructed, genuinely impressed by the boy's ingenuity.

Maybe Brian was not as stupid as he led people to believe, John thought as he watched him hunting through the drawers for a marker pen. Satisfied that everything was under control, he left his student to his work.

Eager to return to his magazine, Brian began the meticulous task of marking up the creatures. He carefully traced a thin black circle around the base of each tumour, ensuring that he got them all, proud that his idea had been used despite his disgruntled actions.

"Stuck up git, they pay us peanuts and get us to do all the shitty jobs by calling it industrial experience," he muttered to himself.

Brian was used to being pampered, living at home until he was eighteen before going to college. There he had moved into the halls of residence with its canteen and other supported living perks. This year had been a different story though; he had been forced to find a place himself and for the first time in his life, there was no one looking after him, a situation he was not happy about.

He reached into the first of the cages and tried to grab the rat. Unlike usual the creature shied away, trying to avoid his probing digits. When he finally caught it, it continued to wriggle in his grasp desperately trying to get away, bearing its teeth and snarling. It was the same with all ten of them and Brian thought it seemed odd; the rats did not usually mind being handled. He thought no more about it and decided it was not worth his time to make a note in the log, preferring to return to his music and magazine.

When he was done, he flopped back into the chair and swung his feet onto the bench after checking there was no one else around. Reaching for his magazine with one hand, he pushed the earphone back into his ear with his other.

"Roll on home time," he said aloud to no one in particular.

Five

After many hours of writing up the experimental logs on his computer, John realised he'd been at work for over fourteen hours and decided to stop for the day. He had discussed the weight gain with Gwen and they had both agreed that it was a very positive sign. As usual, there was so much to do that he could have stayed and worked straight until the early hours of the morning, but for once, he was ready to go home. He saved his work and pulled his worn leather jacket on before switching off the office light and heading into the corridor.

John was surprised to find Gwen's office lights on and decided to check in on her to make sure everything was all right.

"Hi Dr Taylor, what are you still doing here?" he asked, sticking his head round the door. "It's very late, and trust me, it's a bad habit to get yourself into."

She glanced up at the clock and noticed it was already past eight o'clock.

"It's a good thing you stopped by, I didn't realise it was so late already. I probably would still be here by midnight," she said and closed the textbook she was reading, replacing it on the shelf behind her desk.

John took the opportunity to glance around her office and noticed how spotless everything was, just like the woman herself. His office was also an accurate portrayal of him, messy and in a complete state of disorder.

"Don't worry. I've done it myself on more than a couple of occasions. Sometimes, right into the early hours of the morning," he said with a grin.

Gwen looked at him thoughtfully, her head tilted slightly to one side.

"Are you hungry?"

"I suppose so," he replied noncommittally.

"Well I'm starving. Do you fancy popping out for a quick bite? I know a wonderful pub just down the road from here, The Stag. Do you know it?" she asked, pulling her expensive cashmere coat on.

"Yeah, I've popped in a few times after work when I didn't feel like cooking," he replied.

What he failed to tell her was that he only went there as a last resort. The place was quite trendy, full of smartly dressed young men and women, the exact opposite of him. He preferred the relative quiet of a country pub with a traditional home cooked meal and a roaring fire.

"Well come on then, I could do with the company," she said.

Out of nowhere, John felt butterflies in his stomach. He had not been out in public with a woman in over five years and never one as attractive as Gwen. Even as a young man he had suffered from terminal shyness and had always been awkward in the presence of a pretty girl.

"I'm not sure, I really ought to be getting home," he said pathetically, trying desperately to think of a legitimate reason to excuse himself, but Gwen was not taking no for an answer and threaded her arm through his.

"Come on, it's the perfect opportunity to get to know one another a little better. I've not really had much chance to socialise since I got here, so you would be doing me a favour," she insisted.

Seeing there was no way out of it, he decided that he needed a few minutes to smarten himself up a little.

"Okay, I'll see you there in about ten minutes, there's something I have to do first," he told her before hurrying back to his office.

There was a smart ironed shirt in his locker, the one he kept there for emergency meetings, and a shaver that he hoped still worked. He quickly removed a couple of days' worth of stubble and dragged on the shirt, smoothing out the few creases gained from being in the confines of his locker for several weeks.

"What are you thinking of, you old fool?" he asked his reflection rhetorically as he ran his fingers quickly through his unruly mop of hair.

The pub was reasonably full by the time he got there so he found an empty table quietly tucked away in the corner. The place was full of smartly dressed young men and women as he had expected, most of them in groups or with their partners. Loud music was playing in the background, a song by the latest girl band blaring away above the din of people shouting at the tops of their voices.

As he sat down, a group of young women in their early twenties came staggering in, dressed in skin-tight Lycra dresses and tight denim, already worse for wear with alcohol. He watched them stagger over to one of the larger tables, giggling and joking, their faces creased up in silly grins. That type of behaviour made John uncomfortable in such surroundings and seeing all the smartly dressed people, he began to feel self-conscious.

He sat down and immediately an attractive young woman dressed in a short black skirt and a white blouse with 'The Stag' emblazoned across the breast pocket came over and stood looking expectantly at him.

"Can I get you a drink sir?" she asked politely, thrusting her chest forward, proudly displaying her more than ample cleavage.

The pay there was only minimal but she had learnt that the tips could be exceptionally good, especially from lecherous older men. John, however, showed little interest.

"Yes please, I'll have a bottle of alcohol free beer if you have it," he replied, his attention on the entrance.

"Yes we do sir, would you like to order any food?" she asked, writing down his order on a tiny little pad.

"I'm meeting someone, can you give me another ten minutes please?" he asked.

"Of course sir, I'll fetch your beer in a second," she answered politely, reaching across him to remove a used napkin from the table.

John flinched as she pressed her large but firm bosoms on his upper arm; she had perfected the act over several months to induce generosity from her male clients.

Sensing his lack of interest, she disappeared into the bar, her hips wriggling suggestively as she walked, attracting several appreciative glances from some of the other men.

At that moment, Gwen walked in. John stood up and waved frantically to catch her attention in the crowd. Spotting him, she waved back, her face lighting up with a smile as she made her way over to his corner.

"Can I get you a drink?" he asked, offering to take her coat.

She nodded graciously and John could not help but notice the number of men casting their eyes in her direction. One of them even gave him a cheeky wink to acknowledge his respect.

"Yes please, can I have a glass of red wine? In fact we could get a bottle if you wanted," she replied, taking the coat from him and folding it neatly over the back of her chair.

"Normally I would love to join you, but I brought my car and would have to drive back to Worthing," he said slowly.

John detected a slight flicker of disappointment for a second but decided he must be imagining things.

"You live in Worthing too? I live on Offingham Lane, just before you get into town," she asked, surprised.

John knew the area well as he passed through it daily on his way to work. It was just off the A24 and contained some of the most expensive houses in town.

"I know where you mean, those big houses just after the roundabout," he said impressed, suddenly feeling a little ashamed of the scruffy little bedsit where he lived.

Gwen nodded and asked, "What about you, are you close by?"

"I am afraid not. I live on the other side of Worthing in a little one bedroom flat," he confessed reluctantly. Before she could ask any further questions, he took the opportunity to disappear off to the bar. Surprisingly, it was empty, and as he approached, the waitress who'd attended to him earlier came over carrying his bottle of beer.

"Sorry sir, I got a little waylaid," she explained politely.

"No problem, my guest has arrived, so can I have a large glass of red wine as well please?" he asked, scanning the huge selection of bottles behind the bar.

It was a waste of time; he knew absolutely nothing about wine other than the fact that it came in red, white and rosé. He wanted to get her a decent label and was not afraid to pay for the quality.

The waitress watched him patiently as he examined the choices before asking politely, "Anything in particular takes your fancy?"

John just looked bewildered and glanced back over to the table to see if Gwen could give him some sort of hint. She was busily examining the menu so he had no choice but to admit he was out of his depth.

"Could you recommend a good one please?" he asked the young woman pathetically. The waitress had followed his gaze back to the table and spotted Gwen. She smiled knowingly and winked at him.

"It's okay sir, I know just the one. It's a bit more expensive, but I think your lady friend will enjoy it," she assured him, understanding now why he had not paid her any attention previously. Her help, however, would definitely improve the chances of a healthy tip.

John nodded, his ego taking pleasure purely from the fact that the waitress assumed the two of them were together.

"No problem, can you make it a large glass please. Oh, I would like to start a tab as well if that's possible for table twenty-three," he added thankfully.

Smiling sweetly, she handed him the drinks and nodded, "I'll give you a few minutes, then I'll come and take your order."

John thanked her and returned triumphantly to the table, carrying his new prize with honour. He placed the drinks carefully on the beer mats.

He watched with hopeful anticipation as Gwen picked up her drink and took a small sip of the ruby liquid.

"Mmm, that's really nice. Dr Simmons, are you a bit of a wine buff in your spare time?" she asked, impressed by his selection.

"Actually, it's an Italian full bodied Corvina, La Grola 2005 Allegrini," he said with a flourish, reciting the label word for word.

He had purposefully asked the young woman to show it to him for that very reason. John made a mental note to leave the waitress a generous tip at the end of the evening.

"Very impressive," she said, tipping her glass in appreciation.

However, honesty was always one of John's strong points and, although it was only a small matter, he felt guilty that he'd conned her into thinking he was a connoisseur.

"I'm sorry, I can't take the credit. I asked the waitress for a hint and she picked out the wine. I know absolutely nothing about wine, but I'm glad you like it," he admitted, smiling apologetically.

She chuckled pleasantly, "Don't worry, I know even less, so I normally have to settle for the house red. This is a welcome change, trust me."

John joined her in laughter and despite the fact that he felt out of place in his surroundings, he actually felt very comfortable around her.

He noticed how the corners of her mouth turned up sensually at the edges as she laughed, displaying the slightest hint of her teeth. They were not perfect, the front two standing slightly proud of the others, but in her the imperfection only seemed to add to her appearance. Her eyes were the most stunning blue and they sparkled with a vibrancy of their own as she smiled.

He looked away and realised that he was falling for her, a path that would only lead to trouble. He felt immense sadness that she had chosen to date Richard. Regardless of her attachments, he found her company enthralling and decided that the least he wanted was her friendship.

They made small talk until the waitress reappeared and John made a point of nodding to her in recognition for her help. He ordered a wholesome steak and ale pie while Gwen settled for a salad Niçoise.

When John had finished his meal, he could hardly breathe, he was that full.

But he noticed that his companion had barely eaten her salad and realised how she kept herself in such good shape. He thought, however, that the food was excellent and had polished off everything on his plate with gusto.

After eating, they discussed the project in some detail while finishing off their drinks. John found himself becoming even more enamoured by Gwen, and realised that she was not only intelligent and attractive, but funny and honest as well. He found her eyes beguiling and struggled not to stare. John decided to dig into her past, that way he would control his roving eyes.

"So, how did you end up at Swiftgene? I would have thought that someone with your qualifications and reputation could have secured a job at any of the big pharmaceutical companies?" he inquired curiously.

Swiftgene was a great company but there were others within the genetic engineering industry that seemed better, and with excellent research opportunities, especially American companies. John had once considered taking the plunge.

She sighed and leant back in her seat.

"I'm afraid my story is quite depressing. I was lucky enough to get a post-graduate position studying the very work I'm now doing, only the pay was not as good. Unfortunately, one of my professors, a married man, took a shine to me and began stalking me. He pestered me at every opportunity, buying me gifts and flowers. I turned down his advances, but after a while he started to get a lot more persistent. When he started arriving at my house late at night and demanding to see me I knew I had a problem."

"That's disgusting, he's meant to be in a position of trust. You should have reported him," exclaimed John.

"Oh, I did. I tried to complain to the university faculty but it turned out he was a good friend of the dean who swept the whole affair under the carpet. The dean politely suggested that I should leave, offering me a glowing letter of recommendation. When I refused, he spoke to my sponsor who withdrew my grant, and that was the end of my academic career," she said bitterly.

"I'm sorry to hear that," John said, shaking his head in sympathy.

She shrugged her delicate shoulders.

"The best thing was that as I was about to leave, my professor turned up again and began pestering me to go out with him after he'd ruined everything. This time, I had nothing to lose so I just called the police and made sure that he got his just deserts. I was so angry that I went to the papers and told them everything. I embarrassed the dean so badly that he had to resign. Unfortunately, that was when I found out that the professor was married with two children. His wife left him and took everything, which served him right, but I felt guilty because of the children. As you can guess, my glowing recommendation evaporated into thin air and that was why my avenues were rather limited. Talk about poetic justice," she explained, a hint of anger creeping into her tone.

"I know it's no consolation, but it sounds like the misogynistic bastard got his punishment, and for what it's worth, you probably did his wife and kids a favour," John said quietly.

He personally hated men who abused their position to get what they wanted and it was one of the reasons why he had never been friendly with Richard.

"Taking that into consideration and the nature of my research, Swiftgene was the only company that was prepared to take me on, and that came with the condition that I work on some of their other projects as well," she continued, the regret creeping back into her voice. "Unfortunately, thanks to your ground breaking discovery, even that had to take a back seat."

She took a sip of her wine and John looked at her sympathetically, feeling even guiltier than he had for the accusation he had made the day before.

"I'm truly sorry, I didn't realise just how important your research was to you and I was less than sympathetic the other day," John apologised.

"Don't be silly, it's not your fault. As it turns out, you had good reasons to be suspicious, if not of me then of Richard at least," she answered.

"There is a way you could make sure you were given your project back. All you have to do is complain to HR that I had made inappropriate accusations. They would make sure Richard wouldn't force you onto the Methuselah project," he suggested. "And just for clarity's sake, I've always respected your work."

Gwen stopped mid-sip and looked at him, stunned. She was amazed anyone would be sympathetic enough to put their career on the line for her. She grabbed his hand and squeezed it softly.

"Oh Dr Simmons, I would never do something like that just to get my own way. Yes, I was upset the other day, but I understood why you were angry and I have to admit had the situation been reversed, I think my reaction would be the same, if not worse," she said earnestly.

"Well, if you change your mind, the offer stands," he told her, squeezing her hand back.

"Never! I was annoyed at first because I wanted to stay on my project full time, but I've had time to think about it. With you helping me on my project, I'll probably get a lot further than on my own anyway, and it will be interesting to work with you on yours. No, I think things have turned out pretty well for me if you don't mind me saying," she assured him. "Besides, I get to be part of the biggest discovery of the twenty-first century. It's going to be one hell of a ride if the trials are positive."

"Even so, I feel horrible now I have got to know you better. I said some disparaging things to you. If there's anything I can do to make it up to you, please let me know Dr Taylor," he said sincerely.

"Firstly, you can stop calling me Dr or Miss Taylor. My name is Guinevere or Gwen to my friends," she said.

"Sorry, force of habit. You too, please call me John," he insisted.

"Deal," she said, shaking his hand.

"Well Gwen," he said, picking up his drink and lifting it to her, "here's to the new partnership. Let's hope it's long and successful."

She clinked her glass against his and sat back, looking at him curiously.

"What about you John? Your credentials are even better than mine. You actually taught molecular genetics at Cambridge University for a while."

"I am afraid I did, but that was a lifetime ago," he grunted.

"What made you move to Worthing of all places?" she asked with interest.

Watching the pained expression on his face, she knew instantly that something very bad had happened in his life and she instantly regretted asking. People hardly pull a face like that unless it was something very unpleasant.

"My seven year old son died during the swine flu pandemic, and shortly after that, my wife and I divorced. The whole thing was very painful for both of us, so I chose to move away as far as possible to make it easier on her. Swiftgene seemed to be the perfect opportunity for a new start," he replied, speaking quietly as he relived the episode once more in his head.

"John, I'm so sorry, I had no idea at all; no one told me anything," she said, shocked.

He looked into her eyes and could see that her concern was truly heartfelt. She really was a wonderful specimen of a woman, he thought, as she revealed another attractive side to her lovely personality.

"I am afraid that's my own fault; I've never told anyone here about my past. As far as they know, I'm simply a divorcee and I'm happy for them to continue thinking that; people tend to treat you differently when they know such intimate details of your past," he said calmly.

"John, I promise I'll never mention it again, and I give you my word that your secret is safe with me," she assured him.

Realising that the night was now over, she glanced at her watch and noticed that they had been there for several hours.

"Look at the time, I hadn't realised it was this late. Please excuse me for a moment while I arrange for a taxi," she said, climbing to her feet.

John stopped her without really thinking it through.

"Don't be silly, I can drop you off. It'll be no trouble; like I said, your house is on my route home," he offered.

The sentiment was true but he immediately pictured his battered car parked around the corner and regretted his rash offer. He mentally crossed his fingers that his twenty-year-old banger would start for him at least one more time.

"Are you sure? I don't mind getting a taxi if it's too much trouble?" she asked, not wishing to put him out unnecessarily.

"I wouldn't hear of it, and I would rather make sure you got home safely," John insisted, hoping he sounded chivalrous rather than overbearing and chauvinistic.

"Okay then, thank you. That would be great."

Being a gentleman, John insisted on paying for the meal despite objections from Gwen. As a rule, she had learnt to split the bill when dining with male companions as it avoided any confusing signals. However, with John, she somehow sensed that his intentions were purely honourable so allowed him to pay on the condition that she reciprocated later.

Gwen had also noticed something else about his behaviour, for example, he always held the door for her, allowing her to pass in front of him. She knew the gesture was a little old fashioned in the age of equality but still, she felt a strange sense of satisfaction from the attention anyway. Richard was entirely different; he barged through ahead of her and only held the door if it occurred to him.

Outside, the night air was cold and she found herself shivering despite her long cashmere coat. She hooked her arm through John's, enjoying a small respite from the chill. John, however, did not notice the cold, accompanied as he was by a beautiful young woman.

John felt strangely warm all over. The streets were almost deserted at this time of night, with only the odd couple staggering between pubs breaking the silence of the side streets. John winced inwardly as they approached the rusty form of his car and wished he had replaced the ancient pile of scrap a long time ago. He held the passenger door open while she gracefully climbed in.

He could not help but admire her long shapely legs as she climbed inside his rickety car. The door screeched as John slammed it shut to make sure the dodgy lock caught properly. He didn't want the door to fly open inadvertently on their way home. Running round the car, he climbed in and made himself as comfortable as his dilapidated seat would allow.

"This is great. I learnt to drive in one of these as a young girl. Do you like vintage cars?" she asked innocently, pulling the seatbelt over her shoulder.

"Believe it or not my father bought it for me brand new when I finished high school. I kept the car so long because the day he gave it to me was one of the last times my mother and I ever saw him. We assumed he left during the night, but to be truthful, I have absolutely no idea what happened to him. Since then, I've never had the heart to get rid of the old girl," he said, patting the dashboard fondly.

"John, that's really sweet. You really are a bit of an old sentimentalist aren't you?"

Mentally crossing his fingers, John turned the key in the ignition, heaving a sigh of relief as the engine fired into life once again. For the last five years he had not cared what people thought of him, but in the space of a few days, he was becoming self-aware, especially when he was around Gwen. He made a decision there and then to start searching for a new car just in case the opportunity ever arose to give her a lift again.

They chatted happily on the journey home and John hoped that she didn't notice he had driven exceptionally slowly the whole way to prolong the journey. Eventually, however, they arrived at her house and yet again, he opened the car door for her, taking her hand to steady her as she climbed out from the low seat. Smiling, she said goodnight and headed up the drive towards her house.

John watched her walk to her door before leaving, telling himself that he was only making sure that she went in safely. Subconsciously, he just enjoyed the sway of her hips as she walked away from him. When he finally left, John realised he felt better than he had in years, no longer depressed by the prospect of going home.

***

The laboratory was silent but the rats stirred restlessly in their sleep, definitely aware now that they were beginning to change physically. Their bones ached as they grew, muscles becoming so strong and dense that humans would soon detect the changes. The unfortunate creatures afflicted with painful tumours were starting to feel better, the malignant lumps gradually shrinking as the cells returned to their normal functionality.

But in their bloodstream, the virus was spreading. It had started to overpower the immune system, destroying more and more red blood cells.

Their thighbones hurt as the bone marrow went into overdrive, racing to replace the depleted red blood cells.

Their hunger had now become a constant throbbing pain, no matter how much bland dried food they ate. Internally, their bodies were crying out for the raw materials required to make more blood.

Their untreated siblings on the first bench now cowered whenever one of their treated relatives glanced across, sensing that something was severely wrong with them. The odour of the affected rats permeating the air but was noticeable only to the other rodents in the room.

Rat Number 20, a large female, was pacing her metal prison, testing every inch for signs of weakness. She scratched at the plastic base and pulled on the metal bars with strange human-like fingers. Finding no exit, she reluctantly settled into the shredded paper that served as bedding and closed her eyes to rest while she dreamt of escape into a world that only existed in her imagination.

Once again, John arrived early in the morning in a strangely cheerful mood. He strode through the corridors, whistling a tune he'd just heard on the radio. He dropped his coat in the office and made his way to the test facility to make the first observations of the day.

This time, he was surprised to find Richard, Gwen and Brian already waiting for him, huddled around one of the benches. None of them turned to greet him as he approached, all of them totally engrossed by their task.

"Good morning all," John said cheerfully, causing them all to jump.

Gwen grabbed his arm and pulled him hastily over to the results they were scrutinising, pointing to one of the sheets in particular. On it was a range of photos taken prior to the treatment detailing each of the tumours. Next was a similar sheet with photos taken earlier that morning.

"Look John, the tumours are almost gone, you've done it! Finally there's a treatment for cancer that doesn't involve months of debilitating chemotherapy. With Methuselah, the patients actually seem to be fitter than when they started," she said excitedly.

"You're kidding; it's only been a couple of days. There's no way it could have acted that fast," John answered incredulously.

In disbelief, he picked up the photos and checked through every single one of them in detail. Then he walked along the row of cages himself and examined every animal closely. The black ring Brian had drawn on each of them to signify the extent of each tumour was visible and demonstrated a reduction in every case. It was unbelievable, and if he had not seen it with his own eyes, he would not have accepted it. Some of the tumours were so small they were indiscernible.

"It can't be true! Every single one of them shows improvement. Results like this are unprecedented," he exclaimed in disbelief.

Gwen nodded enthusiastically and John saw her face beaming; excitement rushed through him like a tidal wave.

"Look at them; they seem healthier and stronger than the untreated control subjects. How can that be in such a short time?" John asked, looking at her for confirmation.

"I have no idea, but you can't deny the evidence John, just look at them!" Gwen exclaimed with a smile.

"It looks like the Methuselah serum works better than we could've ever anticipated. The increased strength and muscle mass means there may even be applications in wasting conditions such as muscular dystrophy as well as other genetic abnormalities," he said incredulously.

John, however, was a scientist and insisted they reviewed all the results taken over the last twenty-four hours to make sure everything was consistent with the physical appearance of the creatures. John and Gwen checked and confirmed that the rats had all gained muscle mass, increased in size and that the physiological readings had improved consistently. They were looking at creatures that appeared to have grown younger and increased in physical size compared to the control subjects.

John stared in disbelief at Gwen, his face finally breaking into a huge grin.

"Do you really think it's possible? Have we really solved the ancient mystery of aging?" he asked.

She nodded enthusiastically.

"It's undeniable. The proof is right in front of you. You've cracked the ancient mystery, the secret of eternal youth. Healthy people will be queuing up for this treatment, never mind the ill," she said.

Unable to contain her excitement any longer, Gwen rushed forward and wrapped her arms around John;

before he knew what was happening, she kissed him ever so gently on the cheek, her lips lingering for a mere fraction of a second in celebration.

She let go and repeated the action with Brian leaving John reeling from the experience, the first intimate contact he'd received from a woman in a long while. His cheek tingled from the lasting sensation of her lips on his skin.

John noticed with a certain sense of satisfaction that Richard was not included in the display of affection and it brought a wicked smile to his face.

Unseen by the others, Richard stared jealously at John; it was becoming noticeable to everyone how quickly their friendship was developing. In retrospect, he regretted his decision to force Gwen and John together.

"Brian," John said, spinning round.

"Yes Doc," answered Brian, almost displaying a hint of enthusiasm.

"When did you take these readings?" he inquired, passing him a sheet of paper.

"Dr Jennings asked me to repeat them this morning, last night's reading were a little lower," Brian answered, tipping his thumb towards Richard.

John's mood soured at the thought that Richard had been interfering with his project and turned round to face the man he detested.

"Why are you involving yourself with the details of my work? Do you consider me incompetent?" John asked aggressively.

Richard took an involuntary step backwards and held his hands up to placate the angry scientist.

"John, before you get upset there's something I need to tell you. I've arranged for the investors to come in early based on yesterday's results and I wanted some up to date readings to show them," he said, trying to defend his actions.

"And that couldn't wait until I arrived this morning?" John asked sarcastically.

"It's not that; we already have some phenomenal offers on the table from these people and it's in the company's best interest to capitalise on them as soon as possible," Richard tried to explain.

He was desperately trying to avoid another public argument with John, one he knew he would ultimately lose. For now, he would have to put up with the man's insolence, but he consoled himself with the fact that he would have the last laugh.

"Richard, why are you in such a rush to release these results? It's far too early to rely on them, don't you see?" John asked suspiciously.

"I've told you, the sooner we secure external funding, the better," Richard replied, but his resolve was waning.

"Couldn't we wait for another two weeks to gather more results? You know we have detected errant proteins that we can't yet identify. What if one of them turns out to be another Creutzfeldt–Jakob disease? The human form of mad cow disease." John pointed out sarcastically.

"It's very unlikely though, isn't it?" Richard asked uncertainly.

"Of course it is, but you're missing the point! That particular disease has an incubation period of up to twenty years. Do you want to be responsible for another disease that causes early onset dementia or maybe one of the proteins turning out to be a potent carcinogen and creating our own form of cancer? What I'm trying to say is we need to perform a hell of a lot more testing before we can classify the experiment a success and the investors need to be under no illusions about that!" John said in a raised voice.

He was extremely angry that Richard seemed to be willing to do anything to rush the project along; that was how dangerous products were released into the market and there was no way he would allow his name to be associated with anything like that. He had worked hard for too long to allow his work to be utilised in that manner. His primary goal was to alleviate the suffering of patients, not to further enrich the wallets of a few investors no matter how important their money was to the development of Methuselah. To his surprise, Richard agreed without an argument.

"That's perfectly acceptable. We'll make it very clear to them what stage of testing we are at. This is purely a business decision aimed at making sure we have the correct financial backing. The extra funding means that you'll be able to procure whatever you need to complete the trials, the very best equipment, more staff or even a greater share of the available laboratory space," Richard told him in an amiable tone.

"Okay, as long as we make it clear, I have no problem," John said grudgingly, the wind somewhat removed from his sails.

"Not only that John, but the board are aware of your efforts and in recognition of your achievements they've authorised me to offer you a promotion," Richard added.

The news took John by surprise.

"You're to be the new head of research and development here at Hove, making you directly responsible on a technical level for every project underway at this facility," Richard continued, taking advantage of John's silence.

The board of directors had insisted on John's promotion; Richard had resisted because he wanted to retain control of the projects himself but they were adamant. They wanted someone with the right technical expertise running things. Now seemed like the ideal moment to reveal the board's intentions to make sure that John would still be under his control, at least for the short-term future.

John had been at Swiftgene for just under five years and had not moved within the company hierarchy in that time or received the slightest recognition for his work other than a passing mention in scientific periodicals.

He should have been over the moon, but he was still suspicious. Richard had thrown in this promotion at an opportune moment without even speaking to him about it first. Sensing that he was holding all the cards for once, John decided to test just how far Richard was willing to go to keep him on side.

"Okay Richard, bring your investors in and I'll tell them of the potential benefits of the new gene therapy, but I'll also make it crystal clear that we're basing our pitch purely on preliminary results. I can guarantee you now that there will be no human trials for well over a year and they need to be perfectly clear on that," John demanded.

"Agreed. Now is there anything, and I do mean anything, at all that you need for your work? This project is now priority number one at this facility with everything else taking a back seat," Richard said smoothly, offering John a blank cheque.

John glanced over at Gwen and could see that she was ecstatic at the news. He realised this could be the perfect opportunity to put her in the strong position of finishing her project with proper funding.

"The truth is that I can't manage both research and development and still give Methuselah the attention that it requires. I'll take Research and I suggest that you give Dr Taylor the position of development director. She has the necessary practical experience and it will take the pressure off me. Her input on the project has been invaluable and I'll continue to need her support if we're to make this a success," he demanded, the tone of his voice making it clear that it was not a negotiable condition.

Gwen stared at John in disbelief but he kept his focus on Richard's reply. He knew Richard had intended to help Gwen climb the slippery management pole to gain favour, but this way John knew that Richard could not hold it over her.

"Okay, if that's what you think it will take, I'll sort the contracts out with HR by the end of the day," Richard agreed through gritted teeth, a pained expression on his face.

He forced a smile and shook John's hand before leaving, satisfied that he had made the right decision as far as guaranteeing the cash flow he required, but he knew John had outmanoeuvred him with respect to

Gwen. As soon as he was gone, Gwen grabbed John by the elbow and led him gently but firmly out of the room, away from eavesdropping ears.

She had a peculiar expression on her face somewhere between anger and gratitude that confused John immensely.

Gwen looked a little awkward, as if she was not quite sure how to begin.

"Thank you for standing up for me in there, but I told you I don't want recognition by riding your shirt tails. If I'm to be promoted, I want it to be based on my own talents and achievements," she said quietly.

John now realised she had not understood the true nature of his reasoning. He grabbed her by the shoulders and looked her directly in the eyes to show her he was sincere.

"That's just it; I recommended your promotion based entirely on your academic and professional talent. A true expert who understands your achievements has therefore recognised you and not your boyfriend with ulterior motives. Now if anyone comments on how you got the job, you can honestly tell them that you were recommended for the position by me," he said, his eyes imploring her to believe him.

She nodded, realising that even though he had done her a great favour, his motives had been entirely professional.

"I'm a big fan of your work, but even I know there's little profit for the company in that line of research and funding will always be poor. Now you'll have control of the purse strings and can make sure that the techniques you have developed on your project can be used elsewhere. That way, you can qualify for additional funding. The only selfish claim I can make is that I've now removed the only thing Richard intended to hold over you by eliminating him from the equation. I have to admit I took great satisfaction out of spoiling his plans, but it was not my main reason." John's approach was logical enough and was above reproach. He truly had no element of personal gain, and she had to admit that he was right.

"If you really mean that, then thank you, I appreciate your support. You're right, it does mean more to me coming from you than it does from a lecherous fool like Richard," she said, feeling a little embarrassed that she had doubted him. "You really are quite a decent man John Simmons, and I think you'll make an excellent director. I'm looking forward to working with you," she added, shaking his hand.

John gave her a smile and then winked at her.

"Anyway, before you get too big headed in your new role, do you think you can spare a little time to finish looking through this morning's results with me? It looks like we have to prepare a little presentation of some kind to make sure the suits will give us enough money to actually fund our pay rises," he joked.

He did not, however, tell her of his concerns over the behaviour of the animals. He had noticed there was something not quite right with the rats that morning, but he could not quite put his finger on it. For the moment, he decided to keep it to himself but made a mental note to continue observing them to see if the slight agitation increased to anything more suspicious. For now, he would concentrate on impressing the investors.

Six

After the impromptu meeting with John, Richard stalked back to his office with his tail between his legs, annoyed that the belligerent scientist had taken away the one opportunity he had left to impress Gwen. Checking up and down the corridor to make sure there was no one around, he locked his office door and proceeded to dial the number for his contact.

"This is Richard Jennings, I have an update for you regarding the trials," he said unenthusiastically.

"Are the results positive or am I going to be disappointed?" asked the electronically scrambled voice.

"The formula not only works but we have seen positive results after only a few days. The tumours have almost completely gone into remission, but that isn't the best part; the animals are actually growing bigger and stronger. It seems the cellular repair processes are going into overdrive, actually optimising each animal's basic structure. New muscle is noticeably developing and the metabolic processes are through the roof. If the theories are correct, they're actually getting younger," confirmed Richard, the excitement getting the better of him.

The investors would be begging to invest in a product like this, and he would be able to choose the terms he wanted now. As soon as the money was on the table, he would be free to take his slice through the phony company he had created. He was not about to tell his contact, however, that he was still dealing from both sides.

There was silence from the other end as if his contact were contemplating what he had said.

"That's excellent news Dr Jennings, but it's imperative that we begin the next phase of testing as soon as possible. I want you to try the serum on a human subject as soon as possible. I don't have time to wait for the MHRA authorisations," his contact stated.

Richard balked at the idea.

The MHRA was a government run agency which tested dangerous products before their release into the market.

There was no way they would clear a drug at this stage for human trials, and if they did it illegally, the sentences would be very harsh.

"Are you crazy?" he asked angrily, "we are not in a position to start human trials, and besides, where would I find a volunteer with so little research data to rely on?" Richard was beginning to realise the potential trouble he would be heaping on himself.

He still had no idea who he was dealing with and was beginning to suspect that they were not just a rival company trying to poach a product. They were exceptionally well connected and had excellent intelligence on every major player in the industry. Richard shuddered as he also concluded that people like this, when they did not get their own way, were very likely to make him one of the test subjects should he refuse to co-operate.

"Dr Jennings, I don't care how you do it, but I want to see the serum tested on a human subject as soon as possible!" snapped the voice over the phone.

From his tone, Richard knew that his contact was a person who was not used to having their orders questioned.

"Well can you at least help me source a trial subject? You know I can't use any of the normal channels for this, and I'm sure you will have some connections that can help," he pleaded.

"Richard, need I remind you about the money you've already received? If I wanted or was in a position to do the trial myself then I wouldn't be paying you for your services, would I?" the voice snapped at him.

"I know but ...," Richard stammered.

"I don't care how you do it but I want you to test the serum on someone as soon as is humanly possible. If you can't find a suitable subject then as far as I'm concerned, you can start testing it on yourself, which is what I would do if I were in your position. You have twenty-four hours to sort something out or there will be serious repercussions!" the voice threatened, sending an icy chill through Richard's entire body.

Panic gradually crept in, almost immobilising him; he sat there for half an hour racking his brains, trying to work out how he would find a subject and test the drug without anyone at Swiftgene finding out. He was about to give up when an idea jumped into his head and a cruel smile spread across his lips. He knew his time was limited anyway; he would eventually pack up and leave with as much money as he could accumulate. That meant making a good impression on the investors, so with a renewed sense of vigour, he leant forward and began to prepare a presentation on his computer that would convince the investors to part with their cash.

John and Gwen had worked hard all morning preparing a list of key points they were going to present to the investors that afternoon and, pleased with themselves, they had disappeared for an early lunch. However, without realising it, they had stayed chatting in the restaurant for over an hour, forgetting about the imminent arrival of the investors. They were still laughing as they entered the lab and found themselves surrounded by a group of strangers.

They were surprised to see that Richard had already met with the investors and now a dozen pairs of eyes were staring at them, belonging to a group of men and women dressed in expensive business suits. Both of them stopped dead in their tracks and Richard, sensing their surprise, took the opportunity to introduce them.

"Ladies and gentlemen, may I formally introduce the brains behind the whole project, Dr John Simmons, my research director, and Dr Guinevere Taylor, my development director, both of whom are respected internationally in the field of genetic engineering," he said, gesturing towards the startled pair.

There was a murmur as the surprised scientists walked amongst the group, shaking hands and exchanging pleasantries, before joining Richard at the front of the room. Richard allowed a couple of minutes for the investors to settle down before continuing with his pitch.

"Dr Simmons, would it be possible for you to give our esteemed guests a brief overview of the Methuselah project and what we've achieved so far?" Richard asked in his most pretentious voice.

John smiled uneasily and began telling them the history of the project, just as he and Gwen had rehearsed.

The group listened intently, but many of them were not even scientists, never mind molecular geneticists, and John quickly realised that they were beginning to struggle with his explanation.

"I'm sorry. Sometimes I get a little carried away. Maybe it would be better if you asked any specific questions you may have," John offered.

A tall, clean-shaven man in his thirties stepped forward and spoke in a strong Yorkshire accent, "You say you have potentially identified the genes for immortality, is that correct?"

The whole group looked at John expectantly; a true anti-aging treatment would be worth billions of pounds.

"Not entirely, no. We have identified the genes responsible for it in bacterium and have managed to transfer them to a multi-celled creature. However, the effect is not guaranteed to work in that organism due to the complexity of the interactions between the large number of different cells," John answered confidently.

"But is it theoretically possible though?" continued the man impatiently.

"Theoretically, yes, practically, however, the most likely outcome is to extend the life of individual cells and therefore that of the organism itself, but that's not the main purpose of our work. We're more interested in the potential for the repair processes to be used in the treatment of genetic disorders such as cancer," John stressed, trying to hide his frustration at the direction of questioning.

John had hoped that the various applications for treating known debilitating conditions would be of more interest to them, not man's age-old quest for immortality.

A middle-aged woman with short brown hair stepped forward.

She was a little overweight and seemed to struggle with her breathing. John suspected that she was a heavy smoker or suffered from a form of asthma and was hopeful that she would be interested in a medicinal aspect of the treatment.

"You said in that in theory there could be some extension in the life span of a cell, does it also dial back the effect of aging, actually making someone younger?" she asked.

John was surprised in her case; Asthma was one of the conditions he was hoping to treat and he assumed that a treatment would be of more interest to her than turning back the clock a few years.

"Yes and no. Only part of the aging process is caused by cellular and DNA damage and Methuselah is able to help repair some of that damage, but there are still many aspects that we don't fully understand. We've only just begun testing so at the moment, all of the results are still open to interpretation," John answered, beginning to wonder what was wrong with the people in front of him.

He had not worked hard all of these years to have his work turned into a beauty treatment for vain men and women. The tall Yorkshire man already had his hand in the air before John had finished speaking.

"Presumably when you have achieved satisfactory results from the current trials, you'll be moving on to human subjects. What sorts of medical conditions do you feel you will be looking at for the trial groups?" he asked.

Finally, a question he could sink his teeth into, John thought with relief, but Gwen, however, sensing his rising irritation, beat him to the mark, desperate to become involved before John began to get angry.

"That's an excellent question and the truthful answer is we do not yet know the full range of possibilities. We are looking at any condition caused by faulty or malfunctioning genes. A few examples we could begin to look at, with the exception of cancer which in itself is a whole family of conditions, are multiple sclerosis, cystic fibrosis, Parkinson's disease, bipolar disorder and haemophilia to name but a few," she answered, reeling off the conditions from the top of her head.

Unlike John, she had no problem speaking in front of people.

Gwen seemed to have impressed the crowd. Every one of them knew most, if not all, of the conditions and the debilitating nature of them to their victims and families.

A young man stepped forward. He was very dashing with a heavy suntan and was obviously drawn to Gwen.

"When do you foresee these trials taking place, and how do I volunteer for them?" he asked, winking cheekily at her.

John intercepted, this was the point that he had promised Richard he was going to make very clear to them from the start and he wanted to make sure that they were in no doubts as to the timing.

"We've only just begun the first phase of testing, and although the results have been exceptionally positive so far, we need to perform longer term observation before we even think of putting this to human trials. After all, we're talking about fundamental changes at the genetic level. Think about the uproar GM food has caused and then imagine what an outcry there will be with GM human beings. With that in mind, it's likely to be several years before human trials can commence," John stressed to them.

That took Richard by surprise and he interrupted immediately before John could go into too much detail. He had hoped that the potential cures themselves would be of more interest to the investors for now, but he had underestimated their interest in other aspects of the project.

"What Dr Simmons is trying to say is we can only make an educated guess at this point based on the current trial data. Dependant on success, the human trials can be brought forward if all goes well," Richard interjected.

He looked belligerently at John, wishing he would be a little less open until they had discussed the decision a little further in private.

The investors, however, did not appear concerned by talk of delays. They had heard enough to know a potential blockbuster drug when Gwen had reeled through the list of conditions Methuselah could potentially treat.

They nodded enthusiastically and began to talk excitedly amongst themselves. It was obvious they were all interested in this new product and the huge number of potential applications, all of which would lead to an enormous return on their investments. Richard smiled as he watched them chat; it could not have gone better.

They would be snatching his hand off to get a piece of the action.

"If everyone could follow me, I have a presentation on the financial implications of the project and forecasts on projected sales for you to look at," he said, walking over to the lab doors and holding them open, indicating that the group should follow him.

On their way out, many of them took the opportunity to shake hands with Gwen and John again. Several of them complemented John on his new promotion. Richard had told the group about John's importance to the project before Gwen and John returned from their lunch, stressing his continuity plan to ensure he kept him on side. Like the presentation, Richard viewed John as just another tool in the corporate toolbox. When the investors left the lab, he stuck his head back round the door and spoke to them briefly.

"Congratulations both of you, that was fantastic. By the way, I left a little something on your desks that I need you to look through. I would appreciate it if you could get it back to me by the end of the day if possible. Oh and Gwen, can you pop in later this afternoon? I need to speak to you about another matter," he said gratefully, before disappearing after the excited throng of people.

He left John wondering exactly what had just happened. Both he and Gwen had expected a much longer discussion, but it appeared their input was no longer required.

"He really is closed minded when it comes to performing human trials, isn't he? He must know we're nowhere close." John stated rhetorically, not really expecting an answer from her.

Gwen nodded. She had also been unimpressed by Richard's answer to the final question. Richard knew the piles of legislation that applied to the testing of new drugs, which was why so many of them failed before getting close to a human subject.

"What do you think he left on our desks? You don't think it's our new contracts do you?" she asked, half joking.

"I doubt if he could manage to arrange a promotion that quickly, but there's really only one way to find out" John replied, striding off. Gwen ran after him, leaving the lab empty.

When they arrived at John's office there was a fat A4 envelope with 'Private and Confidential' emblazoned in big red letters across the front. John tore it open and unceremoniously dumped the contents onto his desk amidst dozens of unfinished reports and other paperwork.

"Well I never! Richard has kept to his word. There is a new contract of employment, enhanced pension options, bonus scheme information, share options and what looks like an executive car catalogue," he said, leafing through the individual documents.

"Come on then, what does it say?" Gwen asked impatiently, placing her hands gently on his shoulders and peering over his head at the mess of paper.

"He has made me research director as promised and I presume you must have a duplicate of this for the equivalent development role. Bloody hell, look at that salary, it's way over the industry standard and more than two and half times what I'm getting now," John replied suspiciously.

"That's fantastic, isn't it?" she commented.

"I don't know Gwen. I have a very bad feeling about all of this. He only mentioned the promotion this morning and yet here's all the paperwork signed, sealed and delivered a couple of hours later."

He handed the documents to Gwen.

"What do you think?" he asked curiously.

"John, I can't look at your contract, what if it's better than mine or vise versa! It could cause bad feelings," she objected.

"If he's given me more than you, then you have grounds to complain and if he has given you more than me, then good luck to you," John told her, unconcerned about competing with her.

Gwen smiled and began to scrutinise the documents, carefully reading all the sub-clauses to look for some form of legal jargon to prove there was something amiss but she couldn't find anything.

"John, everything looks totally legitimate; you get a full benefits package along with the salary, which is pretty standard for a position at that level. What's making you so nervous?" she asked, a little bewildered.

It was obvious to her that Richard was purely trying to ensure that John would stay because he was crucial to Methuselah. Without him, there was no project and therefore no investment opportunity.

"No, you don't understand. I'm sure the paperwork is legitimate and I know I should be excited about getting the job and a new car et cetera. It's not what's happening but the ease and speed at which it's happening," he told her.

"What do you mean?" she asked, a little confused.

"I'm talking about the rush to get the investors in, the talk of pulling human trials forward and now the promotion sorted all in one day even though I haven't had an ounce of recognition in the past five years. It all seems a little fishy to me," he said seriously, a look of concern on his face. "I know you're involved with Richard, but something in my gut is telling me that we ought to be wary of Richard's motives."

He could see there was something troubling her following his admission. Gwen looked like she was trying to make her mind up whether to say something or not. Handing back the documentation she finally spoke.

"Keep this to yourself, but I think Richard almost divulged something the other night in the lab. I think Swiftgene is having some sort of financial difficulty and he's keeping it from the board of directors. It may well mean he has something to hide and that's why he needs the investors on board as soon as possible."

John was a little shocked but it made perfect sense; Richard's behaviour was completely out of character.

"That's very interesting. I think from now on, we need to watch each other's backs. If he's involved in anything shady, we don't want to be dragged down with him. If he's filtering money from the company, someone could end up serving time in prison," warned John, a little more anxious now than he had been; Gwen was after all the man's girlfriend.

She contemplated what John was saying and old doubts once again began to surface about her association with Richard. She had never been fully happy with the situation and, so far, it had only been a dozen or so nights out with his wealthy friends and their vapid girlfriends. Richard had originally pestered her into dating him, and given the concerns she was experiencing now, Gwen realised it was long overdue that they went their separate ways.

"I think you're right, we have to be very careful," she agreed.

John suddenly smiled and in a much lighter tone changed the subject.

"Well, doubts or not, there isn't any reason why we can't take advantage of the situation. At least the contracts are legally binding so I suggest we sign them, choose a car and get them back to him before he has a chance to change his mind," he advised, chuckling.

John decided to take added advantage considering he had a legitimate reason behind his offer.

"How about we go out for a meal tonight to celebrate our joint good fortune?" he suggested, "We could go to The Stag again, the food there was excellent."

Her face lit up and she rewarded him with a smile.

"That's a great idea but forget The Stag, why don't we go somewhere local to both of us instead? That way neither of us would have to drive and we can celebrate the good news properly with a few drinks?" she countered.

"Okay, but do you have anywhere in mind? I'm afraid I don't go out that much in Worthing."

"Actually, there is a really good Indian restaurant just outside the town centre called The Royal Jaipur that the local newspapers rave about. How about I meet you there at about seven thirty tonight?" she suggested happily.

"Seven thirty it is," he accepted.

When Gwen disappeared to fetch her contract, John suddenly had a terrible recollection of their last meal together. He had not bought a single item of clothing in years and did not want to turn up looking like a hobo as he had the other night. He hurriedly scrawled his signature on the documents and returned them to the envelope provided. On the way to Richard's office, he dropped in at the test facility to give Brian a list of instructions for the rest of the afternoon.

Richard was not in his office and John guessed that he was still sweetening up the investors so he scribbled a quick note and left it on his desk with the signed contracts. John rarely used any of his holiday entitlement and routinely lost them at the end of each financial year, so he always had plenty in reserve. He decided to claim half a day, so he could smarten himself up a little before his date with Gwen.

He left Gwen a note telling her that he would still meet her that evening, with a copy of his phone numbers just in case. Within twenty minutes, he was on his way to the car park, eagerly anticipating his first shopping spree ever.

Richard had been elusive all day and Gwen had not managed to get hold of him as requested, finally deciding enough was enough at six o'clock. He had been ignoring her calls and she was furious at him for leaving her so little time to go home and get changed to meet John.

She had to admit to herself that she was growing more than a little fond of her new partner in crime and she was honest enough to accept that John had played a part in her decision to finish her relationship with Richard. It had taken her only a short time working with him to realise theirs was not a relationship based on love, at least not from her point of view anyway. However, she didn't believe in having that particular discussion at work, so she would have to bite her lip for now and settle for just dropping her contract on his desk. Unfortunately, Richard was now at his desk and wanted to talk.

"I've been trying to get hold of you all afternoon. Why have you not been answering your phone? I'm meeting John for a meal tonight and now I'm late," she complained, irately throwing him the sealed envelope.

"You never mentioned that you were going on a date with John," he accused, his jealousy rearing its ugly head.

"Don't be stupid, we're not going on a date. We're just meeting for a drink to celebrate the promotions that's all, and the reason I didn't mention it was because we only made plans this afternoon after the meeting. If you had answered your phone I could have told you," she snapped back, unhappy with his tone.

It was his own fault that he had ignored her calls and her patience was growing thin.

"What did you want? I've told you I'm running late," she demanded again.

Itching to get home, she made a point of checking her watch to demonstrate her impatience.

"Well, I feel sort of awkward now; I also wanted to take you out to celebrate and I have spent the whole afternoon chasing down tickets for the Theatre Royal. I was going to take you to a restaurant afterwards for something to eat and from there I thought you might want to come back to my place," he said, walking round the desk behind her.

He began to knead her shoulders gently, kissing her neck in an attempt to placate her.

His touch made her skin crawl but she resisted the urge to pull away, very conscious of the fact that both of the contracts were still sat on his desk. If she upset him now, he was just the sort of man to 'lose them in the post' and she didn't want John to suffer for her mistakes. She had, however, made it very clear on previous occasions that she was not prepared to stay over at his house.

"Richard, I've told you before, I'm not going to just jump into bed with you. We agreed we had to take it slowly after I told you what I went through in Cambridge. There's no way I'm going to repeat that mistake in a hurry, so stop pressuring me," she said, pulling away from him, her face seething with anger.

Since they had met, it appeared that nothing she said or did would stop him trying, which supported her decision to break off the relationship.

"So what are you saying? You would rather go out with John? Where is he taking you, to a burger bar and then a pub? You said you were going to give our relationship a fair try?" he accused.

Turning away from him, she rolled her eyes knowing that there was no way she could get out of the date without potentially upsetting him. She remembered how he had plagued her for weeks with gifts and flowers to get her to go out with him in the first place. Finally, because she had no friends in the area, she had reluctantly agreed to go out for a meal. That was where she had first met his arrogant friends and very quickly realised that all he wanted was a trophy girlfriend to impress them. In hindsight, she should have ended it then, but today was not the right time. The funny thing was, Richard had been right; she would rather go out for a burger with John than to some boring play, especially with him.

"I'll try to get hold of John and let him know. If I can't then I'm not going to stand him up, but I meant what I said about sleeping together," she said, reluctantly fishing her mobile out of her bag.

"That's fine; you can stay in the spare room. You don't have to drive home late and it will be easier to get into work tomorrow," Richard responded, trying not to sound disappointed.

"Okay then, I'll have to go home and pick a few things up first so I'll meet you at yours at around eight," she promised as she looked through her bag for the phone number John had given her.

"Just as long as I reach John!" she mumbled.

***

At six o'clock and after spending an absolute fortune in Brighton, John filled the boot and the back seat of his car with bags of clothing, shoes and a variety of other stuff he had been putting off buying for ages. The cost did not worry him too much as he had built up a tidy sum in the bank over the past five years; after all, he only rented a one bedroom flat, very rarely went anywhere and never spent money on himself.

He decided that a major clear out was long overdue when he arrived home, so he left his new shopping in the car and picked up a roll of black bin bags from the kitchen. Without a moment's hesitation, he went through every cupboard, every drawer and every other place he stored his clothing. He threw everything into a large pile on the bed. As he stared at the pile of tattered old clothing, he realised that he had become an old man at the age of thirty-eight. If it had not been for the arrival of Gwen, he probably would have stayed one. Now he had a reason to smarten himself up and worry about his appearance, even though the best he could hope for was her friendship. He decided it was time to start enjoying his life outside work. John crammed every item of clothing from the bed into the bin bags. He dumped them all in the recycling bin outside, stacking the excess on top when it was full.

It took him several trips to and from the car but he finally managed to bring in his new wardrobe. Now every piece of clothing he owned was new and he could happily go out in public without people offering him loose change. He had even gone to the hairdresser's and was now sporting a much smarter 'short back and sides' instead of his normal unruly mop of hair.

He undressed, remembering to put his old clothes straight into a bin bag before climbing into the shower. He began singing cheerfully as he scrubbed himself clean, appearing several minutes later clean-shaven and smelling of expensive aftershave.

John caught sight of his reflection in the full-length mirror on the rickety wardrobe and realised that he was now a blank canvas. His toned muscles were a result of a great deal of time spent cycling across the South Downs in his spare time. At almost six foot, his excessive cycling had given him an impressive muscular frame without an ounce of fat to spare.

John selected a casual pair of khaki trousers and a plain white cotton shirt. He then pulled on the expensive new pair of trainers he had purchased, and the effect was surprising even to him. Staring back from the mirror was a respectable looking young man, no longer a homeless drop out. Satisfied, he pulled on his new leather jacket, its casual design completing the outfit superbly.

He checked his watch and realised that he had over an hour before he was due to leave, but decided to take a steady walk into the town centre rather than book a taxi. There were a couple of pubs along the way and a few pints of ale might be enough to calm his nerves a little before meeting with Gwen. He had just opened the front door to leave when his mobile phone rang.

"Hello, John Simmons, can I help you?" he answered cheerfully.

Gwen heard his cheerful tone and suddenly found it very difficult to speak to him before answering reluctantly.

"Hi John, it's me, Gwen. I'm sorry but I'm going to cancel our date tonight, I hope I've managed to catch you before you set off," she apologized, and it was clear even to him that there was a hint of disappointment in her voice as she spoke.

"No it's fine, I was just about to leave. Is everything alright?" he asked concerned, she did not sound particularly happy.

"Yes, well no, I mean it's not a problem but I was on my way home and Richard decided to spring a surprise theatre trip on me. I would have turned him down but I don't want to risk jeopardising our contracts," she said slowly.

"You don't think he would...?" John asked, not needing to finish the sentence.

"I wouldn't put it past him. I'm ever so sorry, I would much rather go out for a curry than go to the theatre with him and his arrogant friends. I'm really sorry to cancel at the last minute," she said apologetically, hoping that he was not too disappointed.

John understood entirely but at the mention of Richard's name, the cheerful tone in his voice changed. He replied to her in a more civilised and unemotional manner.

"Don't worry about it, we can do it some other time," he replied.

He understood her position but would have felt better if it was someone else and not Richard that she was ditching him for; it hurt a little.

Gwen was quiet on the other end of the phone but she was still there. He heard her soft breathing down the line. She was rehearsing mentally what to say to him without wishing to appear needy or desperate.

"John, I've really enjoyed spending time with you over the past few days and it's great to finally be able to talk to someone who doesn't find me boring when I drone on and on about genetics. We really ought to make other arrangements and soon," she said sincerely, hoping he would pick up on her less than subtle hint.

Beaming like a stupid teenager, he replied, "Of course we should, don't worry, you go and enjoy your night at the theatre and we'll catch up tomorrow."

Gwen was relieved that he seemed to cheer up but was more than a little disappointed that he did not suggest another date.

"Okay, see you tomorrow," she said and the line went dead.

John punched the air and began dancing on his doorstep, much to the amusement of a teenage boy riding past on his BMX bike.

He realised she still wanted to go out with him; he got the hint that Gwen could end her relationship with Richard soon, and that fact made him uncharacteristically happy.

He turned to go back into the flat and then stopped. Making a one-eighty degree turn, he decided to pop over to The Black Dog; he was already dressed for it after all. He crossed the road whistling and disappeared for a couple of pints.

Seven

Gwen put her mobile phone back into her handbag as she walked towards her car. She had given John the perfect opportunity to arrange something else over the phone and he had either not realised or he was too unhappy with her.

She climbed into her bright red Mini Cooper and gunned the engine, annoyed that she was now going to have to rush when she got home thanks to Richard. The traffic was light so it didn't take her long to get home, especially as she spent most of the journey on the wrong side of the speed limit.

As soon as the front door was unlocked, she ran straight into the house and up to the bathroom for a quick shower before throwing on a plain black dress and some flat shoes. Luckily for her, an overnight bag was still packed from a night out she had promised herself with her friends from Doncaster but never arranged, so she grabbed that and a suede jacket before plunging back down the stairs and into the taxi that she had booked on her way home.

By her reckoning, she had made very little effort with her appearance and was wearing no makeup or jewellery. Unfortunately, with her figure and looks she still appeared stunning; the dress clung to her feminine curves provocatively.

Despite her promise to Richard, the idea of staying at his home was not very appealing, especially after the disappointment of her spoilt evening. She had planned to fake a migraine after a few drinks and make her escape.

The taxi dropped her outside Richard's house in one of the wealthier suburbs of Brighton. When he opened the door to her, Richard couldn't hide his lustful thoughts and stood there openly leering at her. She shuddered and could picture him almost drooling. When John looked at her, he made her feel attractive and desirable, not dirty like this. That was the main difference between the two men; one appreciated her beauty and the other just lusted after it. Richard invited her in, revealing a rather grandiose marble staircase with matching marble tiles inlaid into the floor in the hallway. There were erotic statues all around and it made her think of a high-class brothel she had once seen in a documentary about Hollywood prostitutes.

"Thanks for dressing up," Richard said, still staring at her cleavage unashamedly. "You look hot! You make James's underwear model look cheap," he said huskily.

She was less than impressed by his attempt to give her a compliment by comparing her to his friend's nineteen-year-old bimbo girlfriend who liked to say things like 'It is, in it?' or 'Ooooh that looks expensive'.

Richard's friends were all investment bankers, part of a generation of young ambitious 'Yuppies' who had made their money in the early nineties. All but one of them was single and they loved their young models, parading them around for each other's benefit. Compared to them, Richard was a pauper but he loved mixing with them at all the prestigious events in London, splashing his money round like there was no tomorrow. Following her earlier discussion with John, Gwen wondered where some of it might have come from.

Even though the theatre was no more than half a mile away, Richard had ordered a chauffeur driven car to take them and pick them up afterwards. He loved the attention it brought from the hundreds of scantily clad young women that followed the Brighton nightlife scene. When they arrived, Richard waited for the chauffeur to open his door before climbing out, making his way straight into the theatre and leaving her to climb out by herself. She found him inside with his friends, slapping each other on the back and shaking hands, guffawing at each other's corny jokes. As she approached, several of his friends gave her barely disguised lecherous stares before nodding approvingly at Richard who accepted their praise gladly.

Their girlfriends stood to one side chewing gum and looking distinctly uninterested in their skin-tight sparkly dresses and high heels. As soon as they saw Gwen, the little 'green eyed monster' took over and the four of them looked at her with disdain. They may have been younger but next to her understated elegance and class, they looked cheap.

When Richard had finished his horseplay, he finally came over and offered her his arm to lead her into the theatre. It was not because he cared, he just wanted to make sure everyone knew that she was with him. They walked past all the wealthy and influential people.

Later that night, after a rather mundane performance of some obscure independent play, they all sat round a table in the finest French restaurant in Brighton. The meal had been excellent, marred only by the company with the men getting drunker, while they made suggestive comments as the night went on. The girls just giggled incessantly and talked about the latest celebrity scandal. Gwen just sat there quietly, completely numb from their meaningless waffle, desperate to be home and curled up in front of the television. She nursed a glass of red wine, only her second of the night despite the fact that Richard had been constantly trying to top it up.

Despite this, she was beginning to feel lightheaded and found herself swaying a little in her seat. Gwen also noticed that she had started slurring her words and wondered if the wine was stronger than she had first thought.

All through the evening, Richard's friends had been leering at her and making inappropriate comments to him about his plans for her later that night. Gwen had suffered in silence but she had just about had enough of his behaviour.

She leant towards him, finally determined to give him a piece of her mind and smiled gesturing with her index finger for him to move a little closer.

"I know what you're trying do, but it isn't going to work; I'm not going to get drunk," she whispered, the slur in her voice becoming even more pronounced.

She tried to speak but her eyelids felt heavy and the room was beginning to spin.

The food she had eaten was sloshing about in her stomach and threatening to make a repeat appearance when Richard replied.

"Not at all, I just want to see you let your hair down for once, that's all," he said, smiling knowingly as she struggled to keep her eyes open.

"What have youuuu done til mee ...?" Gwen slurred.

Giving up the battle to stay upright, Gwen slumped forward, her head resting against Richard's shoulder, not understanding why she felt so dizzy.

"I think it's about time I got her home," Richard said, addressing his friends and winking at them in a suggestive fashion, causing them all to laugh and give him the thumbs up.

He dropped a wad of twenty-pound notes onto the table and stood up, helping Gwen's almost unconscious form to her feet. Seeing them rise, the maître d' rushed over carrying their coats and helped Richard slide Gwen's arms into her jacket as she struggled to stand. He had already phoned for Richard's limousine and the driver was now waiting patiently outside for them.

The driver helped Richard lift her gently into the car, whilst reminding him that there would be a substantial fee if she vomited in the back. The drive home took less than ten minutes, by which time Gwen was unconscious, quietly snoring with her head rested on Richards lap. The driver helped him to get her carefully out of the car, supported her while Richard drew yet more money from his wallet, and gave him a heavy tip.

"Would you like any help carrying her inside, sir?" offered the driver.

"No, don't worry I've got her," replied Richard, unceremoniously heaving her onto his shoulder and heading up the steps leading to his front door.

The Afflicted

His house was part of a rather exclusive Georgian terrace and it had been costing him a fortune in mortgage payments until his little arrangement had sorted that for him. Now he lived comfortably. He struggled to put his keys in the door but finally managed to push it open and staggered in, heading up the huge staircase and into one of the guest bedrooms.

As per instructions, his housekeeper had prepared the room especially, making the bed with his finest Egyptian cotton sheets and leaving a pile of fresh towels on the dressing table. He swung Gwen off his shoulder and dumped her heavily onto the bed, the impact barely registering with her unconscious form. Richard roughly pulled the blankets from under her and rolled her into position on her back, none of which caused her to wake. He had been trying to ply her with alcohol all night but she had been determined to stay sober. He had instead been forced to resort to 'plan B', slipping a concoction of drugs into her drink when she had not been looking. He finally had the message that she was not interested in him, which made what he was about to do so much easier. He sat her forward and carefully unzipped her dress, slowly sliding it over her slender body before laying her back on the bed. He gazed appreciatively at her semi-naked form; the firm mounds of her breasts particularly caught his attention. Her rounded hips perfectly accentuated her hourglass figure, which led to the shapeliest legs he had ever seen.

He now knew he would never get the opportunity to see her like this again; she had made it perfectly clear that he would never lay a finger on her. He reached down with both hands and cupped her ample breasts, one in each hand, squeezing gently as he relished their firmness, circling her slightly erect nipples with his thumbs. He slowly slid his left hand down her body, reaching beneath the thin material of her panties and rubbing his fingers through her pubic hair. For a moment, he considered going further; she would never remember a thing with the drugs he had given her, but Gwen moaned slightly in her sleep and caused him to withdraw his hand. Much as he would like to fulfil his own fantasies, he had not brought her here for his sexual gratification.

He strode purposefully out of the room, returning moments later with a small green plastic box that he opened up and dropped onto the bed beside her. In it was a syringe and a stolen bottle of Methuselah. Carefully, he pushed the tiny needle through the rubber membrane in the cap and withdrew all of the slightly yellow fluid within. He had no idea what the correct dose would be for a subject of her size and weight; he decided to inject the whole sample. With his limited knowledge of anatomy, he felt along the inside of her thigh until he located the femoral artery, before piercing the skin and carefully injecting the cool liquid slowly into her. The artery bulged momentarily with the additional fluid pressure until the last dregs disappeared into her blood stream. He removed the needle and held a small wad of sterile cotton over the tiny pinprick until he was certain that there was no evidence of bleeding. He had chosen the location carefully, knowing that unless she bruised heavily there was little chance that anybody would spot the injection site.

Placing everything back into the green box, Richard scanned the room to make sure there was no evidence left lying around. He would have a great deal of trouble if he had to explain medical supplies in the morning. When he was confident there was nothing, he stood there for a few seconds, giving her one more appreciative glance before pulling across the blankets and returning her dignity. For a brief moment, he looked at the peaceful expression on her face as she slept and felt a slight prick of conscience, hoping there were no significant side effects. His pity did not last long and he started to smile. All he had wanted was to sleep with her, to add her to his long list of conquests and she had denied him that one simple pleasure. Richard was used to getting what he wanted from women before moving on, all of them attracted by his apparent wealth, but not her. She had resisted him to the end, but now it was his turn to show her. This was the ideal solution to his problem; his contact needed a subject, and he wanted revenge for his humiliation. Besides, if he had not done it, it would be him lying there now and there would be no more handouts. As far as he was concerned, no woman, even one as stunning as Gwen, was worth his health and definitely not that amount of money. Smiling smugly to himself, he left her to sleep, flicking the light switch and plunging the room into darkness. Her gentle breathing was the only sound as he left the room. She lay totally oblivious to her fate.

The bacteriophage immediately began their assault inside her body. The Methuselah particles harmlessly attached themselves to cell membranes and delivered their payloads efficiently.

The contaminant introduced by Richard, despite being altered, began its assault on her red blood cells, mutating as it had done in the rats. The dose she had received, however, was only large enough to treat ten rats and with her greater bulk, her body would take much longer to start showing symptoms, especially with a much slower human metabolism. Over the next few days though, her new improved genes would begin repairing the damage caused during thirty-two years of aging and enhance her body's immune response. Only time would tell if the improvements would tip the tide in her body's favour in its battle against the invading pathogen.

Richard went downstairs and entered his private study. In the centre was his huge professionally crafted and exceptionally expensive leather topped desk. He had spared no expense when fitting out his home office, purchasing only the finest designer furniture, his favourite item being the Italian leather chair in which he now sat.

When he dialled his contact's number on the phone, an unfamiliar voice answered. This time it was a woman and she employed no form of electronic wizardry to hide her voice.

"Please hold the line, Dr Jennings," said the unfamiliar voice.

In the background, Richard could hear someone wheezing and coughing violently. He heard the woman speaking to someone but he could not tell what she was saying. Another voice in the distance, however, shouted a response, which he heard.

"I'll be the judge of that, now do as you are told and fetch me the phone."

The voice was old and broken, but Richard couldn't tell if the speaker was a man or a woman. Richard listened patiently, trying to identify any noises that would give away the identity of his contact but the line was strangely quiet. It was not long before the phone clicked and the more familiar electronic voice returned. Whoever it was, they were still wheezing as if struggling to breathe and it amused him as the scrambler made it sound like he was talking to Darth Vader.

"Have you made your decision, Richard? Have you found me a subject?" his contact finally asked, still struggling for breath.

"I have done better than that; I've already started the treatment. I settled for Dr Guinevere Taylor and she has just received an entire sample, as I didn't know what size a dose it would take. I would expect to start seeing the first symptoms in a few days, but she is unaware that she is being used as a guinea pig so I'll have to be careful. The project could be threatened if she were to find out," Richard informed his contact, quite pleased with his handiwork.

He was a little annoyed, however, that he had to use his back up sample. There would be suspicions if another vial were to go missing so he would have to replace one of the bottles with a sample of coloured saline if he needed more.

"That's excellent news, Dr Jennings, I'm glad to see you're finally on board with our little project. Make sure you keep me apprised of her progress," his contact praised him.

"No problem, I just wondered, however, if ...?" Richard started to ask but the voice interrupted him.

"I want to know the moment you see any of the major symptoms, and don't worry about her finding out. If necessary, we'll move her to a secure facility so that we don't jeopardise the project."

"But what ...?" Richard tried to ask.

"Enjoy the rest of your evening, Dr Jennings; I'll be in touch shortly," wheezed the voice and it was obvious the owner was really struggling to breathe now.

The phone went dead in his hand, as whoever it was did not seem able to talk any longer.

Richard shrugged and reached into his briefcase, pulling out a leather Filofax bursting at the seams with additional bits of paper. This was where he kept his most vital information, particularly a full record of his dealings with the unknown contact. He wanted to make sure that if things boomeranged, there would be records that he had not being working alone. If worse came to worst he was sure the police or a good lawyer would be able to use his scribblings to track them down. He opened it up and found the appropriate page in the diary section, scribbling down a few words to mark the occasion. 'First human trials commenced today. Subject Dr Guinevere Taylor, Female, 32 years old, 175cm tall, weight approx. 70kg. Initial treatment introduced successfully, 100ml of pre-prepared Methuselah serum with unknown additive. Contact informed of trial commencement but subject remains unaware'. He quickly closed the Filofax and dropped it back in his briefcase, spinning the combination to secure its contents. He smiled as he thought of all the money he was receiving for his part in the deception and felt smug that he had taught Gwen a lesson, even if she didn't know it yet. Besides, if the results in the lab were anything to go by, and as long as nothing went wrong, she should probably thank him.

***

Most of the others were asleep, but rat Number 20 was pacing her cage again, grasping the bars intermittently with her tiny hands and shaking them furiously. The hunger that had been growing all day was now a gnawing pain and was driving her to distraction. The other treated rats were feeling it too and she stared into the next cage, sharing a look of understanding with the animal in there; he too wanted out of his miniature prison.

Internally, their bodies were now much improved, stronger and faster with every system working at previously unknown efficiencies. But the contaminant was depleting the red blood cells. Their bodies could not keep on taking this level of punishment without problems occurring. The dry food humans gave them did not contain the correct nutrients to provide their bone marrow with the raw materials to produce enough red blood cells to replenish those destroyed. With every one damaged, hundreds of virus particles were released infecting yet more blood cells.

Slowly but surely, the rats were ultimately losing the battle with the microscopic army of invaders.

***

Gwen opened her eyes woozily as the sun shone straight through a gap in the curtains and onto her face. She turned onto her back and yawned, stretching her arms and legs in the bed. She pushed back the blankets and was surprised to find herself almost entirely naked.

She began to panic as she looked around the strange room. She couldn't remember anything about her surroundings or how she had got there. On a chair beside the bed was her overnight bag, and beside that was the dress she had worn the night before.

Gwen could remember setting off for Richard's house and a few flashes of some tedious modern play they had watched, but that was about it, everything else was a mystery. Her head was throbbing, obstructing her reasoning, but eventually she realised where she was. Placing the palms of her hands over her bare breasts, she climbed out of the bed and dug out some fresh underwear and a bra from the bag, hurriedly pulling them on. Glancing nervously around as she dressed, she pulled out a pair of jeans and a casual top which she realised was a little tight, but it would have to do.

Both items of clothing appeared creased having been crammed into the bag quite roughly, which was unusual of her. She always preferred to look clean and well presented. But her priority was covering her nakedness and finding out exactly how she had turned up there in the first place. She grabbed the items she had worn the previous night and shoved them into the bag, cramming them in with little care for their condition before putting on her suede jacket.

Satisfied that none of her belongings were left in the room, she headed through the double doors onto the landing and went in search of Richard and his explanation. She walked carefully down the stairs, each step causing her head more pain until she finally reached the bottom. The smell of bacon permeated the atmosphere and she followed her nose to the kitchen where she found a short middle-aged woman in a pinafore juggling several pans on the stove.

"Good morning, miss. Dr Jennings said that I should cook you breakfast," the woman said, her accent hinting at her Slavic descent.

"Where is he?" Gwen asked abruptly, her head hurting far too much for pleasantries.

By now, even the sound of the sizzling fat in the frying pan was beginning to hurt her head. Her stomach however was craving the savoury treat that tempted her with the smell assailing her nostrils.

"Would you like some tablets miss, for your poorly head?" the woman asked politely.

Although she was anxious to speak to Richard, Gwen nodded enthusiastically, desperate to quiet the cacophony of hammer blows beating against the interior of her skull. The woman disappeared into what looked like a large pantry and returned seconds later carrying a box of painkillers which she handed to Gwen. She nodded thankfully and hurriedly swallowed two of them with a glass of water. She had no recollection of ever having such a strong headache from drinking before.

"Can you tell me where Richard is, please?" Gwen asked, repeating her original question and dropping a sleeve of the tablets into her jeans pocket, positive that she would need the rest before the day was done.

"Yes, miss; he's in his study," the woman replied helpfully, pointing back into the hallway.

Gwen followed the woman's directions, immediately spotting a set of lavish looking double doors and barged in without knocking, surprising Richard who was busy typing on his computer.

"Morning sleepy head," he said pleasantly as she pushed both doors shut behind her, the fury evident on her face.

"What did you do to me last night and why the hell did I wake up naked?" she asked venomously.

She walked angrily over to the desk and leant on the edge, staring straight into his eyes with a look that would stop a charging rhinoceros in its tracks. Richard pretended to look offended by her reaction while the picture of her beautiful body stayed on his mind.

"You had a little too much to drink, that's all; I just didn't want you to ruin your dress," he said pitifully, but he could see Gwen did not believe him for a second.

"Did you lay a finger on me at all last night?" she demanded furiously, disgusted by the mere thought of him pawing her unconscious body.

"Of course I didn't. You had already made it quite clear that you weren't interested," he said, strongly protesting his innocence.

Gwen looked at him suspiciously, still not sure whether to believe him or not, but she began to calm down at his adamant protestations.

"How did I get so drunk? I know when I went out I had already made a conscious decision not to drink much, did you spike my drinks?" she questioned him, trying to make sense of the night.

"I didn't need to; you were knocking back the red wine like it had gone out of fashion. I tried telling you to slow down but you wouldn't have any of it. I think you were a little annoyed by James's girlfriend; she kept having a dig at you all night, I thought at one point you were actually going to hit her," he lied.

Gwen peered suspiciously at him, looking for any sign of deceit, but with her throbbing head she could not work out if he was telling the truth or not. The story was plausible; after all, she had made no secret of her intense dislike for the floozies his friends seemed to attract, but by the same measure, it was unlikely that she would be drawn into a petty squabble, never mind entertain the idea of using violence. For the moment, she was at a disadvantage and decided to make a tactical retreat, at least until her memory came back.

"I am afraid I don't remember enough to argue with you and it's already eight o'clock, so I'm late for work. You should have woken me!" she stated, determined to blame him for something.

Despite the fact that he seemed to have a logical explanation for her being there and the condition of her head that morning, she still didn't trust him.

"I came into your room earlier this morning but you looked quite rough so I decided to leave you. I rang work and told John that you'd stayed over and would be working from here," he answered innocently.

Richard knew that she would be upset at the thought of John knowing she had stayed at his house. The look of anger on Gwen's face turned to one of horror and it confirmed his suspicions that even if there was nothing happening between them, there was interest there and that was enough for him.

"Well you were wrong; I'm going in anyway," she said to avoid her embarrassment and stormed out of his office, berating herself for being so stupid the previous night and allowing herself to be put in such a compromising situation.

Gwen winced as she thought of John's reaction and was worried that he would assume that she and Richard had spent the night together. The strange thing was that there was nothing to feel guilty about as the pair of them were mere friends, but Richard was the jealous sort and he would have seen a lot more between her and John. She realised that her own reaction to John finding out was quite interesting; if there was nothing going on, then why was she so bothered what John thought of her? Gwen purposefully slammed the front door behind her and strode off, her mood one of self-loathing as she headed for work.

The Afflicted

Richard watched her walk down the street from behind the net curtains and laughed aloud. She had no idea what had happened and he intended to keep it that way, at least for the moment. He even considered fabricating a night of passion just to add insult to injury, but that would only happen when he had finished his preparations to leave. His parting shot before he disappeared for good.

Eight

John entered the testing unit at about half past eight, just as Brian was about to take the mornings weights.

"Morning Brian, any news today?" he asked cheerfully.

Brian turned to answer but stopped dead in his tracks, staring in disbelief at his boss with his mouth agape.

"Wow Doc, is it a job interview or a court appearance?" his young protégée asked cheekily.

John's appearance was a total surprise and Brian liked what he saw. John looked like a different person compared to the scruffy looking scientist who had disappeared home early the day before. He was wearing a smart pair of grey trousers, crisply ironed pinstriped white shirt and a crimson paisley tie. He was clean-shaven and even had his hair cut short, a radical transformation by anyone's standards.

John found himself blushing slightly at the positive attention. He had convinced himself that his efforts were solely to set a good professional example in accordance with his promotion. Subconsciously, however, he knew that his clothes would help impress a certain young woman of whom he had become quite fond.

"Don't be silly Brian, someone has to set a good example to the likes of you don't they?" he replied, trying to shrug off the attention.

John had not realised just how used to his dishevelled appearance people had become. After all, he was only wearing a simple shirt and tie; he must have been quite a mess before if this was going to be everyone's reaction.

Brian came over and shook his hand.

"I never got the chance to congratulate you on your promotion yesterday," he said sincerely.

As he got closer, Brian began to sniff the air.

"Oh Doc, a shave, haircut and aftershave as well...I should have known, who's the lucky lady?" he teased, winking knowingly.

This time John did blush. Turning away from Brian, he picked a pile of results and pretended to examine them, continuing the conversation over his shoulder.

The Afflicted

"There is no lucky lady Brian; I told you, I'm just smartening up my image because of the job," John said curtly, shuffling the papers in his hands to feign attention. "Now, speaking of work, have there been any changes overnight?"

Brian, realising that he was not going to get John to bite, reluctantly picked up the weight logs and handed them over.

"The rats seem to have peaked at about forty percent above the equivalent control animals mass as of last night in both sets of treated animals. The cancerous rats are showing absolutely no evidence of tumours and all the treated specimens are now taking three times their normal intake of food and water," Brian said as John verified the readings for himself.

The trends in weight gain were almost identical in every animal and John decided it was time to look a little deeper at the physiological changes they were seeing.

"Brian, can you euthanize rats one, eleven and twenty-one please and send them for autopsy. I think it's about time we did a full comparison to see exactly what changes there have been physically," he instructed with a hint of reluctance,

It was a part of the job to which he had never grown accustomed.

"No problem Doc, I'll get on it as soon as I have finished this morning's readings," Brian confirmed, holding up both his thumbs and smiling broadly.

John shook his head as he walked away; oh to be young and stupid again, he thought cheerfully, smiling to himself as he left the lab.

It had taken Gwen a little over twenty-five minutes to walk to work from Richard's house and thanks to a surprise downpour she looked and felt even worse than when she had set off.

The throbbing in her head was beginning to dull but was still distracting enough to sap her enthusiasm. She swiped her card through the reader on the front of the building and rushed along the corridor towards her office, keeping her head down to avoid the sympathetic glances of her colleagues. Because she was not paying too much attention to where she was going, she turned the corner and bumped quite hard into a smartly dressed man in a shirt and tie.

Mumbling her apologies, she continued on her way, keeping her head down as much as possible. It was not until she heard a familiar voice that she stopped dead in her tracks.

"Gwen, are you alright, you look a little preoccupied?" John asked, his voice full of genuine concern.

She cringed inwardly and turned round hesitantly, knowing the man she had almost knocked over had in fact been her new partner in crime. Facing him, she felt even worse as she noticed his new attire; the clean shave and, most striking of all, the absence of his unruly mop of hair.

"Hi John," she answered meekly.

She examined him appreciatively, noticing how his new shirt clung to the contours of his body revealing his athletic build.

Typical, she thought, the only day I turn up looking like a drowned rat and he decided to have a makeover.

"Are you okay?" John asked again, breaking the awkward silence.

"It's nothing. Apparently I had too much to drink and passed out in the restaurant. Then I woke up late this morning and had to rush into work, but my head is pounding so I think I'm going to catch up on a little reading for an hour or two," she stammered, feeling like an awkward schoolgirl talking to her first crush.

She had an overwhelming desire to run off and hide somewhere.

"Hey, we've all been there. You take it easy, there's nothing I can't handle this morning," he said sympathetically, his smile soft and understanding. "In fact I have an errand to run and then I could go and fetch you a coffee!" he offered.

"Thanks but no, I'll be alright after a few more painkillers," Gwen answered, lowering her head and dashing off without another word.

She headed straight for the nearest ladies' bathroom and leant against the first of the sinks to peer into the mirror. Facing her was a woman ten years her senior with bloodshot eyes, bedraggled damp hair and dark rings under her eyes. To make matters worse, her mouth felt like she had slept with a stale onion sandwich in it. She groaned. What she needed now was Lorraine, her shallow but exceptionally vain mature student. Lorraine always had a handbag full of makeup with her, so with a mission in mind, Gwen went off in search of vanity salvation.

Brian had been meticulously working his way through the cages, taking out each rat in turn and placing them on the specially designed scales. The untreated animals were easy; they were docile and sat still so it only took him a few seconds for each.

However, the next batch, the treated control rats, were restless and forced him to chase them round the cages.

Once he caught them, they wriggled and struggled, refusing to settle on the scales without the cover on. By the time he came to Number 20, Brian had just about had enough of their behaviour and was ready to start thumping them.

He unlatched Number 20's cage and peered inside. The rat was nowhere to be seen, so Brian correctly assumed that it was hiding in its bedding enclosure and reached in after it.

"Come on ratty, I haven't got all day," Brian said, feeling through the shredded paper.

He touched a patch of fur and began to close his fingers around the errant rodent when he felt a searing pain in the sensitive region between his thumb and forefinger. Reacting automatically, he yanked his hand free, splattering blood all over the interior of the cage and the bench top. He remembered at the last second to slam the cage door shut before wrapping his good hand around the oozing wound. It was then he noticed a sizeable piece of flesh missing from the bitten area.

"You son of a bitch!" he screamed at the top of his voice, slapping his good hand on the top of the cage angrily, startling the already frightened rat.

Hearing the commotion, John came running in and spotted the unfortunate lab technician clutching his damaged hand.

He grabbed one of the spare lab coats and rushed over to wrap it around the young man's hand and stem the flow of blood.

Gwen appeared at the door a few seconds later and John shouted for her to find a first aid kit, which she fetched from the office next door.

Slowly, John unwrapped the hand and instructed Brian to lay it on the bench so he could get a better look at the damage. There was a jagged piece of flesh approximately three centimetres across missing from the web of skin that joined the thumb and forefinger of Brian's right hand.

"Brian, we have to clean the wound to make sure it doesn't get infected, but it's going to sting quite a lot," John warned, reaching into the first aid kit and retrieving a small bottle of hydrogen peroxide.

John held Brian's hand firmly against the surface and carefully poured the clear liquid slowly onto the raw flesh, making sure he got every nook and cranny. As soon as the liquid touched the wound, Brian experienced a spasm of pain, almost causing John to drop the bottle.

"Bloody hell Doc, you weren't kidding!" Brian exclaimed through gritted teeth, desperately fighting back the urge to scream like a little girl.

John took an absorbent pad, applied some antiseptic cream and placed it on the wound before wrapping a clean bandage to hold it in place.

"That should do you for now, but you need to go and get it checked out at the hospital because you're going to need stitches and maybe a little plastic surgery. You'll probably need a tetanus shot as well," advised John, admiring his handiwork.

"You're kidding right?" asked Brian, staring at him with his mouth open in disbelief.

"Sorry, but no, I'm not kidding! Come on, I'll take you down there myself," replied John, "let me just get my coat and we can go."

"Don't bother Doc; I brought the car today and I would only have to come and pick it up later if you take me," Brian said, looking rather depressed. He hated needles.

"Look on the bright side Brian. You better take the rest of the day off, the tetanus shot can leave you a little sore," John told him, smiling.

"That makes me feel a whole lot better Doc," said Brian sarcastically.

"Before you go though, I have to file an accident report. Can you tell me exactly what happened? Anything at all that you can remember," said John, reaching into the first aid box for the accident book.

Brian began to explain how the treated rats had all been resistant to his handling and John wrote down what he said verbatim.

As they discussed the incident, tiny quantities of rat saliva missed by the hydrogen peroxide seeped into Brian's blood stream through hundreds of tiny capillaries in his hand. The few hundred particles of the mutated virus floating in the saliva began riding the flow into the circulatory system. It would not be long before those tiny invaders began to make their presence known. These mutations now carried portions of the Methuselah virus stolen from the original serum and changed the nature of the disease dramatically. What had been a relatively harmless but extremely contagious disease was now a potential killer and it had found its way into a human being. Because the full Methuselah virus was not present, Brian's immune system was not enhanced and the mutated disease had full sway to attack and multiply, spreading at a much higher rate than it had in the rodent test subjects. Within hours, those few hundred particles would have multiplied to a few hundred thousand and would be spreading virtually unchecked. Brian was now living proof that the virus could be transmitted between hosts.

"What do you think made the rat bite like that?" asked John as Gwen examined the animal once Brian had left.

The rat sat on its haunches, clearly unperturbed by earlier events, cleaning its whiskers as it stared back at them. It had eaten the torn piece of flesh and meticulously cleaned every trace of blood from its cage. It now seemed very calm and docile.

"To be honest John, I don't have a clue what could have caused it, unless the animal was spooked in some way. These animals are usually placid and I have never seen one of them bite anyone as hard or aggressively as that," Gwen replied, noticing that the rat now seemed to be very benign and displayed no hint of its earlier aggression.

"Me neither," he said thoughtfully, turning to look at her.

It was the first time John had seen her since their little collision earlier and he noticed as she stared at the rat that she seemed a little more alert than she had done earlier. It was obvious to him that she had applied some make up, something he had never seen her wear before now, and realised that she must have been a little self-aware about her appearance. He personally did not see the need and had still thought that she looked great even when bedraggled and wet.

Gwen noticed him looking at her and her feelings of self-consciousness returned. She noticed how he glanced away and returned his attention to the animals when she spotted him staring.

"Looking at the other treated animals, it appears that quite a few of them look agitated; it could be a side effect of the treatment. From now on, I want everyone who handles the rats to be a lot more careful and I think it would be prudent to use the thick, bite proof gloves," John said, becoming professional again. "I don't think people understand just how powerful a rat's jaws can be; it's entirely plausible that they could sever a digit with very little effort."

Gwen returned her attention to rat Number 20.

"Actually, you are right about the others; they do look a little agitated, but look at Number 20. It appears to be quite docile compared to the others," Gwen observed, subconsciously rubbing an itchy spot on the inside of her thigh that had been bothering her all day. She wondered for a second if an insect of some sort had bitten her.

Rat Number 20 stared up at the hairless giants. She could still taste the heavenly flavour in her mouth and realised that she had found the food she had been craving for the past few days. Sated, at least for the moment, the pain in her stomach had all but disappeared as her body absorbed the necessary nutrients. For a while, her bone marrow had the right nutrients to replenish her flagging red blood cell production. Somehow, she knew though that the hunger would return and instinct would drive her to find more of the crimson nectar.

When the humans had gone, she began to pace the cage, testing again for any weakness she may have overlooked. She grasped the bars of the cage door in frustration and began to shake them, causing the door to move under her weight.

The first human in his anger had only pushed the door shut and had not latched it properly. With a small push, the cage door swung open easily and freedom beckoned at last. She climbed nervously through the gap and scurried along the bench, her fellow captives calling to her as she passed with many of them hanging from the bars trying to follow her lead.

She leapt from her bench to the next and began to wander past the cages housing her untreated cousins, attracted by the familiar odour of blood issuing from their bodies. They cowered in fear at her much larger bulk, instinctively knowing that she was a threat to them.

Number 20 had seen the humans operate the latches on the cage doors a dozen times and with her Methuselah enhanced intellect, she understood that the latch was accessible from the other side of the bars. Rearing up against the door of the nearest cage, she pulled on the thin piece of metal that served as a latch and pulled. It slid across very easily and she suddenly found herself staring at yet another open cage, but this time from the outside looking in. The rat inside began to squeak agitatedly as she pulled the door open and climbed inside, her hunting instincts now taking over. She moved cautiously towards the much smaller male and prepared to leap, bunching the muscles in her hindquarters. Without warning, she lunged forward, sinking her powerful incisors deep into the creature's shoulder, biting so hard her teeth struck his collarbone. Blood gushed into her mouth and she bit down again, this time into the soft tissue of the neck catching the jugular vein and causing blood to spurt more strongly. Her victim shuddered and dropped down dead instantly. Number 20 drank deeply, biting the body repeatedly in her search for every drop of blood. She even chewed on the flesh, squeezing the last remaining dregs from it, before finally dropping the ruined carcass to the cage floor, her own pelt saturated with blood. Strength seemed to flow into her; she felt so powerful after feeding and the hunger dissipated once again. As before, she found herself becoming less agitated so she sat back on her haunches to start cleaning her fur when a loud scream shattered her peace.

One of the humans had managed to sneak up on her and was now staring at her through the bars of the cage, screaming frantically and pointing at her. Following her natural instinct to run and hide, Number 20 jumped out of the cage and onto the floor, leaving a trail of bloody footprints on the polished surface. Panicked, she ran as fast as she could, attracted to a strange odour nearby. The smell led her to the drains of the cage washing area where an unfinished repair had luckily left one of the waste pipes hanging open. She dived straight into the hole without thinking and continued to run as fast as her legs would carry her down the darkened tunnel until the floor sloped drastically away. She found herself slipping, desperately trying to cling on to the walls of the pipe but only managing to slow her descent a little. She hit a curved section of the pipe with a thump that slowed her down before ejecting her onto a metal grate.

With the wind knocked out of her, Number 20 lay there for a few seconds, her senses assailed by a cacophony of new sounds, smells and sights. In all her life, in fact for several generations of her family, she had never been outside in the open like this before and the pure scale of everything frightened her. Amongst all this sensory stimulation, she managed to home in on a familiar odour; the scent of her own kind. Her nose twitched as she searched for the source of the odour and she realised that it was emanating up from the metal grate beneath her feet.

Number 20 forced her muscular bulk through the narrow grill and disappeared into the sewer system. She followed the scent, searching for the other rats and was surprised to find a much smaller creature, its fur brown and matted with layers of dirt.

Unlike its domesticated cousins, this animal was used to taking care of itself, so when she attacked without warning, he fought back fiercely and managed to escape in spite of his wound.

Number 20 only got the smallest of tastes but it was enough to drive her forward, searching for more of these creatures to hunt.

Fatally wounded, the other rat scampered away and crawled into a dark corner to recover, its lifeblood depleted. It lay there licking the open edges of the rent in his haunches, unaware that hundreds of tiny passengers had hitched a lift in the saliva of its attacker. Exhausted and in pain, the rat curled its tail around its head and went to sleep, oblivious to the miniature war beginning inside its body.

Back at Swiftgene, there was uproar in the laboratory as John Simmons tried to comfort Gwen's mature student, Lorraine. She was the one who saw rat Number 20 attack one of the untreated animals, brutally killing it and cannibalising the body.

John waited patiently until Lorraine began to calm down before beginning to question her.

"Lorraine, can you tell me what you saw?" he asked compassionately.

Lorraine blew her nose noisily before answering.

"Because Brian wasn't here I decided to pick up some of the slack because the project is so important," she sobbed, "so I took the rats for autopsy as you requested and when I got back the big rat was tearing the other one to pieces."

"But did you see how it got out in the first place?" John probed.

"It wasn't me if that's what you're asking!" Lorraine answered defensively.

"Sorry, I wasn't trying to blame you, I just wanted to know if you had seen it escape." John countered.

Lorraine seemed to calm down a little.

"I guess Brian must have left the cage door open when the rat bit him earlier. Dr Simmons, why would it have done that? I mean look at all that blood, it was horrible!"

"I know it was, but try and remain calm. We have to find the animal, so did you see where it went?" queried John patiently.

"Yeah, it ran off over there when I screamed," she said, pointing towards the cage cleaning area and the trail of bloody footprints on the white tiles.

John instructed one of the other technicians to take Lorraine to the treatment room and joined Gwen who was examining the remains of the dead rat in its cage. John noticed that there was a great deal of damage to the carcass, suggesting that the attack had been ferocious. There was evidence that what Lorraine had said was right; there was missing flesh, which suggested that Number 20 ate the rat. John knew that rats could be cannibalistic if they were starving but he was not aware of cases where they would attack a healthy creature like this.

"This is very worrying, I've never seen or heard of anything like this before," John said, keeping his voice down.

"I know, but the thing that is worrying me is this, where is the blood? With an attack this brutal you would've expected pools of it everywhere," Gwen said with a frown.

"I wonder if this has something to do with the restless behaviour we have witnessed in the treated animals. Something in Methuselah has obviously increased aggression, which means we need to find that animal before it gets into the ecosystem," he warned.

Gwen nodded in agreement, making it obvious that she was also concerned by the recent turn of events.

"Well John, the footprints say it went that way, so let's go and catch ourselves a killer!" Gwen said, pulling on a pair of the thick bite-proof gloves.

John followed suit as they traced the footprints carefully, peering into every nook and cranny along the way for the missing creature. As soon as they rounded the corner into the cage washing area, the damaged pipe was immediately obvious.

"Damn it, these areas are supposed to be secure!" John shouted angrily, "these drains lead to the sewers and the largest population of rats in the area!"

Gwen flinched. She had never seen John angry and it took her by surprise given his usually calm demeanour.

"John, you get onto maintenance and see if they know where that pipe comes out of the building and I'll go and tell Richard. This is a serious breach of protocol and he needs to take action, whether he likes it or not," Gwen said over her shoulder, already on her way out of the door.

John found a phone and told the switchboard to put him through to the most senior person they could find in the maintenance area. A couple of seconds later, an engineer called Jonathon spoke to him.

"Hello Dr Simmons, how can I help you?" the man answered nervously.

It was not often that one of the senior people from research contacted their department directly.

"Listen, this is urgent. I'm in the trial facility and I'm staring at two pipes in the cage area that I think lead to foul drains. One of them is open and it's possible that one of the test subjects has escaped through it, so I need to know where they connect to the main sewers," John said, trying to keep his voice professional.

"Dr Simmons, all the foul drains in the facility join together in the basement and empty into a holding tank before being pumped into the sewer," Jonathon confirmed. "If an animal has escaped, it should have been washed into the tank."

"Thank you, that means we should be able to find it." John answered with relief.

"No problem Dr Simmons, any time," Jonathon replied, happy that he was able to help.

John had just put the phone down when Richard came charging into the lab, closely followed by an annoyed Gwen.

"What's the big deal John? We have one rat in the sewers! We have plenty more test subjects don't we?" Richard asked sarcastically.

He had been in a conference call with one of the investors when Gwen disturbed him.

"Are you serious Richard? Methuselah is a gene therapy and we've just released a genetically modified super rat into the natural population," John explained.

"And?" asked Richard sarcastically.

"Ignoring the fact that this creature has already attacked a human being and savagely killed one of the other trial subjects, you might be aware that rats can have up to six broods a year. Can you imagine what would happen if a creature like that were to breed with the local population?" shouted John in reply, standing face to face with Richard.

John had always considered his boss incompetent but this was a new low even for him. Anyone in the industry should have been aware of the strict protocols governing trials and their importance.

The outburst momentarily shocked Richard into silence as he tried to process what John had just told him. He glanced guiltily at Gwen who he had secretly treated the night before and wondered what, if anything, was going to happen to her. Everyone in the lab was staring at the three of them, which was enough to bring Richard to his senses.

"Why don't we take this to my office, we can make arrangements from there," he said, grabbing them both by the arm and leading them out of the lab.

He sat down in his office on the edge of his desk and clasped his fingers as he stared at them with a concerned look on his face.

"Listen, we have to keep this amongst the senior staff. Can you imagine the bad publicity if this were to reach the local authorities?" Richard asked, wide-eyed.

He was not worried about the reputation of the company but the ensuing investigation that would follow and more than likely uncover some of his own misdeeds.

"That may be so, but who's responsible for leaving that drain open in there? There's a reason why the unit is supposed to be sealed," John accused.

"How am I supposed to know who left the drains open? We have maintenance for that sort of thing," said Richard, shrugging his shoulders.

"You're not meant to know Richard, but you have overall responsibility so you need to get whoever is responsible in here now and make sure that everyone else is aware of the procedures before it happens again. And while they're here, get them to fix that one; we don't want any more of them escaping, do we?" snapped John angrily, seeing that Richard did not seem to be taking the situation seriously.

"Before we do anything, we need to let the authorities know that we've lost an animal. They can help to catch it and stop the spread of a potentially harmful species," said Gwen, a lot calmer and more level headed than John or Richard.

At the mention of outside authorities, they suddenly had Richard's undivided attention. If any of the external agencies poked their noses in, there was a significant chance they would shut Swiftgene down.

"Actually, according to one of the engineers, there's a holding tank between the building and the sewers so it is unlikely that the creature has escaped, but it doesn't diminish the seriousness of the situation," interrupted John.

Richard gave out a clearly audible sigh of relief.

"That's positive news. I'll get a professional clean-up crew in here immediately to secure the animal. If we can't find it then we'll do the proper thing and notify the authorities. There's no point in being hasty, because if the authorities are involved we'll lose control of the situation and they could close us down. Remember there are more than a hundred and fifty people working here; I'd hate to see them all lose their jobs over something that can be handled more efficiently by us," Richard replied craftily.

One thing he was good at was the personal manipulation of other people, and he knew neither John nor Gwen would risk making so many people redundant unnecessarily. Richard watched the conflict on their faces with satisfaction for a few seconds as they looked at each other for mutual support.

"Okay, but I want to see proof when it's captured. If we don't find it, then we'll have no choice but to involve the authorities, the risks are just too high," said John finally, with Gwen nodding in agreement beside him.

"I'll get straight on it, is there anything else?" Richard asked, picking up the telephone handset.

"No, I think you have the situation under control," said Gwen begrudgingly

She grabbed John's arm and lead him out of the office. Richard waited for them to leave before beginning to dial, but instead of the clean-up crew, he contacted the pathology lab.

"David, this is Dr Jennings. Have you finished the autopsy on rat number eleven yet?" he answered.

"Yes sir, in fact all three are finished and I was just about to send the carcasses for incineration. Do you want the results sending through now?" David asked.

"Yes please, but can you do me a favour and bring me the carcass of number eleven in one of those portable cooling units?" he asked, "There's something I want to check."

"Yes sir, I'll fetch it up myself, right now" David responded.

Richard placed the phone down carefully and reached into his desk drawer. He pulled out one of the RFID tags used to track the animals and lay it on his desk. It was protocol that as the managing director, he had to issue them personally to ensure complete traceability of the system. Taking out the specialised tool, he crimped the Number 20 onto the blank metal tag before hiding it in his top drawer. It would keep everybody off his trail, provided no one scanned the tag properly.

He didn't want anybody, even a clean-up crew, knowing anything about the escape. If word got out, the company may decide to send an internal auditor to see what was going on. Besides, he doubted whether a pampered lab rat would survive for long in the wild anyway, so the problem should solve itself.

Nine

When Brian had first left work, his hand had still been hurting like crazy, but as he pulled up outside his flat, the pain had sunk to a dull throb and he decided not to bother with the hospital. On his way home, he had remembered that last year he had received a tetanus shot after he stood on a nail in his father's garden. He surmised that there was no point wasting time sitting around for a couple of hours in accident and emergency for them just to change his bandage. John Simmons had done a good job of cleaning up his hand, and he decided that he was going to make the most of his unexpected bounty instead and enjoy a free day's holiday from work.

Brian unlocked the front door to his flat and pushed it open. Inside, there was stuff scattered all over the floor of the tiny living room and it looked like someone had burgled him. Unfortunately, it was the same as he had left it that morning.

Pangs of hunger rippled through his stomach and he made his way to the dingy little kitchen and opened the fridge door, peering inside for anything that remotely resembled food. There was a metallic tray with the remnants of a chicken curry he had bought two days ago, so he scraped it onto the cleanest plate he could find in the sink after hurriedly wiping it with a tea-towel and shoved it in the microwave for a couple of minutes.

He wolfed down the lukewarm curry in thirty seconds whilst lying back on the sofa. When he finished, he dropped the plate to the floor and, feeling strangely run-down, he drifted off to sleep.

Internally, the virus was reproducing, rapidly spreading from blood cell to blood cell.

His bone marrow and lymphatic systems were already responding to the invasion but they were woefully inadequate.

The battle waged on his body was horrible, but his body was already losing badly.

Brian woke up a couple of hours later to find that he was still ravenous even after the curry. Again, he searched the kitchen for something to eat but this time there was nothing. Frustrated, he decided to try his luck at the mini supermarket a few streets away.

The Afflicted

Like many of the smaller local markets run by families from the estate, the shop was sparsely furnished. They were usually very friendly and always had a welcoming smile for their customers. Today, however, the shop was almost empty; the only customers were an old couple debating which potatoes to buy, a pretty young woman who smiled at him as he walked past and a thin youth in a black leather motorcycle jacket. There was the image of a heavy metal band called The Raging Dead emblazoned across the back and Brian thought to himself, what a waste of a perfectly good leather jacket. He was a bit of a purist when it came to heavy metal fashion. The youth stood at a large fridge peering through the selection of pre-wrapped cuts of meat when Brian approached. Spotting Brian's own leather jacket he nodded in appreciation, recognising a fellow rock fan, but Brian ignored him, more interested in the smell that was emanating from the fridge. He reached in and grabbed a piece of the bloodiest steak he could find just as the youth reached for the same piece of meat. The youth dropped it immediately and apologised, looking very sorry; it was obvious he was not looking for trouble.

"Sorry man, my mistake, good meat, uhh," he said pleasantly, shrugging his shoulders.

Normally Brian was really laid back, the sort of man who never got riled about anything, but at that moment something snapped inside him and he began to feel rage welling up for no apparent reason. His stomach was cramping badly due to the weird hunger and he felt the sudden need to lash out at somebody.

"Watch what you are doing, you little punk," Brian shouted, shoving the youth quite hard.

"Hey, calm down. I said I'm sorry. It's only a piece of meat," the youth exclaimed, a little shocked by the angry looking Brian who was now bearing down on him.

All logic had ceased in Brian's head and he took the youth's comment as a form of challenge. He launched himself forward, leaping onto the smaller youth and knocking him to the floor. He sat astride the frightened teenager and began to rain punches down about his head and face, the sight of blood spurring him on to hit the guy even harder and faster. Soon the youth was unconscious, but Brian found that he could not stop. He was in fact fighting the urge to bite the young man when a pair of strong arms encircled him.

If the stranger had not grabbed him and dragged him off forcibly, Brian would probably have continued beating the youth to death. The man flung him to the floor and Brian immediately jumped to his feet, turning to face the new threat, but stopped dead in his tracks. He was enormous, standing well over six feet and wearing a denim jacket with the sleeves cut off to display his muscular tattooed arms to great effect. What little logic still flowed through Brian's head suddenly kicked back in and he realised that the man could probably pull his arms and legs off then beat him with the bloody ends.

"Listen pal, I don't know what your beef is with him but he's had enough. Just get out of here and leave him be," the large man pleaded, he did not want any trouble and was not fond of violence, despite his size.

Brian stared around with bloodshot eyes and saw that everyone in the shop was staring back at him in fear. He looked down at the injured boy in astonishment, not really understanding why he had done it. He began to stagger uncertainly backwards, then turned and ran as fast as his legs would carry him out into the street. By the time he had finished running, he found himself in the park breathing heavily and glancing around furtively to see if he anyone had followed. Frightened, he tried to look as inconspicuous as possible and began walking back in the direction of his flat. He couldn't comprehend why he had been so angry, nor remember why he had suddenly wanted to kill a man he'd never met before.

Brian stared at the bandaged hand now covered in blood again, some of it from the bite wound but most of it belonging to his unfortunate victim. Perhaps he ought to get it checked out, he thought, maybe he had caught some sort of infection, even though the supplier had guaranteed that the rats were infection free. Deciding he would go later if the symptoms got any worse, Brian began to feel weary again so headed back to his flat to sleep off whatever it was that was making him feel abnormal.

***

Gwen and John sat in his office discussing Richard's apparent disinterest in the escaped animal. Anyone working in the industry would have been concerned with the escape of a test subject, even if the creature were known to be completely healthy.

"After what we discussed the other day, I'm starting to get more than a little concerned about his behaviour. The strange phone calls, the promotion and now this. This is not the behaviour of a normal person," said John, looking to Gwen for her opinion.

She nodded, a pained expression forming on her face as she did so. The recent problems with Richard were causing her to regret ever meeting him, talk less of agreeing to going on a date with him.

"I think he wants to brush all this under the carpet, because whatever he's up to is not good and if external authorities come in and start digging around, all hell will break loose. I'm beginning to think that he's a lot more unethical than I'd previously imagined and whatever he's into must be quite big," John continued, ignoring the discomfort Gwen was displaying.

"I'm afraid I agree with you, his behaviour is very strange."

"Strange doesn't cover it. He's secretive, unscrupulous and I'm sure he has promised the investors way more than we can deliver," he continued, looking her straight in the eye.

"You don't know the half of it. To understand him, you have to know what sort of a man he really is, not the persona he puts on for work. He's used to getting what he wants, in fact, that's how we started going out. He pestered and pestered until I finally agreed to go for dinner, and we both knew the rest," Gwen said with a slight embarrassed tone to her voice.

"Oh, I didn't know that," John said with interest.

"Not only that. We only go out with the same group of friends. They're exceptionally wealthy and all they ever do is compete with each other on how much money they can spend. Richard does the same, but I know for a fact that he's nowhere near as wealthy as them, so who knows where he's getting his money from," Gwen continued, her tone bitter.

"I'm sure he isn't the first person who has tried living beyond his means," said John.

"The problem is I've dropped myself in it again. I only agreed to go out with him once and after meeting his friends, I knew he was only interested in a trophy girlfriend. I didn't know anyone down here so I let myself go with the flow and once again found myself stuck with the wrong sort of man," she complained unhappily.

"Gwen, that says a lot about your character. To me, it says you're too nice for your own good, and I suppose he's complimenting you in a way if he thinks that you're a catch compared to a bunch of models," John told her, his argument weak at best.

Gwen recognised her opportunity to set John straight as to the intimate nature of her relationship.

If nothing else, it would make her feel better if he knew the truth.

She didn't want John to be under the impression that her relationship with Richard was rock solid.

"No, there was no compliment. He was using me from the very start and I was just too stupid to see through him. All he wanted to do was get me into bed, something I'm very happy to say didn't happen," and her tone hardened, "I won't let myself be used in that manner, which is why last night he tried to get me drunk. His plan backfired though and I passed out; that's why I was late this morning," she said quietly, glad to get it off her chest.

John had not missed the hint and found the information strangely comforting, although he tried not to show it. The last thing he wanted was for her to think he was callous.

He may not be Gwen's first choice in men but it pleased him to know Richard had not faired any better.

"I am sorry to hear it, but it sounds like you have filled in the missing part of the puzzle. If he's trying to compete with his friends then he has a financial motive. Besides, if he can think of a beautiful woman like you as nothing more than 'arm candy' then there's something seriously wrong with him and his friends," said John, immediately blushing.

The comment had not gone unnoticed by Gwen and it pleased her greatly that he found her beautiful, despite the fact that he had not yet acted on her suggestion that they rearrange their date.

She had no illusions about her looks, but it was nice to know that someone decent like John could think of her that way, especially as it was obvious that he liked her for other reasons as well.

"Well, it seems that we both agree that he may be involved in shady deals, but what are we going to do about it? We can't act without proof and he's right, if we get the authorities involved, it may damage the company image and cost a lot of people their jobs. I'm not sure I can have that on my conscience during a recession," she responded, annoyed that Richard could use their consciences to manipulate them.

"I'll tell you what we're going to do; we'll keep an eye on him till we can gather the evidence to single him out whilst protecting the company. People like him are users, they will not hesitate to take other people down with them so we'll need to be careful," John told her, his anger getting the better of him for a moment.

He now understood why he had disliked the man from the very beginning. John hated anyone who was prepared to manipulate other people so readily.

Hearing John call Richard a user was the last straw and Gwen burst into tears, upset that she had been stupid enough to get involved with yet another man who did not care about her.

"I'm sorry John, but I always seem to get stuck with people like him who are only interested in me for my looks or my body. For once I would like a decent man who actually talks to me and doesn't mind if I sit about like a slob once in a while," she sobbed, releasing years of frustration.

Unfortunately, she was doing it in front of the one man who she wanted to think of her as a strong independent woman, making her feel more despondent. John slid across the floor using the castors on his chair and wrapped his arm around her, allowing her to rest her face on his shoulder. He patted her gently on the back until the sobbing subsided and she sat up to look at him.

"Sorry, you must think I'm a little vain," she apologised, wiping her eyes, feeling a little better for getting it off her chest.

"Don't be silly, everyone worries about their appearance at some time, I mean look at me. Anyway, I don't know what you're talking about, personally I've always thought you looked a bit plain," he said, trying to console her.

She looked at him aghast until she noticed his cheeky grin and realised that he was actually trying to be nice. The pair of them began laughing at how ridiculous the situation was.

"That's possibly the nicest thing anyone has said to me in a long while," she said sincerely and squeezed him tightly.

"Tell you what, you stay here and take it easy for a while. I've just had a really scary thought about the test subjects and there's something I want to try," John said, picking up his ragged notebook and patting her on the shoulder yet again.

She looked at him intrigued, her curiosity suddenly piqued, "What is it? Please tell me it's not something bad?"

He tapped the side of his nose indicating that it was a secret and headed through the office door, obviously on a mission. She took a second to wipe her eyes, feeling a lot better that she'd released her pain. Professionally, however, she was far too curious to do as he suggested and followed him towards the trial facility.

"Hi Lorraine, I want you to take a blood sample for me from one of the treated animals please," John instructed as he entered the lab.

"Sure Dr Simmons, which animal do you want testing?" Lorraine asked curiously.

It was not part of normal trial protocol to single out an individual animal.

She looked to Gwen, who had just entered, for confirmation.

"Any one of the remaining seventeen, but I don't want the sample sent for analysis. I want you to inject the blood into one of the untreated control subjects instead," he told her, amused by the bewildered expression on both Lorraine's and Gwen's faces.

This was definitely not normal protocol for clinical trials and John could see that the two women were thinking he had finally lost his mind. After enjoying their confusion for a few seconds, he took pity and decided to put them out of their misery.

"Do you remember asking me the other day whether the low blood count could be because the virus was replicating?" John asked.

"Yes, but you disagreed," Gwen answered.

"That's right, I did; but thinking about it logically, it would be the perfect reason to explain not only the low red blood cell count but it may also have something to do with the aggressive behaviour."

"Agreed, but you said the virus was denatured by you," Gwen stated.

"And it was, but what is Methuselah designed to do?" he asked, guiding her to the same line of reasoning as him.

"To repair damaged DNA... Of course the reproductive cycle could have been re-initiated, in fact the virus would have been mutated all together!" she exclaimed ecstatically.

"Yes, and if that's the case, then the virus may still be in the bloodstream and will in fact be able to transfer to the new host," he said, happy that she had reached the same conclusion as him.

"Well! What do you want me to do Dr Taylor?" Lorraine asked impatiently, she had not followed the logic.

"Go ahead and inject the blood as Dr Simmons instructed," Gwen told her.

Lorraine took a sample from rat number twelve, using the thick gloves as a precaution, and injected it into rat number two. John made a mental note of the time and left strict instructions that the rats were no longer to be handled without protection and only when there were two people in the lab. He wanted no more incidents. Now all they had to do was wait to confirm his suspicions.

Brian had made it back to the flat and felt rough after his unexpected bout of exercise; the virus was now taking a strong hold on his body. Despite the hunger, he was so exhausted that he literally flopped onto the sofa and fell into a deep sleep for the second time that day.

Brian woke up to find himself lying in the middle of the living room floor amidst all the accumulated debris and realised he must have been writhing about in his sleep. His head was now pounding and the pain in his stomach was getting quite intense so he decided to risk going out for food once again. He was just about to open the front door when the doorbell rang, causing him to jump. Waiting on the doorstep when he opened the door was an attractive young woman in her early twenties, staring angrily at him with her hands on her hips. She was dressed in tight denim shorts and a skin-tight Lycra top revealing her ample bosom; however, he didn't notice that, but the anger in her eyes.

"Where have you been? You were meant to meet me in the Student Union bar at half past eight!" she accused.

She stood there pouting with her arms folded, staring expectantly at him waiting for an answer. Helen

Thompson was a student he'd met at the Student Union bar and he had fallen for her straight away. She always dressed in figure hugging clothes revealing as much of her firm young body as was legal. They shared a common interest in music and had become good friends almost immediately. After growing much closer, they had finally started dating three months ago and Brian was smitten. His attraction to her was helped by the fact that Helen was a consummate nymphomaniac, most nights the pair of them rarely making it out of the bedroom.

However, when angry, as she was now, she could be a complete cow constantly digging at him and making him feel miserable.

She poked him in the middle of the chest with her index finger, pushing him out of the way before squeezing past and flopping gracefully onto his old stained sofa. She continued to stare at him expectantly, waiting for his explanation as to why she had to leave the bar and walk all the way over.

"I'm sorry, but I got bitten at work today by one of the bloody rats and I think I've caught something from it," he said pathetically, holding his bandaged hand up as proof.

The bandage was drenched in blood following his fight earlier that day and he was happy as concern replaced her angry expression.

"Oh my God, are you alright? You could catch anything from those filthy creatures. Look at you, you're all pale and drawn," she said, jumping to her feet and placing the back of her hand on his forehead, "and you're all clammy. We need to get you into bed right away."

He gently pushed her hand away, preferring her sudden display of affection to her angry tone.

"Don't worry; I'll be alright as soon as I get something to eat. I'm starving and my stomach is really starting to cramp," he said, pressing his hand to his midriff in an attempt to ease the discomfort.

Helen was having none of it. She pushed him gently but firmly towards the open bedroom door, carefully placing her feet to avoid various piles of material on the floor that she could not quite identify, nor wanted to.

"Tell you what, if you do as you're told, I'll nip out and fetch you something nice. But first I want to take care of my little Bri, Bri," she said, putting on her little girl voice, happy now that she knew he'd not deliberately stood her up.

The backs of his legs hit the end of the bed causing him to sit down heavily and Helen began undoing the zip of his hooded jacket. She carefully removed it, followed by his t-shirt, socks and shoes, hurriedly tossing them onto the already messy floor. She undid the metallic button on his jeans and pulled down the zip, pushing him onto his back she slid them and his boxer shorts expertly over his hips in one swift motion.

"Now get in to bed, you need to rest," she ordered, stepping round the bed to pull back the duvet.

"I've told you I'm fine, all I need is a little food!" he complained, but he could see that she was not going to back down and slid into bed.

He watched with interest as she undressed herself, eyeing her appreciatively.

"Don't get any ideas," she warned, sliding in beside him and cuddling up to him. "The best thing you can do now is get some rest."

Brian lay there for a while listening to the sound of her breathing and gradually began to fall asleep, the hunger he felt growing stronger and stronger. Finally, he fell into unconsciousness and the pain disappeared.

It was pitch black in the room when Brian woke up. We must have slept for hours, he thought, reaching over to try to find the bedside lamp he kept on the cabinet by the bed.

As he fumbled in the dark, he noticed a strange coppery taste in his mouth and a similar smell assailed his nostrils. He found the lamp and operated the switch, flooding the room with light. That was when he opened his mouth to scream; the scene in front of him was one of horror, but his lungs refused to work and not a sound came out.

The bed was soaked with so much blood that some of it had run onto the floor. There were droplets on the wall facing him as if someone had spray painted it. Helen's body lay immobile facing towards the ceiling, her right arm hanging limply over the edge of the bed. There was a wound on her neck that still slowly oozed her blood onto the sheets where her flesh had been torn open. Her face, however, was peaceful; there was no sign of a struggle and she would have looked like she was sleeping were it not for the blood.

Frightened, Brian ran into the tiny bathroom and stared at his reflection in the mirror. His whole body was saturated in congealed blood and he looked like some ghoul from a forgotten horror film. It was obvious to him that he had bitten Helen but he had no recollection of doing so.

His mind wandered back to his outburst at the mini-market and he started to panic, terrified of what was happening to him. No one was going to believe that it was an accident. He had torn a piece of flesh from her neck for crying out loud. Brian knew he would go to prison for the rest of his natural life for such a heinous crime, or maybe worse, into an asylum for the criminally insane. Brian knew he could not go to prison, he knew what happened to pretty boys like him there. He would become some big fat hairy thug's bitch; no, he was not going down for something he could not even remember doing. With those images fresh in his mind, he experienced a moment of clarity and he made a decision about what to do next.

First, he climbed into the shower and scrubbed his body clean, making sure there was not a hint of blood anywhere. Next, he brushed his teeth until they shone to get rid of the taste of blood. When he was clean, he dug out a pair of black jeans, a black t-shirt and a dark blue hooded jacket and hurriedly dressed.

Brian then went out to his car, drove it round the back of the house down the narrow alley and reversed it into the secluded garden. There were tall trees down both edges screening the garden from the neighbours on either side. He happened to know that the neighbours upstairs were away on business for a few days, so he knew they would not witness anything.

Back in the house, he pushed Helen's body onto the floor, wincing as her head bounced loudly off the hard wooden floorboards. He then dragged the blood soaked mattress out through the back door before returning indoors to pull up the living room carpet, which he used to wrap the still bleeding body. After that, he pulled up the bedroom carpet and used that to wrap up any items that had traces of blood on them. Working as fast as he could, he crammed everything into the back of his Volvo, thankful that he had bought an estate so he and his friends could sleep in it after gigs. He forced the tailgate down until it clicked and took a moment to get his breath back before heading back inside.

Finally, he scrubbed away every trace of blood he could find. While he was scrubbing, he had a revelation and realised that his hunger had all but disappeared since the attack.

Thirty minutes later, he was driving down the A27 towards Southampton, flinching at every approaching car, imagining that the police had caught up with him. Even though he stuck to the speed limit and drove with the most care he had ever done in his life, his nerves were in tatters. It took another hour before he finally reached the New Forest, where the moon provided the only illumination as he turned down the track he had hiked along as a youngster.

His parents had taken him there regularly as a child and he knew the area like the back of his hand. The reason he had driven so far with a dead body in the car was the pits he and his family had discovered ten years ago during one of their many walks. They were deep holes entirely covered by thick undergrowth. He guessed they had been used for fly tipping at some point because there was loads debris at the bottom of them, but they had not been disturbed for years so he knew Helen's body would not be discovered.

Brian reversed the car as close as he dared over the rough ground before dragging his gruesome cargo the rest of the way. He dropped the mattress down first. He knew it would not make a difference but he hoped it might break Helen's fall. Before throwing her down there, he unrolled the carpet to take one last look at his first real girlfriend, the woman who had introduced him to carnal pleasure.

"Helen, I'm so sorry this happened. I know you would never believe me but I loved you and would never have hurt you intentionally," he said, bursting into tears at the sight of her naked body.

He covered her carefully and threw her down the hole, wincing when he heard the dull thump as she hit the bottom. Still crying, he emptied the rest of the evidence down the hole and then jumped in the car, desperate to put as many miles between him and the dumping site as possible. He wondered what he needed to do next and realised that he needed to talk to Dr Simmons to see if he could help.

Woken by the impact of hitting the floor of the pit, Helen opened her eyes and began to wonder why she found herself in absolute darkness.

She was cold and there was something wrapped around her preventing her from moving her arms and legs.

Helen began to panic and started to thrash about on what seemed like piles of broken glass until eventually, the carpet loosened and she was free. She climbed to her feet in the darkness and could tell that she was not in Brian's bedroom anymore.

Her head hurt badly and she was struggling to think straight. Looking up she could just about make out what looked like stars, but her eyes were having difficulty adapting to the poor light. Walking cautiously forward with outstretched arms she finally managed to find the wall of what appeared to be a cave of some sort.

Clawing frantically at the wall she began to pull herself upwards, but about two metres from the ground her hand slipped and she came tumbling back down, banging her head again. Once more, she slipped into unconsciousness and peace returned.

The virus, transferred to her from Brian, was now attacking her blood cells vigorously and, severely drained of blood, her body was already weak and the mutated virus was spreading much quicker in her than it had in Brian. When she woke up the hunger would be much more intense, but for now, she lay on the floor of the pit, sleeping as the tiny invaders robbed her of the last vestiges of humanity.

Ten

Rat Number 20 had made great progress overnight and had put a great deal of distance between herself and the prison she had previously called home. Ahead of her lay the sewage treatment facility and the main sewer leading into Brighton.

She could hear more of her own kind ahead, pattering around and scavenging the few bits of food available. The majority of their diet was found above ground around human buildings, but it was only safe to venture out during the dark. She had already found a few other rats and had attacked them all, her taste for blood now fully developed, draining their bodies fully. Two of the rats she had attacked had not died and they now followed her with a blood-based connection. They were willing accomplices, following her wherever she went, assisting in the kill but not taking a single drop of sustenance unless she allowed them to do so.

She had copulated with one of them prior to attacking it, her urge to reproduce almost as strong as her hunger. By now, she was almost twice the size of the other rats and significantly stronger. Whenever there was contact with their kind, the unfortunate creatures met a gruesome fate. Some of them died but one in six of them recovered, waking up with the same blood-thirsty hunger that affected her.

Every hour of freedom, her miniature army grew exponentially and all of the afflicted followed her loyally. She had hundreds of followers by the time she reached the main sewers under Brighton city centre. They were spreading rapidly through the network of darkened tunnels, leaving a wildfire of infection in their wake.

At Swiftgene, John was looking for Brian. He wanted the results from the little experiment they had knocked together the day before but he couldn't find him anywhere.

"Brian, are you in here?" shouted John, walking into the trial facility.

"I'm sorry Dr Simmons, but Brian didn't come in today. Maybe his hand still hurts after the bite, or perhaps it got infected," Lorraine informed him.

She had decided to cover for him because of the importance of Dr Simmons' project. She enjoyed working with him; he was always very helpful and she had to admit he was quite dashing, especially after his recent makeover.

"Hi Lorraine, have you been covering the animals instead?" John asked, thinking that he ought to check in on Brian to make sure there was nothing seriously wrong with him.

"Yes, I took all the readings this morning and we have yesterday's pathology results back," she said, handing him a pile of paperwork.

John glanced quickly through them but there were no major changes in conditions until he got to the results for rat number two, the rat on whom they had performed his impromptu experiment.

John had boasted to Gwen that the reproductive cycle of Methuselah had been sterilized, but these results suggested that he had been mistaken.

Rat number two had started to display the same symptoms as the treated rats, only she had developed the infection much faster than the other rats with the serum. These results confirmed that the disease was transmittable by blood, so it was very likely that it would be present in other bodily fluids like saliva, sweat or semen. He turned to Lorraine with a worried look on his face.

"Could you do me a favour and give Dr Taylor a call urgently while I check the rest of these," he said, indicating the pile of results.

John walked over to rat number two and leant towards the cage to look at the newly infected rat. It sat on its haunches, watching him with yellow bloodshot eyes. As he leant even closer for a better view, the rat surprised him by leaping against the bars, baring its teeth and snarling as it hung there trying to get to his face. Hearing the commotion Lorraine came rushing over, scared.

"Sorry Dr Simmons, I meant to tell you, this animal is exceptionally more aggressive than the others. I did make a note on the chart," she said apologetically, indicating her scribbling on the associated results.

John stood up shakily.

He had never seen a laboratory animal, or even a wild rat for that matter, behaving in such a fashion, attacking with no provocation. There was a serious problem and he had to make sure that the escaped animal had been re-captured.

There were now two problems; one, the potential cross breeding issue and two, the risk of spreading the infection. Gwen came charging through the door on cue, looking a little startled.

"What is it? Has something else happened?" she asked, looking agitatedly around the lab.

John pointed to the creature that was now hanging off the bars of the cage, giving off a weird growling sound.

"This proves that the Methuselah bacteriophage is now contagious and the worrying thing is that the new form seems to act much faster. I think it's somehow responsible for the aggressive behaviour we've been witnessing," he said, pointing to the animal ranting in its cage.

"We need to make sure that Richard has acted on our little escapee; it's essential that we prevent it reaching the local population.

This creature was infected last night and it's already displaying massive levels of aggression. If the escaped rat isn't caught the affliction will spread like wildfire, especially with the aggression element driving them to attack more frequently," said Gwen, the worry evident in her voice.

She really hoped that even Richard could not have been stupid enough to ignore their warning.

Holding the door open for Gwen, John took one last look at the creature and shuddered.

Fear ravaged his soul as he wondered at the possibilities of his serum turning into something else.

This should not have happened with my serum. I had fully removed the reproductive gene. John thought uneasily.

In his office, Richard was on the phone with a look of extreme agitation on his face as he spoke to his secretive contact.

"Look, I know you said it wasn't important but we've made a rather disturbing discovery here at the lab. Can you tell me what I contaminated the samples with?" he pleaded, anxiously running his fingers through his hair.

He was beginning to regret tampering with the serum, especially now one of the rats had escaped.

If John's results from his experiment yesterday were correct, they were potentially responsible for releasing a hazardous disease into the external environment.

"Despite the fact that you don't need to know, I explained that the introduced material simply impedes the functionality of the inserted genes and it can do no harm. Perhaps Dr Simmons has messed up and his material was not as pure as he first thought," countered the electronic voice.

"I doubt it. Much as I don't like the man, he's meticulous. He denatured the virus to prevent reproduction so there is no way it could be contagious, yet this morning they have proven that the rats are now able to transmit the disease and they are becoming very aggressive. Looking at the results, I suspect that the disease can be transferred using saliva, so whatever you made me add must be responsible," Richard accused, momentarily forgetting whom he was talking to.

"Dr Jennings, I don't care what you think the results show. If you think you have a contagion then you simply have to put the animals under quarantine. They can do no harm if they can't get out," the voice shouted back at him angrily.

"But I told you yesterday, it's already too late; there has been an escape. Dr Simmons and Dr Taylor wanted to go to the authorities so I covered it up and have taken action to make them think the animal had been recaptured, but in truth it's still out there," he moaned pathetically.

"Dr Jennings! Under no circumstances are you to allow the authorities to become involved, I don't care if there has been an escape. There's far too much riding on this project and if you mess it up there will be serious repercussions," threatened the voice, and Richard knew that his contact did not just mean a slap on the wrist.

A knock on the door startled him and before he had time to react, Gwen and John barged into his office without waiting for an answer. It was obvious that they needed to see him urgently.

"Thank you Dr Spencer, it was good to hear from you again," improvised Richard in a pleasant voice, "but I'll have to go now. It appears that Dr Simmons and Dr Taylor are here to see me," he said, knowing that his contact would understand.

"Deal with them in any way you can, but mark my words Dr Jennings, the authorities are not to get involved. We'll talk again soon, and you would do well to remember I don't tolerate incompetence," the voice warned before hanging up.

"Goodbye for now, we'll speak again soon," Richard replied, speaking to an empty line.

He placed the phone down carefully, hiding the slight tremble in his hand and looked up at his colleagues, forcing a fake smile as he did so.

"I guess this couldn't wait, that was quite an important call."

Richard stated, his tone displaying a hint of irritation.

Gwen walked over and leant on the edge of the desk to bring her face level with his.

"It's desperately important. You need to warn the exterminators to wear strong protective equipment. We have confirmed this morning that the infection is communicable," she blurted out.

John noticed with annoyance that Gwen had been correct about Richard's behaviour. The man immediately stared at her cleavage, despite the seriousness of what she was saying.

After a few moments of staring, Richard smiled and then walked over to the portable cooler he'd received from the pathology lab.

"That won't be necessary. They have already captured the rat and this is the carcass right here," he said, lifting the lid to show them the animal as if it was his own personal trophy.

John didn't trust Richard.

He examined the RFID tag and noted it was marked quite clearly with the Number 20 and the rat's internal organs were exposed.

John and Gwen examined the creature closely and although everything seemed to be as expected, John had a sneaking suspicion that something was not quite right with the carcass.

He could not put his finger on whatever it was, so he decided that he was just being paranoid.

"Are you sure it was captured before it managed to infect anything else?" asked John, turning to look Richard in the eye.

For some reason he felt Richard was hiding something from them, but it was just a gut feeling; after all, the evidence was right in front of them.

"As you said John, the waste pipes all connect before emptying into the holding tank. They found the rat on the filter grate looking rather confused and disorientated. The exterminator reckoned it had spent so long in captivity it just didn't know what to do or where to go. He said they literally walked up and grabbed it without a struggle, so I had the creature autopsied to see if there was anything we need to be concerned about. I sent the results to you both via e-mail if you would care to take a look," Richard explained to them in detail, although John had to admit it fitted alongside what the guy from maintenance had told him.

John nodded, satisfied for the moment that they had dodged the bullet and looked at Gwen to see if she agreed. She too nodded, but she had one more thing to say.

"That may have dealt with one problem, but it appears that we may have another, Richard. There is the potential that some aspect of the virus has mutated and it seems that it may be transmittable through saliva. The animal that we infected yesterday has developed the symptoms much faster than the others and is displaying a higher level of aggression. We've already warned the technicians to be extra vigilant when handling the creatures," Gwen informed him reluctantly.

Richard turned to John feigning concern.

"John, you said the virus was sterile, yet here we are, facing quite a serious contagion," said Richard sarcastically.

Richard knew what the real problem was but could not avoid taking the opportunity to have a dig at the man he was rapidly growing to hate. If it was possible to pin the blame on John for what had happened, he would do it in a heartbeat.

"That's the problem Richard, we don't know what has happened and because of that, I think the reasonable thing to do is stop the trial. We need to destroy all the afflicted animals and I'll start again by constructing a new genome from scratch, this time paying attention to the size and structure of the leftover pieces. The first ones treated definitely showed evidence that my DNA fragments worked and that is why the infection took longer to develop; their immune systems had been fortified. Those infected by blood showed an accelerated degeneration and I suspect it will be the same for saliva induced infection," John explained.

He was surprised to see the look of horror on Richard's face at the suggestion that they stop the trial. It was the logical thing to do until they could explain what had happened.

But Richard seemed to have other plans.

"Just wait a minute; I don't think we need to be so hasty. Don't you think it might be useful to study the animals for a little longer?" Richard asked desperately, realising his dig at John had backfired.

Richard had to convince John and Gwen to continue with the project, failure to do so could bring dire consequences from his contact. He doubted whether they would be willing to wait for another couple of years for a satisfactory result.

"The project has been fraught with setbacks from the beginning. We can't run the risk of testing this strain any further; I mean, can you imagine what would happen if we tested the serum on a human being?" John asked with a short laugh.

Richard flinched at that, sneaking a guilty glance at Gwen, wondering exactly what was happening within her body as they spoke.

Was she developing the same contagion as the treated animals? Because if she were, it would not be long before the first symptoms began to show, and when that happened, he knew he had to be far away from Swiftgene. In fact, he aimed to be on a different continent.

"No, I disagree. I say that we need to keep the animals alive. Watching them may lead us to some clue as to what went wrong and maybe give us an idea how to avoid it in Methuselah II. Also this is a unique opportunity to study a previously undiscovered virus; you never know, there may actually be some beneficial results if we look hard enough," Richard said positively, appealing to the scientists in them.

Richard watched as his words sank in and knew he had won them over for the time being. He needed to bring his escape plans forward though. Gwen and John were intelligent and he may not be able to fool them for long.

Later that afternoon, John tried to isolate a sample of the secondary mutated form of the virus in the hope that they would be able to identify it and possibly determine where it came from. Although the evidence suggested otherwise, John was still convinced it didn't come from his Methuselah genome. He had actually sliced out the appropriate section of RNA to ensure there would be no reproduction.

To isolate the virus, they took a sample of rat number two's blood and sent it off-site for analysis, leaving them with nothing to do for the moment.

Gwen, infected by the virus, was starting to feel the first effects as her metabolism accelerated and made a suggestion.

"John, do you fancy something to eat? I'm starving!"

John gave her a curious look as she had eaten only a few hours ago.

She normally had such a small appetite.

"You're hungry already? You must have hollow legs, you ate a massive lunch this afternoon," he said incredulously, "people must hate you for your ability to eat like that and still have such a slender figure."

She blushed slightly at the unexpected compliment, which he seemed to have made without realising it. Whatever his intentions, she fully appreciated the attention he had been giving her.

"Flattery will get you everywhere Dr Simmons, but now you mention it I don't normally eat so much do I? It must be all the stress with the new project," she admitted.

"Do you fancy a bite or what?" she asked, subconsciously rubbing her hand across her perfectly flat stomach.

John was completely engrossed by his work, causing him to miss the opportunity to spend time with her.

"I'd better not, thanks; I think I'm going to hang around here for a while and keep an eye on our friend over there. The results of the blood tests will be ready soon and I would love to know what is making the rats so aggressive," he muttered his attention on his work.

A brief look of disappointment crossed Gwen's face but John missed it.

If he had seen it, he may well have realised his mistake, but he was a scientist and his work always came first.

Not to be beaten, Gwen offered him another opportunity to make amends for his little slip.

"Do you want me to hang around? We can always pop out a little later if you want?" she asked optimistically.

Again, without looking up from his work, John politely declined. Gwen gave up, walking off disheartened. Short of physically twisting his arm, it did not look as if she was going to cash in her rain check today, and she had been so sure he was keen on her. She decided to put it down to the devoted scientist in him and headed off to her car. She was not going to give up on him yet, even if he was a little slow on the uptake.

***

Over in the New Forest, at the bottom of the pit, Helen opened her eyes once again. The transformation induced by the virus had taken a lot out of her physically, along with the bump on her head, and she'd slept for almost twenty-four hours.

She could see stars above her, but it was so dark she could not differentiate between the wall of her prison and the sky. Driven now almost purely by animal instincts she struggled to process the situation with no recollection of where she was or how she got there. All she knew was that she was ravenous. Her blood had been almost fully drained, allowing the virus to spread very quickly through her system, her higher brain functions no longer working due to the lack of oxygen-carrying red blood cells. The muscles in her stomach began to spasm and she screamed out in pain; she needed to eat, and soon.

Standing up groggily, she held her arms out in front of her and walked slowly forward until her hands touched something solid. The rock was cold to her touch, almost wet and she could feel it rising way above her. Driven by hunger, she reached over her head and with super human strength dragged herself slowly upwards. Painfully, she felt her way to the top until finally, at the edge, she managed to swing her legs up and over the edge, dragging her aching body into the night air.

The moon provided little illumination, yet her vision seemed near perfect. The new virus did carry one or two beneficial genes but was nowhere near as effective as Methuselah itself.

She heard a noise in the distance and peered in the direction it came from and a faint glow between the trees caught her attention.

It was so indistinct that anyone else would have missed it, but to her it was like a beacon in the dark. Having no other ideas, she curiously set off to investigate, wondering if she would find something to eat.

Half a mile away, Paul and Donna Smith were trying to sleep in their new tent.

The Afflicted

They were in their forties and had decided to try out camping now that their children had both left for university, although Donna was not quite keen on the idea.

They had arrived that afternoon and cooked lunch over an open fire, realising they should have brought a book or some playing cards to pass the night away.

Instead, they had decided to go to bed and get an early start in the morning.

Paul took advantage of the opportunity by snuggling close to Donna with the hope of making love, but Donna would have none of it, claiming that there was no way she was going to do 'that' in public.

In truth, she was still upset with him for dragging her out into the wilderness rather than booking a comfortable bed and breakfast like the one they had passed not a mile down the road.

Outside the tent, Donna heard a twig snap and sat upright, frightened out of her wits.

She shook her husband roughly by the shoulder.

"Paul, I think there is something out there. Can you go and check it out please?" she whispered nervously, looking around the tent.

In the faint glow of the night light, she saw her husband roll his eyes as he sat up. Indignant, she punched him on the arm.

Paul was not a happy man; her rejection disappointed him and now she was panicking about some tiny creature stumbling about in the woods.

"Donna, it's probably an animal; we're actually in the middle of a forest for crying out loud. Scraps of food from dinner probably attracted it, so there's no need to worry. There's nothing dangerous living in the New Forest," he said with a yawn.

"Shhhhh," she said, holding her finger to her lips, "they will hear us."

"Good, it will probably scare them away," he answered, raising his voice to prove a point.

Another twig snapped outside with a loud crack and this time Paul froze.

"I think you're right; that sounded a lot bigger than a rabbit. I'd better check it out," he said, suddenly feeling a little apprehensive.

He stared straight ahead and he seemed flustered; maybe camping was dangerous after all.

"Be careful Paul, you hear stories about those big cats that have escaped into the wild!" Donna told him, unable to hide the fear from her voice.

Paul climbed out of his sleeping bag and headed towards the zip, pulling it down as quietly as he could to avoid spooking whatever it was in the dark.

He didn't want to get stampeded by a herd of cows after all. He stuck his head out into the cold night air and was surprised to see what looked like a naked young woman covered in something he took to be mud. He might have been a little more hesitant if he had realised it was actually dried blood, but at that moment, he saw nothing to fear from the tiny woman.

Helen crouched by the fire, scraping the burnt remnants of their evening meal from the dirty pans. She was snorting as she ate and glanced furtively around as if she was frightened.

"What is it?" whispered Donna in his ear, causing him to jump as she tried to peer over his shoulder.

"Stay here woman, there's a young girl out there, and I think she may be in trouble so I don't want to scare her off," he said, suddenly realising that he was only wearing pajamas bottoms.

He decided to move towards her; it wasn't right for a woman to be out naked in the woods. Paul climbed out of the tent and approached her with his arms stretched out to the side to show he was not carrying a weapon. As he got closer, the girl rose to her feet and watched him, her head tilted to one side like a curious animal.

Paul could see that she was entirely naked and took the opportunity to admire her lithe young body, finding her firm breasts particularly appealing. Her hair was badly matted and she was filthy from head to toe, but she didn't seem to be frightened of him.

"Are you all right love?" Paul asked cautiously.

Helen did not answer. She just stood there watching him approach. He noticed that her nose had started twitching as if she had smelled something interesting. He continued to ogle her body, feeling himself becoming aroused. When he was close enough to touch her, he reached forward to try to place his hand on her shoulder to comfort her. She began to snarl at him baring her teeth and Paul took an involuntary step backwards, wondering if the girl was mentally unstable.

Without warning, Helen leapt forward, wrapping her arms and legs firmly around his torso with unusual strength and he found he could not move his arms. He staggered a few steps and fell backwards, landing heavily in the dirt with Helen sat astride him, still pinning his arms. With lightning speed, her head lunged forward and she sank her teeth into the soft tissue of his throat. In one swift twist of her neck, she tore a huge chunk of flesh and spat it to the ground before wrapping her lips around the wound. Blood spurted all over her face as she drank, slurping loudly at the crimson liquid.

Paul's mind began to fade as his body struggled with the massive loss of blood. He mercifully sank into complete unconsciousness. Donna watched in horror as the filthy little creature fed from her husband and she knew he was dead. Finally, Donna came to her senses and screamed at the top her voice before jumping through the tent flap and running off into the night. Helen watched with interest as the strange figure dressed in a white nightshirt disappeared into the darkness, intent on finishing her meal.

When the blood flow from her current meal began to slow, Helen lost interest and instead listened intently for the sound of Donna's noisy escape. It did not take her long to ascertain the woman's direction and she leapt to her feet in hot pursuit.

Spurred on by the opportunity to run down her prey, Helen ran faster, sniffing the night air. It wasn't hard to track the woman as she was making a ruckus as she ran blindly through the trees.

Donna was unable to see a thing in the pitch darkness, her throat was sore from the prolonged screaming and she ran blindly through the forest. Her mind struggled to comprehend what she had witnessed. The girl looked like she had been drinking her husband's blood like the vampires in the movies. Her night vision was not as acute as Helen's and it was not long before she ran headlong into a large beech tree. The trunk was almost a metre in diameter and it stopped her dead in her tracks.

Donna's head bounced off the solid wood, breaking her nose and knocking her unconscious. She fell backwards onto the floor and lay perfectly still, her breathing now slow and regular. Donna was unbelievably lucky; Helen passed within metres of her position, completely oblivious to her presence. She'd narrowly escaped the same fate as her husband and would live to tell the tale. Helen gave up the pursuit and headed off into the woods looking for new victims.

Eleven

Number 20 was comfortable at last; she had found herself a nice burrow and surrounded herself with her surviving victims. The blood stained body of her latest suitor lay immobile in the corner. She had mated with the strongest and fittest males she had come across since her escape but had accidentally killed her latest conquest.

As most animals do, she knew the moment conception had occurred and was now carrying a brood of her own. With her maternal instinct sated for the time being, she began to feed again, but she no longer had to search for prey; her loyal victims fetched any terrified creature unfortunate enough to enter her territory. She had become the matriarch of the diseased community, responsible for the infection of thousands.

Her kingdom was spreading very quickly, with every infected rat infecting several more. The death toll was high, significantly reducing the population of rats in the area to a sixth of its original number. Those that remained, however, were ten times more dangerous.

Prey was becoming hard to find in the darkened tunnels, so most were venturing above ground looking for new prey. Other creatures, normally common around towns and cities, were becoming targets. Cats, dogs, squirrels, birds and foxes, everything was fair game to the ravenous hordes. With their new victims much larger, the rats began to attack in packs, and fortunately, the prey usually ended up so badly wounded that very few of them survived to contract the disease themselves. For now, humans were still oblivious to the growing threat, but soon the mounting bodies would give away their existence.

***

John arrived at work and as usual, he headed straight to the trial facility. He suspected the answer was within their grasp but still evading them. He had only been there a few minutes when Gwen arrived and he noticed she somehow looked different. It was subtle, but he couldn't quite explain it. She was literarily glowing with health.

Gwen noticed him staring at her curiously and began to feel a little uncomfortable.

"What is it? Do I have something on my face or something?" she asked, self-consciously feeling around with her hands and looking rather embarrassed.

"Sorry, I didn't mean to freak you out, it's just that you look different somehow. Have you had your hair done or something?" he replied, still staring.

"Typical man, go for the haircut every time," she teased, relieved there was nothing wrong.

John began to blush as he realised there was a natural answer he had not considered.

"I'm sorry, I should have realised. The increased appetite, the healthy glow; you're pregnant, aren't you?" he asked undiplomatically, forgetting that many women liked to keep pregnancy private until they were a number of months gone.

John knew he had made a terrible mistake by the shocked expression on her face.

"No I'm not, you cheeky sod. You might as well go the whole hog and ask if I've been putting on weight," she said, pretending to be offended.

"Sorry, I wasn't thinking," he apologised.

Embarrassed, John decided to shut up and buried his head back in the pile of papers he was studying. Gwen, however, seemed to be contemplating what he had said.

"Actually John, it's funny you should mention that I was in glowing health. When I woke up this morning I have to admit I felt very good about myself; you know, one of those days where you leap out of bed and start singing. Perhaps it's the weather," she said, just in case John had taken her comment to heart.

"I'm not saying another word, I know when to shut up," John answered without looking up, his tone worried.

Realising his discomfort, Gwen decided to change the subject.

"I'm going down to the restaurant for a bacon sandwich, do you want one?" she asked

That was too much for John, she had set herself up too well and he could not help but laugh.

"Food again?" he asked, "are you sure you're not eating for two?"

Gwen threw a pen at him and pretended to storm off, chuckling to herself and happy that they were becoming comfortable enough around each other to make jokes that would be inappropriate from others. She much preferred banter to the constant attempts at chatting her up.

After finishing with the first set of results, John decided to grab a coffee from the vending machine while he waited for the remaining results from pathology. He disappeared into his office to read the newspaper while he enjoyed his warm drink. A couple of particular articles caught his eye.

The Afflicted

Attack in the New Forest

A woman was found hysterical in the New Forest early this morning. She claimed that a young woman had attacked her husband in the early hours of this morning. The bloodstained tent has been found, but there is no sign of her husband's body. The woman has been taken into custody for her own protection after claiming the young woman had bitten her husband's throat like a vampire. No murder weapon was found at the scene but the police are continuing with their enquiries...

Mystery of Disappearing Pets

The police have reported an alarming rise in the number of missing pet reports in the Hove and Brighton district over the last few days. Residents are advised not to allow their pets to wander unescorted in the city. Animal Rights groups have accused local pharmaceutical companies of taking the animals for testing. Anyone with any details is advised...

John shuddered. He immediately thought that the woman had murdered her husband and was probably building a temporary insanity plea. The missing pet story only made him angry. He had a lot of respect for the animal rights groups who showed conviction in the sanctity of all life, but it annoyed him when they made

243

spurious claims like that in the national press. It had been decades since some of the less ethical companies had resorted to using stolen animals for experimentation; the MHRA were very strict on the conditions and types of animals that could be used for clinical trials. There was a lot of investment these days into alternative methods for testing and he personally expected to see changes soon.

He was about to continue when Dave from the pathology lab stuck his head round the door with the missing results.

"Morning Dr Simmons, or should I call you 'Sir' now?" he joked. "Sorry the results are late, we have a bit of a backlog," he added apologetically.

John had always got on well with Dave; they were well known for their comical banter.

He hoped the situation would not change at his promotion.

"Morning Dave, 'Sir' will do fine but I think you ought to add a curtsey for good measure!" John answered wryly.

Dave responded by curtseying very low, as far as his aging knees would allow.

"There are some interesting results there, what are you looking for John? Some form of Leukemia?" Dave asked with interest, his natural curiosity piqued with anything to do with diseases of the blood.

"No, in fact we're more interested in a viral contaminant. What makes you say Leukemia?" asked John with interest.

"Well the blood constituents are all out of balance, the red blood cell count has dropped significantly compared to the control rats, whereas the white blood cells and other lymphatic immune components are also vastly higher than normal," Dave explained. After all, he was an expert in his field.

An idea popped into John's head and he started to connect the dots - the rats' behaviour, the results and the attack.

"Dave, are these conditions likely if, for instance, a virus was specifically attacking red blood cells? And what else would it cause physiologically?" John asked. If anyone knew the answer, it would be Dave.

"Well I'm not aware of any condition like that, but theoretically, the bone marrow would become active to replenish the supply, but they could only create them if the body had a regular influx of iron to produce Haem for Haemoglobin," Dave explained, in his element.

"Of course, that's it," John exclaimed.

John jumped out of his seat and headed out of his office door, shouting over his shoulder as he went, leaving a rather confused looking Dave in his office wondering what had happened.

"Thanks Dave, that's brilliant," he said excitedly.

On the way to the trial facility, he bumped into Gwen who had the latest set of weight results from that morning.

"I was just coming to see you," she told him.

"Me too, I think I have a clue as to what's going on," John said with excitement.

"Does it explain why all the treated rats have suddenly started to lose weight or why their health appears to be deteriorating?"

The last piece of the puzzle slotted into place for him with that piece of news.

"That's fantastic," he said as she stood looking at him, confused, "I think I know what's causing the problem."

He handed her the results but she didn't make the connection.

"There is a virus but I couldn't work out why we were getting the odd results from pathology until Dave gave me an idea. The reason we didn't make the connection is because there is no virus that works in this fashion, at least not at these accelerated rates," John tried to explain, but his mind was going a hundred miles faster than his mouth.

"I still don't get it," Gwen moaned out of frustration.

"Think about it, the rats treated in the trial were also treated with the Methuselah genome that enhanced their bodies and allowed them to fight off the infection for longer. Any rat infected after that doesn't have the benefit of enhanced genes, and hence they develop the condition so much faster," John explained.

"How does that explain the aggression and the attacks?" asked Gwen, still not seeing where he was going with his line of reasoning. She ran her hands through her hair staring at John.

"It's simple, with low levels of red blood cells, the brain doesn't get the oxygen it needs and the body starts acting on instinct. In this case, the instinct is to replenish the raw materials required to manufacture red blood cells, the best source of course being healthy blood. They're simply experiencing a form of blood lust, the same way you or I may crave something sweet when our blood sugar is low," he finished, glad that they now had a theory to explain the animals' strange behaviour.

Her face went through a series of emotions.

"So if what you're saying is true, we could provide a constant infusion of blood directly into the circulatory system and the symptoms would subside. If we could then cure the virus the patient would be back to normal," she said, realising at last.

"Yes, it looks like we have the beginnings of a viable treatment. Shall we get started?" he asked, beaming broadly.

"Well, what are you waiting for, let's ..." Gwen started to say and then stopped mid-sentence, her smile disappearing.

"What is it Gwen?" asked John, looking worried.

"Oh John, I've just had a scary thought. Do you think the virus is able to jump between different species?" she asked, suddenly concerned.

"It depends. The original bacteriophage casing was designed to target any eukaryotic cells so if the mutated virus retains this, it will be able to attack any multicellular organism. Basically any species that's not single celled," intrigued by her line of questioning. "Why?"

"John, Brian was bitten!" she said.

It was John's turn to lose his smile.

"Oh my God, we need to find him immediately and hope that a higher organism like a human being has better control over the blood lust. This time Richard has to act," said John and they ran towards Richards's office.

***

Little Emma climbed down the creaky old steps leading to the cellar in her house. Her parents had told her a dozen times not venture down there, but Emma liked the adventure. It was dark and smelled funny, but there was some great stuff to play with. She especially liked to pile up the suitcases, pulling the tarpaulin her father kept down there over the top to make her own little den.

Emma had no brothers or sisters so she was used to playing alone and could stay down there for hours. She especially liked pretending to be Princess Emma whose real parents were the king and queen of a faraway land. They were coming to rescue her, taking her to their magnificent castle to live happily ever after; every seven-year-old girl's fantasy.

She was peering across her vast lands that stretched all the way to the cellar wall, when she noticed some movement accompanied by a strange wheezing sound and she clambered out to investigate. There was an injured rat struggling to drag itself along the floor. Having never seen one before, Emma assumed it was a small kitten. It left a sticky trail of blood from several nasty wounds as it crawled along, half-dead from an attack. Its attackers had left it for dead, but the virus had already begun to work, giving it extra strength. Alas, the damage was too severe and even with enhanced healing, it could not tolerate the wounds; the continued blood loss was a fatal blow. The rat spotted the little girl as she approached and, driven by hunger, it changed direction, redoubling its efforts to move, almost able to smell the fresh blood in her veins. Emma walked over and reached out her tiny hand to pet the injured creature.

"Come on kitty, are you poorly?" she asked, innocently stroking its blood soaked fur.

Dorothy Johnson stood at the sink drying the dishes as she listened to the breakfast show on the radio when she heard the ear-piercing scream. For a second, she paid no attention assuming it was part of the broadcast before realising the sound was coming from the cellar. She dropped the plate she was drying, and it smashed into a hundred pieces on the tiled floor. Dorothy ran for the stairwell leading to the cellar. She took the darkened steps two at a time risking a serious fall before coming to a dead stop, not able to believe what she was seeing.

Her daughter stood there, screaming at the top of her lungs as she clasped her right hand, tears flowing from her eyes in torrents. Blood flowed over her hand from the stump of her missing index finger. Dorothy screamed in fury and kicked the rat with all her strength as it lay half dead consuming the last piece of the child's finger. The rat crashed against the wall, its body crushed instantly, finally out of its misery. Emma fainted as the shock finally hit her tiny body and Dorothy barely managed to catch her in time before she fell. She carried her daughter's limp body up the stairs crying out for her husband, leaving a trail of blood behind.

The Afflicted

***

Bill Jones sat with his feet on the scruffy old desk in the makeshift office, his large girth shoehorned into the P.V.C. bound office chair that one of his shift buddies had brought in. It was relatively comfortable compared to the standard four-legged piece of plastic the council provided, but he had to admit it was made for someone a lot narrower than him.

He hated this particular shift rotation down in the pumping station. The smell was atrocious, he couldn't acclimatise to it, and for eight hours, it seeped into every pore of his body.

The only thing he did was keep an eye on the main pumps and make sure that the pressure remained within certain tolerances.

Some of the younger guys that were bright enough to go to college loved it down there and utilised the free time to study, but Bill was 'old school' and preferred getting his hands dirty.

If they were able, the council would have an automated system, thereby getting rid of people, but the pumps serviced the whole of the Brighton and Hove area, moving thousands of litres of sewage every hour to the treatment plant. They were usually very reliable, having triple redundancy built in and today was no exception, but on the odd occasion they failed, someone had to be there to fix it immediately or toilets would back up in the city within half an hour.

Bill plodded over to the control panel and wrote down the hourly pressure readings on the log sheet before returning to lie back in the chair and put his feet back on the table.

He opened the top drawer and pulled out one of the well-thumbed adult magazines, opened it up in the middle and allowed the central pinup to unfold. He stared at the particularly buxom young brunette and daydreamed about what he would do with someone like that. It never occurred to him that based on the age of the magazine the girl was now older than he was.

Bill made his way through three of the magazines before a strange whinnying sound, which came from the direction of the pumps, disturbed him.

Disgruntled, he dropped his reading material into the top drawer and took a steady walk over to have a look.

Pump number three had begun to labour badly, the whining sound building intensity until there was a loud clunk and the motor driving the pump tripped out, coming to a complete standstill.

"Oh shit!" he exclaimed. "The bloody filter must have backed up and caused a blockage," he muttered to himself, reaching into his pocket for the adjustable spanner he always carried.

Bill might moan and complain but he preferred to be busy rather than sit about doing nothing. He sauntered down to the main filter and began unclipping the fiberglass housing.

"What's it going to be today I wonder? A bit of carpet, some cardboard or maybe we have a dead body again," he chuckled to himself.

The casing came away with a squelch and a wave of sticky black detritus slopped out of the gap, all down the front of his overalls and onto his boots.

"Bloody typical," he shouted, the stench assailing his already battered nostrils causing his gag reflex to go into overdrive.

He scraped off what he could and sprayed some of the bleach and disinfectant solution provided to prevent contamination over the stain. It didn't really do that much but the smell was preferable to the rancid smell of raw sewage.

Bill dragged his maroon elbow-length protective gauntlets on and one of the filtered facemasks before reaching into the unit through the disgusting, foul smelling slime. Eventually, his finger brushed against something solid and he grabbed it firmly. He attempted to pull it out but his hand couldn't and it slipped free, sending him skidding backwards.

"Right you awkward piece of crap, let's try that again shall we?" he muttered.

He grunted in annoyance, reached in with both hands and got a real firm grip this time. The object was in there tight so he pulled as hard as he could but was initially unable to shift whatever it was. Finally, the blockage began to move and it suddenly freed itself, coming loose with a sickening squishy sound causing him to fall backwards. The oozing, rotten carcass of what looked like an Alsatian dog landed firmly across his chest. He screamed in disgust throwing the rotting dog to one side and climbed to his feet retching, his vomited splashed out adding to the disgusting smell.

As he bent over wiping his mouth, he noticed a multitude of shiny eyes watching him from underneath the exposed section of pipe work. He leant over curiously and peered into the darkness. He switched on his torch just in time to witness two of the largest rats he'd ever seen launch themselves sadistically at his head. One of them landed directly on his face and bit down hard, piercing his eyeball and tearing a strip of flesh from his cheek. The other landed on his shoulder and bit into the soft flesh of his neck causing blood to gush from the wound.

The pain was excruciating. Blinded in one eye, he staggered backwards, slipping in his own vomit and landing on his back. The corpse of the Alsatian exploded underneath his weight, releasing an overpowering stench of decay, making it difficult to breathe. As he lay there catching his breath, hundreds of the creatures rushed out in unison, swarming all over his body, even biting him through the thick cotton material of his overalls. He felt a pain in his groin as one of them bit through the shaft of his penis and mercifully, he blacked out, not caring whether he lived or died. In the dimly lit tunnel, a mound of wriggling fur formed a grotesque mask as the rats drank the ample blood supply.

***

Brian had woken in the morning after sleeping for almost thirty hours, his body sated by the blood he had taken from Helen. During his slumber, however, his red blood cells had been severely depleted and the hunger had returned with a vengeance and his capacity for rational thought had gone.

He went outside and made his way back to the park, somehow knowing that there would be people there. He hid in the bushes not far from a young couple holding hands as they stared at each other lovingly. His sense of smell had increased and he could actually smell the sweet coppery scent of blood flowing through their veins. He knew that he had to be cautious and waited until there was no one else around before grabbing a broken tree branch.

He ran directly towards the pair and swung his makeshift club hard, straight into the face of the man, eliminating the likeliest source of retaliation. The man collapsed to the floor holding his face, barely hanging onto consciousness and the woman started to scream. Brian cut off the sound quickly by grabbing her by the windpipe and digging his fingernails in hard. With one smooth motion, he tore out a huge chunk of her throat. The smell of the fresh blood sent his senses reeling and he went wild, leaping astride the prone body and slurping enthusiastically at the free flowing coppery fluid.

Despite his badly broken face, her boyfriend dragged himself painfully to his feet and ran over to the body of his girlfriend. He kicked the blood-covered fiend as hard as he could and noted with satisfaction at least two of the attacker's ribs breaking under the force. Brian barely felt anything, instead he rolled smoothly off the carcass and was on his feet in less than a second. Without hesitation, he dived headfirst at the boyfriend, sinking his teeth deep into the soft tissue of the man's throat. He was dead before the pair of them hit the ground, but his body continued to thrash about like a fish out of water for several seconds before lying still. Brian drank his fill, gorging himself on the two bodies, then disappeared off once again into the bushes. This time, the infusion of blood did not bring any clarity to his mind, instead it drove him to hunt for more prey, his actions now that of a mindless beast.

Twelve

For the second time, Gwen and John took Richard by surprise as they barged into his office looking both irate and worried. They spared him even the pretence of a knock.

"John, Gwen, you've saved me a trip, I was just coming to drop these off."

Richard blurted, distracting them before either could open their mouths to speak.

He handed them the keys to what they assumed were their new company cars along with a wedge of paperwork and instruction booklets.

"Thank you," they said in unison, taken a little by surprise.

But John was not going to let Richard distract them from the task at hand.

The potential harm that Brian could cause was much too high.

"Richard, we believe the virus can be transmitted through a bite and we believe there's been a release," John stated.

Richard involuntarily glanced at the portable chiller at the back of his office, wondering if they had seen through his deception

"That's not possible. I told you, we captured the rat before it had a chance to infect anything else," Richard began to rant, immediately going on the defensive.

And Gwen's words changed everything.

"Not the rat! He means Brian Travis, John's student technician who was bitten a couple of days ago and has not returned to work since. It's highly possible that he has contracted the condition, even if he isn't showing the symptoms yet, and is a risk to anyone he comes in contact with"

Richard was relieved, again he had dodged a bullet, and no one would hold him responsible for the new revelation.

"That's quite worrying isn't it? I'll tell you what I'll do, I'll send a security detail to go and pick him up straight away for treatment," he said, picking up the handset of his phone.

"Don't jump to conclusions; he might not have developed the symptoms yet. There's the wildcard factor that the mutated virus appears to work much faster when transmitted through bodily fluids than when contracted through the serum. If that's the case, then there's a chance that he may already have passed the condition onto someone else. This time I think it would be prudent to contact the authorities about a potential threat out there," cautioned John; he didn't want Richard to be able to sweep this under the carpet.

"Yes they need to be aware so they can quarantine any carriers to make sure that they can't transfer it as well. They will descend into a sort of sub-human state driven by pure instinct in their search for nourishment," added Gwen, watching the look of horror spread across Richards face.

"Before we go panicking and overreact, what exactly are we looking for? I thought only bodily fluids could transmit the virus. Do you seriously think he's out there biting his friends?" Richard said with a hint of sarcasm, desperately trying to make light of the situation.

"Richard, we can't guarantee that he isn't. The virus depletes red blood cells causing the body to crave blood and it depresses the mental capacity of the host. Effectively, anyone or anything that becomes afflicted with the condition effectively becomes a crude animalistic form of vampire, a sort of sub-human state as Gwen has mentioned," John stressed, trying to explain the potential effects of an afflicted human to the populace.

"Do you expect me to believe that you've created a modern day vampire?" Richard asked, laughing heartily. "Hang on a second, it just so happens that I have Professor Van Helsing on speed dial."

John was furious and slammed both fists hard onto Richard's desk, causing him to jump back startled.

"We're not talking about some horror movie Count Dracula. We're talking about a creature driven by instinct, medically requiring blood to survive. You have to take this seriously because if it starts to spread, we're going to be in one deep pile of shit. You must know that several diseases over the centuries have been attributed to the vampire myth. It just so happens that this condition actually does produce a living breathing vampire!" he shouted angrily.

He struggled to stress the importance of what he was trying to say, unaware that Richard already knew the consequences and was desperately trying to keep his involvement a secret by playing dumb.

He'd monitored every aspect of the experiment and was well aware of the effects on the secondary infected rat.

Richard sat forward and stopped laughing, the look on his face turning mean in a second.

He stared at the pair of them seriously before beginning to lecture them on the potential outcome of releasing the data.

"I'm not going to contact the authorities and tell them there's a vampire roaming the streets of Hove. I said I'll get someone on it immediately and we will bring Brian back here for treatment. Do you understand? I don't want this to get out, you would make a laughing stock of the company and I would personally make sure that you took the fall for that abomination of a product you have created, now get out!" he shouted, finally resorting to veiled threats to silence them.

The outburst and vindictive tone in his voice took Gwen and John by surprise. It was obvious he was not going to listen. They left the office a little unsure on how to progress, discussing the situation as they went.

"He's right you know, and it's my fault. I'm the one who created this monstrosity. I will go down in the history books as the man responsible for 'The Affliction,'" he said, submitting to self-pity.

"John, don't blame yourself, how could you have known this would happen? He's right, let him find Brian and we'll work on a treatment to save him. We can go back and try to find what caused this later when the situation is under control. For now, we need to concentrate on a treatment," she reassured him, putting her arm around his shoulders.

Despite her reassurances, Gwen was worried.

John may have developed the serum but gross incompetence had allowed the rat to escape in the first place. Besides, no one could have predicted what would happen to Brian, if in fact anything had.

As soon as his subordinates left, Richard picked up the phone and spoke to the security manager, Frank Brown. He instructed him to put a team together urgently to go and find Brian. He told them to make it their priority job; he could not afford for this to become a big problem. Richard did not give them the full details of Brian's condition for fear of the secret getting out, but he did warn them that he was very ill and needed specialist treatment. He informed them that one of the symptoms could be violence, so they were authorised to use reasonable force to capture him. As soon as he had finished talking to Frank, Richard immediately called his contact

"Hello, it's Richard Jennings. We now have a real problem! The condition is a lot more serious than we previously thought. If John is correct, the affliction can spread through saliva, so the escaped rat could already be spreading the virus as we speak," he said hastily, as soon as the contact answered the phone.

"I thought you said you had taken care of that particular situation," replied his contact angrily.

"I said I had taken care of John and Gwen's suspicions by providing a dummy rat for them to see because they were going to warn the authorities. The rat itself is still out there." Richard explained guiltily. The voice on the phone was silent for a while as his contact took time to contemplate the situation.

"I don't think we need to worry about the rat for the moment, they are no threat to humans if left alone; besides, how long could a laboratory reared animal survive in the wild? At least you convinced Dr Simmons and Dr Taylor that you had captured the escaped animal so we have plausible deniability." the voice assured him, surprisingly calm given the news.

"There's something else, and this one sounds more serious. One of the lab technicians was bitten a couple of days ago by one of the infected rats. He hasn't returned to work and we have reason to believe that he may now have contracted the affliction. Even worse, John suspects that the secondary form of mutated virus may progress even faster than the serum induced variety and is worried that Brian will devolve into a sub-human state and may already have transmitted the disease to others. I've sent the Swiftgene security officers out to fetch him but we need to minimise the potential damage," Richard said nervously.

There would be very little chance of covering up their involvement if things continued to go wrong. Richard knew as well as his contact that, unlike a rat, a human victim would be able to point the finger.

The voice exploded on the phone letting out a tirade of foul language, screaming with rage and taking a couple of minutes to calm down. Richard just listened without daring to interrupt, his hands physically shaking.

"You fool, if this condition appears in the populace it can be traced back to Swiftgene and you. There is also the possibility that you could implicate me, and trust me; my organisation will be far from happy about that. When your people find this Brian fellow then the official story will be that he disappeared without a trace, do you understand?" the voice instructed ominously.

"You mean kill him? How am I going to do that? I am a scientist, not a hit man!" Richard was shaking as events spiralled out of his control.

"I'll sort that part out. You just find him, get him somewhere secure and then let me know when it has been done," the voice ordered with no hint of emotion, even though he was talking about the life of a young man.

"Okay, I'll sort it out," Richard replied meekly.

He now understood the sort of organisation he was dealing with, they were ruthless and dangerous. For all he knew, someone else could be getting a duplicate of the phone call.

"What about Dr Taylor? Has she started to develop any of the symptoms yet?" the voice asked calmly.

Richard was surprised that his contact seemed so interested when they knew the serum was flawed.

"The only symptom I've noticed in passing is an increase in her appetite. She normally eats like a sparrow, but lately she's eating like a horse. A full meal at lunchtime and quite often sandwiches through the afternoon," Richard told them.

He was so blind towards the woman he was supposed to love that he had not noticed her general improved image of fitness and overall healthy glow as John had.

"Given that we may soon be facing a problem at your end, I'm going to move things along. I'll make arrangements to transfer her to me and we'll continue to monitor her ourselves," the voice informed him.

The potential of this alone gave Richard a warm glow of satisfaction given her recent coldness towards him. That would teach the teasing bitch for tempting him and then walking away for that nerd in the lab, he thought. He knew that whatever awaited her at the hands of his contact would not be pleasant. It would also remove the evidence that he'd undertaken an illegal and unauthorised human test.

"Fine, just let me know the arrangements when you've decided," Richard confirmed, gloating silently.

***

Deep in the New Forest, Helen's first victim, Paul Smith, was starting to regain consciousness. She had sensed that he was not dead the night before when she had returned to her kill and had dragged his unconscious form to the overgrown hideaway in which they were now hiding. He would be good to have around considering he was much bigger and stronger, a useful characteristic if you were hunting prey as large and intelligent as a human being.

Helen crouched about a meter away, staring at him inquisitively, noticing that he smelled different now. The sweet coppery smell was gone and had been replaced by a strange, sour smell. Paul opened his eyes and stared around, slightly bewildered by his surroundings, moving his hand to the partially healed wound on his throat.

She cocked her head to one side curiously, any means of communication long forgotten as the neurons in her brain began to deteriorate. Paul grasped his stomach; he was beginning to feel the first pangs of hunger and would have to feed soon. He attempted to stand but Helen pulled him back to the floor as she watched the multitude of police officers searching the woods for his missing remains. Helen watched, unable to move, waiting for them to make a move. But they didn't find what they were looking for. Later, when they had gone, the two of them would venture out to hunt.

***

At lunch, John watched as Gwen polished off a starter, a main course, and two sweets in a single sitting. This time he knew her well enough to know she would not appreciate any amusing comments. When she had finished she stacked her empty crockery on to the wooden tray and pushed it to one side. She then looked at John who had only eaten a main course and smiled sheepishly, her cheeks turning a slight shade of red and she decided to divert his attention from her for the moment.

"If Brian has become afflicted, we know that we can ease the requirement to feed, but do you have a particular treatment in mind to cure the condition itself? After all, some of the changes are at the genetic level," she asked, leaning closer to him.

"I've already considered that, and I think we need to treat the condition on three fronts. We'll give the patient a heavy infusion of blood to replenish the depleted red blood cells, a strong anti-viral to remove the free form virus and then some form of gene therapy to actively target the inserted genes. That's going to be the most dangerous step, if we get it wrong we could damage the viability of the host's DNA, possibly leading to death," he theorised.

"That all sounds good, but I think you might be over thinking the problem. I don't think the inserted genes are causing the problem, it's just the wayward virus, so I think we might get away with just the first two steps," Gwen suggested.

"Actually, I think you're right and to be honest it will take a great deal of the risk out of the equation," John agreed, nodding his head.

"Good, because we have to prove a method as soon as possible so we can treat Brian when he arrives," she told him.

"Don't worry about that, I've already made plans by creating a few more creatures with the secondary infection to give us a few attempts to prove a cure. It's certainly going to be easier and a lot faster if we're not messing around with any form of gene therapy," John confirmed.

"Well there's no time like the present. Let's go and see if your theory is correct!" said Gwen, climbing to her feet.

They dropped their trays on the kitchen trolleys and left the restaurant, chatting about the potential causes of the transmission. They both agreed that they needed to work out the original cause of the affliction if they wanted a chance to stop the disease properly.

The Afflicted

***

Dr Trevors was at a loss following seven admissions already that day with alleged rat bites. One of the cases, a water authority worker named Bill, could be explained by his frequent exposure to rodents in his line of work. The others, however, were unusual; a seven-year old girl attacked in her own cellar and losing a finger, a woman attacked by five rats in a florist and even a postal worker bitten through someone's letterbox. He could not see a common factor between them other than the rat bites themselves.

All the victims were now showing signs of some sort of infection and he was not familiar with the condition. He knew rats carried many diseases such as Weil's disease, murine typhus, salmonella and even meningitis, but none of those explained the symptoms he was seeing.

The victims were displaying a strong fever and the blood work showed that something was damaging the red blood cells, but he was personally at a loss.

Bill, the water authority worker, showed the worst signs of infection after sustaining more than a hundred bites. The attack had been brutal, leading to the loss of his nose, both of his eyes, genitals, and three fingers. He had also lost an incredible amount of blood. Alt-

271

hough the paramedics had seen no evidence of heavy bleeding at the scene; he had required eight pints of transfused blood to stabilise him.

He placed a call to the Health Protection Agency (HPA) for advice as none of the doctors at the hospital had seen anything like it. On his way back from making the call, Dr Trevors went into Bill's room to assess his progress, although if it had happened to him he would have preferred to die.

Surprisingly, Bill was sitting on the edge of the bed staring out of the window.

"Mr Jones, it's good to see you're beginning to recover. How are you feeling?" Dr Trevors asked politely, looking at where the man's eyes would have been below the bandages if he still had them.

Bill moved his head, uncannily staring straight into the doctor's eyes, although he had just been guided by the sound of the doctor's voice. He made no sound at all, probably too traumatised by the attack, the doctor assumed.

"Bill, my name is Dr Trevors; you're in Brighton General Hospital. Your co-workers found you unconscious in the pumping station. Do you remember what happened?" he asked, and the man's head moved again, as if he was trying to lock in on the source of the sound.

The Afflicted

Dr Trevors took his stethoscope from round his neck and leaned over to listen to Bill's exposed chest, finding a piece of flesh large enough to place the circular metal instrument between the stitched up wounds. Bill began to sniff the air as the doctor leant over before suddenly grabbing his arm and gripping it tightly. Dr Trevors assumed Bill was just looking for comfort through the feeling of another human being and tapped his hand reassuringly.

"Mr. Jones, everything is going to be alright, you're just in shock. Now please let go of my arm, I need to check your heart beat to make sure it's stabilised," the doctor said kindly but firmly, trying to retrieve his arm.

Bill's face, or what was left of it, curled into a mask of sheer hatred as he pulled the doctor physically towards him. He sank his teeth into the exposed flesh of the doctor's throat, tore away a huge chunk and spat it onto the floor. The jugular tore like a piece of cooked spaghetti and blood sprayed out into the room. Bill instantly began to drink with gusto, swigging away at the doctor's life giving essence.

The last thing Doctor Trevors heard were the screams of the other patients and the nurses in the corridor. Mercifully, he sank into unconsciousness, unable to hear the horrible slurping as Bill drank his blood.

***

It had been another long and stressful day when Gwen and John walked over to the executive parking spaces to examine their brand new company cars. John was exceptionally pleased to see that Gwen had chosen the exact same model of Mercedes as his, albeit in red instead of black.

"I think you have excellent taste in cars," joked Gwen as she moved round to the driver's side.

"Oh I don't know, I think mine is much better than yours," he teased, trying to work out which of the many buttons on his remote opened the doors.

He surveyed the car happily. Until recently, he would have been satisfied with any vehicle with a working heater, although he had experienced deep sadness when the tow truck had come earlier to take away his old Honda for scrap.

John could not complain though; he'd gone from a severely out-dated little town car to this powerful and prestigious vehicle, and when all was said and done he knew which one he would rather be driving.

As he sat on the luxurious leather seats Gwen distracted him as he watched her climb into her own car.

Being a sporty model, the seats were much lower than his Honda and John was transfixed as he watched her swing her long slender legs into the car. Just as she was about pull her door closed, she swung them back again and climbed out before walking round to the driver's side of his car. He pressed the button to lower the window and she leant over staring at him.

"John, you never did take me up on that 'rain check', so I was wondering, do you fancy coming over for a bite to eat tonight? I'll cook us something simple," she asked nervously, brushing her hair out of her face and tucking it behind her ear.

John felt an involuntary flutter in his stomach as he wondered whether she was actually making a pass at him.

He replied, still making a concerted effort to focus on her face and not to admire the pert swellings peeking at him from her blouse.

"That would be great, what time would you like me to come round?" he asked nervously; he had not been on a date in over ten years, if not more.

"Why don't you make it around seven thirty, that will give me time to knock something together. You'll need this just in case you can't remember where I live," she said, holding out a folded piece of paper, where she'd written her address and telephone number earlier that day.

Not giving him chance to change his mind she straightened up and walked back to her car. Her blonde hair blowing freely in the slight breeze and the sway of her hips was almost hypnotic. She turned to wave goodbye and for a second he could have sworn she was blushing; he had no idea how uncomfortable she had found it building up the courage to invite him over after he'd turned her down the last time she asked. Gwen had been waiting impatiently for him to ask her out, but he was as naïve as a teenage boy so she had decided to take the initiative herself. He watched her drive off, gunning the powerful engine across the car park, leaving him slightly stunned.

John sat there admiring his car and all the modern gizmos when he realised that he only had a couple of hours to get home, get changed and make his way over to her house.

With that thought in mind, he fired up the engine and planted his foot firmly to the floor, exhilaration overtaking him as the car surged forward with horse-power.

"This is definitely not a Honda Civic!" he grinned, easing off the accelerator to maintain a more reasona-ble speed as he drove through the narrow streets of Hove.

***

The scene at Brighton General Hospital was chaot-ic. It appeared as if all hell had broken loose. Police cars had surrounded the front entrance with their flashing blue lights illuminating the unusual activity. Reporters had described it as the worst catastrophe since the terrorist attack on the political conference in the Grand Hotel in 1984.

Inspector Michael Devon had never heard of anything like it in his whole career. One of his officers had told him that there were bodies lying everywhere at the hospital. He'd thought the officer involved was playing a prank on him, it sounded surreal.

If only that was the case.

It appeared there had been a multiple unrelated attacks resulting in the deaths of twelve people with at least another fourteen seriously wounded and many more with minor injuries. At least the hospital authorities had identified seven people as the perpetrators of the attacks. It appeared that all of them had been unrelated, but the motives had been the same; the attackers had assaulted anyone they came across, several of them biting their victims.

The first had been a water authority worker who had torn out his doctor's throat with his teeth, killing him instantly. It had taken several members of staff and relatives of the other patients in the ward to subdue him, even though the guy was blind and severely injured. Unfortunately, angry relatives had given him quite a beating and he was now in a coma in intensive care unlikely to wake up.

Less than half an hour later, in two separate incidents, a florist and a seven-year-old girl had simultaneously gone on the rampage in two different parts of the hospital.

As with the first attack, they had targeted anyone close by, scratching, biting, and clawing at them. Luckily, the police were already on the scene and they quickly restrained them, minimising any casualties.

As soon as the second incident was under control, four men in the same ward had woken up and commenced a brutal attack on one of the female nurses. One of them had brutally raped her while the others had literally torn her to shreds.

The police in attendance were heavy handed and the four men were nursing a few broken bones and split skull between them.

All of the assailants were now under lock and key back at the station, secured as much for their own safety as anyone else's.

Michael had been quite disturbed when he saw them covered in blood and behaving like wild animals. It was then that the chief inspector had called and told him to come down to the hospital to lead the investigation.

As he pushed his way through the throng of people on his way to the front entrance, he began to wonder what he was getting himself into; many people there were trying to get into the hospital to see relatives, as well as the usual sick-minded ghouls who were just trying to get a look at the scene of a horrific crime and maybe snag an interview on the television.

Michael had abandoned his car a street away, unable to get any closer even with blaring sirens. As he reached the front of the crowd, he noticed that reporters and TV crews corralled to one side, presumably to watch more closely. Reporters were notorious for breaking into crime scenes for that one big story, contaminating evidence and essentially making a nuisance of themselves.

A row of burly police officers held back the crowd and Michael slowly made his way over to them, waving his warrant card at a frightened looking young constable who recognised him immediately, even in civilian clothing.

"Thank God you are here sir. They've set up an emergency room just inside the hospital foyer. The chief inspector is already there, flapping about like a headless chicken," he said to Michael.

Michael had come through the ranks after earning the respect of the officers who worked for him.

The chief inspector, however, was barely out of university and was the butt of many jokes back at the station. Officers knew him to be petty and vindictive on occasions.

"Thanks Constable, are you managing to keep everything under control, or do you need reinforcements?" Michael asked, concerned for his men.

"We could certainly do with a few more men sir; a couple of relatives have fought their way through but luckily the team inside has intercepted them. The hospital has set up a relative's area inside for anyone with family in the hospital. Sir, I know it's not my place but it might be worth considering riot gear, if this crowd gets any more rowdy we're not going to be able to hold them," suggested the young police constable.

"I'll get the reinforcements first and then we'll see where we go from there when they arrive. The last thing we want to do is cause a panic, there's enough tension already," Michael said, slapping the man on his shoulder as he passed.

Heading for the entrance he made a point of ignoring questions from the press, he would leave that to his superior officer.

As soon as he was inside, he spotted the remarkably inexperienced chief inspector talking to a couple of men in white coats, presumably doctors, near the front desk.

"What's the situation sir, have we called for more reinforcements yet?" Michael asked, approaching the man wearing the impeccably presented uniform.

Michael could see straight away what the young constable had meant; his superior had very little experience walking the beat or dealing with people.

He was limited to being a figurehead, good for talking to the press in situations like this, his proper English making him seem like he was fully in control.

"Inspector Devon, glad you could finally make it. We have ourselves a very nasty situation here, it will not do our public relations much good at all," he said insolently, and Michael fought back his usual urge to punch the man.

"What do we have so far?" Michael prompted.

"We have spoken to several witnesses from each of the individual incidents and it appears that all of them were identical MO's. The attackers were all patients brought in earlier today after suffering rat bites. The medical staff are telling us that they're suffering from some form of infection and they suspect that it may be an aggressive form of rabies," the chief inspector said, shaking Michael's hand.

Despite his comments, he knew Michael was very experienced and was desperate for his help.

"Are you sure they said rabies, sir? The disease is very rare in this country and it has a long incubation period. How do you explain so many incidents in such a short period of time?" Michael queried.

It appeared to him that the doctors were clutching at straws if that was the best explanation they had.

In response to Michael's question, the chief inspector grabbed him by the arm and led him over to an important looking man wearing the traditional doctors' apparel of white coat and stethoscope. He was busy issuing instructions to a number of medical staff whom he sent running off as the police officers approached.

"Inspector, this is Mr. Andrew Ridgemount, one of the senior consultants here at Brighton General. Mr. Ridgemount, this is Inspector Michael Devon who is going to be leading the investigation from here on," the chief inspector said, introducing the two men.

Michael noticed the look of contempt on the consultant's face for the chief inspector, obviously seeing him for what he was, and instantly, Michael liked the man.

"Pleased to meet you, Inspector Devon. Sorry about the commotion, but we are trying to regain some form of order," the surgeon said, offering his hand.

Michael shook it, noticing that he had an exceptionally strong grip for a man who lifted nothing heavier than surgical instruments.

"Well Mr. Ridgemount, we need to work together to get you up and running efficiently. What do you want from me and my men that you're not currently getting?" Michael offered.

The Afflicted

It was important they regained control before there were any further casualties.

"Thanks for the offer, but your men are doing a fantastic job keeping the crowd back. I know only one or two have made it past and even they were apprehended quickly," the surgeon said, complementing the police help and recognising their efforts.

"Well rest assured, there will be reinforcements here shortly. I intend to get that crowd even further back and give your guys room to breathe. Because of the unexplained attacks, I'm going to assign three or four officers per floor to make sure your staff are safe," Michael promised.

"That would certainly help take some of the pressure off our security staff. I'll get them to report to your people, they will be at your disposal," Mr. Ridgemount assured him.

"Mr. Ridgemount, if you have the time I would like to hear a little bit more about the condition," Michael requested, mainly to demonstrate that he was now in charge at the hospital and not the chief inspector.

"Inspector, can I be honest? I have no idea what it is and have never seen anything like it before in all my years as a medical practitioner. The closest disease I can think of is rabies, but this condition presents itself within hours of infection. That's unheard of in any disease, the fastest usually taking more than twenty-four hours before symptoms develop," Mr. Ridgemount informed him.

"Is there anyone who can help with the diagnosis?" Michael queried.

"The MPA have been contacted to bring their contagious disease specialists and they will have much more experience than me; we have to face the fact that we may have a potential outbreak," replied the doctor honestly.

Michael felt a little uncertain all of a sudden, if a guy like this was confused and worried then what chance did the rest of them have?

"Can't we control the outbreak now that we have isolated all the assailants?" asked Michael, not entirely comprehending what he was talking about.

"We may have controlled the assailants but my money is still on the rats that passed the disease along initially. The condition seems to be making them more aggressive, hence the large number of attacks in one day. We would normally only get seven or eight a year, so just think about all those people out there who have been bitten but have not reported it. Then we have to consider how many people will get bitten tomorrow or the day after and we find ourselves looking at an epidemic," Mr. Ridgemount explained, finally giving Michael a true picture of the situation, a picture he wished he did not understand.

The chief inspector was listening patiently to the discussion but was now starting to feel like the fifth wheel that he was.

"Listen gentlemen, this is all very interesting but I have promised a press release to update the public on the situation. What should I be telling them?" he asked impatiently.

"Sir, I think for now we release only the pertinent details or we'll have a mass panic on our hands. The last thing we want to tell them is that those bitten by rats become crazed killing machines. I would suggest that we tell them that there has been a small outbreak of a yet unidentified condition but we have it contained. The condition can only be transmitted through the bite of a rat, so warn them to avoid the creatures at all costs and to bring anyone who has been bitten to the hospital for treatment immediately. While you do that, I'm going to do my best to clear all those idiots outside who are holding up the smooth operation of the hospital, so Mr. Ridgemount here can do his job undisturbed," Michael told him, and he noticed the surgeon was nodding in agreement.

"Yes, the inspector is right; we have to avoid a panic. The MPA will make any further announcements as required when they have determined what we are dealing with,"

Dr Ridgemount added, supporting Michael.

He was pleased to see that they would finally be getting somewhere now Michael was there.

The chief inspector trotted off, happy as the face of reassurance, yet safe from any of the operational decisions should anything go wrong.

"Mr. Ridgemount, I didn't want to say anything in front of him but we need to isolate anyone injured during the attacks, new admissions and anyone who arrives at other hospitals or surgeries. We don't know yet if human victims can transmit the disease," Michael advised, speaking quietly.

Andrew Ridgemount nodded in acknowledgement and immediately began giving orders to senior members of the staff, making sure none of the public was alerted to the possibility.

The fewer people knew the full details for now, the less chance someone would panic and attempt to leave the area, spreading the disease further afield.

Michael stopped one of the police sergeants who was directing the action and gave him instructions to get more reinforcements on the scene.

"Tell them to gradually move the crowd back and off the grounds. I want the entrance clear of people, and if anyone gives you any trouble, arrest them. They must get the message that we will not tolerate this mob mentality," Michael ordered.

"Yes sir, I will get right on it," answered the sergeant, turning to leave.

"Oh, by the way sergeant, where are the witnesses? I would like to have a chat," he asked.

The sergeant did not speak but pointed to the corner of the foyer where a group of frightened people were sitting. Whatever they had seen, Michael could tell that it had severely affected them.

"Well, here goes ...," he said, bolstering his reserve.

Thirteen

Even though it was late, Richard was still working in his office. The security officers he'd sent to look for Brian had come up with a blank so far and he was on the phone with Frank Brown, not yet aware of the outbreak at the hospital.

"Dr Jennings, we have been to the target's flat and there is no sign of him," said Frank Brown over the phone, "it looks like he hasn't been back there for a few days."

"Crap!" shouted Richard, banging his desk in frustration.

He could see his plan to escape crashing down around him if he didn't get control of the situation.

"I want you to call everybody you can from your team and tell them that I'll pay you triple until we find him. It's imperative that Brian is in our custody as soon as possible," Richard barked down the phone.

"Yes sir, we'll start a sweep of the local area immediately. With overtime on offer, I should be able to get another couple of teams on this within the next half an hour," the voice replied confidently.

"Do that, but remember he's suffering from a rare mental illness which means he may become very violent so take every precaution. You may have to use force but don't hurt him too badly, we're trying to help him before he hurts someone. In addition, it would be bad press if someone knew he worked for us, so make sure you keep this as quiet as you can. You know what the press are like; they will be blaming Swiftgene for his condition if we're not careful," said Richard, giving them a long list of instructions.

Richard knew that the longer the situation was under wraps, the better the chance he had of escaping the country without being stopped.

"Yes, sir," responded the security officer, well trained in dealing with the press.

Working in a controversial industry like pharmaceuticals, they were often approached by animal rights protestors trying to get the dirt on the company.

Richard placed the phone back on its base and leant forward onto the desk, holding his head in his hands. If he did not get the situation under control soon, he was going to be in trouble whichever direction he chose. Either the MHRA would have him imprisoned or worse, his contact's friends would be looking for him and he definitely did not want that. For now though, all he could do was wait for news.

***

John arrived outside Gwen's house a little before seven-thirty, paid his taxi driver and nervously walked up the brick paved drive. The house was enormous, maybe five or six times larger than his squalid little flat and he made a mental note never to invite her over to his.

He pressed the doorbell and stood back, admiring the ivy-covered brickwork, while the butterflies in his stomach did acrobatics.

The porch light came on and a familiar silhouette appeared in the glass.

The door swung open to reveal Gwen standing in a figure hugging black dress, the hem of which was high up her thighs, revealing her shapely legs to devastating effect.

He could not help but notice the plunging neckline that reached all the way to her waist, displaying enough of her cleavage to be utterly tantalising.

"Wow! You look absolutely amazing," he said appreciatively, his mouth open as he took in the overall effect.

Gwen blushed and smiled bashfully. "Thanks, you scrub up quite well yourself," she said, eyeing his apparel.

He'd chosen a casual pair of beige chinos and an expensive tailor-made shirt to complement his athletic build, topped off with a brown leather jacket.

It was his turn to blush as he handed her a bunch of red roses.

"These are for you," he said.

Gwen took the flowers and sniffed them carefully, before leaning forward to kiss him delicately on the cheek.

"They're lovely, thank you," she said gratefully.

He stood on the doorstep feeling quite awkward, rocking a little on his feet when Gwen spoke.

"Oh I'm sorry you must think me so rude, please come in," she laughed, stepping to one side.

John stepped through the porch into the huge, brightly lit hallway and glanced around at the richly decorated interior. The work was professionally finished with exposed wood adding character and yet imparting the same elegance he had come to associate with Gwen. Her taste certainly seemed to be expensive.

"This is amazing, did you decorate it yourself?" he asked, truly impressed.

"No, I'm afraid my father brought a team of his builders and decorators down when I first bought it," she replied, pleased by his approval, "he virtually re-built the house from scratch, no expense spared."

As he stared at the décor, Gwen took the opportunity to observe him in the light. The dishevelled look she had once known was entirely gone.

She surveyed his athletic body, his broad muscular shoulders, apparent even under the leather jacket. He was still clean-shaven, revealing a strong jaw line and even though his hair was thinning slightly on the top she found him attractive.

"Your dad's in the building trade?" he asked, turning to face her.

"That's an understatement; he virtually owns the building trade. That's where all the family money came from. I think that was what attracted Richard in the first place; he does seem to levitate towards wealth. Unfortunately for me, my father still tries to control my life and thinks I can't provide for myself. The house is nice but I would have liked to put my own touch on it to make it feel a little more like a home," she sighed, a little harsh but still demonstrating that she loved her father.

"Don't knock it, he is showing you in his own peculiar way that he still cares for you. I wish my father had hung around to help me with anything," he said bitterly, the way he always felt when he thought of his father.

She smiled understandingly and realised he still had his jacket on.

"I'm sorry, I'm not a very good hostess am I? Please let me take your coat," she offered.

John placed the bottle of wine he was carrying on the dresser while she carefully took hold of his coat from behind and slid it slowly from his shoulders, feeling the warmth of his skin through the backs of her fingers.

He picked up the wine and passed it to her, making sure the label was visible.

"A rather full bodied Italian Corvina, La Grola 2005 Allegrini, I would strongly recommend it," he said, laughing. "I remembered that you liked it so I picked it out especially."

"You remembered," she said, covering her mouth, pleasantly surprised.

He nodded, smiling.

"Come, please make yourself comfortable," she said, leading him by the arm into the dining room that was centred with a twelve seat exquisitely constructed dining table.

Again, the room was superbly decorated, the walls adorned with many watercolour landscapes, some of which he recognised as local landmarks.

He had spent many a happy hour escaping onto the South Downs during his free time, sometimes on foot, sometimes taking the harder routes on his mountain bike.

Gwen returned carrying his bottle of red wine and a corkscrew. "Will you do the honours please?" she asked.

He removed the cork and poured the ruby liquid into a couple of lead crystal glasses she had already placed on the table. He offered one to Gwen who took it delicately, her fingers feeling cool and smooth to his touch as her hand lingered temptingly for a moment. She smiled broadly, staring into his eyes, realising what a beautiful, cool shade of blue they were; the strong eyes of a true gentleman.

"Cheers," they said in unison, and clinked their glasses gently.

He watched as Gwen placed the glass to her lips, appreciating the sensuousness as the ruby red liquid disappeared past her perfect and even pearly white teeth. Every time he looked at her, he found himself appreciating her beauty more, a masterpiece crafted by the most gifted of sculptors.

"Dinner will be another fifteen minutes," she informed him, breaking the spell. She pulled out a chair and invited him to sit, patting the velvet seat cover invitingly. He sat down and she squeezed his shoulder affectionately as she left for the kitchen making John begin to feel a little hot under the collar. It had been a long time since he had been in a situation like this and never with someone as stunningly attractive as his current host.

The kitchen door was ajar and he furtively watched her as she moved around preparing his dinner, appreciating her long slender legs displayed to perfection beneath the thigh length dress, the material of which stretched provocatively over her firm buttocks as she bent over to check the contents of the oven.

For a moment, it appeared to him that Gwen had grown even taller, but he quickly dismissed the idea, putting it down to the slimming effect of the dress and the slightly raised heels. If only he knew exactly how much trouble she had taken to choose her clothing specifically to display herself at her best, the finished effect elegant and classy.

She didn't have to worry; John appreciated her efforts.

John was transfixed, unable to take his eyes off her until she reached down to remove plates from one of the bottom cupboards and he saw her breasts swell forward in the dress; he could take no more. He began to examine the watercolours in an attempt to bring his heart rate back to normal.

Dinner was excellent, and John decided that Gwen was in fact the perfect woman. She was intelligent, funny, charming, sweet, stunning and a chef to boot.

He began to wonder why someone had not snapped her up a long time ago.

Her appetite had impressed him again for someone with a figure like hers. He chose not to say anything following his comment about her suspected pregnancy, but he began to wonder if she truly did have hollow legs.

They chatted through the whole meal discussing the ethical intricacies of modern genetics and the approach to genetically modified designer children. It was an unusual topic for a normal dinner table, but these people were scientists and loved their field of work.

Neither had ever experienced such an evening before and they honestly enjoyed each other's company. For John, the fact that she was tremendously gorgeous was purely a bonus; he actually found her company to be immensely stimulating. He began to wonder for the first time since they met whether she could possibly return those feelings to a slightly older, distinctly less attractive, thinning haired scientist.

When she offered him a glass of her finest single malt, he accepted, even though he was already light headed from the wine. He was therefore surprised when she returned with a glass beaker half-full of the amber liquid, possibly enough to knock him on his behind. She led him into the front room and invited him to sit on a leather sofa in front of the largest flat screen TV he'd ever seen.

"Thank you Gwen for tonight, I've really enjoyed it. I haven't had a home cooked meal like that for years and your culinary skills are second to none," he said, complimenting her.

"Thank you, I've enjoyed it too; it's the first time I've entertained anyone here since the house was finished," she said, smiling broadly.

Gwen sat next to him on the sofa and he became intensely aware of the proximity of her leg, a mere fraction of a centimetre from his own, so close that he could almost feel her touching him.

John suddenly began to feel warm again, his heart rate increased dramatically and his nerves danced.

He fought the sudden urge to reach down and stroke her smooth, creamy white thighs, imagining how her soft skin would feel under the palm of his hand.

He shuffled uncomfortably, embarrassed by his own immoral thoughts when she spoke.

"Would you mind if I switched on the T.V? I like to catch up on the news at night time," she asked thoughtfully.

"No, not at all," John replied and passed her the remote control from the arm of the sofa, again noticing as her hand lingered in his.

Gwen had noticed how awkward he seemed to be behaving and wondered if John was not noticing her less than subtle hints. She decided that she needed to be a little more direct in her approach. She switched on the television and selected the news channel whilst she kicked off her shoes. Sitting back on the sofa, she curled her long slender legs beneath her, making sure they rested against John's thigh, noticing how he flinched at the contact. She then laid back and laid her head firmly in the centre of his chest, snuggling her body up to him to get comfortable, sure that even the shyest of men would not fail to read a signal as direct as that.

John reacted by jumping to his feet.

Gwen had severely underestimated how nervous he was and the move had taken him completely by surprise.

His reaction horrified Gwen, and she wondered if she had misjudged his feelings for her. Her cheeks turned a deep shade of red with embarrassment.

"I am so sorry John. I didn't mean to offend you. Please forgive me," she stammered, not knowing where to look.

John was mortified by his own childish reaction to such close contact.

"No, please, it's my fault entirely; you took me a little by surprise that's all. I just haven't been that close to a woman ... since ... since my wife," he said, very ashamed by his immature reaction.

Realising that he was just shy, she reached over and took the tumbler of whiskey from him, carefully depositing it on the coffee table. She moved closer to him until her breasts pressed firmly against his chest and placed her hand delicately on the back of his neck.

"There's no need to be sorry," she promised him.

John was still confused. He knew what he wanted, but he was also exceptionally nervous. He could feel the warmth of her breath on his face as she moved forward to kiss him. Making a decision, he placed his hands on her shoulders and softly pushed her away, wincing at the look of disappointment she displayed.

"Gwen, I'm so sorry, but I can't. It wouldn't be right with us working together and you and Richard ...," he said, having to exercise amazing restraint.

His heart was telling him to submit completely to her; his logical mind was considering her feelings and dignity.

"John, I thought you would have guessed by now that there's no Richard anymore. The only thing I can think of is that you think there's something wrong with me," she stated with confusion, her eyes glistening from the tears that were threatening to come.

"Absolutely not! You're an exceptionally beautiful young woman who is talented and charming. You can't begin to understand how flattered I am, but I would be taking advantage of you. I'm much older and we hardly know one another," he tried to explain, watching with surprise as the look on Gwen's face changed from embarrassment to a knowing smile.

"I'm afraid that isn't entirely true, Professor Simmons. I have known and liked you for years. You seriously don't remember me at all, do you?" she asked, smiling, a new look of relief now showing.

This time it was his turn to look puzzled.

He had not been called professor for over four and half years now.

John examined her features but could not place them anywhere apart from Swiftgene.

"I'm sorry, but I'm not sure what you are talking about. I'm positive I would remember you if we'd met before," John assured her.

"It was my fourth year at Cambridge and I took your molecular genetics lectures for a couple of terms, you were famous in the academic community even then. That was when I first fell in love with you, your comments on one of my essays are what made me branch away from chemistry and into genetics," she replied, fondly recalling the time.

"I must have marked thousands of essays from hundreds of students over the years, I'm not sure I would have written anything special in yours; I prided myself on being fair and unbiased," he said, struggling to picture her from the hundreds he taught.

"You were fair, in fact you tore my essay to bits and I don't blame you. Quite frankly, it wasn't very good. What you wrote was 'You have missed the point this time, but trust me, keep on trying; you are a smart and talented young woman and I am positive you will go far'. From that moment on I was enamoured," she explained.

"But why, that's not very good; you messed up the essay," he said, really beginning to get confused.

"It wasn't the essay it was the support. You don't remember me because I was fifteen kilos heavier and covered in acne. I wasn't used to men being nice to me and at that moment, you changed my life. I joined a gym and went to the doctor's to fix the acne. I was just starting to lose the weight when I saw you at a faculty dinner with your beautiful young wife and your perfect little boy and I knew I had lost my professor forever. It wasn't long after that you disappeared, and until the other night I didn't know that it was because of your son, and it was then I knew there was nothing to stop us," she said hopefully. "The problem was, I was stuck with that jerk and no matter what I did, you just didn't seem to make your move to the point where I decided if there was to be anything between us, it was up to me," she continued, half berating him for his lack of effort.

The Afflicted

"Gwen, don't be ridiculous, of course I noticed you; you're the most attractive woman I've ever met," he replied, "I just never thought that in a million years you would even look sideways at someone like me," he said, letting go of her shoulders.

"Well, now you don't have a choice," she said.

This time she wrapped both her arms round his neck and pulled him more forcibly towards her, kissing him passionately on the lips. His hands reached down her slender body, following the curves and coming to rest on her shapely hips, pulling her firmly against him. She felt him begin to stir immediately and she pushed him urgently against the settee where he dropped backwards into a seated position.

Finally, she had the man she had dreamt of for all those years.

Gwen lay there nestled up against John, enjoying the feeling of his naked body against her back, his strong arms wrapped protectively around her. He slept the deep sleep of the contented while she idly flipped through the television channels when a familiar sight caught her attention, so she turned up the volume.

"Following a spate of attacks at Brighton General Hospital earlier today the police have issued a public safety warning. Patients bitten by rats carrying an unknown disease caused the incidents. A representative

of the hospital has warned that in the last twelve hours, there have been over forty reported cases of rat bites around the city. People are advised to avoid contact with rats and keep away from places they are likely to congregate such as sewers and other underground locations. Anyone bitten should immediately contact the number at the bottom of the screen. Police have also warned that the victims could become violent and should be avoided at all costs. Again, if you see anyone behaving in this manner, contact the number below. Further news...,"

The newsreader on the screen continued, but Gwen had heard enough to realise there was a problem. She noticed the flashing lights of at least a dozen police cars on the screen and jumped to her feet, startling John awake. He looked at her, bemused as he watched her naked body dancing around in front of him while she picked up her dress and shoes.

"Hurry John, get dressed. There has been a major development. It looks like the contagion has spread already. There have been loads of victims; would you believe it? From rat bites," she said, pointing to the news report that was now repeating the warning.

Much as he enjoyed ogling her, John's attention was quickly transferred to the screen when he heard the term 'infected rats' and he realised from the sound of it that their little science experiment was free.

The Afflicted

"My God, that's way too much of a coincidence. We have to do something," he exclaimed, jumping to his feet, searching for his own clothes.

"Either Richard lied to us and he didn't even look for the rat, or the exterminator didn't catch the test subject in time and it must have infected at least one other animal before it was captured. Probably an unfortunate creature it encountered within the building." Gwen added.

She dismissed the first explanation as she couldn't believe even Richard would be so negligent.

"Do you have Richard's number? We need to let him know straight away," John said, hurriedly pulling on his trousers, "and I think we need to get back to work. If this turns out to be what we think it is, the authorities are going to need our help sooner or later."

"Okay, but give me a minute, I don't think they would appreciate me turning up at work in this," she said, holding up the dress.

"Oh Gwen, I think you're very wrong about that. But I agree you need to change; I personally would find it very difficult to concentrate," he contradicted.

She smiled and kissed him on the forehead before running out of the room.

John took one last appreciative glance at her naked buttocks disappearing up the stairs before dragging on the rest of his clothes.

Fourteen

Deep in the expanse of the New Forest, Helen and her new friend, Paul, skulked in the darkness surrounding the campsite they had found. A small fire still burned in the centre of the clearing but the campers, some cub scouts and their adult supervisors, had retired for the night.

Helen had begun to grow impatient as they watched the arguing boys forced into their tents, all of them desperate to spend a few more minutes telling scary stories around the campfire. She and Paul quietly crept up to the adult's tent, knowing they needed to subdue the two men first if the attack was to be a success. As they approached, Paul stumbled and dropped to his knees, the sound of which could be heard quite clearly inside the tent. Helen heard rustling as the silhouette of one of the men approached the zipper. The tent zip shot down and a man's face protruded through the opening, trying to spot the little trouble maker who had got out of his tent.

"Who is that creeping ...?" the man asked, expecting to see one of the cub scouts.

He did not know what hit him as Paul lunged at him, knocking him backwards into the tent snarling and growling as they fell. Helen quickly targeted his companion, attacking him before he had time to react to the commotion beside him. The two men were dead within seconds and the feral attackers paused to drink their fill, unaware of the curious children approaching.

The cub scouts had heard the commotion and were now filing out of their tents to investigate.

It was traditional for the scout leaders to select the name of one of the animals from the Jungle Book and the boy in the lead whispered them on approach.

"Baloo! Shere Khan! Is everything alright?" he asked, shining his torch through the open tent flap.

The boy stared in disbelief at the slaughter inside. Letting out an ear-piercing scream he turned and ran straight towards the darkened woods.

The other boys followed suit, screaming into the darkness without seeing the two feral creatures inside the tent.

The two hunters finished their meal of fresh blood and then silently set off in pursuit of the frightened children. They disabled each one in turn, returning only when all of the children had been located to feed. When Helen and Paul had finished, they lay immobile on the forest floor, glutted with blood. Hunting had been very good tonight.

***

Brian didn't return to his flat; he no longer remembered where he lived. Instead, he patrolled his new territory, hunting whatever prey he could find. He was currently peering through the open downstairs window of a bungalow, watching an old woman sleep. She shifted slightly in her sleep causing him to duck down, but he resumed his vigil once she settled. Confident she was not going to wake up, he pushed the window open fully and stealthily crawled into the room like a big cat.

As he approached the bed, he noticed an odd odour; she did not smell as sweet as his previous victims. The scent was older and muskier, but he was hungry and could not afford to be fussy. Without making a single sound, he sunk his teeth into the sleeping woman's throat, covering her mouth with his hand to stifle a scream and began to drink.

The blood flow did not last for long, her heart rate petering off quickly as the last vestiges of life departed her ancient frame. As he stood to leave, another sound attracted his attention. He walked towards it, sniffing the air.

***

Richard was still in his office waiting patiently for a phone call from security, hoping they would find Brian soon, not that it made much difference now as he knew the trouble at the hospital was down to them. The story was all over the news and he knew it would only be a matter of time before John and Gwen found out. It would not take them long to join the dots and work out what he'd done considering he could not blame Brian for a series of rat bites.

The authorities were blaming a rare strain of rabies instead and giving him a little more time for his plans to come into fruition. He knew it would not be long before things got out of hand as the hospital ran out of space and people to deal with the situation. So far, he did not think that they had made the connection that humans could also spread the disease but he would be surprised if they did not suspect it. At the rate things were going, he knew there would be a serious problem soon and he did not intend to be around.

He'd already decided that it was time to leave and make arrangements for his own protection. It was not just a case of the authorities anymore; he didn't want to run into one of the creatures. He had stashed his latest cash payment at the house and had squirreled away a significant amount in foreign holdings so that he would be comfortable for a long time.

Tomorrow, he would head for the port of Dover and in less than twenty-four hours he would be out of the country, out of the danger zone. The phone rang shrilly, jolting him back to reality.

He took a moment before answering and could almost guess whom the caller was and he tried to compose himself.

"Hello, who is it?" he inquired cautiously, and was horrified to find out it was his contact.

"Dr Jennings, can you tell me why I'm assailed by reports of an outbreak of an unknown virus all over Brighton, and that sounds very much like the affliction created by Methuselah? It's all over the news!" shouted his contact angrily.

"Oh you've finally heard. What do you expect me to do about it?" asked Richard arrogantly.

Knowing he would be leaving shortly he saw no point in pandering to the unknown person who had been threatening him for so long. He doubted that whoever it was would be able to do anything about him before he had the chance to escape.

"Be careful Dr Jennings. I don't think you know whom you're dealing with. I can have someone take care of you permanently!" the disembodied voice threatened.

Richard winced physically.

He'd never heard his contact so angry but he had reached a point where he really didn't care anymore.

"You're absolutely right, I don't know whom I am dealing with, but I promise you that I'm out of this ridiculous arrangement as of now. Before you threaten me, you need to know that I've been doing a little research myself and if anything happens to me, I've left strict instructions for all that information to fall into the hands of the authorities. I'm sure they'll be able to track you down with what I have collected," Richard told him.

His bravado was false.

Although he'd kept detailed records of every conversation, every delivery date and many other details, he was not sure that the authorities would be able to use any of it.

"If that's the way you want it Dr Jennings, I'll be seeing you soon, and trust me, you will not...," the voice began to say before Richard slammed down the phone, a cold shiver running down his spine.

He sighed, looking round like a caged animal.

"I think it's time I disappear," he muttered as he began to select specific items from the drawers of his desk.

He doubted if anyone would be able to find him if he made his move now. He was just about to open the wall safe when he heard voices in the building.

Gwen had only drunk a couple of glasses of wine, so they decided that since she had eaten so much it was safer for her to drive. John knew he could never drive in his condition, especially after the tumbler of whisky.

Several police cars drove past them with their sirens blazing but they were more interested in the Brighton incident than a couple in a car. When they arrived at Swiftgene, they noticed Richard's silver-grey BMW parked in front of the building in its usual spot.

"Richard must already be here, maybe that's why he wasn't answering his mobile," said Gwen, heading towards his car. John suddenly grabbed the steering wheel and urged her to park over at the far side of the car park.

"I don't know why, but I'm beginning to doubt Richards's integrity. I think it may be prudent if we sneak in through the rear entrance, just in case he's up to no good. I would just love to catch him unawares," he cautioned.

Richard never came in this late; he definitely had something to hide. John's suspicions were further confirmed when they found the building in complete darkness. It was company policy to leave one or two lights on and they were disturbed by the lack of security; there were always three or more men around during night shift.

"Maybe they're all out looking for Brian; although, that's disputable at the minute," whispered Gwen as they entered the corridor leading to Richard's office.

"No it isn't, think about how protective Richard has been about contacting the authorities. If they locate Brian, there's no way they would be able to trace the outbreak back to Swiftgene, and that means there's no blame on him," John said in a whisper.

"I'm sure he wouldn't be that callous. And besides, he must know we would say something?" she suggested, looking at John for confirmation, although she had a strong suspicion what he was going to say next.

"Maybe he thinks we can be bought?" he replied, and Gwen sighed.

For a moment, she had thought he was going to suggest that Richard would harm them.

They made their way to the office without switching any lights on and it was then that Gwen noticed how well she could see in the dark, an effect of her genetic enhancements. Unaware of the Methuselah in her system, she joked to herself that she must have been eating a lot of carrots.

When they arrived outside Richard's office the lights were off, but John tried the handle anyway and was surprised to find the door unlocked. Richard was sitting at his desk with only the illumination of his computer screen, but despite the suspicious circumstances, they could see nothing out of the ordinary.

"Have you seen the report on TV? There's no way we can sit on this anymore, Richard. The virus has escaped and people have died so we need to contact the authorities and tell them everything we know," said John, a little taken aback by Richard's flustered appearance.

"I know. I caught the late news too. It looks like there's a bit of a problem down at the hospital," he replied, "but there isn't much I can do now, is there? We're too late to help, the disease is already spreading."

John and Gwen looked at him with utter contempt at his dismissal of a situation that he was heavily involved with, and in part responsible for.

"Have you contacted the authorities yet? There was a number on the TV for people to ring if they had anything to report. We need to tell them absolutely everything and make ourselves and this facility available for them to use," hissed John, desperately trying to keep his temper in check.

"Oh that! Yeah, I've already contacted them. The chief inspector is on his way and there's a team of specialists coming from the hospital to use our laboratories. I told them about the serum and they think they may be able to isolate the virus if they have a sample of the original treatment," Richard said, suddenly snapping out of his trance and realising they were in the room.

His thoughts seemed distracted and they assumed he'd been worried about what was about to happen.

"Have you managed to find Brian yet?" asked Gwen, "He was the first human infected, so it would be exceptionally useful if we could get him back here to finalise a treatment. The sooner we do, the sooner we can start treating any other cases."

"No, not yet, but the security guys are still searching the area near his flat. They have strict instructions to call me as soon as they find anything and I am sure it will not be long now," he tried to reassure them.

He looked around quickly, nervously trying to think of a way to get out of there without attracting undue attention.

It would only be a matter of minutes before they realised the police were not coming.

"We are going into the lab to work on isolating that virus, but let us know as soon as the chief inspector arrives. We have devised a treatment that we think will help," said John, about to leave.

"Wait a minute John, there is something I noticed on the rat we captured I think you should take a look at. Gwen, could you do me a favour and go to the entrance to let in the visitors when they arrive?" he said pleasantly, smiling at the pair of them.

Gwen left the office and Richard walked round the desk to the portable chiller that was still sitting on the cupboard at the back of his office. Concealed in his hand was a heavy granite paperweight from his desk. John opened the unit and looked inside, wondering if Richard had spotted whatever it was that had eluded him from the previous day. Even as he looked at the splayed body again the same feeling began to plague him once more.

"What was it you found inter...," John started to say, but did not get a chance to finish as Richard struck a blow to the back of his head.

The rock landed with a dull thud and the scientist collapsed instantly, falling first to his knees and then dropping onto his back as blood trickled from the wound. Richard took the opportunity to swing a spiteful kick at the unconscious man, catching him solidly in the midriff.

"You almost spoiled everything, you arrogant piece of crap," he shouted, knowing that if John had been awake he would be no match for the younger man.

Richard grabbed his briefcase and ran, forgetting about the material in the safe. He knew that as soon as John came round the alarm would be raised and he needed to be out of there before that happened. Using the same route through the rear of the building that John and Gwen had used to enter, he made his way outside, his intention to catch Gwen by surprise. He would take great pleasure in tackling her; in his warped mind he still had unfinished business with her. He laughed in anticipation, tossing and catching the lump of bloodstained granite up and down in the air as he walked alongside the facility.

When he arrived at the corner of the building, he spotted the solitary figure standing on the edge of the expensively finished courtyard. He smiled, thinking of how much satisfaction he was going to get from finally teaching her a lesson. He crept up as quietly as he could with the rock held high above his head, ready to strike. He did not get a chance though as Gwen sensed his presence and turned to face him. It took no more than a second for her to figure out what he was up to.

"What are you doing, you piece of scum? You're doing a runner, aren't you?" she said, backing away from him.

Now she had seen him, Richard dropped the rock and placed his briefcase carefully on the floor. He outweighed her by about thirty kilos and he was confident that he could physically outmatch her. He lunged forward and landed a punch hard in her stomach causing her to bend over in pain, but she managed to stay on her feet. She kicked out hard, hitting him square in the chest and knocking him back several steps. Despite being unaware of the effects, she had the influence of Methuselah to thank for her improved strength.

A worried look replaced his confidence as Richard realised he had completely forgotten about the serum he had given her. Suddenly, he wondered if he had bitten off more than he could chew, she was obviously growing stronger already.

Knowing that he had no choice if he wanted to get away, he decided to rely on his superior weight and ran at her, rugby tackling her to the ground. Gwen's head bounced hard against the brickwork of the drive but still she managed stay conscious. Dazed, she grabbed him and tried to force him off, pushing with amazing strength against his arms and almost succeeding. While Richard temporarily had the upper hand, he punched her twice in succession right on the jaw, this time knocking her out cold.

Richard climbed to his feet realising just how lucky he had been; it had taken everything he could muster to hold her down. It was obvious the formula had started to work, which meant that eventually the bloodlust would start and she would become a danger to the people around her.

He doubted her new healing abilities would take long to kick in so he grabbed his briefcase and ran for his car. He had one quick stop to make and then he was out of there for good.

John came round slowly, the back of his head throbbing and his vision slightly blurred. What the hell had happened, he thought, reaching up to feel the sticky patch on the back of his skull. It all came rushing back to him and he remembered that Richard had brained him from behind.

"That slimy bastard, I knew he was up to something!" he groaned to himself.

It was clear to him now that Richard must have something serious to hide. It also occurred to him that Gwen was between Richard and his car and, unaware of his treachery, she would be an easy target for him.

"Gwen, where are you?" he shouted, starting to panic as he climbed groggily to his feet.

He staggered out of the office using the walls for support and made his way to the front of the building. He spotted her through the huge plate glass windows as he approached the foyer, lying unconscious on the forecourt floor. An icy hand grabbed his heart and squeezed; he could see that she was not moving. Panicking, he sprinted outside, almost taking the door off its hinges, and dropped to his knees besides her prone form. He sighed with relief when he realised that she was still breathing and began to gently slap her face to bring her round.

"Gwen, are you alright?" he asked tenderly, checking her from head to toe for any sign of injury.

The only injury he could see was a slight red mark on the side of her jaw where Richard had obviously punched her. He felt a surge of pure hatred for Richard and made a promise to himself that if ever he saw the man again he was going to teach him a serious lesson.

Gwen opened her eyes and smiled sweetly when she saw it was John. Sitting up she kissed him tenderly on the lips.

She reached her hand round the back of his neck causing him to wince when she accidentally poked him right on the bump at the back of his head.

"Is that blood? Are you alright?" she gasped, panicking and jumped to her feet as if nothing had happened, pulling him up with her.

"C'mon, we have to get that treated, you could have a concussion. What are you doing out here? You should be looking after yourself," she said, fussing over him unnecessarily.

It had taken her five years to get her man and she was not going to risk losing him on their first date.

"Alright, but first we have to contact that emergency number and get the authorities involved. Not only do we have the problem in Brighton to be helping out with, but I am sure they would like to speak to Richard as well," he said with a wicked smile.

They headed back inside with John leaning against Gwen for support.

The dark alley was only illuminated by the lights from a few of the windows of the surrounding shops. Brian hid behind a large skip and was peering out to watch the homeless woman bent over one of the wheelie bins, industriously searching for her evening meal. She was very quiet; the shop owners did not like her going round there, even though she never did them any harm or left a mess. One of them had actually thrown a lump of wood at her the other day hurting her knee so she avoided them completely now.

Brian slunk out from behind the skip and began to stalk the woman, creeping up slowly from behind, ready to pounce. It was then he sensed there were others hunting him. He stopped dead in his tracks and dropped to one knee, hastily searching the darkness for their location.

"I have found the target. I repeat, I have found the target. He is in the alley behind the Golden Palace Chinese takeaway," said a voice in the darkness.

Brian froze. He could not see who had spoken or their location, but he sensed their presence. He scanned his surroundings, desperately looking for any clue as to their whereabouts. He did not have to wait long as four men dressed in blue uniforms walked sinisterly out of the shadows on one side of him. He turned to escape before another two men emerged in front of him causing him to panic. There was nowhere to, go so his sub-human instincts kicked in and he crouched down ready to fight.

Taking no chances, the men all rushed at him simultaneously just as Brian leapt at the closest of them, raking the man's face with his nails. Something hit the back of his head hard and he dropped to the floor, down but not out. The men, worried that he would get up again, piled on top of him, their combined weight only just enough to stop him wriggling free.

"The boss was right; this scrawny little turf is crazy as a shithouse rat," yelled the leader, placing his knee in the middle of Brian's shoulder blades while he twisted his arms behind his back. One of the others hurriedly fastened a pair of handcuffs around his wrists. To hold his feet they used several thick tie-wraps and slowly managed to get him under control. Brian writhed and snarled at the men until the leader, a large, heavily built man, raised his fist and punched him hard on the chin causing his body to go limp.

"Right, go get the van and bring it right up to the entrance of the alleyway," the large man instructed, rubbing his bruised knuckles, "we don't want anyone to see us loading him up!"

***

Michael Devon was beginning to feel stressed as the situation grew steadily worse. He was on his way to find Andrew Ridgemount, the surgeon in charge of the medical efforts, to help bring the problem under control. He finally spotted the doctor and was making his way over to him when his mobile phone rang, the number showing the emergency room in the foyer.

"Inspector, we have a very unusual call on one of the emergency lines from a company called Swiftgene just down the road in Hove. The man seems to think he has critical information about the current situation," said the female police officer.

"Get some details, but whatever you do make sure you keep him on the line, I'll be right down," he answered, breaking into a run.

He hoped this was the break they were waiting for, considering they were all chasing their own tails. As he sped through the hospital, it was becoming obvious that the situation was getting severely out of hand. Reports of attacks by rats were increasing with every passing hour and on top of that there were now rumours of incidents involving dogs, cats and other animals, as well as human beings. The MPA were due any minute now to assess the situation. Personally, he thought it was time to bring in the armed forces and declare martial law, but that would be their decision when they got there. He arrived at the makeshift emergency room a couple of minutes later seriously out of breath, which was unsurprising given his unhealthy lifestyle and the fact that he spent most of his time behind a desk nowadays.

He remembered his days on the beat fondly when he could outrun any criminal, but age and promotion had taken care of that. A middle-aged woman in uniform waved to him as he entered the foyer, beckoning him over urgently.

"Inspector, he says his name is Dr John Simmons and he claims to be a geneticist over at Swiftgene. He seems to have a good understanding about what is happening over here," she said as he approached.

The inspector grabbed the phone enthusiastically and spoke to the unseen scientist.

"Hello, this is Inspector Michael Devon. I am in charge of the operation here at Brighton General. How can I help you, or should I say how can you help me, Dr Simmons?" he asked earnestly, hoping for some shred of good news.

He was about to be disappointed.

"Inspector, I don't have time to explain in any detail over the phone but suffice to say you need to come over to Swiftgene and bring the MPA with you. We have some of the answers you need here as to what caused the disease, but I am afraid so far we only have a theoretical way to treat it," John told him.

The claims to know what was going on made Michael very suspicious; it sounded too good to be true.

"This had better not be some sort of hoax or paparazzi trick, do you know what we are dealing with down here? People are dying," he threatened, the last thing he had the patience for was some time waster looking for a quick thrill at the taxpayers' expense.

"I assure you Inspector, this is no joke, but if you don't believe me please have the telephone number checked. I am calling directly from Swiftgene and my credentials can be easily confirmed," John answered, "but please hurry, there's a lot you're not aware of."

"As soon as we have verified who you are we will be back in touch, but for your information the MPA have not yet arrived. I am sure they will be able to confirm your identity," Michael promised before handing the phone back and giving the woman a quick instruction.

"Check him out immediately. If he is telling the truth this could be important. Oh, and when the MPA arrive can you give me a call," he instructed the police officer, watching her nod as he spoke.

"Sir, they are here now," she answered, pointing to a convoy of white vans being escorted through the crowd outside.

The three vehicles stopped parallel to the front entrance and a number of people began climbing out, one of them a short, plump middle-aged woman with dark cropped hair.

"Can someone please direct me to Inspector Michael Devon immediately," she shouted to a bunch of nearby police officers.

"He's just over there miss, the man coming towards you," one of them responded, pointing in his direction.

She turned to the group who were still climbing out of the vans, "Everyone please wait here until I have discussed the situation with the inspector. I don't like the look of this scene so we may need to move to another location," she ordered, and they immediately stopped what they were doing.

The group consisted of a number of specialist scientists plus several medical staff. They had a number of pieces of high-tech analytical equipment in the van.

"Hello, I am Dr Tracy Roberts and I have been informed that you are the officer in charge here," she said, offering him her rather large hand, much too big for her small body.

"Yes Doctor, and are we happy to see you. The situation is growing worse with every passing minute and there appears to be no end in sight. The number of people afflicted is increasing exponentially, way too fast for the first day of an epidemic in my opinion," Michael told her, shaking her hand enthusiastically.

He explained everything he knew, most of which had already been relayed to her on the trip down from London.

"There's something you may be able to help with though. A couple of minutes ago, literarily as your vehicles were arriving, we received a phone call from a Dr Simmons over at Swiftgene claiming to know something about the outbreak, but as yet we have been unable to verify his identity or credentials," he said, knowing she would have more resources in that line of enquiry.

"Would that be Dr John Simmons, the world renowned molecular geneticist?" Dr Roberts asked, her interest suddenly piqued.

"That's what he maintained but I have someone checking him out. He actually suggested that we move the MPA over to Swiftgene to use the laboratories there and said that he would explain a little more about the condition," he confirmed, guessing by her reaction that the caller had been genuine.

"Inspector, I suggest you call him back; if this man is who he says he is then we need to get over there immediately. He is one of the most accomplished in the field of genetics and his help will be invaluable, especially if he has prior knowledge of the condition. Also, looking at the situation here Inspector, I think it would be safer to set up our scientific operation away from the centre of the outbreak. That may sound a little cowardly but these men and women are going to be the ones who find the solution and we must preserve their safety no matter what the cost," she said indignantly.

She headed back towards the vehicles, barking orders as she went. Michael watched her with a sense of admiration; she was a woman who knew how to take charge.

Michael began organising police support for the scientists. He agreed with Dr Roberts' assessment of the situation and also decided he would be more useful at Swiftgene acting as a liaison and notified the emergency room to keep him appraised. Before leaving he went to find Andrew Ridgemount and explained the situation, offering him a seat in his car but the man refused. Andrew Ridgemount was a surgeon and he knew that he would be of more use at the hospital treating the ill. Michael shook the man's hand.

"Well, good luck Mr. Ridgemount; let's hope for all our sakes that these people know what they are doing," Michael told him.

"You and me both, Inspector; you and me both," he replied sincerely.

***

After receiving the confirmation call from the inspector, John and Gwen were getting ready to receive the team.

They had cleared the conference room and called in several of the laboratory assistants to make sure there was enough labour. All the laboratory equipment that might be needed for analysis had been switched on and was now warming up, ready for use.

"Gwen, the MPA and the inspector are on their way, have you managed to get hold of the security teams yet? We need to find Brian as soon as possible," John asked, pacing back and forth in the foyer.

He was concerned at the way events were unfolding as he knew they were complicit in recent events. Richard may have been largely responsible, but John had a conscience and was fully prepared to be held accountable.

"No, not yet. I've left a few messages with Frank the security manager but I've heard nothing back from him so far," she answered, barely hiding her disappointment.

Gwen was beginning to get impatient as they waited for the specialist team to arrive. Every wasted minute was keeping them from working on a cure. Also, she was beginning to feel hungry yet again, despite the fact that she had eaten a large meal with John only a few hours earlier. She appreciated the fact that they may have burnt off a few calories in their lovemaking but she was ravenous.

"We need to find some evidence to prove what Richard has been getting up to; it looks like he has been keeping everyone in the dark about one or two things," John told her.

"On that we are agreed," she confirmed.

"We also have to identify why the experiment went wrong in the first place. It could well be that Richard contaminated the original samples. I have reviewed my results thoroughly and I am certain the reproductive ability was removed completely and could not have been reactivated even by accident," he said, sharing his theory. "If they can identify any interference it could help treat the disease."

"If you think he tampered with the original samples then it's simple, we should run a test on the remaining serum and if there is anything in there that doesn't belong, you should easily pick it up from the results.

John suddenly felt stupid.

The answer had been obvious and it had been right under his nose the whole time.

He had traces from earlier experiments; all he had to do was compare the current results to see if they were different.

The security buzzer sounded, causing them both to jump.

"That must be them now," John said, "let's get this show on the road."

The pair went to meet the officials from the MPA, swiping open the main front doors and leading everyone into the main conference room. It took several minutes for everyone to settle down before John was able to call for silence.

"Good evening all, my name is Dr John Simmons and my colleague here is Dr Gwen Taylor," John told them.

"Dr Simmons, your reputation precedes you. I am Dr Tracy Roberts, leader of the emergency response branch of the MPA, and I believe you have already spoken to Inspector Michael Devon of the East Sussex police force," Dr Roberts answered.

The four people nodded respectfully to each other.

"I believe the condition you've been dealing with is directly related to a research project called 'Methuselah' that I initiated here at Swiftgene," John informed them nervously.

"So, I am led to believe Dr Simmons that perhaps you can tell us a bit about the condition?" Dr Roberts suggested.

"Forgive me for interrupting," said Gwen, "but the situation is a little more complicated than just a straight forward condition. John, why don't you start from the beginning and let everyone know how much we have figured out?"

"Good Idea. Well first things first, Methuselah is a gene therapy that ...," John began.

John, with occasional help from Gwen, walked the room full of people through the project, the theories behind Methuselah and the circumstances surrounding what they believed to have caused the epidemic. They made it clear that Richard was at the centre of the calamity, exposing his suspicious behaviour. John then highlighted their theories regarding potential treatments for the disease.

For over an hour, the crowd of people sat in silence as they listened and even Michael managed to start making sense of some of the behaviour he had seen in the victims.

There were several gasps as John described some of the more distasteful behavior, but Dr Roberts' team were professionals and listened intently until the pair had finished.

"Dr Simmons, Dr Taylor, thank you for your update, we now have something to work on," said Dr Roberts, "Inspector Devon, I agree that Richard Jennings has been hiding something. Can you and your team see if you can track him down? I am very interested in what he has to say."

"No problem, I'll get a team on it straight away. I'll personally begin in his office and start going through everything to see what I can find out," Michael replied.

"Dr Simmons and Dr Taylor, I think you have already identified where your focus should lie. We can assume nothing; start from the very beginning and see if you can identify what went wrong with the original serum, especially if you suspect sabotage of your work," Dr Roberts continued.

John and Gwen nodded. Out of the whole group they knew the most about the condition to date and hence were her most precious assets.

"My team, I'd like you to set up our equipment in one of the spare laboratories, familiarise yourselves with the technical aspects of the project and provide Dr Simmons and Dr Taylor with anything that they need," she instructed.

Gwen introduced the Swiftgene laboratory technicians to instruct them.

She offered their help to show the newcomers how to use the Swiftgene equipment. It was the latest and most high-tech in the world and was set up, ready to use. Dr Roberts thanked her profusely. Every saved minute would inevitably mean less people dying in the future.

When Dr Roberts had finished, John alerted them to another situation.

"Dr Roberts, there is one other matter the inspector's police connections may be able to help with. Brian, the very first human infected, is still unaccounted for and our security teams are currently out searching for him. However, we have been unable to contact them. Perhaps the inspector can help to locate him. We have proposed a treatment that we are going to try on a few of the rats first, but we are very confident that it should work," he said, looking hopefully at Michael.

"No problem, I'll get the details out to my people on the street straight away," confirmed Michael, scribbling the details in his trusty notebook.

"Now people, we have some good intel so we can make headway at last. Don't forget, everybody is to use full microbiological protocols. I do not want any accidental infections, I cannot afford any of you to be compromised," Dr Roberts warned.

"Remember, inform me of any significant breakthroughs immediately, other than that we will meet back here in two hours," instructed Dr Roberts.

As everybody rushed off to perform their various tasks, Dr Roberts asked John, Gwen and the inspector to stay behind for a minute.

"I didn't want to frighten everyone but I have serious question for the three of you. Given what we are seeing at the moment and what you now know about the condition, what can we expect to see over the next few days?" she asked, staring at each one of them in turn.

The expression on her face was showing a high level of concern. She knew the situation was serious, but there was the option of involving the military if things got too dangerous and the sooner she had the information to make an informed decision, the better it would be for everybody.

"Honestly, we don't know. The disease is very infectious by contact and because of the sub-human blood-lust it induces, the hosts are forced to go and infect new people. Add that to the fact that the incubation period can be as low as a few hours, we will have several hundred cases by tomorrow morning, if not more. Twenty-four hours after that there could be thousands," said John, trying not to sensationalise the problems.

That did not stop the horrified expressions forming on all their faces, Dr Roberts so affected that she sat down heavily. Never in her career had she faced anything quite so virulent and destructive.

"I knew it was going to be bad, but you've put it into perspective for me. I now know that I have no choice but to quarantine the entire area. We cannot risk this disease spreading, so I'm afraid I have to request the armed forces to back us up," she said, standing up, slightly recovered from the initial shock.

The Afflicted

"Don't forget the rats are going to be spreading the disease through their own unseen community below ground. I think we will start seeing isolated cases popping up everywhere, radiating out from this location. That is if we do not take some action to exterminate them before their food source dries up and they are forced to hunt above ground, if they are not already doing so," warned John.

"What about the people? Is there anything we can possibly do to reduce the impact?" Dr Roberts asked hopefully, for every one of the afflicted walking around today could very quickly become five or six tomorrow and so on.

"At the moment the only thing I can suggest is sedation and isolation," John replied. "We have a potential treatment but it will take time to kick in and during that time a sufferer of the affliction would be capable of attacking new victims. At least unconscious the hosts are unable to spread the disease any further, and that has to be a bonus,"

"We may be able to combine the treatment with a sedative at a later date, that way we will kill two birds with one stone," Gwen suggested helpfully.

"Can you get hold of tranquiliser guns quickly and in large volumes?" John asked Dr Roberts, taking Gwen's lead.

"Of course! That's an excellent idea. I have a few contacts within the animal welfare community and I am sure that I can secure a number of weapons," laughed Dr Roberts, relieved to have good news at last.

"You're going to shoot the afflicted?" Michael asked incredulously.

"Only those that are active and attacking victims, those already restrained can be sedated, pending the discovery of working treatment," Dr Roberts answered compassionately.

"I suppose, but we had better get the weapons issued to the police armed response units. I don't want just anyone running round with those things," Michael conceded reluctantly.

"It might be worth getting some of those tranquiliser poles as well. Even restrained, if the bloodlust has a grip on the victim then we need to be able to treat the afflicted at arm's length," John suggested.

"I'm sorry Dr Simmons, you won't be treating anyone, nor you Dr Taylor. As of this moment you two are the most important people on the planet and we cannot risk any harm befalling you," Dr Roberts ordered, and by the tone of her voice John, Gwen and Michael knew that she was serious.

"How do you suppose we do our jobs then?" John asked sarcastically.

"You can complete the research but you are not to handle infected specimens or the afflicted. My people will do that for you; as far as you're concerned they are expendable, but you two are not," Dr Roberts told them coldly.

"I'm sorry, but no one is expendable on my account," John protested.

"Nor mine," Gwen agreed angrily.

"Well, let's hope it never comes to that shall we? For now we all have work to do and time is running out," Dr Roberts answered.

To stress her point she walked over and held the door open for them.

"I'll see you in two hours!" she said, smiling politely.

Fifteen

Richard screeched his powerful BMW to a halt outside the gates of his house and jumped out. He rushed up the front steps, knowing that he didn't have much time before Gwen and John notified the police, if they had not done so already. He was in so much of a hurry that he did not notice the two men sitting in the grey transit van parked on the opposite side of the road, watching him fumble for his keys. Once inside he ran straight up the stairs, into the master bedroom and grabbed the two large suitcases from the top of the wardrobe. He threw everything he could into them, cramming them as full as the straining zips would allow. He then dragged a briefcase from under the bed and opened it to reveal a stash of money in bundles of ten and twenty pound notes. He took one of the bundles of tens out and shoved it into the inside pocket of his coat before relocking the briefcase. Swiftly, he grabbed all three cases and headed back down the marble staircase for the last time. He had already made provisions to sell the house, the proceeds of which were to go into an offshore bank account.

He dropped the cases at the door to his study where he retrieved his passport, driver's license and a few other important documents. They joined the money in the inside pocket of his coat and then he was ready to leave. He turned in a full circle and took a good look at the house, regretting for a moment that he was being forced to leave. It had taken him six years to renovate the house to his exact standards and now he would be forced to start again from scratch. Luckily, property prices in Brighton were at a premium so he would still make a handsome profit, despite the thousands he'd spent.

Sadly, he turned to the front door. When he opened it he was surprised to find two very large men with short military haircuts in smart grey suits staring at him. They had turned the van around, pulling it directly in front of his house and pushing his BMW out of the way, much to his distress. His desperate hope that they were Jehovah's Witnesses evaporated when they spoke.

"Going somewhere in a hurry, Dr Jennings? That's a shame, because our employer has specifically requested the pleasure of your company. He wants to talk a little more about your last conversation," said the one on the right, grabbing Richard's arm in a vice-like grip as he spoke.

Richard pulled back trying to free himself, but it was no good; the man was far too strong for that to work so he chose a different tactic.

"Let go of me you thug, what do you think you're doing? Help, I'm being robbed!" he shouted at the top of his voice, trying to attract attention.

The only passer-by, a young woman over the street, looked over curiously but carried on her way, not wishing to get involved. It did not pay in this day and age to play the hero, there were too many unscrupulous people wanting to take advantage of the unwary.

The man on the left pulled out a small shiny handgun that looked just like the one Richard had seen so often in the James Bond movies and pressed it hard into his ribs.

"If I were you Doc, I would keep my voice down. You wouldn't want to startle him and cause the gun to go off accidentally, now would you?" said the man on the right sarcastically.

Realising there was nothing he could do for the moment, Richard relaxed and stopped struggling. The man with the gun reached down, took the briefcase from him, and led him down the steps to the side of the van. The other one grabbed his cases and took them before shutting the door. He had been instructed to make it look like Richard had actually done a runner.

The door to the van was one of those sliding affairs without a window and when open it revealed another two men crouching inside.

Richard was shoved roughly inside and one of the men punched him in the midriff, astounding him; the other used tie-wraps to secure his hands and feet. While one of them tore off a strip of duct tape to cover his mouth, the man with the gun turned round to face Richard from the driver's seat.

"The boss told me to give you a message from him. He told me to say, 'Nobody speaks to me like that and gets away with it', I think that was it," the man said, a moment before he drew back his fist and punched him hard in the face. Richard was not physically tough and passed out immediately, falling to the hard, dirty floor of the van with a dull thud. The tape was placed carefully over his mouth, making sure that he could still breathe through his nose.

"Right, you take his keys and get rid of the car, we'll get the woman and meet you where we arranged," the driver said to the front seat passenger.

As soon as he climbed out, the driver gunned the engine and headed towards Hove. After the discussion with Dr Roberts and the inspector, Gwen and John went to his office to formulate a plan of action.

"I think with all the labour available to us it would be better if we split up and covered more avenues," John suggested, retrieving the Methuselah folder from his desk.

He grabbed his scruffy notebook and dropped it into his lab coat pocket.

"Agreed, how do you want to split it up?" Gwen queried.

"I'm going to work on the analysis of the serum itself to see if I can spot something in there," he answered.

"What if there is something in there? Isn't it likely that Methuselah has mutated the original specimen in the host's body? It would explain the virulence and why we have never seen a condition like this before," she countered.

"You're right, I think we need to screen the infected blood to see what we've got. I'll get some of the MPA personnel on that, it will be interesting to see if there are any differences."

"What about me? I think I would be most useful working on a treatment," Gwen suggested.

"Good idea. We need to be ready for Brian when he finally gets here. He's patient zero, the only person we know that was bitten by a directly treated rat. I just hope the virus or whatever it is doesn't mutate or jump strains," John agreed.

"Okay then, we have a plan," Gwen said.

At that moment, her stomach rumbled audibly causing John to laugh aloud.

"It's not funny, I'm really hungry," Gwen grumbled, placing the palm of her hand over her tummy.

She had a craving a rare steak, which was unusual, as she usually liked her meat very well done.

"I'm not saying a thing," John chuckled.

"John, I think I'm going to raid the restaurant before I get started. Can I fetch you anything?" she offered, wondering if there would be any food accessible at that time of night.

John looked at her in amazement; he had seen what she had eaten for supper and despite their bout of 'exercise', he could not believe that she could be hungry again already.

"You do realise us normal people hate you, don't you? You eat like an elephant and look like that," he teased, fascinated by her ability to consume huge amounts of food.

She pulled a face at him and stuck her tongue out before disappearing out of his office.

Bemused, John went to the secure refrigerator in his lab and unlocked it to retrieve one of the original samples of Methuselah.

He noticed that sample number 29 was missing and checked the log sheet. He spotted Richard's entry and noticed that he had removed the sample several days ago, supposedly to place in the company vault. John knew that it was company policy to store valuable samples in a separate location but he had a sneaking suspicion, given what they now knew, that Richard may have taken one for himself. Had Methuselah worked as predicted, the pale yellow liquid in that jar would be worth hundreds of thousands of pounds to an unscrupulous scientist, and still might be if sabotage was to blame for the virus.

He made a mental note to inform Michael and Dr Roberts when they next met, just in case. He then set about preparing his sample for analysis. Gel electrophoresis had been used to identify smaller components like proteins and DNA fragments based on the minute electrical charges on the molecules.

However, working with the larger bacteriophage and other virus capsids he would have to change the method. There should be only one trace, so if he discovered any other peaks then it proved that there was something else in there. Then they could work on identifying what it was.

When Gwen arrived at the restaurant it was in almost utter darkness, the faint emergency lights providing only enough illumination to guide someone out in the event of a fire. She felt her way along the wall in an attempt to locate the bank of switches she knew would be somewhere while trying not to notice how ominous the restaurant looked in the dark. Her hand happened on the switches and thankfully, the huge room was flooded in bright light causing her to squint a little, her eyes seeming to be a little more sensitive than normal.

Without hesitation, she headed for the food counters near the electronic tills. There were glass cabinets to display all the sandwiches, cakes and other prepared foods at meal times. It appeared, however, that at night these areas were cleared and all she could find was a series of locked cupboards underneath the counters. She had no idea where the keys may have been stored; they were probably with the restaurant manager who was safely tucked up in bed.

Determined to find something she pushed open the kitchen doors to find this area also in darkness, and once again found herself groping in the dark for a light switch.

Something metallic clanged to the floor on the other side of the kitchen causing her to freeze, her eyes probing the darkness. Surprisingly, her eyes were already beginning to adapt to the low levels of light. but she could still not see anything of use.

"Hello, is anyone there?" she asked loudly, suddenly feeling a little nervous.

There was no answer, but instead of getting out of there, she continued to feel along the wall for those elusive light switches, her hunger pangs giving her false courage.

"I said who's there?" she asked again, becoming a little frightened but still refusing to retreat to the safety of the restaurant.

She sensed rather than saw something moving to her left just as her finger happened on one of the switches. The fluorescent lights flickered briefly as the tubes began to charge and she spotted the silhouette of a large man in the kitchen.

"Who are you?" she demanded boldly, assuming now that it must be one of the many police officers patrolling both inside and outside the building.

As the lights came on properly she noticed the intruder was an exceptionally large, well-dressed man with short crew cut hair.

"Don't be frightened Dr Taylor, I'm Ben Cavendish, Brighton CID. I was just trying to find a snack and I couldn't find the light switch," the man told her, and Gwen began to relax.

Just then, a pair of arms encircled her from behind, one of them restraining her firmly and the other one holding a rag of some form over her mouth and nose. She recognised the odour of chloroform immediately and began to struggle frantically. Unfortunately, Gwen just succeeded in speeding up the process and very quickly she began to lose consciousness.

"Sweet Jesus, she was strong for such a skinny little runt. For a moment I didn't think I was going to be able to hold her. That chloroform should have worked almost instantly; I used so much I was starting to feel dizzy myself," commented the man holding her.

They dragged her out of the kitchen and across the service road to a hole in the fence that led to a playing field behind the building.

"Jonas, of course she is, she has been treated with the serum you idiot. Why do you think the boss wants her? So make sure she's securely tied. And another thing, whatever you do, don't let her bite you. The boss said you would turn into one of those bloody creepy zombie things that have been attacking people," Ben warned his colleague as they dragged her towards the open side door of the van.

Dan, who had remained in the van, helped them carefully lift Gwen inside, a lot more gently than they had with Richard. Ben was Nigerian and a death squad leader with a penchant for machetes while Jonas and Dan were South African paramilitary. All three were mercenaries but they were frightened of the people who hired them. They had been given strict orders that Dr Guinevere Taylor was not to be harmed, so they carefully tied her hands and feet before laying her out on a sleeping bag. They tossed Richard to the rear of the van on the dirty hard wooden floor.

***

Ben slid the door shut and climbed into the driving seat before heading away from the well-lit profile of the Swiftgene building. They had a few more errands to run and some equipment to collect before heading back to base. None of them knew exactly what their boss wanted the girl for, but they were paid big bucks not to ask questions.

"C'mon, let's get out of here before they notice she's missing. Dave will probably be back by now," said Ben, driving the van carefully over the bumpy surface of the field with the lights off to avoid drawing any unwanted attention.

At the time specified by Dr Roberts, the whole team began to make their way to the conference room for a progress meeting. When John and Michael arrived, only Dr Roberts was around and she was just finishing her telephone conversation as they entered.

"Have either of you seen Gwen? The last time I saw her she was going to find something to eat in the restaurant and I have to admit I forgot all about her until now. She should have been back in the trial facility by now but the place was empty as I came past," John inquired, feeling a little uneasy for some unknown reason.

"Actually, come to think of it, I was down there a little earlier and she wasn't there either. Is it possible she might be working somewhere else or skipped outside for a smoke or something?" asked Michael innocently.

"No, she should have been there and she doesn't smoke. Something is wrong; we came in specially to help so there is no way she would disappear without telling me. She might have had an accident or, god forbid, one of those things got in here," said John, really starting to worry.

"How long ago did you say it was?" asked Michael, beginning to agree with John.

Michael had picked up the bond between John and Gwen as soon as he had met them.

There was no way she would have disappeared without letting John know something.

He was generally a good judge of character and had instantly liked the pair, so he was a little concerned too.

"About an hour and a half ago. I'm going to look for her," John told them, heading for the door.

"Hang on, I'll come with you," said Michael, running to catch up. "This won't take long Dr Roberts," he shouted over his shoulder as the door swung shut.

They were even more worried when they reached the restaurant and found Gwen's lab coat still hung over one of the chairs near the door.

All the lights were on and from where he stood, Michael had spotted that the kitchen light was also on.

They could hear a rhythmic tapping sound coming from that direction and they both released a sigh of relief, assuming Gwen was still preparing some food from whatever she had found.

They wandered over feeling a little reassured and Michael stuck his head round the kitchen door.

"Hi Dr Taylor, are you in there?" Michael asked cheerfully, glancing around the immaculately clean stainless steel kitchen.

He spotted the source of the sound immediately. The back door leading to the bins was open and the breeze was causing a ladle to bump into the colander next to it.

He spotted a woman's shoe in the middle of the floor and a little further away, a rag folded over several times, abandoned by the kidnappers.

Michael hurried over and picked it up just as John pushed through the doors behind him, still smiling. "Are you still eating?" John asked, before taking in the scene in front of him, noticing the inspector looking at him worriedly.

"What's happened here, and what's that?" John asked, pointing at the solvent soaked material in the inspector's hand.

"I think it's chloroform, John; you should be able to tell better than me," Michael said, holding it out for the scientist to examine.

John sniffed it gingerly. The majority had evaporated away but the remaining odour was quite distinctive to him, the odour of trichloromethane; the chemical name for the solvent chloroform. There was only one reason he could think of for it to be used in this manner.

His heart dropped even further when he noticed the rear door swinging open.

John headed outside with the inspector, hoping beyond hope that they were not too late and she was still there, but the roadway was empty except for her other shoe lying there abandoned. John picked it up and cradled it in his arms, tears beginning to form in his eyes as he accepted she had been taken.

"John, listen to me. Can you think of anyone who would benefit from taking her? Did she have any enemies?" Michael asked, placing his hand supportively on the scientist's shoulder, upset by the man's obvious despair.

John shook his head at first. There were a few people who had spread rumours about her, but essentially it was done out of jealousy; he did not think any of them meant any harm. It was then that a horrible thought entered his head. She had told him that Richard had been trying to bed her for ages and she had refused.

"Richard Jennings. They were dating for a while but nothing came of it and she broke up with him. Gwen and I were also responsible for flushing him out, maybe he is just after teaching her a lesson?" John suddenly blurted out. He had attacked them trying to make his escape after all.

Michael lifted the mouthpiece of his police radio to his lips and began to speak.

"Bravo One Four, this is Inspector Devon. I want you to widen the search for Dr Richard Jennings. He is wanted in connection with the outbreak in Brighton and it is possible he has kidnapped Caucasian female, approx. in her thirties, blonde, tall, slim and attractive going by the name of Dr Gwen Taylor. He is to be considered armed and dangerous," he said, speaking into the crackling mouthpiece.

"Yes sir, I'll get right on it," came the reply, almost immediately.

Michael turned to John and tried to console him.

"Don't worry, I will get all his details and pass them on to control. Every police officer for a hundred miles will be looking for him. If he shows his face in public anywhere, we'll have him. I don't think he wants to hurt her, that's why he used the chloroform; he wants her alive."

Michael tried to reassure him, patting him between the shoulders blades. "Leave my men to it and we shall continue with the job at hand."

They returned to the conference room, Michael leading the dejected scientist by the arm. He stopped outside the room to talk to him.

"I know you don't feel like it but you are our best hope of solving the bigger problem and we desperately need your help. I promise you I will do everything in my power to find Dr Taylor," he promised, staring John in the eye to show him this was the promise of an honourable man.

John could see that he meant what he said and he felt a little better knowing that.

Dr Roberts and the others were sitting around, idly discussing the situation but had waited before commencing the meeting.

After all, John and Gwen were the two most important people in the operation.

Michael went up to her and explained what had happened quietly before stepping back out of the room to arrange the search.

He dispatched police units to Richard's home and ordered a search of all known associates.

"Dr Simmons, I am sorry to hear about Dr Taylor but I am afraid we have a crucial service to perform at the moment. Have you any further findings to report?" asked Dr Roberts, her voice compassionate yet determined.

John looked up half-heartedly and replied quietly, "I have initiated the analysis of the original serum and some of your people are doing the same with samples taken from the blood of some of the afflicted rats. It should be finished within the next half an hour and I'll fetch the results through as soon as they are ready. I will be able to tell you whether there is a contaminant present in either source."

"Thank you Dr Simmons. I know it is asking a lot of you, but can you take over the treatment regime for Dr Taylor as well? You can use any of my people you might need to help. It's crucial we confirm a method of treatment as soon as possible," she requested hopefully.

"No problem, we have already discussed a plan of action and I can get your people started on it pretty quickly," John confirmed unenthusiastically.

Michael re-entered the room and she singled him out.

"Inspector, do you have anything to report so far?" she asked.

"Yes, unfortunately reports back from the emergency room are not good. We are getting reports of attacks all over Brighton now. Initial estimates are telling us that we have already had about three hundred attacks from rats, humans and other animals combined. Although I suspect the real figure is probably double that, with many people being too frightened to report incidents. Based on Dr Simmons' recommendation we are issuing tranquiliser guns and Tasers to try to sedate the afflicted. We have limited numbers but we are receiving more from all over the country as we speak; even so, I think we may have to go international before long," he informed the team.

"Is there anything else?" Dr Roberts asked.

"Yes, we have been through Dr Jenning's office with a fine-tooth comb and have found nothing of any pertinence except for a wall safe. There may be useful documentation in there but I have had to call a demolitions expert to blow off the door as apparently a locksmith would not be able to touch it," he continued.

Even the best locksmiths they had been able to contact were unwilling even to attempt to open it. The door itself was approximately ten centimetres thick and was constructed to a very high standard.

"Thank you Inspector. Once my team manages to isolate a sample of the virus or whatever it is from the rats, it will be been sent off to London for analysis. These particles are usually very complex so it may take several days to correctly identify the culprit. If there is nothing else to add for now, we need to get back to work. We will meet again in two hours to catch up, if anyone needs me in the mean time I will base myself here," Dr Roberts instructed.

Sixteen

Richard started to come round as the van bounced around on an uneven surface of some kind. He tried to move, but his hands and feet were tied. All he could do was shuffle far enough to see a rather shapely pair of legs covered in figure hugging denim. He recognised them immediately as Gwen Taylor's, although he could not quite see the rest of her body.

His head felt fuzzy from the extremely hard punch he had received and he could feel his swollen lip throbbing underneath the duct tape. There were two men sitting in front of him looking directly over him towards the front of the van. It was not long after when he felt the van reach a halt and he heard the front door open and then slam shut. A second later the side door slid open from the outside, revealing the night sky. Someone pulled on his ankles and he was dragged un-

361

ceremoniously out, dropping the gap of almost a metre to the floor and banging his head on the step on his way down. Ben and Dan lifted him to his feet then Jonas cut the tie wraps holding his ankles and tore off the tape covering his mouth. Richard took the opportunity to check out his surroundings, seeing nothing but a derelict church and miles of countryside in every direction. There were no familiar landmarks and as he had been unconscious for the whole journey, he had no idea how far they had travelled. He watched with interest as Jonas carefully lifted the still unconscious form of Gwen carefully out of the van before slinging her easily over his heavily muscled shoulders.

Ben shoved him hard between the shoulder blades, urging him to walk.

"Where are we? And what are you doing with her? Has your boss finally decided to bring her in?" Richard asked, hoping one of the men would slip up and give up some morsel of information that would help identify where he was.

All he received for his troubles was another shove, so he started walking, following Jonas and his precious cargo round to the back of the church towards the graveyard.

Remembering the gun from earlier, Richard started to panic when he saw the gravestones. This would make an ideal spot to hide a couple of unwanted bodies.

He was just thinking of making a run for it when Ben spoke.

"Take them both down to the lab; the boss wants to get started straight away. I'm going to move the van so it can't be seen from the air. Keep your eyes open for any of those freaks before you go opening any doors. We don't want one of them sneaking up on us," he ordered the others, referring to the afflicted with hatred.

There were a few other cars parked in the overgrown copse about two hundred metres away from the church. They were hidden from any unwanted visitors by a huge camouflage net suspended from the branches overhead but were close enough to the facility should they be needed in a hurry.

Richard was led to the front of a large mausoleum in the graveyard with the aid of several shoves from Jonas and Dan. Its ancient stonework looked in even worse condition than the church. Dan lifted a tarnished brass memorial plaque next to the huge wooden doors to reveal a hidden switch, a modern addition to the aging structure. The doors may have looked rotten on the outside but they were solid. Inside was a dusty passageway leading to a flight of steps consisting of massive slabs of limestone, worn smooth over the ages. They stopped facing a blank wall that Dan and Jonas leant against, forcing one edge of it to spin open on a huge central pillar. Inside was a large modern elevator platform that looked completely out of place amongst its crumbling surroundings. To one side was an older flight of steps, presumably leading down to the same location. Richard made a point of committing them to memory just in case he got a chance to escape; he doubted their plans for him were friendly.

Dan shoved him hard onto the platform causing him to slam his head into the back wall, unable to stop himself with his hands tied behind his back. They joined him and the elevator began to descend, dropping through a shaft of solid rock. Richard guessed that they descended for about thirty metres before stopping with a jolt at the bottom. He was forced through a set of reinforced steel doors similar to those used in old-fashioned fallout shelters, courtesy of the cold war.

Inside was a different world altogether. Heading to the left, right and straight ahead were large corridors, the ceiling of each forming arches above their heads. Richard guessed they had been designed that way to provide structural strength; they were a long way underground after all. The place was spotless; everything was painted white and illuminated with fluorescent lighting giving the hidden facility a sterile appearance.

There were dozens of doors off the various corridors but Richard had not yet seen any other people around. Dan shoved him again and they took the sterile corridor straight ahead leading a hundred metres away to another perpendicular corridor, the junction of which contained a set of double doors with glass in the top half.

He could see through them as he approached and could make out what looked like an enormous laboratory, three times the size of any at Swiftgene but just as well equipped, if not better. He was forced through these doors and was faced with an interesting sight. Ahead of him were four tables similar to the ones used by surgeons, with some form of padding attached to them. There were obvious restraints built into them for the arms and legs and what looked like some form of head brace. The tables were mounted on a central rotating axle that allowed them to be spun into the upright position once the patients had been firmly secured.

It was towards one of these that Richard was forced and Gwen was taken to another. He was physically lifted and slammed down onto his and held securely in place while the restraints, thick leather straps with heavy stainless steel buckles, were fitted. Richard struggled wildly as Dan fastened the last restraint, desperate to be free but there was no way he was going to wriggle out of them once they were fastened.

"Remove her outer clothing first, I want to see how much her body has changed already," said a man's voice from behind Richard's table.

They lifted Gwen onto a table and now Dan and Ben were rather roughly removing her blouse, jeans and socks, taking full opportunity to ogle her semi-naked body. They fastened her still unconscious form in place and then waited patiently for further instructions.

Richard strained as far as he could to try to see the owner of the voice. It sounded very familiar and he realised that he was about to meet his contact face to face for the first time.

"Rotate the tables into the vertical position please," instructed the unseen man.

The men operated the ratchet handles and the tables slowly drew into the upright position as an old man rolled into view in an electric wheelchair. He was bent almost double, obviously suffering from some defect of the spine and he had an oxygen mask in one hand, the bottle for which was secured on a little shelf at the rear of his vehicle. He pulled up in front of Richard and drew in a lungful of pure oxygen as he examined the man who had betrayed him.

"Dr Jennings, it's good to finally meet you in the flesh, especially following our little misunderstanding on the phone. I told you that you would regret speaking to me in that manner. And now I will tell you something that may distress you; we were coming to pull you out to safety tonight anyway as a thank you for your hard work. Your little outburst cost you a lot more than the money I have reclaimed everything, and yes, that does mean the foreign holdings as well. I have some good news for you, however; you will not be facing any charges for your incompetent handling of Methuselah. The bad news is that you will die a poor man at my hands, but not before you have provided me with one last service," explained the old man.

Without the electronic scrambling device, his voice was old and broken.

"Look, whoever you are. I was just a little frightened, that's all. I didn't mean any of it. Just tell me what you want and I'll do it," Richard pleaded, tears of desperation forming in his eyes.

"Who I am is of no consequence to you Dr Jennings, especially now. All you need to know is that I am never going to give you the opportunity to make a fool out of me again. I dragged you out of debt and helped you cover the company funds you had misappropriated and you still tried to cheat me. The sad thing is that if we had pulled you out as we had planned, we would also have set you up with a new identity. You would have had a new home somewhere warm and enough money that you'd never have to work again. You messed it up in the last few hours with your abject greed," the old man taunted, enjoying the pained expression on his captive's face.

"I mean it; I can put this right and help you develop the drug. You have Dr Simmons' work and I could help you patent it first. We can falsify the results to show that you thought of it before Dr Simmons; you would make millions, if not billions," continued Richard, desperate for his life.

It was true, at that very moment he would have done anything, even sell his own mother if she had still been alive.

"You pitiful little worm," the old man scolded, cackling so hard that he was forced to snatch a lungful of oxygen.

"Please, you have to help me!" Richard begged, any semblance of dignity forgotten.

The old man gestured to Dan and pointed at the now trembling form of Richard. Still sobbing, he managed to straighten himself up, expecting that the large man was about to free him.

Instead, Dan drew back his fist and punched him hard in the face, instantly breaking his nose.

"That was for your arrogance, Dr Jennings, in imagining that I would ever trust you again, you maggot of a man. I have all Dr Simmons' research and my people are more than capable of performing the work on my behalf, I don't need you at all!" the old man said, laughing.

Unnoticed by them all Gwen had started to come round and she listened to the discussion with interest, keeping her eyes closed and her body limp. She decided it would be useful to hear what they were saying whilst they thought she was unconscious.

"Now I will explain why I asked you to add the contaminant to Dr Simmons' serum. His work and theories are flawless; the serum will work exactly as foreseen in its uncontaminated form and that is why we couldn't allow him to test it successfully. The viral strain we asked you to add was meant to just attack the red blood cells and make the patients ill, hopefully preventing any further testing. However, we did not count on the effect that Methuselah would have on it. It appears to have repaired damaged viral RNA making it exceptionally potent and then, as you are aware, it began working too well, causing 'The Afflicted'. This strange bloodlust is just a rather unfortunate side effect, if I do say so myself. It is enough, however, to take Methuselah off the trials schedule, because if it had been allowed to succeed, many people like me would have lost millions, if not billions. Hundreds of existing drugs would have become redundant, not to mention any new drugs that we had already developed. Now my colleagues and I are the only ones who control Methuselah and I have the only untainted serum ever produced," he mocked, knowing that Richard could do nothing about his predicament but enjoying torturing him anyway.

"You bastard Richard, how could you?" screamed Gwen, her eyes opening at last. "We trusted you and you have perverted John's work for money. Now look what you have unleashed on the world, a disease that could literarily wipe out humanity!"

"Now, now, Dr Taylor, your good friend's work is still perfectly safe, it just won't belong to him anymore," the old man said in a condescending voice.

"Why?" she asked, "was the money really worth it?"

"It wasn't just the money, you foolish girl," the old man said, moving over to her table. He stroked his finger along her muscular thigh and tight abdomen, amazed at the increased muscle tone, "I want what you have now. I want to be young and strong again with enhanced healing, just like you."

"What are you talking about, you crazy old man? I've not been injected with Methuselah, unless...?" she started to say, but could not finish as suddenly everything began to fall into place; the appetite, the improved muscle tone and the disappearing subcutaneous fat deposits.

She stared across at her ex-boyfriend with murder in her eyes, knowing that if she were now free she would have killed him on the spot for the unsanctioned violation of her body.

Richard looked away guiltily, staring instead at his own suspended body as the old man began to laugh heartily. The truth of the situation was that Richard only felt sorry for being captured. He did not regret using her to save his own skin and would happily do it again if it suited him.

"Richard, even you couldn't be that unethical. Please tell me he isn't telling the truth?" she beseeched, somehow knowing the answer already.

Richard could not even look at her and she took his silence as an admission of guilt, but the old man was not so shy.

"Yes, Dr Taylor. He used you as a guinea pig for the Methuselah serum, didn't you, Dr Jennings? And all because he needed money to pay off his various gambling debts," he happily informed her, the sadist within him taking great pleasure in her discomfort.

"How could you," Gwen screamed, "Did you ever have any feelings for me at all?"

Richard looked at her vehemently as he remembered all the times she had refused him her body, reason enough in his twisted, selfish mind to betray her.

"I did it to save my own life, but also to teach you a lesson. All you were to me was an acquisition to show off to my so-called friends. When I realised you were never going to let me touch you I decided to make you pay. Especially when I noticed how close you and that freak John Simmons were becoming, laughing at me behind my back. I mean, what has he got that I haven't? I was rich for crying out loud and he lives in a tiny one bedroom crap hole," Richard shouted, finally happy to get it off his chest.

Gwen hung her head allowing the raw emotion to filter into her being as she comprehended what Richard had done to her. Her mind drifted back to John and the limited time they had spent together. She felt rage building within her and decided that she was not going to give these two monsters the satisfaction of seeing her break down. She gritted her teeth to harness the rage and lifted her head to return the old man's stare, showing no sign of weakness. The old man was visibly shaken by her resolve and the smile disappeared from his face.

"Enough small talk, we have business to attend to. Fetch me the uncontaminated serum please," the old man barked angrily at one of the assistants standing at the rear of the lab.

A young man retrieved the sample from one of the steel refrigeration units and brought it over with a syringe.

Gwen noticed how the sample was almost entirely clear with no evidence of the yellow tint that she had seen in the other samples, confirming that something had definitely been added to them all.

"Administer half the sample to Dr Jennings and start monitoring him every half an hour. If the previous results are anything to go by we should start to see major changes within twenty-four hours without the contaminant to slow things down," the old man instructed.

The assistant approached Richard, and removed half of the fluid from the vial with the syringe.

Richard's face dropped and he began to shake his restraints, trying to escape as he realised the old man was serious.

"No, you can't do this; that serum is untested and you have no idea what the side effects could be in a human being," screamed Richard as he felt the tell-tale scratch of the needle piercing his skin.

He watched in horror as the clear liquid disappeared into his arm and Gwen began to laugh at his predicament, finally satisfied that he was getting his comeuppance.

She was glad that Richard got what he deserved.

Richard started to writhe about in panic until someone hit him for the third time that day and he slipped mercifully into unconsciousness.

Gwen was, however, wide awake.

"Don't you have a conscience at all? Because of you, people are dying by the hundreds, maybe even thousands!" she accused the old man.

"Don't give me your holier-than-thou rubbish. Maybe you will understand when your perfect body begins to wither and die," he snapped back at her.

"If you really thought that, you would have left John alone to complete his work. People like you are interested only in power and money," she accused.

"Well played, Dr Taylor. It appears you are not as easy to con as your friend there," he conceded, pointing at the limp form of Richard.

He nodded to one of the assistants who walked over carrying a syringe. The young woman injected Gwen who immediately began to feel drowsy.

"You won't get away withhh ...," Gwen started to say, before giving up the fight for consciousness.

"Oh yes I will Dr Taylor, it is you who will not!" the old man chuckled, before heading out of the lab leaving the two sleeping forms to rest.

***

Richard's office was a hive of activity as dozens of forensics officers went through his belongings with a fine-tooth comb, pulling out the contents of drawers, filing cabinets and any other place containing documentation. They inspected every single piece of paper and log entry looking for evidence to show Richard had been up to no good. One or two financial transactions had raised interest so far but there was nothing solid. John had just popped his head round the office door looking for the inspector when Richard's phone rang, causing them all to jump.

"John, would you do us a favour and answer the phone. It may be one of Richard's contacts and we don't want to tip them off. You never know it might even be the security detail he sent to find the young man," Michael said, gesturing towards the phone.

John gingerly picked up the handset, "Hello, this is Dr Jennings' phone, Dr Simmons speaking. How can I help?" he asked nervously.

"Hi sir, this is Frank Brown, the security manager, I am just calling to say we have located Brian Travis and have taken him to the secure location as instructed by Dr Jennings," said the voice on the other end of the line.

Inspector Devon frantically made hand motions for John to write down the conversation and shoved a pad of paper and a pen at him. Subtly, he walked round the desk and peered over John's shoulder as he sat in Richard's luxury office chair trying to interpret his doctor-like scribbles. John was no secretary but he managed to write down the odd helpful word.

"Hi Frank, how's it going? I haven't seen you for a couple of days, I miss you kicking me out when I've stayed too late. You say you have found Brian, well that's great. Richard said you might call but there has been a change of plans concerning the location. Can you bring him straight here instead so that we can begin the treatment straight away?" urged John, thinking on the spot.

He was not aware of any secure location other than the facility in Hove but played along with Frank anyway.

"I'm not sure sir; Dr Jennings was very particular about keeping the boy out of public view. Is he there? Can I speak to him?" Frank asked suspiciously. "He said he wanted to deal with this matter personally."

Dr Jennings had not mentioned anything to him about involving Dr Simmons and he did not want to upset his boss. After all, they were being paid good rates for the night's work.

"Frank, he's not here at the moment; he had to nip home for something, that's why he called me in to take care of this. Just bring the boy to Swiftgene before anyone sees you with him. We must treat him before his condition gets any worse," John lied, doing his best to keep his voice composed.

Michael gave John the thumbs up to say he was doing the right thing, because even he, a non-scientist, understood how urgently they needed to find the missing lab technician, "still, I better talk to Dr Jennings first to confirm. I'll try him on his home number because he isn't answering his mobile," Frank said apprehensively.

Frank could tell by the tone of John's voice that something was not right and put the phone down suddenly.

"No, you don't need to...damn it, he's gone," said John, angrily slamming the phone handset down in its holder.

"That was our missing security manager, Frank Brown. It appears they have Brian somewhere secure but he refused to bring him here until he had spoken to Richard."

"And where would that be?" Michael asked eagerly.

"I am not aware of any secure locations and he wouldn't elaborate any further," he said, banging his fist on the table out of frustration.

He was beginning to get a little angered by all the deception and double talk that seemed to surround anything Richard had been involved in.

Michael had already picked up his radio handset and was calling central headquarters.

"Bravo One Four this is inspector Devon, I need an emergency phone trace on the office phone line of Dr Richard Jennings at Swiftgene. While you are at it can you also get me the phone records for the same number over the last six months please? When you have fixed the location, please ready an armed squad. We have to secure the safety of a civilian, one Brian Travis. We suspect that he is being held against his will by Swiftgene security forces, but beware, he is probably one of the afflicted," Michael ordered the voice on the other end.

He turned to John and queried him.

"They will be able to triangulate that position very quickly, are you sure you are ready for him?" he asked, now satisfied they were getting somewhere.

John nodded. This was the breakthrough they needed finally, the one chance they would have to test the cure on the most potent of all the victims.

"Inspector, the reason I came to see you was I have found a problem with the Methuselah serum, well at least the samples I have tested already. Every one of the samples has a contaminant peak in them and based on my previous attempts, it should not be there. If I were a gambler, I would say someone deliberately added it. I would also hazard a guess that this original virus has been mutated by the curative properties of Methuselah and that is why it's turned into some sort of super-bug. Whoever put it in there couldn't have known the effect it would have, but they must have desperately wanted to disrupt my work," John explained.

Michael's curiosity grew with every passing minute.

"Why would Dr Jennings want to sabotage your experiment? Surely he would lose out if it didn't work?" he asked inquisitively.

"Gwen and I were speculating that Richard was having money troubles, so he may have attempted to sell my work. For him to succeed he would have to make sure that my project was a failure. He could have received millions for a project with the potential of Methuselah. That is why I was wondering if you had found anything; a project as complicated as this would definitely leave a paper trail," John answered.

"Have you mentioned this to Dr Roberts yet?" Michael asked, looking more than a little confused.

"Yes, her people are checking my results now against the first small scale experimental results, just in case it was me that contaminated the samples. I am, after all, still a suspect," replied John, trying to demonstrate a good reason for Richard's disappearance.

"I am afraid there is nothing in the office itself and we are still waiting for our demolitions expert to open the safe. Only explosives or the combination is going to open that safe, but we are hopeful if there is anything to be found, then it will be in there. We are hoping that you and Dr Taylor disturbed him so he didn't have time to clear everything out," said Michael, and realised that he had let her name slip.

"Any news about Gwen?" John asked hopefully, not being able to hold off any longer.

Michael shook his head despondently.

"I'm sorry John, there has been no news whatsoever," he told him, "but I promise you, you will be the first to know."

"I don't mean to put you under pressure but she is very important to me," John tried to explain.

"No apology necessary. I'm hoping there are some clues in there," Michael said, pointing to the safe.

"Anyway, I'd better get back, there's plenty to do," said John before wandering off.

The weight of the world was on his shoulders.

Seventeen

There were only a couple of hours of darkness left, which was why the virus was not spreading more rapidly. Those who were aware had locked themselves away securely for the night, but many were not, and in a few hours the streets would begin to fill up with unsuspecting victims fresh to the slaughter.

The hospital was full to overflowing and new victims were turning up by the dozens. The medical staff were no longer treating them, with new victims being tranquilised or sedated and locked away in rooms that were becoming dangerously overcrowded.

An attempt had been made to procure extra staff, but news of the outbreak had spread quickly and there were few takers given the number of staff that had already been injured while dealing with the afflicted. Those injured medical staff now shared the hospital lock-ups with the very people they had been trying to treat.

There were armed police officers all over the hospital carrying the new tranquiliser guns and they had been ordered to shoot first and ask questions later. As a precaution, they all carried handguns with live ammunition as well, but so far, they had not been necessary.

In the streets, the afflicted that had not made it to the hospital before the sub-human blood lust had kicked in now roamed the back alleys and darker areas of the city.

Alongside them were their much smaller cousins, the infected rats and other animals. It was now hazardous to be out in the open. Those in less secure accommodation were also at risk; some of the more adventurous of the afflicted or the hungrier were not above breaking their way in to find the inhabitants, usually the vulnerable in their beds. Any victims that did not die during the attacks lay dormant for several hours, depending on the amount of blood lost. Later, they too would wake up and go on the prowl themselves, adding to the numbers out hunting.

Now the afflicted numbered about five hundred, a lot of whom doctors had sedated at the hospital. When the sun came up, those figures would climb significantly, reaching thousands in a very short time.

The Afflicted

Deep in the New Forest was a sleepy little village called Lyndhurst, isolated by miles of forest and countryside. The inhabitants lay asleep, the trouble in Brighton a world away from them, or so they thought. On the outskirts of the village, a group of the afflicted now gathered, with Helen as their adoptive leader.

Three men and a handful of filthy cub scouts, all of them covered in dried blood, were waiting for her directions.

They had spent most of the day under cover, the men taking it in turns to fulfill one of their sub-human desires with their naked female leader. Now they gathered patiently behind her as she surveyed the closest property with curious eyes, sensing the inhabitants inside.

Helen began running around the edge of the field along the wall that bordered the property. She kept herself low behind the hand built dividing wall, her instincts telling her that stealth was required. Her little gang carefully followed, guided by her naked bottom as it bobbed along through the tall grass.

As they entered the yard, they heard a lone dog whimpering in fear through the open window to the kitchen having sensed their approach.

It was normally a good guard dog, but something about the scent of these people frightened it and it had crawled under the kitchen table out of sight.

Helen tested the back door to find that it was unlocked; crime was not a problem in this secluded location and many of the residents had grown up leaving their properties unlocked at night. She pushed the door open and they crept in. One of the boys noticed the cowering canine and leapt on it without warning, killing it swiftly with barely a sound.

Upstairs the distinctive sound of snoring could be heard so Helen began to climb the stairs with the others cautiously following towards the unsuspecting homeowners. As she entered the first room, the man who had been sound asleep suddenly woke with a start and sat bolt upright, grabbing the shotgun he kept by his bed in case of errant foxes. He swung the weapon towards them, intending to shoot, when he actually comprehended what he was seeing. A grubby, naked young woman surrounded by a bunch of what appeared to be cub scouts, their uniforms in tatters and covered with blood, gathered by the bedroom door, staring. His hesitation cost him his life as they all charged at him at once, tearing into his flesh with their gnashing teeth. The shotgun accidentally went off during the foray and one of the boys was sent flying backwards with part of his head blown apart. As his life slipped away, the last thing the man felt was regret for killing a child. His wife woke with the discharge of the weapon and screamed at the scene before her, but only for a second, as the sub-human horde turned their murderous attention to her as well.

When they had finished at the farmhouse, the hunters worked their way through every property in the village, spending no more than a few minutes at each isolated house, dispatching the owners quickly and efficiently.

There were few survivors following the ferocity of the attacks, but those that did lay dormant, the virus working its way through their damaged systems, all condemned to rise later that day.

***

The police had finally located the elusive Swiftgene security guards in an industrial estate on the outskirts of Brighton bordering a run-down housing estate. The armed response unit had surrounded the old building with officers to the front and rear.

"Jones, is the rear of the building secure?" crackled a voice over the radio.

"Yes Sarge, we have the rear exit covered," answered the young police constable, his hands shaking slightly.

"Are all of the team ready?" asked the voice. "Yes Sarge, we are all ready," Jones replied, checking round as his colleagues gave him the thumbs up.

"Okay then, we are going in, be prepared," the sergeant ordered.

Jones sat behind the low wall facing the rear of the building, his hands shaking almost uncontrollably now. It was only his second day in the unit and it had been a trial by fire having attended five incidents in his first day.

The most memorable had involved a young mother who had not made much sense over the phone, but when they arrived at her house, they had walked into a scene from Dante's visions of hell. The mother was bleeding in the corner, there was a dead eight-year-old boy on the floor and worst was the four-year-old girl. She was covered in blood from head to foot and was snarling and growling as she drank from the wound in her older sibling's throat until she had spotted them.

Jones had been physically sick when the girl had lunged at him and he had swung his nightstick, feeling the crunch as her skull fractured under the weapon. She had dropped to the floor, dead in an instant.

They'd been warned not to take any chances with the afflicted, not even with children, but that would never take the innocent look on the girl's face away as she lay dead.

Shaking his head to clear the vision, he focused on the situation at hand. At least these people were not afflicted.

Round at the front of the building, the sergeant approached the front door of what appeared to be an old medical supplies warehouse and banged on it with his fist. They had been told there was one of the afflicted being held in there and that he was of extreme importance to the MPA.

A large man sporting the dark blue Swiftgene security uniform, the bright insignia splashed across the breast pocket, opened the door just a crack and peeked through at the police officer.

"Hello officer, can I help you?" Frank Brown, the security manager, asked politely.

"Yes sir, you can. We have received intel that you are holding Brian Travis who we believe is one of the afflicted. He is wanted for urgent questioning in relation to the current outbreak," said the sergeant very professionally.

Frank stood immobile for a few seconds, pondering what to do before replying.

Dr Jennings' instructions had been to let no one in, but these were armed police officers and therefore represented the law.

Not that he would want to take them on, even on triple pay he was not being paid enough to cross the police. Besides they only had a couple of Tasers and a few cans of pepper spray between them.

However, he decided to push his luck verbally first.

"Sorry, there's nobody here by that name," said Frank, and he began to push the door shut.

The sergeant was well versed in these sorts of situations.

He wedged his foot in the door and raised the muzzle of his weapon so that it pointed directly at the man's chest.

"If you do not allow us access to the property sir, you will be arrested and charged with obstructing an on-going police investigation," the sergeant warned, again keeping his tone professional.

You did not get to be sergeant in the armed division without having a calm disposition and the skill to defuse potentially violent situations without the use of force.

"This is a private research facility containing confidential materials, so unless you have a warrant I suggest you leave," replied Frank, still trying to push the door shut.

"Sir, the man you are holding has been decreed as critical to national security. Release him into our custody or we will have to use force," the sergeant warned, signalling his men to reveal themselves.

A dozen police officers armed with tranquilizer guns stood up from their hiding places behind the sergeant, weapons all pointing at the hapless security guard. That was enough for Frank to know he was beaten and he raised his hands while moving back from the door to allow them access.

"He's in there," Frank said, nodding his head towards an office to one side of the hallway. "Guys listen carefully, it's the police. They're armed so don't try anything," Frank shouted to warn his men, hoping to stop them from doing anything stupid.

However, they had all been listening at the door and panicked, deciding to make a run for it instead.

The sergeant was knocked from his feet as three of them barged past him only to be stopped dead in their tracks by a barrage of tranquiliser darts from the waiting police officers. With the sergeant on the floor, Frank decided to take his chances with the rest of his men and headed for the rear entrance of the building, knowing the van was parked in the alley round the back.

To the rear of the building Jones was distracted. He thought he had seen something move in the bushes but he could not make anything out in the poor light.

The other officers did not seem to notice, so he returned his attention to the rear exit.

All of a sudden, four men in blue uniforms rushed out, banging the door hard against the wall. The entire squad stood in unison with their weapons held ready and the men skidded to a halt, raising their hands in submission.

"Lie down on the floor and, put your hands behind your head," Jones shouted, pointing to the floor with his free hand.

The men looked around, desperately searching for a means of escape.

Finally, they accepted the inevitability of the situation and began to lower themselves to the floor as instructed.

What happened next took everybody by surprise, including the armed police officers.

The bushes to the right hand side of the building erupted as a dozen or more of the afflicted burst into the yard howling and screaming like a pack of animals. They attacked the four security officers from Swiftgene first, allowing the police officers a couple of seconds to pull themselves together.

"Open fire!" ordered Jones.

His teams were well trained and did not need instructions more than once. They released a barrage of tranquiliser darts with extreme accuracy, but there were too many to control. The noise of the attack was attracting too much attention and they could already see more of the afflicted bearing down on them.

"Sarge, we're under attack from the afflicted," Jones shouted into the mouthpiece of his headset.

"Get out of there! We've secured the target, so do not risk any casualties," the sergeant responded.

"Everyone, we've been ordered to retreat," Jones shouted to his colleagues above the din, but they had already started moving towards the alley that led to the front of the building.

"Switch to live ammo, there are too many to track!" Jones ordered.

Walking backwards and firing at the same time they all began to leave, swapping their tranquiliser guns for the lethal handguns.

Attracted by the noise, more and more of the afflicted were coming through the hedge, focusing on the police officers now that the security officers were already dead or dying.

The officer bringing up the rear stopped to provide cover and managed to shoot three of their attackers in quick succession.

They just kept coming, climbing over the bodies of the dead to get to him.

His dying scream and the discharge of his last few rounds spurred the survivors forward. Turning to run, Jones and the others sped up the alley and piled into the armed response van, the officers inside providing covering fire.

"Go, Go, Go!" shouted the sergeant, and the driver floored the accelerator, sending the frightened police officers in the back flying as he raced down the street with sirens blaring. Brian Travis lay unconscious on the floor, the first known human to become one of the afflicted.

***

At Swiftgene another two hours had passed. The senior scientists and police officers were now gathering in the conference room for their scheduled meeting with Dr Roberts. As usual, she was leading the meeting and stood up, clearing her throat to get the attention of the group.

"Welcome back, everybody. I am sure you don't want to be here so I will get straight down to business. It has become clear that we are losing control of the situation in Brighton town centre and the surrounding areas, so the Home Office has taken charge and the military has been dispatched. The whole area within a twelve-mile radius of Brighton city centre is to be placed under enforced quarantine until further notice. No one will be allowed in or out of this area without passing through one of the strictly controlled decontamination facilities that are being installed. Unfortunately, for the moment, those facilities will not be accessible to the general public, they are reserved purely for military and support personnel until the government can provide more trained personnel. The whole zone will be subject to martial law and a strict curfew will be implemented; no one will be allowed to move around without a military escort. It is in the country's best interest that the virus does not escape from this region," she informed them sadly amidst cries of protest erupting from around the room. "You will, however, be perfectly safe here. Because of the importance of your work we will be providing you with a full armed guard," she assured them.

"What about all those innocent people still within the affected areas, they will not stand a chance if they are trapped there like animals. Surely it would be better to get them out and reduce the potential number of afflicted we have to deal with?" asked John angrily.

He had no intention of leaving but he knew many people at the company had families and loved ones in the area.

"Dr Simmons, this is upsetting for everyone, but we have limited resources at the moment and our duty is to protect the majority: the innocent people who happen to be on the outside of the quarantine zone. When the armed forces arrive en-masse, they will attempt to set up safe zones where survivors can congregate, but you must appreciate the difficulty. If just one of the afflicted, animal or human, gets into one of those zones it could be catastrophic. Our only option is to provide them with a viable treatment and put an end to the disease once and for all," she answered apologetically.

Dr Roberts had never been in a situation like this before, but she knew someone had to make life or death decisions.

John sat down more frustrated than angry as he realised there would be very little chance of him getting out of there and finding Gwen while the quarantine was in force.

Rescuing one scientist was not high on the list of priorities when there were hundreds, possibly thousands, of people dying out there.

It was a harrowing situation.

"We have one bit of good news though. Brian Travis, the first human to become afflicted, has now been apprehended. The police team that recovered him is on its way here now, so our first priority is to attempt Dr Simmons' treatment on him. Are you in a position to attempt a cure, Dr Simmons?" she asked with interest.

The whole room turned to him hopefully. He cleared his throat before speaking.

"I have treated several of the animals with a strong anti-viral agent, Acyclovir. This seems to be neutralising the pathogen and allowing the body to catch up with red blood cell manufacture. Once nullified, the body's immune system will start producing antibodies against the virus and will offer immunity to re-infection," he advised.

"Will the same process work on a human being, especially one that has been afflicted for so long?" Dr Roberts inquired.

"I think so, although I am going to give him a couple of transfusions during the initial phase to assist the body's recovery. I cannot, however, predict whether there will be any permanent brain damage due to prolonged lack of oxygen carrying red blood cells," he answered, shrugging; it was difficult to assess that from a rat.

"Dr Simmons, you previously discussed removing the Methuselah DNA sequences from the host. If we disable them surely the viral DNA repair functionality will also be deactivated?" asked one of the MPA microbiologists.

"We thought that Methuselah had something to do with the virus but we have since discovered there was a contaminant added to my serum, possibly by Richard Jennings. So we now know that the introduced DNA vectors are nothing to do with the virus other than helping to mutate it. This is good news because it means we can treat the virus with a simple procedure and do not have to worry about any sort of gene therapy," John replied gruffly, watching everyone in the room with veiled expression.

He had not realised how protective he had become of his discovery, especially now he understood that it had not been to blame for the outbreak, at least not directly.

"Dr Simmons, you will have as many of my staff as it takes to do this. We need something positive to report, something we can use to fight the outbreak," she offered, noticing how disgruntled he seemed even though they had good news at last.

She turned to Michael next.

"Inspector Devon, have you found out anything more since our last discussion that can help us shed light on who is behind this?" she asked.

"I'm afraid not, the demolitions expert has only just arrived and until we get into the safe there will be nothing to add," he informed the room. "You all need to be aware though that there will be a small explosion. Nothing more than a muffled bang, but no one here is at risk so please don't panic when you hear it," he continued, looking around the room to make sure that everyone understood.

"I'm sure we will be fine. Do you need anything else?" asked Dr Roberts.

"At some point I could do with Dr Simmons' help. We may need him to go through whatever material we find to help us sort it out," he answered, looking at John who nodded reluctantly.

"Okay, but make sure he is not distracted from the treatment," she confirmed.

"As before, I want everyone to keep me updated, so I will see you all here in a couple of hours," Dr Roberts finished, dismissing them back to their various tasks.

***

In the lab below the abandoned church, Gwen was trying to have a good look around, searching for anything that would help her to break free. She was struggling to concentrate as the hunger grew stronger, although at this stage a good portion of food would have held it at bay. If she did not eat soon, however, the balance in her blood stream would shift in favour of the virus and she would begin to experience a decline into sub-human bloodlust.

Her body had begun to change significantly; her musculature was clearly defined through her skin and she had grown in the past few hours.

She was the only human carrying the primary infection and she assumed the influx of Methuselah and her human conscience were all that were keeping her from fully turning into a beast. Those with the secondary infection were not so lucky; the mutated virus worked much faster without Methuselah's enhancements to keep it at bay. All that would become debatable if she could not convince someone to give her food though. She could hear a couple of technicians working in the lab behind her and began to shout to get their attention.

"Hello there, you behind me! Can I get something to eat and drink?" she shouted, turning her head as far as she could in the restraints to try to see them.

She assumed that as they had not tried to harm her so far they needed her alive, at least for the moment. A little food and water should not be a problem, or so she thought.

A short, thin man with a strangely pointed face and prominent front teeth that made him look like a rodent appeared in front of her. She shuddered as she realised he was literarily standing there gawping at her near naked form with a cruel smile on his face. He licked his lips before actually looking up at her face and she realised he was just a perverted opportunist who had probably never seen a naked woman in his life.

"Hi Dr Taylor, it's a pleasure to meet someone with your credentials, but I'm sorry, we have strict instructions to withhold nourishment. The old man believes that a lack of food will cause your condition to progress more rapidly. You can have some water though if you like?" he offered, his voice nasal and high pitched, reminding her of a weasel she had once seen on a children's cartoon.

"Some water would be fine, thanks," she replied politely, trying to hide her feelings of contempt.

The Afflicted

She began to wonder how her captors managed to find people like this who were prepared to torture a fellow human being with no qualms. He picked up a water bottle from the bench, one of those fitted with a straw you often see children drinking from, and walked over to her. He stood on a portable step to bring his face level with hers, purposely pressing his body against hers. He held the straw to her mouth, obviously taking a sick pleasure from humiliating her. While she drank, the weasel man once again started to admire her semi-naked body. He touched her cheek with his free hand. Using his index finger, he gently stroked her, running his finger down her face and under her chin. She shuddered involuntarily as it moved towards her exposed cleavage, trying to ignore him as she thirstily gulped down the water knowing that anything in her stomach would ease the hunger pangs, even if just for a minute or two. The man's finger ran over the swelling of her left breast, lingering for a moment before continuing over the thin material of her bra, stopping to run it back and forth over her nipple, the sensation of touch causing it to harden slightly. This excited him and he grabbed her whole breast, squeezing it hard and enjoying the firmness in the palm of his hand.

Her repulsion for the man was too much and she began to wriggle, desperately trying to move out of his grasp. This excited him more, thinking that he was actually beginning to turn her on. He dropped the water bottle and moved his face closer to hers in an attempt to kiss her. That was exactly what she had been waiting for; she thrust her head forward as far as the restraint would allow and sank her teeth into the soft flesh of his cheek. She bit down hard, her enhanced strength causing her teeth to sink easily through his flesh. He desperately pulled away and in the process, a chunk of his cheek tore from his face and Gwen spat at him in contempt. She tasted the sweet coppery fluid and found the sensation strangely pleasurable but was disgusted by her own excitement. She spat out any traces of blood in her mouth, trying to desperately to get rid of the taste.

The man fell to the floor and she felt a sense of satisfaction as she watched him writhe about in pain. The man climbed to his feet and was screaming and staggering away from her holding his face when Dave and Ben rushed in to see what the commotion was about, and the scene shocked them.

"Look at this, the bitch bit me for no reason. I'm going to kill her," the weasel man threatened, lunging forward to strike her with his fist.

Gwen flinched but Ben was too quick for him. The much larger man dragged him away from Gwen and threw him to the floor.

"She's restrained you little pervert, what were you doing to her that she could reach your face in the first place? The boss told you she was not to be touched," Ben threatened, raising his own much larger fist to the man's face.

"I was just giving her a drink, that's all, and she went nuts," the man whimpered, touching his tender cheek, cautiously examining the damage with his fingertips.

"Keep that filthy little freak and his roving hands away from me. It's one thing to be a science experiment, but to let creeps like that maul me is another matter altogether, you animals," Gwen ranted as she noticed the old man come rolling in.

The old man looked at the blood running down her chin and then at the little weasel man and worked out in a second what had happened.

"Ben, get him out of here and treat his face. He doesn't come near Dr Taylor again," he ordered without raising his voice.

Ben grabbed the man's arm and started to lead him through the doors when Gwen took a parting shot at him, just to add fear to his injury.

"I would be careful if I were you, Ben. Remember, I carry the infection and my bite is contagious, but his will be too in a few hours," she shouted after them.

The frightened look on the man's face was retribution enough as the reality sunk in, knowingly exactly what she had meant.

He began to struggle but Ben and Dave held him firmly between them.

"Please help me! She's right, I'm going to turn into one of those things," he pleaded with the old man.

The old man smiled at him deceptively. "Don't worry, we look after our own here," answered the old man generously, "We will make sure you are alright," he promised, motioning to Ben to escort him out.

The weasel man calmed down and seemed much happier as he walked out, chatting away nervously to Ben. The old man waited until he had vanished through the doors before speaking to Dave.

"She's right, take care of him. We cannot afford to have an outbreak here. Make sure you dispose of the body safely, I don't want to attract any unwanted attention," he told Dave with no hint of emotion.

Dave nodded and smiled knowingly as he reached into his shoulder holster to retrieve his handgun. From another pocket, he removed what looked like a small piece of pipe that Gwen instantly recognised as a silencer.

She shuddered but had to admit to herself that she would not lose a great deal of sleep over the man's demise.

Gwen looked at the old man who was once again admiring the muscle tone of her body and for once, she wished he were like any other lecherous man.

She now preferred ogling to being examined like a specimen.

"Why are you trying to make me change? You know what I will become if you don't get me the nourishment I need. I'll be a lot stronger and more dangerous than the afflicted with Methuselah in my system," she sneered at him, wondering what sort of a monster this twisted old man was.

He just smiled at her and pointed to Richard's slumbering form where he hung limply from the upright restraints.

Gwen's gaze flickered in Richard's direction briefly.

"He has been treated with the pure Methuselah serum and if I am correct, we will see physical improvements in him very soon. He will change faster than you or the original rodent test subjects because his body is not fighting the virus," he said proudly.

"What does that have to do with me?" she asked, her curiosity getting the better of her.

"If Dr Simmons' theories are correct, Methuselah improves the body's systems and reverses the aging process which means that Dr Jennings' immune system should be much stronger than yours or mine. What I want to see is if he can survive an attack from you without contracting the mutated virus; after all, you're the only other person treated with Methuselah. If I'm right he will not develop the affliction, and that's the final piece in the puzzle for me," he explained with some gusto.

"What sort of a crackpot are you? You could have achieved the same results by injecting him with my blood," she exclaimed, disturbed by his utter disregard for human life.

"You are right, I could. But I also want to see you both in action. I can already see the physical improvements in your body. Imagine what they will be like in his as he already outweighed you by about thirty kilos," the old man chuckled, taking more than a little pleasure from the prospect.

Gwen strained against the restraints with all her strength, which was considerable now, but even she could not budge the thick leather.

"You are a bitter, twisted old man, and if I ever get out of this contraption I am going to take great pleasure in killing you myself," she threatened, writhing and struggling for all she was worth.

If she had escaped at that moment, she would probably have ended his life with her bare hands.

"You are right, Dr Taylor. I'm old and twisted, as you can see. I have a range of debilitating conditions that I am hoping Methuselah will correct. All I need is a successful trial to see that there are no ill effects, and that is why Richard is going to be useful. However, I wanted to see what I would be capable of first hand while disposing of the two of you at the same time. Although, looking at your fine physique I can see why Dr Jennings was so interested in you. I might just keep you around as a distraction, if you survive," he said cruelly, enjoying her reaction to his comments.

Gwen was angry and she began struggling once again, this time so violently that she shook the whole table unit in her rage. When she finally calmed down, the thought crossed her mind that she was getting more and more aggressive with time. If this continued then soon she would not be able to control herself at all.

"Save your energy my dear, you'll need it soon enough," the old man laughed, turning his electric chair around and gliding noiselessly out of the lab.

He was looking forward to the display; John Simmons truly was a genius, and if the experiment worked, he would be able to ditch his damned wheelchair for good.

Gwen could hear him laughing as he rolled down the corridor and shuddered involuntarily. It did not bother her for long as a few seconds later a technician appeared with a large needle in her hand. The woman hesitantly reached forward towards Gwen's struggling body, taking great care not to get too close, and jabbed the needle into her leg. Gwen felt the cool liquid pump into her veins, and within seconds her eyelids began to grow heavier until she collapsed forward asleep against the restraints.

Inside her body, the virus had almost gained the upper hand and her red blood cell count was decreasing with each passing hour.

Eighteen

John barely recognised his placement student, Brian, when they brought him into the lab, kicking and screaming. He had turned from a docile young man to a manic monster, snarling and snapping at people like an animal. He was covered from head to foot in blood, some of it dry and hardened, some of it fresh and sticky, making him smell like an abattoir.

"He's all yours Dr Simmons," one of the police officers said before hurrying away, glad to be out of the lab.

John stared at the wriggling creature in front of him and wondered what the boy must have done to end up looking like that.

His nails were all broken, his fingers pulped as if he had been scratching at concrete, and the bone of his left index finger protruded from the damaged flesh. His face was pale and drawn, making him look twenty years older than he actually was. John noticed that his gums had receded, making his teeth look more pronounced, especially his canines. John's mind drifted to vampire folklore and he now understood why disease had often been blamed for the supernatural creatures commonly portrayed on the big screen. John was truly seeing the instinctual sub-human potentially present in all of us.

"Nurse, can you please give him a mild sedative, I want him calm but conscious," he asked one of the MPA medical staff.

The woman reluctantly obliged, afraid of getting too close to the gnashing teeth, but soon after, Brian gradually began to calm down, looking half dazed around the room.

He made a half-hearted attempted to bite the nurse before finally relaxing back onto the padded surface of the table.

"I want blood samples taken immediately, and can you cross match four units of blood. The sooner we get him onto transfusions the quicker his treatment will progress. Direct injection into his bloodstream will be a lot more effective than him ingesting the stuff," John instructed the nurse, who was a little less hesitant now the boy was calm.

The first nurse took the samples and a second ran off to source the blood for infusion.

The Afflicted

"Can we also begin a saline drip, I want to add the Acyclovir in diluted form as the dose is going to be very strong and it may be too toxic at high concentrations," John asked a third nurse, who immediately followed his instructions.

It was not long before Brian had a number of needles piercing his circulatory system with a mixture of fluids dripping steadily away. When Brian finally lay still, contentedly staring at the ceiling, John began to relax. All they could do now was monitor his progress and cross their fingers that the treatment would work on a human being.

"Can we monitor blood pressure, temperature, Oxygen saturation and heart rate at all times. Please let me know if anything changes," he instructed taking off his lab coat.

A few rooms away he heard a muffled bang and realised that the police must have removed the safe door. He hurried off in the direction of Richard's office, eager to see what they had discovered and if it could lead to Gwen's whereabouts. He had already lost one good woman and he was not prepared to lose another.

When John reached the office, the demolition squad were just re-entering the room and a cloud of dust and smoke billowed out through the open door.

"Any luck?" John asked Michael eagerly, wafting the dust away from his face.

"Patience Dr Simmons, we are just about to find out," Michael replied, understanding the scientist's eagerness.

One of the police officers opened a window and the metallic tasting smoke began to dissipate. A member of the demolition team had to rush out of the office as the dust reached one of the smoke detectors in the corridor setting off the fire alarm. The man hurriedly instructed control to send a message over the tanoy system, negating the alarm before everyone in the building began pouring outside.

As the view cleared, they could see the safe door, blackened around two of the edges, sitting on the floor near the opposite wall. There was a dent in the plaster where it had struck with the force of the blast. The door was intact, but the lock and the hinges were nothing but twisted metal. John was impressed by the precision as he looked at the interior of the safe where there was not even a scorch mark on the paperwork inside.

"Now it's up to you John, is there anything in there that looks familiar?" asked Michael, turning to face him.

John examined the contents. There were piles of files, CDs and notebooks inside, but the thing that caught his attention was a leather-bound Filofax on the second shelf. He had seen Richard with it on several occasions and with it were several folders and CDs with the word 'Methuselah' scrawled on them in Richard's distinctive handwriting. Alongside the paperwork was the missing sample bottle number 29, but after picking it up, John noticed that it was completely empty. He could not understand where Richard might have used it.

"These are copies of every document associated with my project; he has all my notes, all the results and analytical printouts. Basically everything that you would need to reproduce my work," he told Michael, who took the material from him.

"What about this?" Michael asked, picking up the Filofax.

John opened it and pored through the pages, stopping to read an excerpt from over a week ago.

"John Simmons' new Methuselah project is coming on well. The results are promising so far as John has managed to isolate all twelve RNA vectors required. He is now trying to insert these vectors into a sterile viral genome. My contact is pleased with the progress and had provided a sample that he wants me to add to the final bacteriophage serums. He will not disclose its purpose, but who am I to argue, he continues to pay well and I'm now straight at the casino."

John dropped back into Richard's large chair with a look of astonishment on his face as he read the confirmation of what he had already suspected. It was different, however, seeing the facts in Richard's own handwriting.

"This is the proof we needed! Richard was working with someone else on the outside. He spiked my serum on purpose with a contaminant; the slimy two faced greedy bastard is directly responsible for the outbreak," John said, still struggling to believe what the man had been capable of, purely for personal gain.

John was now frightened for Gwen's well-being.

"John, you need to read through that in detail and find out what Richard was up to, anything that will be useful to help fix this," urged Michael.

"No," John replied, pushing the Filofax back towards the police officer. "I know more about Methuselah than any man alive and we already have a plan of action to deal with it. We need you and your team to go through it with a fine-tooth comb and find out who these people are and where he has gone, because I guarantee wherever Richard is we will find Gwen there too."

John stood up and was about to leave when he noticed the portable chiller still plugged into the wall at the back of the office. Inside his mind something stirred, but he still could not think what was wrong with the specimen. Still curious, he decided to take one last look to see if something would click. He opened the container lid and stared again at the carcass.

It took almost a minute to hit him unexpectedly as it stared him straight in the face.

"Oh my God! How did I miss that? It was so obvious; the bloody rat has a penis!" he shouted, causing everyone in the room to stare at him confused.

"Sorry, but you have lost me. How is that important?" asked Michael, wondering if the scientist had finally lost his marbles.

"Remember when I told you how Richard had captured the escaped rat and we confirmed it with the tag? Each one has a unique number on it and this says the number is twenty," he said to the bemused inspector.

"Yes, but like you said, it has the number on it," Michael pointed out, growing more and more confused by the second.

"The difference is, Inspector, all the even numbered rats in the trial were female, so even though the tag number is correct it can't be the right animal because this rat is male. That means Richard just put a new tag on the body of another rat to cover up and ignored the fact that a genetically modified creature had escaped. He could have prevented the whole thing if he had done what he said he was going to!" answered John excitedly, rushing out of the room.

He returned thirty seconds later carrying the radio frequency scanner and held it over the tag reading the resultant display.

"I knew it, the tag is unassigned and Richard was the only one who held these tags. By law, he was responsible for issuing and recording them. He must have got the carcass of another animal and marked up a new tag to put us off his trail. We wanted to go to the authorities, but we didn't because we thought there was no threat. How stupid could we have been?" John said, berating himself for believing the lying scumbag.

"Are you sure?" asked the inspector, "Because if you are right the charges against him won't be manslaughter, they will be murder."

"I am positive Inspector, but I want you to do everything you can to find Gwen. There is no telling what he will do to her if he is capable of this," John said with a new sense of urgency.

He grasped the inspector by his shirt and looked him solemnly in the eye, "And I do mean everything."

John let him go and headed back to the laboratory, a new spring in his step; he was not going to lose Gwen to a monster like Richard.

Michael picked up his radio handset and spoke.

"Bravo One Four, this is Inspector Devon. I requested the phone records for every number associated with Dr Richard Jennings yesterday. I know things are crazy out there but new evidence has become known. It is of the utmost importance that we have those records immediately. Fax them for my attention to the emergency headquarters at Swiftgene and let me know as soon as you do!" he ordered, hanging it back on his belt without waiting for a reply. As a police officer, he could not worry about the safety of one person, but the identification of the external contact and Dr Jennings was now a priority. If they found Dr Taylor at the same time then it would be the cherry on the cake as far as he was concerned.

***

Richard began to stir and he looked groggily over to Gwen, who he noticed was also starting to wake up. His body ached having stayed in such an awkward position for so long, most of which he had spent unconscious.

He worked his jaw to assess the damage from the several blows he'd received and was surprised to find that there was no pain. He peered at Gwen as she started to open her eyes, taking a little longer than he did to come round and he wondered if she had in fact been drugged. He was amazed at the increased amount of muscle she was displaying, the high definition visible through her minimal body fat. Her skin, however, was beginning to look pale, probably due to the change in her blood chemistry caused by the virus. He glanced around the room trying to see and hear if there were any other people present, but as far as he could tell, they were completely alone.

"Gwen, can you hear me?" he whispered, desperately trying to get her attention.

Gwen lifted her head and stared threateningly at him, her eyes bloodshot and yellow.

There was dried blood on her mouth, neck, and chest, making Richard wonder if she too had been beaten. He decided that despite their differences, they were in a similar predicament and it would make sense to form a temporary alliance against their captors.

"Gwen, look, I'm sorry, I was desperate. I had lost a fortune and was in real trouble until the old man helped me out," he tried to explain.

"Richard, you can keep your excuses for someone who gives a damn. Do you know what you have done to me, all because you couldn't control your gambling addiction? What is money compared to someone's life, you piece of scum?" she asked, her voice full of hatred.

She was angry that he did not even contemplate the enormity of his actions on the public.

"If it helps, it was nothing personal," he lied, "you were just in the right place at the wrong time."

But Gwen didn't believe him.

"What I am confused about is how you did it? I would have noticed if you had injected me with anything, and you couldn't have put it in my food or drink because the treatment has to be intravenous," she asked, trying to make sense of her situation.

After all, she had been purposefully avoiding him to spend more time with John.

"Remember the show I took you to and you woke up half naked in my spare room? Well the reason you passed out was that I dropped a couple of sedatives in your drink. I had been trying to get you drunk all night but you weren't having any of it. When you were unconscious I gave you the serum," he told her proudly, impressed by his own cunning way he had tricked her and remained undetected.

"You mean you planned the whole thing just to use me as a specimen? That was why you were so keen for me to go that night, even though I had already made plans with John. That is cold Richard, even for you!" she accused with utter contempt.

"Did you do anything else to me while I was unconscious?" she asked, suddenly concerned.

"No, I was totally honest about that. All I did was have a bit of a fondle, but you have to understand you had been waving it in front of me for weeks. I even gave you a big pay rise, so it was the least I deserved," he said, actually seeming proud that he had limited himself to sexual assault rather than rape.

Gwen had never been more relieved that she had dumped someone in her entire life.

If it were not for the fact that his actions had landed her in this situation she would have taken solace from leaving him hanging.

"You really are a self-righteous piece of scum. You really don't see what you have done wrong, do you? Women are just objects to men like you, and you deserve everything that happens to you, no wonder I fell for John," she said, realising too late that she had expressed her feelings for a man she knew he hated.

Richard's expression changed in a second, turning from one of pleading to one of utter hate at the mention of John's name.

"I knew it! You were just stringing me along for what you could get. I bet you didn't make lover boy wait though did you, you whore!" he shouted angrily.

"Not that it matters now, but you are wrong. When you pestered me I was lonely and weak, I agreed to go out with you purely because I knew no one down here, even though I knew you were using me to impress your snobby friends. John is a real man, he loves me for more than my appearance, and for your information, no, I didn't make him wait; I threw myself at him because I love him," she said, finding it very liberating to express her true feelings for the man she had wanted for so long.

"I know what they have planned for me, and when they release me I am going to beat you to within an inch of your life and take what I want just to spite John. Then I am going to find him, and as I kill him I will tell him exactly how unsatisfying you were," Richard threatened, the veins bulging in his neck as he strained against the restraints to face her.

His face twisted into an evil smile showing exactly how he felt for her. He could handle being dumped but not because of John Simmons, and if he was going to survive this, then he was going to make sure they both suffered.

Barely controlling her temper as it was, the threat against John was too much for her to bear. Her rage spiked instantly and the little control she had evaporated causing her to thrash wildly against the restraints, screaming and shouting obscenities at her fellow captor. The more she ranted, the more he laughed, happy that he could still illicit a response from her. Hearing the noise, the old man came rolling in, this time pushed by Jonas as he sucked oxygen through his mask. He signalled for his bodyguard to stop in front of Gwen.

"Dr Taylor, I've just learnt an interesting fact from my contact at Swiftgene. It appears that they've discovered Richard's little plot. Did you know that he didn't even try to capture the escaped rat? He just tagged another carcass to keep you off his trail. You will be happy to know that he is directly responsible for all the deaths in Brighton and is now wanted for mass murder," he informed her, determined to anger her further.

Gwen realised that the longer she reacted like this, the quicker her transformation would take. She surprised him and became silent, determined to resist them for as long as she could. She wanted to be in control.

***

The treatment was going far better than expected. When John examined Brian a couple of hours later, he could already see signs of the colour returning to his cheeks as the transfusion began to work.

He had stopped thrashing about whenever anyone approached and appeared calm, even though the sedatives had worn off quickly. John was very surprised when Brian opened his eyes and looked at him, speaking for the first time in days.

"Doc, is that you? Where am I?" he asked in a quiet croaky voice, his vocal chords still sore from the repeated growling and snarling.

The MPA medical doctors turned simultaneously, excited by the sound of his voice and began checking his vital signs.

Brian looked nervous at the number of people around him, still unsure what was happening to him.

"Brian, relax, you are back at Swiftgene. You have been extremely ill, but it looks like you're finally recovering. How do you feel?" John asked him, curious about any potential after effects.

"I feel like someone has driven a steam roller over me," he said, trying to sit up against the restraints.

When he found himself restricted, a look of panic began to form and he started to struggle.

"Don't panic Brian; we had to restrain you for your own good. You are getting better now and we will be able to let you go soon, but for now just relax while the treatment takes effect," John said, gently pressing him back to the treatment table.

The boy relaxed slightly but John could tell he was still a little confused. His brain had been starved of oxygen for a long time and John hoped that the memories of his actions were not available to him, but part of him already knew that was not the case.

"Doc, what happened to me? My memory is coming back, but what it's showing me can't possibly be true, can it? I can remember doing some awful things and I think I hurt Helen," he said weakly, his whole body trembling uncontrollably.

As the red blood cell count increased, the tiny part of Methuselah the virus carried had served to protect the tissue of his brain quite well and it had preserved his memory.

"Who is Helen, Brian? Maybe we can help her," asked John sympathetically.

At the mention of her name, Brian's memory of the tragic event came flooding back and he began to sob uncontrollably.

"Oh Doc, I think I killed her. She was the first, when I still had a little control left and I was so frightened that I dumped her body in the New Forest. I don't know why, but I just panicked. After that, I just didn't care anymore, all I can remember is wanting blood, lots of blood. Please tell me I didn't do those things," he sobbed, pleading with his mentor as he recalled every one of his victims.

John stroked his head and looked at him with a kind expression, knowing that the young man would have to live with his actions for the rest of his life, and although nothing he said would console him, he was going to try anyway. He signalled for one of the nurses to come and give Brian another sedative to calm him down.

"Brian, you couldn't help yourself. The man that committed those acts is gone now. It was not your fault, but you may be able to help us," John tried to persuade him.

John remembered an article he had read in the newspaper before all the bloodshed had started about the supposed attack by a young woman on a married couple. He had automatically condemned the wife as a crazy woman who had probably murdered her husband. However, he realised that it may well be that Helen had not died after all, so John hurried off to find the inspector. If his suspicions were correct, they could have another outbreak epicenter.

John found Michael still poring through the mountain of paperwork in Richard's office trying to make sense of some of the scientific language.

Michael acknowledged John as he walked in with a smile that quickly disappeared when he noticed the look on the scientists face.

"We may have a problem," John told him.

John quickly explained his concerns about the potential for another outbreak way outside the quarantine zone and the inspector's heart fell.

Just once, I would like someone to bring me good news, he thought to himself.

"Are you sure?" asked Michael.

"Of course I can't be sure, but the attack mimics the MO of the afflicted. The New Forest is fairly isolated, which is why I don't think we have had any reports, but there are plenty of small villages and campsites scattered all over that area. It could be that there is a pocket of the afflicted growing in that area, and when they breach the forest, there are several larger towns nearby. We could have another Brighton on our hands!" John stressed while the inspector got more and more disheartened by the second.

When they saw Dr Roberts she acted immediately by contacting the Home Office with a warning. In the relatively small quarantine zone, it would be easier to control the spread, but in an area the size of the New Forest it would be impossible, especially with the amount of wildlife to take into consideration.

"How's Brian, I hear he seems to be recovering?" Dr Roberts finally asked, trying to lighten the mood.

"It's looking very positive at the moment. He has retained brain function which is both a blessing and a curse, depending how you look at it. It was his warning that alerted us to the potential second outbreak," replied John.

"Do you think the virus will flare up again within him or can we consider this a cure?" she asked, her interest spiking at a potential treatment for the growing number of the afflicted.

"No, the virus is gone, and with the help of the Acyclovir his body has now developed the correct antibodies to fight off any re-infection. We can possibly use a sample of his blood to develop an immunization. However, the treatment itself is too long and the patients would still be able to run about and spread the virus for several hours while the anti-viral takes effect if they are not restrained. Especially as we only have a limited supply of blood in the country," John informed her, disappointed that he could not offer a better option for the treatment of others.

"Well, what are we going to do?" she asked.

John shrugged his shoulders, "At this moment in time we can only treat a limited number of the afflicted at any one time. I suggest important people like soldiers, doctors, nurses and police officers, anybody who can be useful. We could, however, tweak my original solution and mix the anti-viral with a tranquiliser. When the afflicted are targeted they will immediately be knocked out. If the dose is strong enough they could actually be kept sedated long enough for the virus to be destroyed," John suggested.

It was a long shot but it would mean the difference between mass treatment and selective cures. Dr Roberts pondered for a moment.

"And you believe that this method will work?" she challenged.

"Maybe not every time, but with the right mix of anti-viral and tranquiliser there should be a high success rate," John assured her.

"I have to admit that it's a messy solution, but what other choice do we have?" Michael asked in support of John. "Especially when you consider the alternative."

"It will have to do. I'll get my team on it right away," Dr Roberts said. Any hope, no matter how small, was better than nothing. "At worst it should help to slow the spread of the virus, and at the moment I will take any positive action."

***

Following Dr Roberts' advice, the various branches of the armed forces were deployed to multiple points around the Brighton quarantine zone. They were ordered to secure the area and prevent the egress and access of people by any means necessary. Painful as the choice had been in Parliament, the decision had been unanimous that the risk of the infection spreading far outweighed the number of lives that would be lost, the sort of decision usually reserved for war.

The main problem was the coastline area itself. The sea along the south coast was very shallow in places and could only be patrolled by smaller craft. Instead, an aircraft carrier had been deployed and now dozens of heavily armed helicopters patrolled the area, watching for escapees. Despite some being prevented by deploying men at the various marinas and harbors along the twenty-plus mile stretch of sea facing land, a few boats still managed to launch in an attempt to break the quarantine.

Several camps had been established, mostly in rural areas where the non-afflicted civilians were being protected. These areas were supported by airdrops but they were already desperately short of supplies as more and more people arrived. The decision was made to turn away anyone except mothers with children or people with critical skills such as medical staff.

There was no issue of keeping people out of the main quarantine zone though. Even the press, who turned up in their hundreds at the border, did not intend to enter the danger zone and were content pestering staff at the decontamination centres. Those trying to escape were another matter. It was not easy telling a family with children that they couldn't leave.

Twelve miles north of Brighton a platoon of soldiers had closed both lanes of the A23 dual carriageway. They looked tired but were alert.

The Yorkshire Regiment had been due in Afghanistan at the end of the week, but everybody's orders had been changed.

Most of them had never been in combat and were happy for what they saw as a safe assignment.

"Lieutenant, sections three and four are in position and awaiting your orders," barked a khaki clad soldier, the three stripes and crown on his arm marking his rank.

"Carry on, Sergeant Major," replied the man, saluting in response.

The lieutenant scanned the horizon. They had a good field of view there and he did not anticipate any major problems.

There had already been one or two cars but they had turned back without too much of an argument once they had seen the weapons. There had been only one issue when a group of young men had challenged the decision and threatened to ram the barricade. A few warning shots had sent them racing back towards the city.

"Lieutenant, command is on the secure line for you," said a young corporal, holding out the battlefield hand held unit.

"Lieutenant Barker here!" the officer said, taking the handset.

"This is Major Brown. I have an update to your orders, Barker. The Ministry of Defence is upgrading the status of the current situation and we are now at the highest level of alert. We have had several reports of violence at some of our positions and even some small weapon fire resulting in armed forces casualties. You are now authorised to use live ammunition as the primary method of defense; anyone attempting to cross the quarantine is to be shot. Give them fair warning, but we can't take the risk anymore; the situation has grown worse in the city and some of the camps have fallen. Between the afflicted and the civil unrest it is becoming more difficult to keep our men safe. Do you understand?" instructed the major with authority.

The order shocked Lieutenant Barker. It was unprecedented to fire on civilians even in a war zone.

"Please repeat that sir, can you confirm that we have been ordered to use lethal force if necessary?" asked the lieutenant, a cold shiver running down his spine.

"Affirmative! Live ammunition is the primary means of defense as of now, make sure all your men are issued with it," confirmed his superior.

"Yes sir, over and out," the lieutenant answered with a sense of dread.

The order for live fire was never given lightly, with one of the key teachings in all of the British armed forces being to respect the sanctity of life. The situation in Brighton must be serious for the order to have been issued against civilians and he wondered just how safe he and his men actually were, exposed in the open like this. He returned the handset and shouted to his second in command.

"Sergeant Major, please issue all men with their SA80 rifles and live ammunition," he shouted as the soldier approached, a few of the men turning to look at their commanding officer in surprise.

The sergeant major walked over and, like his commanding officer, asked for confirmation.

"Live ammunition, sir? Are you sure?" he asked, the shock obvious on his face.

Until then, they had been issued the tranquiliser guns and their side arms for emergency use only.

"You heard me, Sergeant Major; we have been ordered to use lethal force if required," the lieutenant barked.

"But these are innocent civilians," said the sergeant major, the concern in his voice evident.

"Listen Sergeant Major, there is no one less happy about this than I am but we have to follow orders," the lieutenant told him.

"Yes sir, okay sir," the sergeant major confirmed.

"But make sure you tell the men that live fire is only to be used as a last resort. It must be getting serious in Brighton for the top brass to make a decision like that, but we are well outside the city and should have more time to assess any situation before we act. Do you understand?" the lieutenant explained carefully.

He always expected his men to follow orders but he respected them enough to be honest with them when he could. An explanation of a difficult order made all the difference to morale in his experience.

"I understand, sir," the sergeant major responded.

He saluted before turning and headed towards the men. The lieutenant shouted one more instruction as he walked away.

"Sergeant Major," he shouted, "careful or not, I think a couple of snipers covering our position may be prudent just in case!"

The sergeant major nodded and set off to follow his orders.

***

At number 10 Downing Street, the prime minister, Mark Philips, and the defence minister, Jason Holden, sat in front of an array of screens in the communications room.

They were watching the images of several world leaders from the United Nations in digital clarity. Great Britain had been under the microscope since the outbreak had started.

Ally countries had very quickly withdrawn their assets and people from the country.

Mark had only been in office for eight months and already he was frightened that he would go down in history as the man in charge when Britain had fallen.

"We have been a member state for decades and you are telling me that you are prepared to quarantine the whole country. Are you really threatening to open fire on any craft leaving the mainland of Great Britain?" Mark asked incredulously, struggling to comprehend what they were suggesting.

"I'm truly sorry Prime Minister, but it is obvious that the situation is rapidly getting out of control. It is only pure luck that you are an island state, without the water barrier we feel the virus could easily have spread to the continent," responded the French president trying to be as diplomatic as possible.

"You can't do this. We need supplies and our business's need to export their goods. There's only a small area on the south coast that is affected and we have already quarantined the area ourselves," the prime minister tried to assure them.

"That is not entirely true though, is it Prime Minister? Our sources have revealed that there is another potential outbreak site further down the coast that you have not quarantined. Anyway, it's not the human contingent we are concerned about; as I understand it, the disease is spread by rodents and other small animals that could easily sneak onto boats and planes. It only takes one to escape and the entire European continent is at risk. This also applies to many other landmasses around the globe. Unfortunate as the situation is, Prime Minister, we as a community cannot allow it," interrupted the Spanish president.

"There's no point discussing this further, the UN has voted unanimously for this action and as of this moment, the island of Great Britain is under strict quarantine. We appreciate your position and have made provisions to drop food, medicines and other essentials as required. We will let you know when we have made firm arrangements for their safe delivery," the French president instructed.

Mark was about to commence pleading but the screens had already started to go blank as they all signed off from the secure connection.

"Sir, we need to start taking drastic action to bring the situation to a rapid end; every day we spend under quarantine our country will suffer," advised the defence minister.

He had spent twenty years in the military, eight of them in the SAS, and was no stranger to tough decisions.

"Well, first things first, we have to conserve what little resources we currently have for emergency use. Ground all flights, put a ban on any form of aquatic travel and stop the flow of fuel to the public. We need to reserve as much as we can for military and civil defense. I will speak to the cabinet and come up with a plan for rationing; the only food we can rely on is what we can produce ourselves," ordered the prime minister.

He could already foresee the unrest these measures would cause but he had no choice.

"I am not just talking about the rest of the country, have we got any news from Dr Roberts in the quarantine zone? That and the New Forest have to be dealt with swiftly and decisively. While there is the slightest trace of the virus, we'll never get the UN to remove the quarantine."

The defence minister said, subtly hinting that they needed to take military action.

If he got the message, the prime minister chose to ignore the defence minister's suggestion.

"Dr Roberts and her team have successfully trialed a cure, but at the moment it is too labour intensive to implement. They have a solution and are working on it as we speak but it will take time," the prime minister said, referring to Dr Simmons' tranquiliser idea.

"Prime Minister, you can't afford to delay. We have to eliminate the threat by any means available. It may be painful now but it will save us a lot of trouble in the end; we have to begin exterminating the afflicted. Every one we kill today will mean six or seven less tomorrow!" the defence minister elaborated, this time being as clear as he possibly could.

"I know, I know, but these are innocent people. Make your preparations for now, but I have to trust Dr Roberts will come through for us. I will give them another twenty-four hours and then we put your plan into action," the prime minister answered reluctantly.

"The people will be easy to deal with, but what about the animal population? I think we need to eliminate every living creature in the danger zones. Like the French president kindly pointed out, it only takes one tiny mouse to start spreading the virus again," pointed out the defence minister.

"You know full well there is only one solution; we have to destroy both areas entirely. We will raze Brighton to the ground; destroy every tunnel and every hiding place. The New Forest is simple, we will burn it down but the whole area will have to be written off. A permanent barrier will need to be built around both areas with decontamination facilities used to enter and leave. We cannot take the risk of a single infected rat escaping," the prime minister stated, angry at having to make the decision no matter how necessary.

"What about the people? There are still thousands of uninfected people in those areas. What do we do about them?" the defence minister probed.

"If we cannot find a practical solution we will remove VIPs via the current armed forces decontamination facilities. That means all military personnel, medical staff, engineers; basically anyone with a trade or profession that will be useful to maintain order. Everyone else will have to make do until the permanent barrier is constructed and we can handle larger volumes of people," the prime minister told him sadly, knowing it would be a death sentence for many of them.

"We have no choice sir, the future of Great Britain depends on it," the defence minister admitted, looking out of the window at the clear sky, "because if we don't do it to them, then the rest of the world will do it to us!"

Nineteen

Brian's recovery had been nothing short of miraculous and he was now sitting up unaided, restrained by only one arm as a precaution but ultimately enjoying the freedom to move about once again.

"Hi Doc, how am I doing?" he asked cheerfully as John entered the room.

John smiled; the young man looked almost human again. His skin had regained its normal complexion, his eyes were not blood shot and he was fully lucid.

"The good news is, your results are clear and your body is now producing the necessary antibodies to fight the infection. The bad news, however, is that we need to take as much of your blood as you can possibly spare, with your permission of course, to begin manufacturing an immunisation against the disease," John told him hopefully.

"Dr Simmons, if it helps you can take all of it. I did some nasty things that I will never be able to make up for; if I can help prevent anyone else going through that, then I will do anything." he answered with utter sincerity. "Is there any news of Helen?" he asked, still feeling guilty about his part in Helen's current situation, if she was alive at all.

"That won't be necessary, we need you alive to keep producing more antibodies, but I am afraid you will be giving blood every other day for the foreseeable future. As for Helen, I have passed the message on but we have had no news yet. Trust me as soon as I know anything, you will be the first to know," John said, patting him on the back reassuringly.

The first rats treated with Methuselah were also doing brilliantly, the infection had fully vanished but the enhancements all remained. They were bigger, stronger and fitter than any other rat in history. Methuselah had worked beyond expectations, so it was a shame that no one would ever touch it after what had happened. All it took was for another virus to be mutated and the world would be facing yet another superbug; possibly worse, it could be airborne next time.

Those infected by the secondary mutated strain were a different story. When the virus was gone there were no lasting changes to the genome, which was a relief to John.

The Afflicted

The last thing humanity needed was a few thousand super humans walking around amongst the normal population. One thing the whole situation had taught him was that too much power led to bad things and that those with no power would do anything to obtain it, often at the expense of others.

He was just about to go and report the success to Dr Roberts when Michael appeared at the door with a serious look on his face.

"Dr Simmons, do you have a moment please?" he asked ominously.

"Sure, have you found something?" John asked expectantly.

Michael motioned for him to follow and John discerned the news was not going to be good.

"I have been through the Filofax in great detail and there is one bit of information you need to be aware of," he said, leading him towards the conference room and the waiting Dr Roberts. Once they were safely in the room, Michael closed the door and Dr Roberts began to speak.

"Dr Simmons, we have discovered a little bit more about Richard's activities. An external number crops up repeatedly on his work phone, his home line and his mobile. Do you recognise it?" Dr Roberts asked.

Michael handed him the phone records on which the same number had been circled several times.

"It doesn't look familiar, have you managed to trace it yet?" John answered.

"That's the problem; this number is redirected all over the place. Whoever set it up is a professional; the trail grows cold at a remote exchange on the South Downs near an old abandoned church. As a precaution, we sent a unit up there to investigate just in case they had a mobile unit in the area. It is after all very secluded with little chance of discovery but the area is deserted as expected. It is more likely to be just another link in the chain of deception," explained Michael. He had seen similar setups used by hackers and peak rate phone fraudsters, although nothing that sophisticated.

"You must have other leads, what is the name of the account holder, can we find them?" John asked desperately.

"I'm sorry, as I said, it's a professional job. The recorded account holder is a false charity and we can't even trace the payments. There is no way of finding out. Whomever Richard was involved with has serious connections. This is no ordinary industrial espionage, we are talking government agency level technology and I just don't have the clout to press it further. Besides, if we push it through the wrong channels we could be alerting those involved," Michael told him.

He was completely out of his depth and there was nothing he could do about it.

John dropped heavily into the seat behind him; all possible hope of finding the woman he loved was dissipating with Michael's obvious despondency. He wanted someone to blame but the only person responsible was the one person he could not find.

"Not to add to your woes Dr Simmons, but there is another revelation. It appears that Richard used the vial of serum we found in his office to perform an unofficial human trial, and the worse thing is, it was not a volunteer. He gave Methuselah to Dr Taylor. He was keeping a log on her behaviour and it appears that the first sign was...," Dr Roberts started to say.

"...That her appetite had increased. Damn it, how did I miss that? The woman was built like a supermodel, but ate like a sumo wrestler. That bastard!" John shouted, as all of a sudden the pieces dropped into place.

He jumped to his feet and kicked a waste paper bin clear across the room in frustration. Two armed police officers came rushing through the door with weapons trained on John.

The inspector immediately jumped up placing himself between them and the irate scientist.

"Stand down, he's just had some bad news and is letting off steam. I'll take care of it," Michael ordered hastily, following them to the door and closing it behind them.

John, who was still ranting, suddenly stopped and slapped himself across the forehead as he realised an important point.

"That's great though! That means she is primary infected, the Methuselah enhancements will hold off the affliction at least for a while. Also, she is more than a hundred times heavier than a rat with a slower metabolism. Even if she had the full dose, that is still only ten times more than we gave each of the rats. The change should be much slower, so we have plenty of time to find her and she should still be safe," he blurted out excitedly.

"What does that mean?" the pair of them asked in unison.

"It means that as long as she's still taking nourishment her body will be able to maintain the balance for much longer. Add that to the fact that she is a sentient being, not an animal, and it means we have longer to find her," he said, picking up his trusty leather bound notebook and scribbling furiously.

"Will Richard and his contact know this if she is being held captive? We have to consider that something may have happened to her!" advised Dr Roberts, sharing his concerns.

"I believe that Richard has sent full copies of all my work so they know almost everything. Their intention is to study the effects of the serum on a human being, so they will want to keep her alive. Inspector, where is this church? I think I will go and take a look myself. Your guys may have missed something," John said, looking up from his writing.

"I am very sorry Dr Simmons, but the contaminated zone is under martial law and you are far too important to national security to put yourself at risk. We cannot spare any more manpower to go on a wild goose chase. Even if we let you leave, you're likely to get shot; the area is under full military quarantine," explained Dr Roberts apologetically. She was officially in charge of the operation and carried full authority.

John slumped back in the chair and he knew he was stuck; there was no way they were going to let him go.

"Look, maybe I can get some of my men to have a more thorough look around; there may be something we missed the first time?" Michael suggested.

"I'm sorry Inspector, but the situation has become a lot more complicated since we last spoke. The UN has quarantined Great Britain, forcing the government to take drastic action. We've been given twenty-four hours to come up with a practical cure that can be applied quickly and safely or we evacuate and write off the population in this area. So, as you can appreciate, we cannot afford to waste any more time, and I am sorry if that affects Dr Taylor, but that's the way it is. Special Forces have already been deployed to exterminate the afflicted; if you are mistaken for them or, god forbid, become afflicted yourself they will not hesitate to shoot. Basically gentlemen, we have run out of time," she explained.

The prime minister had called her to give her the news personally and despite knowing there was no option, it was still a bitter pill to swallow.

***

Lieutenant Barker watched the speeding Land Rover approach through his binoculars as it headed straight for the barricade.

He could see a man and a woman through the windscreen and thought he had seen the heads of a couple of children in the back seat but, it was difficult to tell at that distance. As it drew closer, the driver spotted the soldiers and the vehicle began to slow down. Four armed soldiers surrounded the vehicle as it pulled to a stop and signalled for the driver to wind down his window.

"Hello soldier, what's the problem? I need to get to London urgently," said the man behind the wheel nervously.

"Sorry sir, but the whole area is under strict quarantine and we have been given orders not to let anyone past this point. You must understand we cannot risk the virus spreading any further," the soldier replied, peering through the window cautiously.

There was something strange about the man, so Lieutenant Barker joined his men and added his authority to the discussion by relieving the soldier.

"Sir, please turn your vehicle round as you have been asked and report to one of the rescue centres. You and your family will be taken care of there," Barker instructed, using his most official sounding voice.

"I don't want to go to the rescue shelters, most are overrun now. I have family in London and I just want to get my wife and children to safety," the man said, staring uneasily at the automatic weapons the soldiers had trained on him and his wife.

While this discourse was underway, one of the soldiers leant against the rear window to check the back seat.

He took one glance inside before jumping back from the vehicle, raising the muzzle of his rifle and pointing it straight at the driver's head. The other soldiers followed his lead, assuming he had spotted an afflicted passenger.

"Sir, the children in the back are covered in blood. They are tied and gagged; I think they are afflicted," he stuttered. It was the first of the afflicted they had seen, but the briefings had not done the condition justice.

"Sir, you know it's against the law to break quarantine. You and your wife need to step out of the vehicle slowly," ordered the lieutenant, raising his pistol and pointing it into the car.

The woman in the passenger seat had not moved until now and Lieutenant Barker had assumed she was gripped by fear. There was a blanket over her lap which she now whipped to one side revealing a pump action shotgun, the barrel of which she pushed past her husband's face and pointed it at the lieutenant's head.

"Tell your men to lower their weapons and stand aside; I'm not afraid to use this. All I want to do is get my children to a safe hospital and get them the treatment they deserve," she threatened, pushing the barrel closer so that it was almost touching the end of his nose.

The soldiers all cocked their weapons and switched them from safety to full automatic fire.

"I said tell them to move, soldier. If they open fire, I promise I'll kill you before the first bullet lands," she warned, the barrel wobbling from her shaking hands.

The lieutenant lowered his weapon slowly and dropped it to the floor in an attempt to diffuse the situation before someone got hurt.

"Okay everybody, stay calm. Lower your weapons men, no one has to die here today," he said calmly, gesturing with his hands for them to follow his orders.

There were two snipers further up the road that could happily stop the Land Rover should it break free.

"Listen to me, your children need immediate medical attention and the rescue centres now have a cure which is not available outside the quarantine zone. They will be alright if you go back, but if you attempt to leave you risk spreading the disease to innocent people," he continued steadily, keeping his voice low and level.

He could see the look of desperation on the woman's face as she glanced around, trying to calculate their odds of getting away.

He knew that if she panicked, it was likely she would shoot him in the head and that was the last thing he wanted.

"Don't try and fool us, I've seen the death squads. They're hunting the infected and killing them like animals. I won't let them get my children," she declared, unwilling to listen.

Her husband decided he had heard enough and put his foot down hard on the accelerator. The vehicle shot forward, forcing the two soldiers in front of the vehicle to dive out of the way as the huge vehicle bore down on them. The woman, taken by surprise, squeezed the trigger, accidentally knocking the barrel to one side and the shot whizzed harmlessly past Lieutenant Barker's ear.

The soldiers were trained professionals and those who had been in front of the fleeing vehicle hit the ground rolling and got straight back to their feet. All four soldiers opened fire with their powerful weapons, but the heavy-duty spare wheel fastened to the back of the speeding four-wheel drive deflected most of the rounds.

Still shaking from his close encounter, the lieutenant calmly picked up his handgun and pointed it straight in the air, firing three quick shots in succession.

Five hundred metres further up the road, the two hidden snipers had been watching the whole altercation with interest.

The lieutenant had given his signal authorising lethal force and the pair of them looked through the high specification scopes on their rifles. One targeted the driver and the other the passenger, lining their frightened faces directly in the crosshairs. They fired two rounds each simultaneously, and the blood spattering the cracked windshield confirmed the hit. The Land Rover sped up dramatically, swerving across the carriageway before striking the central reservation. It rode up onto the metal dividers and then tipped over onto its roof. Sparks sprayed out as metal scraped along the tarmac, gradually stopping as the vehicle skidded to a halt.

The soldiers at the checkpoint were already three quarters of the way to the upturned vehicle, finally dropping to their stomachs and pointing the rifles into the interior as they drew level. The lieutenant jogged up at a more respectable pace behind them.

"Check for survivors," he ordered.

One of his men crawled cautiously up to the vehicle and peered through the broken windows, confirming quickly that the adults were dead.

"Sir, one of the children is still alive, shall we call for medical backup?" the soldier shouted over his shoulder as Lieutenant Barker finally caught up.

"Withdraw from the vehicle," he ordered, calmly striding past them and dropping to his knees. Without hesitation, he raised his pistol and fired two shots into the rear seats as his men stared on in horror.

He climbed to his feet and began walking silently back to the barricade.

"There is no medical backup, soldier," he informed them, tears running down his face, "we have to shoot the afflicted on sight, especially this close to the quarantine boundary."

Holstering his weapon, he shouted to the sergeant major.

"Torch the vehicle," he ordered, his voice emotionless and without breaking step. He had only walked another ten steps when the incendiary grenade went off and the Land Rover exploded into flames, its occupants now beyond harm.

***

The airfield at Shoreham was huge and it had not taken the four friends long to find access through the fence near one of the hangars. They dashed from building to building, avoiding the infrequent patrols until they arrived at their target destination.

Like all airports in the zone, the military were in charge. Its runways were short but they could still be used to launch the powerful Tornado GR4 fighter jets, three of which sat there on the tarmac, ready to deploy.

Belinda opened the service door at the rear of the hangar with her keys, out of view of the airfield beyond.

"Come on, hurry," she said, motioning for her friends to follow once she had checked that the hangar was empty.

Her father's plane sat alone in the middle of the hangar looking tiny in the huge building. Her father had bought a brand new Cessna Skyhawk two years ago as a treat after selling his rather successful plumbing supplies business. He had been a pilot in the RAF and had made do with teaching others to fly to keep his licence current, but he had always dreamed of owning his own plane one day. Until now, the family had used the Cessna for popping back and forth from Shoreham to the Channel Islands and France. She had been ecstatic when he had paid for lessons for her twenty-first birthday eight weeks ago, and she had completed several accompanied flights already, working her way towards getting her own pilot's license.

"Tony and Tanya, I want you to remove the chocks. Dave, you go and get ready to open the hangar doors, the switch is over there," she said pointing to the door controls.

"Are you sure about this Belinda? The broadcast said that any plane attempting to leave would be shot down!" Tanya questioned, nervously twisting her long brown hair between her thumb and forefinger.

"We'll be fine, this is a small plane and we will be flying well below radar. Once we are in the air I am going to head straight out to sea where they will not be able to track us at low altitude," Belinda reassured her nervous friend.

Belinda climbed into the pilot's seat and began flicking switches and checking dials, her heart beating wildly in her chest. Tanya and Tony pulled out the chocks and climbed into the back seat, hurriedly fastening their seat belts. Belinda switched on the fuel and pressed the starter causing the engine to kick momentarily to life before spluttering to a stop.

"Hurry up, someone will hear," Tanya hissed at her through clenched teeth, her heart beating like a drum.

Belinda tried again; the engine stuttered a couple of times but this time fired into life causing the three of them to cheer enthusiastically. When the huge doors began to slide open, Belinda pulled back on the throttle slightly and the plane began to roll forwards sluggishly.

The doors were barely open enough as she drew close to them when a shout came from the rear of the hangar near the very door they had used to enter.

A lone soldier had sneaked round the back to have a cigarette and had heard the plane's engine start up. Spotting the open door, he had gone to investigate just in time to see the tiny aircraft clear the doors.

"Air Traffic Control, we have an unscheduled flight from hangar B13. Requesting instructions," he shouted into his walkie-talkie.

Inside the plane, Belinda heard him shout and panicked, pulling back hard on the throttle to open it up fully.

The plane lurched forward, barely missing Dave as he walked forward to meet them. He saw that Belinda was not going to stop.

He sprinted alongside, managing to leap onto the wing support and wrap his legs around it, clinging on for dear life.

"Please don't leave me, Belinda," he screamed at her, barely audible above the sound of the revving engine.

The plane picked up speed rapidly and Dave attempted to get the door open without losing his grip. Tanya leant over the front seat and tried to help him, but the rising air pressure outside held it firmly shut. Starting to panic, Dave began banging desperately on the window and shouting obscenities at his girlfriend as she refused to slow down, her fear of the soldier overriding her love for him. They all heard gunshots from the hangar as the soldier received the order to fire but they were already too far away and travelling too fast for him to get a good shot.

By now, the wind was beginning to batter Dave as he clung on for dear life. Belinda pulled back on the column and the plane rose into the air momentarily before bouncing back to earth with a jolt. The runway was ending fast but she allowed the plane another hundred metres to gain speed and then tried again, this time lifting off and beginning to climb rapidly. Belinda levelled off at an altitude of about fifty metres where she started to bank the plane out towards the sea.

The soldier winced as he saw the young man fall, his body landing out of sight somewhere behind the row of bushes beyond the runway. He hoped for the boy's sake that the fall had killed him outright, because from that height if he survived he would be severely injured and possibly even crippled for life.

"Air Traffic Control, the plane has taken off and is heading south straight out over the channel; it looks like they are heading for France," the soldier hollered into the mouthpiece of his radio.

"We'll take it from here soldier. Air support will pursue the plane, tower over and out," responded a voice from the main control room.

Belinda kept the plane as low as she dared and made her flight path erratic.

Being an amateur, she fought with turbulence at low altitude. She wiped the tears from her eyes; she had met Dave in primary school and they had been life-long soul mates. He had not deserved to die like that, but she could not risk the rest of them been caught; it was too dangerous to go back to the camps.

She kept the radio on the Air Traffic Control frequency but ignored the constant babble of threats it spewed out, concentrating instead on keeping the plane level.

They had been in the air only ten minutes when Tony spotted the jets approaching fast from the north.

"Oh shit! Belinda, I thought you said they couldn't detect us this low," he said fearfully, pointing at the approaching aircraft.

She swallowed hard and said crisply,

"Don't worry, we're almost out of British air space, only a couple of miles. They can't touch us."

Belinda hoped she was right.

Even at full throttle, the Cessna was no match for the powerful Tornado fighter jets as they approached at supersonic speed. Belinda jumped when the radio began to crackle as it relayed a message from the lead fighter.

"Unscheduled flight 009, please turn your aircraft around immediately and return to the airport. You're attempting to leave a military enforced quarantine zone and I have full authority to shoot you down. I repeat, turn your aircraft around," said the metallic voice over the airwaves.

Belinda ignored the warning and began to rock back and forward in her seat, urging the plane to move faster.

There was only a mile and a half to freedom and she was not prepared to give up now.

"Unscheduled flight, this is your final warning, turn the aircraft round or we will fire," reiterated the voice.

"Belinda, maybe you better listen to them, they sound serious," said Tanya.

"We're almost there. Besides, they're not going to shoot down a civilian plane," she said confidently, attempting to convince herself more than them.

Andy Strutt

Just as she finished speaking, the lead jet fired a volley of bullets, just missing the right wing and causing the plane to wobble briefly as she panicked.

"Oh my God," she screamed, grabbing up the pilots headset. "Please hold your fire, I am turning back!" she shouted, turning the steering column, making the plane bank hard to the left.

In front of them on the southern horizon, four fighters appeared coming from the direction of France. She had begun to climb, making sure that the wings stayed well away from the water as the plane continued a one hundred and eighty degree turn.

Belinda gritted her teeth and her hands shook.

Seeing them beginning to comply, the British jets turned before reaching the Anglo-French boundary and flew parallel to the invisible border before spotting the incoming aircraft.

"This is Wing Commander Bennett of the RAF calling the approaching French attack formation; we have the situation under control. Illegal flight is now returning to British airspace, please withdraw," signalled the lead plane.

"That is a negative, plane is currently in French airspace and we have orders to shoot down any unauthorised flights from Great Britain," came the reply.

"Listen, they are turning; they will be back in British airspace in a matter of seconds. I repeat, please withdraw, we will take them in. You must understand that they are only frightened," replied the Commander.

"Sorry Wing Commander, we have our orders. Section leader targeting unauthorised flight, missile launching in three, two, one," came the voice over the airways.

The UN had given very clear instructions that any British traffic entering foreign airspace would be made an example of to deter other offenders. A flash appeared from under the wing of one of the jets as a missile detached itself and accelerated towards the defenceless Cessna.

Inside the cabin, Belinda pulled hard on the steering column and tried to bank in the opposite direction to no avail. The missile was heat seeking and could out manoeuvre a fighter jet, never mind a crude propeller driven plane. The missile collided with the Cessna, causing a huge explosion that blew the tiny aircraft into a million pieces, leaving nothing but a shower of burning debris raining down on the waves below.

"You murdering bastards," shouted Wing Commander Bennett as the French planes banked away, "they were turning back. You didn't need to do that!"

No answer came from the radio, and in his anger he considered for a second going after them and teaching them a lesson, but he knew Great Britain was now alone and even with the best-trained armed forces in the world they could not take on the rest of the planet. Reluctantly, he banked away, heading back to the tiny airstrip. As he reported the needless waste of life to his superiors, Wing Commander Bennett clenched his teeth in a grimace of frustrated rage.

***

Across the country, several incidents came to light during the day. The majority were fishing boats and other marine craft trying to escape the island. The United Nations gave them no quarter; any craft leaving Great Britain was shot down.

Twenty

John sat alone in his office, deep in thought. Brian had now fully recovered and the essential immunoglobulin had been harvested from his blood. They were now ready to be turned into an inoculation. Samples of them and details of the manufacturing procedures were now on the way to every microbiological processing facility in the mainland. The government was trying to negotiate with the UN to get facilities all over the world involved, which had been agreed in theory. The only problem now was the paranoia about getting samples out of the international quarantine area without the risk of spreading the disease.

Brighton city centre and the surrounding metropolis had become a war zone. Soldiers on one side, the afflicted on the other and everyone else trapped in-between. The armed forces had been issued with tranquilisers, but many of them simply ignored them and concentrated on putting the afflicted out of their misery, reducing the danger to those who had managed to survive.

Initial reports hinted that there were thousands dead, murdered for food by the afflicted or exterminated by the armed forces. The government had already begun its campaign to demolish the city and the first bombings had already commenced with the ground crews following shortly behind to target specific structures in the city where the afflicted may have been hiding. When they had finished, poison and traps were laid to kill off any remaining afflicted animals that may have survived the blast. It was becoming commonplace to use toxins that had been banned for decades due to the damaging effects on the ecosystem. The area would be uninhabitable for many years to come, but no one seemed concerned given the alternative.

Flamethrowers and incendiary devices had been deployed in an attempt to eradicate the threat from animals. Every subterranean system was targeted, from the sewers to cellars and other underground structures. Unfortunately, there were also many humans hiding out in some of these areas but the soldiers had been ordered to use force as needed. It was too risky to search these areas first for fear of coming up against the afflicted in close quarters. Initially, the conscientious among them would tanoy warnings but after several attacks by the afflicted, the soldiers even stopped doing that.

John had listened with interest to the bi-hourly updates on the radio, making notes of where pockets of incidents were taking place. The whole operation would take weeks or maybe even months to get anywhere near eradicating the virus, if indeed they ever could. This meant that no one would be allowed to roam without permission and that would be too late for any chance of finding Gwen alive. She had brought new meaning to his life and he was not going to give up that easily, so he sat and planned an exit strategy from the heavily guarded facility. John knew there was no chance of him being allowed to go out into the quarantine zone unescorted, and as such decided his only possible choice was to escape. He had now given them a cure in the form of a tranquiliser-antiviral dart as well as the more involved transfusion method. He had also helped to develop the immunization, so as far as he was concerned he had played his part and did not feel any guilt about leaving.

At around ten in the morning John went to his personal locker, grabbed the old rucksack he used on his occasional cycle rides to work and emptied out his cycling gear. Next, he went to the laboratory and grabbed a range of samples, some anti-viral, a strong tranquiliser, syringes and a couple of small packages he had prepared earlier that day. He stuffed them all into his rucksack, making sure no one saw him. On his way back, he stole Gwen's car keys from her handbag as they had arrived together in her car following their night of passion. It was only a few days ago but to him it seemed an age away, his fond memories of their passionate lovemaking keeping him focused.

Now it was time for phase two and when the opportunity arose, he would have to move quickly. He sat with the door to his office propped open so he could see down the corridor, growing more and more nervous every minute. He had just about given up hope when an opportunity finally presented itself. He grabbed the rucksack, strode out of his office and headed up the corridor towards the men's room, following the soldier who had just entered.

"Morning, sir," said the soldier, standing at the urinals without looking back at John.

John noticed his tranquiliser gun was leant against the wall next to the sinks, and his rifle slung securely across his back.

"Morning," John replied pleasantly, moving over to the sinks and switching on the taps to create the impression he was washing his hands.

John slowly picked up the tranquiliser gun, holding it butt forwards like a club. He crept up behind the soldier who turned to speak as John got closer, his eyes widening as he saw the heavy rifle butt racing towards his face. It connected with a sickening crunch, rocking the man's head sideward. The unfortunate soldier was already unconscious before he hit the floor.

"Sorry son, it's nothing personal but I need your uniform," John explained to the man, hoping that subconsciously he would hear his apology.

He quickly injected him with tranquiliser to make sure there was no chance of him coming around unexpectedly and giving the game away. He then dragged the soldier's body into the disabled cubicle and began to remove his uniform before quickly taking off his own clothes. Propping the unconscious form up on the toilet, John took the trouble to push the soldiers feet into his own disregarded trousers and slipped his shoes on him for good measure, just in case someone came in and spotted his legs under the cubicle door.

Nervously, he pulled on the soldiers uniform while thanking his lucky stars that it was only slightly too large for him. Finally, John gagged the soldier and tied his hands securely to the stainless steel disabled support rail on the wall. It was designed to help the more unfortunate users lever themselves into position, so it was securely fastened to the wall. He retrieved the two weapons and carefully moved all the samples from the rucksack into the pockets of his combat jacket, leaving the two mysterious packages inside the bag.

Opening the door a crack, he checked up and down the corridor and when he was sure it was clear, he quickly headed to the foyer. The main front doors were securely locked but there were no guards his side of the glass, the commanding officer having ordered them to build a sandbag barrier fifteen metres in front of the building. They would only withdraw back inside as a last resort in the event of an attack.

John knelt down behind the glass, positioning himself so a huge plant pot outside the window obscured him from view should any of the guards happen to look in his direction. He carefully placed the packages against the glass and tugged on the magnesium fuses, one of the packages having a slightly longer one than the other. Checking the corridor was clear behind him, he pulled out a lighter and carefully lit the ends of both fuses simultaneously, giving them a couple of seconds to make sure they stayed lit before he set off running. The fuses burned slowly with an intense white light that was too bright to stare at directly. John made his way towards the fire door in one of the labs along the side of the building. He had already isolated the door from the security alarm in preparation for his daring escape, or so he hoped. He then waited impatiently for his homemade devices to activate.

The intense white spots of heat moved towards the packages, the one on the left reaching its target first and appearing to go out as it entered the plastic container. A second later the package split open from the pressure within and it produced billowing clouds of dense purple fumes into the foyer. A couple of seconds later, the second package exploded with enough force to shatter the plate glass window, sending a loud booming sound echoing through the building. Because of biological protocol, the building pressure was kept artificially high so that external contamination was kept out, and this blew the fumes out into the courtyard, rapidly spreading them across the whole car park.

There was mayhem as police officers and soldiers in the building ran towards the source of the explosion while the soldiers outside made their way blindly back towards the building. None of them noticed a solitary soldier running down the edge of the car park.

When they had arrived the other night, John and Gwen had parked at the far side of the car park out of view of the main building to sneak in, and he was glad of their unintended foresight. As he approached the bright red Mercedes, he saw the indicators flash once indicating that the keyless entry had activated and he climbed into the driver's seat, throwing his weapons onto the passenger seat. The ignition was also keyless so he just thumbed the button and the engine roared into life. The fumes were already beginning to disperse as he thrust the gear selector into drive. As he pushed the accelerator hard to the floor the rear wheels span slightly, the powerful three and half litre engine roaring into action before the stability control kicked in and brought them under control.

Producing a little over three hundred brake horsepower the car accelerated wildly, reaching fifty miles an hour on the short stretch to the main gate.

John sat up properly, hoping he was out of rifle range just before the vehicle tore through the flimsy red and white barrier, snapping the plastic clean in two and skidded sideways onto the main road where he struggled to bring the car under control.

By now, the soldiers had seen the car racing away and several of them raised their rifles to fire when Michael stepped forward.

"Hold your fire, we need him alive!" Michael shouted angrily, guessing immediately who it was.

He was simultaneously impressed and disappointed by the ingenuity of the scientist's escape.

He could do with men like that on his team, he thought irrelevantly as he watched the car disappear into the distance.

"Secure the building; I think I know where he is going. We will make other plans to apprehend him," Michael added, watching the soldiers reluctantly lower their weapons, a little embarrassed that one of the boffins from the facility they were meant to be guarding had hoodwinked them.

Michael turned and walked back into the building, muttering under his breath. "Good luck Dr Simmons," he said, chuckling. He actually liked the man and hoped that he found what he was looking for before they caught up with him.

***

The demolition underway in Brighton was not the only action against the afflicted in the south of the country. A convoy consisting of three army Land Rovers and a four tonne personnel carrier sent to look for evidence of the afflicted pulled into the central square at Lyndhurst in the New Forest. The soldiers were surprised to find the village streets empty. Although the village was relatively small, they were expecting to find people milling around on the high street at midday. Instead, they were faced with an eerie silence. The soldiers were already leaping out of the camouflaged vehicles before they came to a complete stop, hitting the ground and forming a defensive perimeter, all of them eyeing the village apprehensively.

Sergeant Davis wasted no time; he separated the men into groups of four and sent them searching house-to-house, looking for any signs that the afflicted were present. Many of the houses displayed evidence of a struggle, but there was not a single body anywhere; the village was a landlocked Mary Celeste.

Sergeant Davis was in the last group to return and got straight onto the field radio with confirmation that the results had been the same for each team.

"This is Sergeant Davis calling strategic command. We have reached the target location, Lyndhurst village, and have searched the entire area but the town is abandoned. Awaiting further orders," he declared.

"Have you found any evidence that there may be an outbreak at this location?" responded a crackly voice, the reception poor due to the surrounding trees.

"Not directly sir, but there are several locations showing signs of a struggle with evidence of severe blood loss at some of them. I would hazard a guess that whatever happened here was finished over twelve hours ago at least," the sergeant replied.

"Okay, secure the vehicles and await further orders. Strategic command out," finished the voice.

The sergeant motioned for his men to gather round.

"This is the situation as discussed in the briefing. Until now, there has been no evidence of the affliction spreading outside the quarantine zone but it appears this may be the case here. We have been ordered to secure the area until further notice. Now, get on with it," he instructed.

The Afflicted

The soldiers all ran off to their various duties, unaware that less than five hundred metres away, hiding in the trees, unseen eyes were watching their actions. Helen's group had grown in number. There were about a hundred of them, mostly made up of residents from Lyndhurst, but there were also a few visitors and campers that had been caught unawares in the surrounding forest.

Pickings were slim in the area now that this group of sub-human hunters had decimated the local animal population. The appearance of potential victims made them excited and they looked towards their unofficial leader for guidance. Helen watched the soldiers scampering around, but something about the long sticks they carried made her nervous. She no longer recognised a rifle, but some long lost memory served to caution her against foolish action. Instead, she crept away into the trees towards their hideout, determined to return at nightfall when they would have the advantage. Then they would hunt.

***

In the lab deep below the abandoned church, Gwen was not doing very well. Her health had begun to deteriorate without the input of fuel to drive the beneficial changes of Methuselah whilst fighting the virus. Her stomach noticeably growled as she sensed the blood in the others around her while they prodded and poked her, recording every aspect of her transformation. Mercifully, for the moment she slept, unaware of her location and the impending brutality.

"Sir, Dr Taylor's temperature has begun to drop and her red blood cell count is extremely low," the laboratory technician informed the old man.

He spun his wheelchair to face the young woman excitedly.

"Is she still coherent? Is she still able to communicate?" he asked, eager for the opportunity to see her in action.

"Yes sir, but her eyes are extremely bloodshot so I think the change is almost upon her," the technician answered.

The old man guided his wheelchair to the foot of the upturned restraint table and examined her body. Gwen's musculature was drastically enlarged now and the individual variations could be seen through the skin. All subcutaneous fat had disappeared to reveal a network of pulsating veins and arteries. Her gums had begun to recede, giving her a ghoulish appearance. He estimated that she had gained almost twenty percent of her bodyweight since the initial treatment and, if the rats were anything to go by, she would also be much stronger by now.

Richard was also unconscious, kept sedated to maintain control having also developed amazing musculature. They had placed him on a high-energy intravenous drip to ensure that his body had all the nutrients required to drive the change as quickly as possible. His resting heart rate had dropped significantly, requiring less effort to drive blood through his much healthier body. Richard had carried quite a bit of excess weight when he arrived, but his body had absorbed the fat as fuel in the last eighteen hours. His metabolism had shot through the roof, increasing the required dose of tranquiliser to keep him under control.

The serum had improved the efficiency of every bodily process, which suggested he was ready to face the afflicted Dr Taylor.

"Is the room ready? Because we need to get these two in place before they begin to wake up. Give them just enough tranquiliser to keep them unconscious for another couple of hours to make sure," the old man ordered.

Ben Cavendish came in holding a walkie-talkie in his hand and approached the old man.

"Sir, the police have been back, but this time they just drove past as if they were looking for something, but they didn't even get out of the car," he informed the old man.

Ben was a little worried that perhaps their location had been discovered. They had not seen any police in months and then they'd had two visits in as many days.

"Is everything topside secure? Are the vehicles hidden and anything else that could give us away all cleared away?" the old man questioned.

"Yes sir, everything outside suggests this is just an abandoned church. They wouldn't be able to find the entrance to the bunker unless someone knew exactly where to look for it," Ben answered with assurance.

"Well, keep on your toes, it may well mean they have traced the phone number, but if they can't see anything they won't make the connection and look any closer," the old man instructed.

"Yes, sir," answered Ben.

"What about the afflicted? Have we had any further trouble from them?" the old man enquired.

The bodyguards had been taken by surprise when they had gone for the van the night before and two of the afflicted dressed in hiking gear had jumped them.

Fortunately, the men had been armed and were very accomplished when it came to handing out physical violence.

The two bodies now lay in shallow graves in a copse of trees not far away.

"No sir, we haven't seen a single person since the attack," Ben told him.

"Okay then. We are going to begin the first experiment in a couple of hours. I would like you and the other men to be present to help escort the prisoners, but make sure all of you are armed. Looking at the recent changes to their bodies even your men will be no match for the two of them should they get loose," the old man ordered.

"Yes sir," the guard said as he left to gather the men.

He found it a little insulting that he should have to worry about a couple of scientists. After all, the four of them had the best military unarmed combat training in the world; what could the freaks possibly do to them, he wondered.

***

Having escaped from the facility, John was now heading through the strangely silent streets of Hove. It was eerie to see a normally bustling town abandoned by humanity, relinquished to the growing ranks of the afflicted.

Occasionally he would spot movement in his peripheral vision, but so far he had not encountered a soul, afflicted or otherwise. It was disconcerting; John knew that there were many dead, but he couldn't see a single body. He somehow knew that the afflicted, starving as they were, had probably consumed them in an attempt to extract the nutrients required for them to live.

It was, however, interesting to note that there were thousands of the afflicted hiding out there. He assumed that they must prefer to remain out of the sunlight, although he had detected no evidence of photophobia in the rats. He could only assume that their enhanced eyesight made them sensitive to bright sunlight.

John made slow progress negotiating the streets littered with abandoned and damaged cars, having to mount the pavement on several occasions. Above him, he heard the drone of plane engines as the air force approached for their next bombing campaign. He had heard them from the facility and knew that very soon, there would be sounds of multiple explosions from the direction of Brighton city centre.

John shuddered; there were still thousands of people in the city, a lot of who were afflicted, but many who were not. Those that had been too frightened to make a run for it had holed themselves up instead.

Finally, he saw the sign ahead for the A23 and headed towards it. Even after all these years working in Hove, he rarely ventured this far east towards Brighton itself and was hopeless at directions. As he rounded the junction, he was faced with the remnants of a huge pileup. It looked like a small lorry had overturned and the other vehicles had piled into it. There was a gap down the edge but he was not sure the large Mercedes would make it through; he had no choice but to try. He mounted the kerb for the umpteenth time that day and the passenger wing mirror just missed the brick wall. There was a loud metallic scraping sound as a piece of wreckage scratched the side of Gwen's car badly, causing him to wince.

"Crap!" he shouted, imagining the look on Gwen's face when she saw her car; he was definitely in for the high jump.

He began to laugh, amazed at how little a thing like a damaged paint job would worry her when the whole country was facing the outbreak.

John was brought crashing back to reality when he noticed a partially eaten body in one of the cars, the hands frozen to the steering wheel with rigor mortis. The windows were shattered, so he assumed that whoever had broken in had done so long after the driver had died and had been unable to pry loose the hands so had attacked the corpse in situ. The sight enthralled John, and he did not notice a middle-aged woman running towards him. She leapt into the air and landed heavily on the bonnet. Kneeling there, she stared through the windscreen at him, a manic grin spreading across her face. Seeing him, she began to claw at the glass and John realised that he was facing one of the afflicted for the first time. Without thinking, he grabbed the automatic rifle and as one of the soldiers had shown him, he switched it from safety to single shot and pulled back the cocking mechanism, chambering the first round. He raised the barrel and pointed it straight at the woman's head. With no chance of missing at this distance, he steadied himself to shoot. Another bang from the rear of the car distracted him and he noticed a man in a dishevelled suit beating against the glass of the rear window. Glancing around him, he saw that there were more of them streaming over the wreckage and through the broken windows of the surrounding buildings.

A sudden scary thought occurred to him; if he fired the high-powered rifle at the glass it would shatter. It may kill the woman, but it would allow the others to break through easily, so he dropped the weapon back onto the seat. Instead, he pressed down on the accelerator causing the car to jerk forward, feeling the wheels bounce over the bodies of the unfortunate few who were in front of him. The woman on the bonnet was thrown face forward onto the windscreen by the acceleration and as soon as he was clear of the mob, John slammed on the brakes to loosen her grip from the car. She was thrown from the vehicle, rolling across the tarmac like a rag doll, Gwen's windscreen wiper still clutched in her hand as a weird trophy. The angle of her head made it instantly apparent that her neck was broken and John shuddered. He had never killed anyone before, and for a moment he sat frozen in horror at his own actions. The snarling and screaming of the approaching mob shook him from his trance and he set off as fast as the road conditions would allow.

Once he was out of Brighton, the main roads were much clearer and he was able to build up to a decent speed. He entered the coordinates Michael had given him for the derelict church into the on-board satellite navigation system. It showed him there was a tiny little road leading from the A23 that turned back on itself into the South Downs a little further north from his current position.

John was able to maintain a steady speed of around forty miles an hour and it was not long until he saw the exit for the road approaching on the tiny neon screen, but what it did not show was the army barricade just beyond. As he approached the parked vehicles blocking the road, he could see that they were too close to the junction he needed for him to avoid being stopped. He slowed the car down to a crawl, wondering how to handle the situation when one of the soldiers began to walk towards his car, motioning for him to lower his window to which he obliged.

"Afternoon Private, I must be in the wrong regiment if this is what they are issuing to the light infantry these days," the man said pleasantly, his demeanour seeming rather friendly, as he perceived John to be a fellow squaddie.

John, however, was a little confused and froze, not understanding what the soldier was referring to.

He relaxed slightly when he realised that he was wearing a soldier's uniform and decided that his best option was to try to bluff his way past the checkpoint.

"I'm on a special mission to deliver these trial drugs to a secure test facility on the Downs,"

John said holding open his pocket and displaying the selection of glass bottles and syringes he was carrying.

"What test facility? I am not aware of any test facility. You will have to wait here while I check back with Lieutenant Barker. Hang on here a minute, will you?" the soldier instructed, turning back towards the control vehicle at the barricade.

"Private, hang on a second. You won't be able to confirm the location because it's top secret. I shouldn't have even told you about it, but I know I can trust a fellow army buddy," John said, thinking quickly. "You wouldn't want to get me in any trouble, now would you?" John pleaded.

The soldier was fascinated and leant on the edge of the window so he could speak a little quieter.

The Afflicted

"What do you mean 'top secret'? Is it like a government job where they are performing tests on those zombie things?" he asked with morbid curiosity.

It was obvious by his reaction that he had not seen much of the afflicted in action, and like many of his type, he wanted to be in the thick of the excitement. John leant towards him and lowered his voice as if worried that the others at the barricade over fifty metres away would hear.

"The mission is so top secret that all we were told was a location and ordered to get these drugs there, no matter what happened. We were in a Land Rover when we left, four soldiers and two scientists, but we were attacked on the outskirts of Brighton. Only one of the scientists and me survived, but he was bitten so he gave me these, told me the coordinates and made me promise to make sure they got to the facility. I knew they were important so I stole a car, pretty nice don't you think, and headed straight here," improvised John, coming up with what he thought was a credible story. Unfortunately, it was too credible.

"No shit! That's wicked! Listen, you have to tell the others. Trust me, they will keep it a secret, they're a good bunch of lads. We don't get to hear much news up here, so it's good to see somebody actually doing something at last. Wait here a minute!" the soldier said excitedly, and ran off to go and fetch the rest of his section.

John watched as the man ran back the last few yards waving his hands about excitedly and he knew there was no way he could keep this up. Dr Roberts would have raised an alert that he had escaped, and if they had not received it yet, they would soon. One slip and he would be arrested, if not shot. He wondered if it was treason to impersonate someone from the armed forces, and he began to panic.

Reaching over to the passenger seat, he grabbed the SA80 rifle and hung it out of the open window, pointing it with his right hand way above the heads of the soldiers but in their general direction. Swallowing hard, he pulled the trigger and simultaneously pressed the accelerator, shooting the car forward. John had never fired a weapon before and was surprised at how loud it was, but he saw the soldiers dive for cover giving him the chance to close the last few yards to the small road he needed. From their position he would only be visible for ten to fifteen seconds before he disappeared over the brow of the hill, and he gunned the engine for all that he was worth. The sporty Mercedes accelerated like a rocket but remained firmly planted as its sophisticated electronic systems assisted him. Very soon he was doing in excess of ninety miles per hour and the brow of the hill was in sight. The weapon's firing pin finally closed on an empty chamber, so he drew it back into the car and threw it into the passenger seat. As soon as he stopped firing, the soldiers were on their feet and he had multiple weapons pointing in his direction, all of them carried by soldiers who had been trained how to use them with some proficiency. He heard the rattle of distant gunfire, all of the soldiers firing in short, controlled bursts and the rear window shattered. He heard bullets pepper the side of the car several times before he felt a sharp pain in his right leg, just as the soldiers disappeared from view. He continued at high speed, not daring to ease off for fear of them following him.

The car was going so fast that he felt the wheels temporarily lift off the road as he cleared the brow of the hill. He hit the peak at about a hundred and five miles an hour, any faster and the car would have tipped in mid-air, but he was lucky and the car landed squarely on all four wheels, bouncing several times on the strained suspension.

The back end began to fishtail and John fought with the steering wheel, only just managing to retain control.

He did not dare pull over to check the wound in his leg as he was expecting one of the army vehicles to come charging up the hill after him, but he eased off slightly for the narrow country lanes.

The soldiers at the blockade were all cursing and swearing, embarrassed at having being tricked so easily. What sort of an idiot opens fire on a bunch of armed men with an automatic weapon and cannot manage to get one clean shot? As far as they could tell, he had not even struck one of the vehicles. Lieutenant Barker became suspicious and decided to check in before sending anyone in pursuit.

"Hello strategic command, this is blockade number 192 on the A23 north of Brighton. We've just had a single Caucasian male in his mid to late thirties open fire on us. He's dressed in light infantry uniform and claimed he was on a top secret mission before opening fire on our position. He is driving a bright red top of the range Mercedes and is carrying a bunch of drugs, please advise; should we pursue and apprehend?" the Lieutenant queried.

"Confirmed, has the target left the quarantine zone?" inquired command.

"No sir, he has turned back into the zone, do you want us to pursue?" asked the Lieutenant again.

"That is a negative, we have a fix on your location and we'll send air support. Have you taken any casualties?" asked control.

"No sir, either he was a terrible shot or he was just trying to create a diversion. We'll stay in position till we receive further orders, over and out," Lieutenant Barker finished.

"What the hell Lieutenant, are they just going to let that guy get away with it?" one of the soldiers asked.

"I think they know who the man is, otherwise they would not be sending air support," the lieutenant answered coyly. "Now get back to your posts; we have a job to do," he ordered.

The disappointed men returned to their posts, hoping that whoever it was would be coming back the same way sometime soon. He would not make fools of them a second time.

John watched his rear view intently, expecting to see the army Land Rovers on his tail at any moment. When nothing appeared to be following, he started to reduce speed and pulled over to the side of the road, which was becoming more of a track by this point. He took the soldier's knife from his belt and cut the material of his combat trousers where the bullet had struck, desperately hoping the injury was not too severe.

After examining the wound, he was relieved to see that the bullet had passed straight though the edge of his thigh and out of the other side without doing any major damage.

It felt like it had clipped the bone on the way through, and his thigh was throbbing painfully, but it was not life threatening, just extremely sore.

He climbed out and limped around to the car boot, retrieving the basic first aid kit. In the middle of the road he dropped his trousers and placed an absorbent pad on both the entry and exit wounds before holding them in place with a bandage. He limped back to the driver's side, examining the bullet-ridden bodywork when he noticed there was something dripping from underneath the front of the car. Kneeling down to examine the damage he ascertained that some sort of lubricant was dripping out which did not bode well for the engine.

"Crap," he shouted, and kicked the car, wincing at the ensuing pain from his wounded leg.

He had about another three miles to go and knew he would not make it very far over the rough hilly terrain on foot without getting his leg properly treated. He hurriedly climbed back in the car, noticing that the engine was idling erratically. He set off steadily, praying that he would at least get closer to his destination, the noise coming from the engine getting worse by the second. He headed for the last portion of hill and crossed his fingers. If he could just make it up this stretch then he would make do with walking the rest, he thought. By the top there was a metallic grinding sound, and a dozen warning lights started flickering on and off on the dashboard. Luckily, according to the satellite navigation system, he only had a few hundred metres until he reached the church and would finally see if his hunch about Gwen and Richard was correct.

Twenty-One

When Michael had first informed Dr Roberts of John's daring escape she was furious and spent the next half an hour speaking to various authorities on the phone to make sure his description was circulated to everyone. She gave them orders to capture and restrain John, even if he had been afflicted; his help would be needed in the near future until the situation was under control.

Later, when she appeared to have calmed a little, Michael took the chance to go and pass her a message he had just received.

"Dr Roberts, we have just received an urgent message from strategic command. It looks like someone answering to John's description was spotted on the A23 near one of the army barricades, just north of Brighton," he told her, hoping the good news would ease her mood.

"Thank God he made it out of the city safely! We need to go and collect him as soon as possible. He is the only one who truly understands Methuselah. What was he thinking trying to escape the quarantine zone? Surely he must have realised there would be precautions in place; he could have been shot," she said, exasperated by John's actions.

"No, the road he took leads up to the Downs and the derelict church where we tracked the phone number we were trying to trace. I think he has gone there to try to find Gwen Taylor," Michael corrected her.

"I thought you said the place was abandoned?" she queried, a little confused that a man of John's intelligence would pursue such a wild goose chase.

"It was. I mean, it is. We've sent two units out there and both report that there is just a church and a graveyard, both of which have seen better days. The good news though is that it is very isolated from any of the major afflicted areas. John should be in relatively little danger, and we know that he is armed with both tranquilisers and live ammunition as he took the soldier's weapons."

Michael said, pointing to the location on the large map they were using to track the progress of the sterilisation efforts.

"Get someone out there as soon as possible, and make sure you take plenty of security. I don't want him, or anyone else for that matter, getting injured," she ordered.

"I have already liaised with strategic command and arranged for some transport and a security detail for protection. The area is a no fly zone, so we are going to have to follow the correct channels, I've been assured it will only take a couple of hours," he told her; it was the first thing he had done upon receiving the news.

She nodded, glad that something was going right. On the table in front of her was a confidential progress report from Parliament. It made scary reading; the village of Lyndhurst in the New Forest had been checked and it was confirmed that there had been attacks that looked like the afflicted were responsible for, although no firm evidence had been found.

Things were also starting to hot up with the UN; European, American, Russian and Chinese governments had combined forces and were now patrolling British boundaries with ships and fighters. A small plane, believed stolen by a young woman, had been shot down mercilessly according to two fighter pilots sent to intercept them. And a Spanish fishing trawler, carrying sixty plus civilians, mainly women and children, had been torpedoed by a Russian nuclear submarine.

Actions by the British government were becoming more direct and brutal. The order to burn the New Forest to the ground, a major ethical and ecological decision, had been given in addition to the destruction of the Brighton quarantine zone. It seemed cruel, but it was necessary. The numbers of afflicted were growing exponentially and the more there were, the bolder they grew. If enough of them were allowed to survive, it would become impossible to prevent them over running one of the barricades, and everyone appreciated that could not be allowed to happen. The one advantage was that decontamination facilities for the public were being pushed through with greater urgency. Not only would it save the lives of thousands of innocent people, it would also prevent more of the afflicted from being created in the first place, hitting the problem from both sides simultaneously.

"Inspector, let me know as soon as the arrangements have been agreed. For the moment Dr Simmons is the single most important man on the planet!" she said, turning to her activity boards to indicate his dismissal.

The decision to destroy the New Forest area had been made for some time before an operator, used to transfer details to the RAF wing responsible for the bombing run, realised that no one had informed Sergeant Davis and his men.

There was a mad rush as everyone began throwing the blame back and forth when the operator interrupted to ask one question, "Is someone going to tell Sergeant Davis that the bombers will be there in a little under thirty minutes, and that they are right in the middle of the attack zone?'

Sergeant Davis had passed the time by drilling the soldiers on the SA80 fully automatic assault rifle. As with most drills, the men were very competitive, desperate to be the fastest in the platoon. They were just cheering one of the corporals for breaking his personal record when the radio began to crackle.

"Sergeant Davis, this is strategic command, do you copy?" asked the voice over the radio.

"Davis here, what's the situation? We are sitting on our hands here" he said, picking up the large handset and holding it to his right ear.

"Sergeant, there have been new orders issued for your platoon. Please withdraw from your co-ordinates and return to base. A bombing run has already been ordered to cleanse your location, please withdraw immediately," the voice ordered nervously.

"Roger strategic command, how long do we have?" Davis asked.

"The attack will commence in thirty minutes, you and your men need to get out of the area by that time. You have been ordered to take the A337 to the northeast of your position as the escape route, that route will be the last location attacked, over and out," the voice responded.

Sergeant Davis dropped the handset and swore at the top of his voice. What sort of idiot leaves it until thirty minutes before an attack to warn troops in the area, he thought angrily as he jumped off the back of the four tonner.

"Right men, we have no time to waste. Pack everything up and make it snappy. I want to be on the road in five minutes," he ordered.

They scattered immediately; most of them had heard the message and no one wanted to be around when the planes arrived. Equipment was haphazardly loaded onto the vehicles, their normal care and precision totally ignored.

Across the square, along the edge of the tree line eager eyes watched with interest as the men scuttled back and forth. The sun was low in the sky, and the edge of the woods was in complete darkness, hiding the hunting party from view.

Helen peered curiously and noticed that many of the men had rested the long objects they were carrying against the vehicles to help them load faster.

Although she no longer recognised a rifle, she somehow knew they were safer while the soldiers did not carry them.

She ducked behind the solid stone wall and ran as fast as she could, hiding from view and headed for the gateway just behind one of the soldiers. Her pack watched with interest as she ran round the outside of the square, keeping hidden behind the low stone wall.

Without making a noise, she crept through the gateway and began to stalk the unsuspecting squaddie, moving slowly towards him unseen. However, the soldier had been in many sticky situations. Suddenly, he froze sensing that someone was watching. He turned and luckily managed to grab his tranquiliser gun when he spotted the naked form of a girl running madly towards him. He dropped to one knee and fired in one fluid motion, catching Helen with the dart just below her left breast.

Furious, Helen snatched the dart out and threw it to the floor, still charging as the chemical entered her blood stream.

She managed to run only a few more steps, each one getting heavier and heavier before she collapsed unceremoniously to the ground, landing straight on her face.

"Hey Sarge, I bagged myself one. Come and look at this," the soldier shouted with pride.

Sergeant Davis glanced over wondering what all the commotion was when he had ordered them to pack up.

Then he saw the motionless form lying on the floor. Sergeant Davies dropped the ammunition can he was loading and jogged over as the soldier turned the naked girl onto her back.

He stared at her and shook his head.

"Good Lord, look at the tits on that!" the young soldier exclaimed as he leaned forward to grope the unconscious girl.

The sergeant's booted foot hit hard him in the gut and sent him flying backwards onto the floor with a surprised look on his face.

"You little prat; one, she's afflicted, so make sure she is unconscious or you are next on the menu, and two, this young woman was, or rather still is, somebody's daughter," the sergeant scolded angrily.

He reached forward and shook the girl quite hard to make sure she was truly unconscious and then reached into his pocket and pulled out his scarf. He poured water onto it from his canteen and carefully wiped Helen's face, revealing a rather peaceful expression on the features of the attractive young woman.

She looked about the same age as his youngest daughter, so against his better judgement he decided to give her a chance. Reaching into his pocket, he pulled out the emergency Acyclovir injection they had all been given and cracked off the plastic top. He raised his hand and jabbed the girl in the thigh with the exposed needle before discarding it over his shoulder.

"Tie her hands and load her into the back of the Land Rover; use the one with the dog cage fitted. That will keep us and her safe," he ordered the downed soldier.

494

"Yes Sergeant," the young man snapped arrogantly, picking himself up off the floor and dusting himself down.

With his ego bruised by his superior, he muttered an obscenity under his breath and gave the sergeant the double 'V' salute before bending down and grabbing the slumbering form under her armpits. He checked round to make sure the sergeant was not looking and grabbed both her breasts, defiantly squeezing them firmly for a second. Satisfied, he dragged her to the Land Rover and slung her roughly into the back, making sure he locked the rear door before returning to his duties.

The watchers stood dumfounded as their unofficial leader was thrown into the vehicle and came to the unanimous conclusion it was time to hunt.

Setting off en masse, the wall of people began running towards the parked vehicles, screaming and snarling like a pack of wild dogs.

Sergeant Davis stopped what he was doing and stared in disbelief at the men, women and children heading towards him and his men.

He knew immediately they were well outnumbered, and there was no time to dig in and fight with these sub-human victims of the epidemic.

He knew what he had to do.

"Everyone to the Land Rovers, now," he shouted at the top of his voice, "do not engage. There are too many of them; we need to get out of here."

He grabbed his own weapon and ran to the rear vehicle where the girl was sleeping peacefully. He raised his weapon and using the telescopic sight, began picking individual targets one by one as his men clambered aboard. Like a true leader, he stayed there until every last one of his men were on board, and the creatures were only ten metres away before he climbed up and slammed the door shut.

"Get us out of here, and make it snappy," he ordered as the crowd slammed against the vehicles, pounding and kicking the armoured bodywork.

Seeing him close the door, the lead Land Rover was already on its way and the second was not far behind. The final one was a little slower to set off but caught up and drove close to the rear of the middle vehicle in convoy whilst they put some distance between them and the chasing fiends.

Gradually, the afflicted slowed to a standstill, watching as their leader and the potential meal escaped into the distance.

As with many animals, if there was nothing to eat, nothing to drink and nothing to mate with they quickly lost interest and headed back into the woods to look for any unfortunate creatures they could find.

It had taken the soldiers about ten minutes to load up the vehicles and stash the girl. After abandoning the four-tonner, the Land Rovers were very heavy and slow to respond. The drivers, professionally trained for any terrain, made short work of the paved roads and were now blasting their way along the A337. They had spotted the bombers approaching about two minutes ago and with less than a minute to go they were still on the outskirts of the target zone. The soldiers sat quietly, some of them praying under their breaths as the drivers coaxed more speed out of the lumbering vehicles.

There were dozens of planes passing overhead and it was not long before they saw the payloads being deployed. The first ones landed and the huge flash of the explosion began repeating itself, growing steadily closer and closer as thousands of incendiary weapons found their targets. At this rate, they only had a few seconds before the advancing wall of flame caught up with them.

Sergeant Davis picked up his radio and urged the lead driver to speed up even more, even though the vehicles were already doing eighty miles an hour. They were not designed for these speeds carrying heavy loads and were rocking quite alarmingly on the suspension with every bump on the surface of the road. Luckily, they were on a relatively straight section of road and were making good progress. As the explosions closed in on their position, the lead driver watched the devastation through his rear view mirror, taking his attention from the road ahead.

Bert had just come from his favourite dog walking spot in the forest. He liked it there because all the paths were nice and level and at seventy-five years old, he was not up for the hill climbing he had enjoyed as a younger man. Monty, his twelve-year-old black Labrador, had also seen better days but he did enjoy a waddle through the underbrush every day.

There had been warnings on the television all day, and even the radio had been telling people to stay out of the forest due to reports there may be some of the afflicted there. But Bert refused to change the daily routine he had followed for the past ten years because of a few rumours. He liked a couple of cigarettes as he walked, something his wife Joan no longer allowed him to do at home. His eyesight had been deteriorating for months now, so he knew he would have to stop soon and should probably not be driving at all. His son and daughter had both threatened to report him to the police if he got behind the wheel one more time, but he knew they would never carry out the threat. The roads round there were usually empty, so he continued to take the risk for now at least, reluctant to relinquish his last vestiges of freedom to age.

The Afflicted

He could see there were vehicles approaching as he drew up to the junction but they seemed a long way off so he began to pull out onto the A337 as he had done a thousand times before. His wife was still the best cook he had ever known, and he was busily contemplating the meal that would be waiting on the kitchen table when the lead Land Rover struck him. Large and armoured, it tore through his car like a hot knife through butter, killing him and Monty instantly.

Sergeant Davis screamed out a warning as he saw the car pull out, but it obviously went unheard as the front vehicle smashed into it, sending a shower of metal and plastic into the air. The second Land Rover smashed into the first a second later. Both vehicles skidded along the road dropping hard into the ditch, the impact causing the generator fuel inside to ignite and explode violently. The two off-road vehicles full of ammunition and grenades went up like one of the bombs being dropped in the distance.

The third driver swerved hard, sending his car into a sideward skid, the chunky tyres digging hard into the tarmac and sending the vehicle spinning over onto its roof several times in succession, throwing the passengers around inside. It slid along on its roof, sparks flying everywhere as it scraped along the road, finally coming to rest against a tree after narrowly missing the edge of a solid wall. Everyone in the car survived, albeit a little worse for wear, and began dragging themselves out of the vehicle.

"Come on, come on, we are still too close to the blast zone, we need to move now!" Sergeant Davis shouted at the confused men.

"What about the girl, Sarge?" one of them asked.

The rear door was pinned against the wall and they could not budge the heavy four-wheel drive.

"There's nothing we can do," Sergeant Davis answered reluctantly and started to run. "Poor little bugger," he said, looking over his shoulder guiltily as they made their way along the road, the wall of flames getting closer every second. The bombs were approaching their position fast, each detonation seeming closer than the last as they neared the edge of the blast zone.

They were close, but not quite close enough as the last of the incendiary devices landed directly behind the fleeing men; flames erupted, coating them in pyrophoric liquid and throwing them to the ground with the force of the explosion, all of them mercifully dead within an instant.

The Land Rover, protected from the flames by the wall, was pushed forward by the blast, spinning the front end round and exposing the rear door. The unconscious Helen slept peacefully in the back, blissfully unaware of her surroundings as the flames leapt up around her, protected from the heat by her metallic prison.

***

The car finally died. A huge cloud of steam erupted from under the bonnet and John knew it was time to walk. He had to admit he was impressed the car had lasted that long given the harsh treatment it had received.

Thanks to the painkillers the pain in his leg had sunk to a dull throb, but he knew he would need to get it looked at if he came through this. Grabbing the weapons, he found spare ammunition in one of the soldier's many pockets and pulled out a fresh magazine. He got rid of the spent one from the rifle and clicked a fresh one into place, cocking the weapon to make it ready for business should the need arise. He slung the heavier SA80 over his soldier and carried the tranquiliser gun ready to use at a moment's notice, although he assumed that he would be pretty safe from the afflicted this far from the city. Cautiously sticking to the sparse cover where possible, John made his way towards the church.

When he reached the decrepit building, John nervously pushed open the ramshackle doors with the barrel of the tranquiliser gun and immediately noticed the footprints in the dust, presumably from the police officers Michael had sent to investigate. He searched the interior from top to bottom looking for any evidence of occupation but it was obvious only a few animals had set foot inside for years. Frustrated, he returned outside and began to stroll around the perimeter, unaware that he had attracted some unwanted attention in his clumsy rooting around.

The woman, if you could still call her that, was in her late forties and had been on her way to go hiking when she had stopped in her car on the way out of Brighton, long before the warnings had become commonplace. Three of the afflicted had caught her unawares and had tried to drag her from the car, but she had fought them off assuming they were car thieves. Racing off, she had managed to get away, but not before being bitten on the hand by one of them. It had hurt quite badly, but she thought nothing more about it, especially as the news of the afflicted hadn't spread at that time. She had simply continued to the isolated car park where she often parked before hiking on the Downs.

The virus had spread, and with her increased heart rate it had finally changed her, causing her to collapse from exhaustion right at the very top of the hill. When she awoke, she felt the hunger like many others but could not make her way back home before the virus finally managed to steal the last remaining dregs of her memory. Since then she had been wandering aimlessly, growing hungrier and hungrier with every passing hour, finding nothing but a few small animals for food. When she saw John, her sub-human instincts kicked in, and she began running towards him, her footfalls masked by the overgrown grass in the graveyard.

John did not see her coming until the last second. Turning to face her, he had been too slow to raise his weapon. The force of her hitting him knocked him to the ground, and he was immobilised as a pain shot through his injured leg, almost causing him to pass out. She now sat astride him, her gnashing teeth inches from his throat as he struggled to hold her off, amazed at the strength of the tiny woman. Slowly, her teeth inched closer and closer until he knew he was done for. Gritting his teeth, he waited for the inevitable pain.

Seconds later he felt the splash of warm liquid hitting his face, and the woman's body went limp in his arms. Opening his eyes, he saw that where her eyes had been was now just a gaping bloody hole and he involuntarily yelled out in surprise. Panicking, he rolled over, threw her body to one side and for the first time noticed the two men staring at him, both of them holding handguns.

He reached down for the tranquiliser gun, but they were too fast for him and both Ben and Jonas grabbed him, picking him up off the ground. They stripped him of his rifle before dragging him towards the front of the mausoleum and the entrance to their secret lair. At the door, Ben dropped him onto his feet and forced his left arm up roughly behind his back as Jonas activated the hidden switch.

"Who the hell are you?" John shouted, trying to break free.

Both of them were taller and better built; he did not stand a chance. He also suspected by the ease with which they handled him that they had some form of hand-to-hand combat training.

"Don't worry about us soldier, worry about yourself. You were just in the wrong place at the wrong time. Now tell us, where are the rest of your men?" Jonas demanded of him once they were safely inside and out of view from any prying eyes. They did not want to attract any further attention by killing him outside and starting a firefight with the armed forces.

"I am not a soldier. I'm Dr John Simmons from Swiftgene. I'm looking for a man called Richard Jennings and a woman called Gwen Taylor," John told them as they forced him to his knees and Ben placed a gun to his head, ready to execute him.

"Did you say John Simmons?" Ben asked, withdrawing the weapon and peering straight into John's eyes curiously. "I know someone who's going to be very surprised to see you if you are," he said, laughing. He dragged John to his feet, this time a little gentler, but still fully restrained.

John suddenly felt a euphoric sense of relief; something told him these were the people Richard had been dealing with and hoped that they would still have Gwen safe and sound. He gave up resisting and went willingly, hoping to be reunited with the woman he had fallen in love with.

"I'm looking for a young woman; she's tall, slim and attractive. Her name is Gwen Taylor, do you have her here?" he reminded them hopefully as they forced him to the hidden door and through to the elevator.

"Yeah, she's here, but there is someone else who will take a great deal of pleasure from finally meeting you. He's quite a fan of your work," Ben said, chuckling as he operated the lift controls.

As they began to descend into the depths, John looked around in amazement and now understood why the police officers had been at a loss.

He would never have found this place in a million years and, unfortunately, that meant that no one who followed him from the emergency centre would be able to either, so he was totally at the mercy of these animals.

Guiding him by the shoulder, Jonas pushed him through the doors at the base of the shaft and into the gleaming white corridor. The size of the hidden facility astonished John.

The strangest thought entered his head as he pictured the dozens of James Bond films he had watched over the years, expecting at any moment for a man in a black eye patch to walk out carrying a white Persian cat. He did, however, understand the trouble he was in; whoever had built this facility was powerful and must have had access to funds he could not even imagine. Jonas shoved him forward and led him to the first door on the left in the corridor straight ahead. He knocked quietly and waited for an answer.

"Yes, what is it?" asked a rather brusque voice from within, "it had better be important, I'm very busy."

"Sir, we have apprehended a visitor who I think you are going to want to meet personally," Jonas said, seeming quite amused by the situation. "We found him snooping around above ground dressed as a soldier," he continued, still not giving away the name of his captive.

"What visitor? Bring them in here!" snapped the irritable voice from within the room.

They shoved John unceremoniously through the door and forced him to kneel on the floor behind the old man in his wheelchair.

The old man operated the controls and spun round to face him, setting his breathing mask down on his lap.

The Afflicted

John stared at him incredulously and a look of pure amazement crossed his face as he gazed at the man he had not laid eyes on for twenty years or more. His face had aged, but it was still recognizable; the one thing that had changed significantly were his eyes. The warm, generous look had been replaced by a cold, steely appearance like that of a large predator for its prey.

"It can't possibly be you. We assumed you were dead after all these years," John said, the contempt on his face clearly apparent as he stared into the eyes of his long lost father, George Simmons.

The man had been a god to him, always there to help with whatever the problem was, from homework to his first forays into the mysterious world of the opposite sex. John remembered the day he had handed him the keys to a brand new Honda Civic, the same car he had kept for all those years. He left without a word a few days later, and they never saw him again. His mother had cried for weeks and had never been the same ever again, becoming a shadow of her former self. All those years mourning his passing turned into a complete indifference to men in general, although she would never hear a bad word about him from John. She scolded him on the odd occasion when his father's name cropped up.

"I'm afraid so John, it's me, but I am just as surprised to see you as you are to see me. You were never meant to find out about me," he said, curiously examining John's face.

He had seen photos of his son, but it took seeing him face to face to realise how much he had given up. He turned to Jonas and barked an instruction.

"One of you go and warn the surveillance team. There is no way he could have found us on his own; he may have back up or been followed at least. I want you to go and double check around up there that there is nothing to give away our position," George ordered forcefully.

"Yes sir, but I have already sent a clean-up crew. There was one of the afflicted attacking him when we went to apprehend him," Jonas answered, looking a little frightened.

The old man was not very tolerant of incompetence, as his predecessor had found out. George Simmons hurriedly moved his wheel chair away from John with a worried look at the blood soaked into his trousers near the bullet wound.

"You fool, has he been bitten?" he said, looking at the blood soaked bandage on his thigh.

"No sir, I was there. We got to him before he was bitten; the wound was already bandaged. I think it's a gunshot wound; from what I have been hearing on the military frequencies, he was shot at by the barricade patrol," the man answered, backing off slightly.

George rolled forward again and resumed staring at the man in front of him, noting how much his son's eyes reminded him of the wife he had been forced to abandon.

"I suppose you have one or two questions for me?" George asked, his voice lower and a little kinder.

"How? Why? I mean what are you doing here? You left without saying a word; if you were alive and well, then how come you didn't get back in touch?" asked John, examining the twisted malformed body in front of him.

Warped by some disease of the spine, John assumed.

His hands were also twisted, with painful looking nodules and they seemed quite debilitating when he moved his fingers.

Without the electrical motors driving the wheelchair, the man would not be able to move.

"I had a new life, one you and your mother had no business becoming involved with," he replied with a hint of regret.

"Surely you could have contacted her, just to let her know you were alive. She died inside the day you left, you inconsiderate bastard," John shouted, attempting to rise to his feet.

Jonas rushed up behind him and pressed him back to his knees. His grip was strong, and John was in no condition to resist.

"John, my life is a long and tragic story, something we may discuss at a later date, but if you want the short version, here goes. I worked for the government as an industrial espionage agent responsible for searching out and eliminating threats. They sent me to infiltrate a top secret organisation known as 'The Establishment' and made up of some of the world's most powerful and influential people. They were responsible for controlling and manipulating the stock markets, especially the life cycle of certain profitable drugs. They would steal new discoveries, preventing their release and ensuring longevity of the existing market. That way, there was always a revolutionary drug in the pipeline somewhere to make them lots of money. I managed to break into their ranks and, for a while, we managed to pick off one or two of their smaller players, the main men being too far out of reach even for us. Unfortunately, my cover was blown, but because of my distinguished career in pharmaceutical circles, they attempted to recruit me. At first I refused, preferring to die rather than give in to them, and that was when they threatened you and your mother. They had found my Achilles heel, and I had no choice. They forced me to leave the pair of you, never to return, to remove me from our government's radar. Since that day, I have always made sure that you were both safe from the shadows, but I was never able to re-join you. So you see, I had no choice, and your mother knew it. I told her everything before I left, but part of the agreement was that the two of you would always be looked after," he explained, a solitary tear running down his cheek as he recalled that painful moment two decades ago.

The truth sank in and John realised his feelings of hate had been based on a lie.

No wonder his mother had always defended her missing husband and never remarried. He was starting to feel sorry for the man when he remembered the actions taken by Richard, whom he now knew had been working for his father.

"If all of that little sob story is true then how could you have allowed the outbreak to happen? You are the one responsible for spiking my work with that horrendous virus. Because of you, thousands have died already, which will become tens of thousands by the time we get a handle on the situation. That is if we ever do; do you know how difficult it's going to be to eradicate a virus that is coded to target every living thing on the planet larger than a microbe?" John asked venomously. "All that because you and your friends want to make a quick buck. You make me sick!" he continued, angry again.

Jonas pushed him back to the floor, and this time his wounds began to bleed more freely, disturbed by the exertion.

He grimaced, watching his father.

"Firstly, the virus I used is a minor strain of a low grade blood disorder. At worst it should have just made the test subjects ill and lose a bit of weight, enough symptoms to stop you from going any further. We never expected it to mutate thanks to the curative properties of Methuselah, and you can thank that moron Jennings for covering up the rat's escape. Secondly, I may have been forced to join but once I was in the inner sanctum I began to understand what they were about and I actually agreed with their ideals. Modern companies are now manufacturing wonder drugs and giving them away free to third world countries, where is the profit in that? Despite the effort that goes into creating new medicines, various governments are now restricting the amount spent on drugs, forcing companies to kill their research budgets and halt the discovery of new and wonderful cures. We're trying to prevent this, because if they succeed, pretty soon the large pharmaceutical companies will fall, the economy will suffer and God help us if some new superbug appears; we won't have the trained people to deal with it," George explained, obviously fully convinced that his views were sane.

The Afflicted

There was some truth to what he was saying. In Britain especially there had been a downturn in new drug production for the very reasons he had mentioned, but none of it was a good enough reason for the man's actions.

"How can you possibly think that? As a species we have to help those who can't afford it, it's what makes us human. Besides, your actions this time may have cost you dearly. Those people dying out there, they cannot buy your drugs; in fact, they can't buy anything!" John retaliated angrily.

"Wrong my dear boy. The Establishment has the majority of shares in most of the major antivirals on the market, Acyclovir being only one of many. We also have major stakes in the inoculations market; can you imagine the demand for those products now? Thanks to the mismanagement of Methuselah by Dr Jennings, we have opened up a market containing billions of frightened people and tens of billions of animals, both food stock and pets. Now that we have Methuselah, we have a more privileged customer in mind. We can sell the pure form for hundreds of millions to the select few wealthy enough to afford it. They would become the elite of society, super fit, super strong and with vastly extended life spans. When you have that sort of money, the only thing you are short on is time. I'm sorry if it means your career, but I am willing to sacrifice your

513

insignificant career to fix this," George continued, pointing to his wasted physique.

"After everything that has happened, I cannot believe you and your friends are still thinking of profit. I accept that you couldn't have predicted the mutation, but you kept quiet once you realised, you and your dogsbody Richard Jennings. As far as I'm concerned, you're both just a pair of dirty rotten murderers and I will do everything in my power to make sure you pay for your crimes," John threatened, this time throwing every ounce of effort into climbing to his feet.

John pushed backwards against Jonas, knocking him off balance, and this time Ben had to rush forward as well and grab him. It took both men to restrain him, forcing him face down on the floor. The bullet wound was severely aggravated, both sides splitting open under the bandage and blood began haemorrhaging onto the pale woven rug where he lay. The old man looked on in dismay as his expensive hand woven acquisition began to turn a nice shade of crimson.

"Get him out of here and get that leg fixed up. I do not want him harmed though; he may not like it but he is my son. There may be hope for him yet," he shouted at the two men as John continued to struggle.

He turned and wheeled himself over to the ornate looking desk before turning to speak one last time.

"And when you're done get someone in here to clean that up!" he ordered, pointing at the priceless Persian rug.

John was picked up bodily and half-dragged, half carried back out into the corridor and towards the large double doors leading to the lab. One of them leant against the doors to open them while keeping a tight grip on John's still struggling form, dragging him over to one of the specially designed restraint tables. They lifted him onto it and quickly secured him firmly in place with the leather straps. Once they were fastened, John realised he was not going anywhere and decided to save his strength, taking the opportunity to take in his surroundings. That was when he spotted the two forms hanging upright in the middle of the room, both unconscious now.

When he saw that Gwen was covered in dried blood running from her chin and down her chest, John finally knew despair. It looked like she had bitten someone, and that could only mean one thing; she had succumbed to the bloodlust. He barely felt the scratch as a thin-faced woman injected a small amount of clear liquid into his arm.

"Don't worry Dr Simmons, it's just a little sedative to calm you down while I take a look at your leg. Please try to remain still," she instructed him, starting to cut away the rest of his trouser leg to get to the blood soaked bandage.

John ignored the woman and fought to remain conscious.

"Gwen, try to focus on my voice. What have they done to you, are you still coherent?" John shouted, his eyelids beginning to feel heavy from the sedative.

He fought to keep them open and watched her briefly raise her head.

"I love you, I am so sorry," she said, the sound barely escaping her lips before she sank back into oblivion.

Tears began to form in John's eyes as he watched her collapse; too weak to fight the effects of the tranquiliser she had been given. He felt the woman begin to clean his wound before he too succumbed to the darkness. The last thing he remembered was the sound of the woman's voice as she examined the wounds.

"Ooh, that is quite nasty isn't it," she said in a matter of fact tone and started to prepare a laser cauteriser.

Twenty-Two

Michael Devon watched fascinated as the RAF Lynx helicopter began its descent to the far end of the car park at Swiftgene, aiming for the makeshift helipad they had cleared. It had barely touched down when one of the occupants sporting a khaki helmet jumped out and headed towards them, ducking his head to avoid the spinning blades despite being well above his head.

"Dr Roberts, we have the location and description of Dr Simmons, do you have any special orders?" the soldier asked, handing over a wad of documents containing his orders.

"Yes, consider this man the most important person alive. He's the only one who knows anything about the disease and he's your number one priority. Use any force necessary to capture and restrain him, but no harm should come to him, even if he's afflicted. If he was correct, there might be a Dr Gwen Taylor and a Dr Richard Jennings there. If possible they are to be taken alive, but be aware, the female is known to be afflicted so don't risk any of your men. We have reason to believe there may also be another unknown contact there. Whoever they are, they must be apprehended, alive if possible, but whatever happens they must not escape. Do you understand?" she instructed them, returning his written orders.

Listening to her cold instructions and how she had just ordered them to actively destroy a target rather than let them escape, Michael stepped forward.

"I think I would like to go with them, just in case. A familiar face may help to placate John when we find him; I'd rather not see him harmed," Michael requested, looking expectantly at the little woman.

"Good idea Inspector, in fact why don't you take one of the MPA doctors just in case he's hurt? In addition, they will be able to treat Dr Taylor before she is returned to the facility if they find her. Dr Simmons is going to be a lot more cooperative if she's safe," Dr Roberts agreed, covering her eyes against the debris the helicopter was throwing around.

Michael grabbed one of the doctors, explaining the situation briefly as he dragged the young man behind him towards the chopper. He pushed him inside, climbing up behind to join the ten heavily armed men already secured in the rear. They were dressed in black with no insignia or rank, and he did not have to be a rocket scientist to realise these were the SAS, Great Britain's elite fighting force and the most highly trained soldiers in the world. Their faces were covered with balaclava masks designed to protect their identities, and Michael suddenly felt a whole lot safer with them in tow.

There were also four heavily armed RAF personnel in the back, and one of them helped him and the doctor into the sideward facing seats. His buttocks had barely touched metal when the ground outside seemed to drop away rapidly, as if the earth were falling away from them. Michael took a deep breath and grabbed the seat harness nervously, ensuring that it was still fastened as within seconds they were already tens of meters in the air.

He tried to speak to one of the RAF guys, but all he could hear was the steady 'Phwut, Phwut, Phwut' of the blades and the roar of the powerful Rolls Royce engines.

One of them reached into the cockpit and grabbed a headset to hand to the inspector, indicating he should put it on.

"We are heading for the blockade first Inspector Devon, sit back; we will be there in about fifteen minutes," said the pilot through the headset, briefly turning to look at Michael so he knew who was speaking.

"Why so long, the church is only ten to twelve miles away?" Michael asked impatiently; they had already wasted enough time waiting for the transport.

"Airspace is severely restricted at the moment, so we have to follow the given flight path to ensure we are not intercepted by the fighter patrols. Don't worry, if your man is there we will get him out safe and sound," the pilot reassured him.

Michael glanced back at the special forces personnel, all of them staring forward without a hint of emotion and he sat back, relaxed. There was nothing he could do but wait; if they were not safe with these men then who would they be safe with?

***

An hour later, the woman had returned and injected him with what he guessed was some form of stimulant. Ben, Jonas, Dan and David, the old man's bodyguards, had all untied him and escorted him to a small room filled with dozens of flat screens showing scenes from around the complex.

Four of them were showing the interior of a rather strange looking room that his father had constructed especially for his experiment.

The Afflicted

The room was large, approximately twenty metres in length by ten metres wide. The walls, ceiling and floor were covered in a strange padded material. At each end of the room sat an enclosure built from iron bars at least three centimetres thick stretching from floor to ceiling. In one enclosure sat Richard, who had just started to come around and was shaking his head trying to clear the grogginess. In the other stood Gwen; normally tall and beautiful, she now looked wild, her face drawn and pale. She was dressed only in her underwear, her face and chest stained with the remnants of the perverted little technician's blood. Her attention was focused on Richard as she remained stationary holding onto the bars with a look of hatred for her counterpart so strong that it would stop a charging bull elephant.

When the technician had first switched over to the view John had gone mad, struggling and swearing until George ordered the nurse to sedate him just enough to calm him down. He wanted his long lost progeny to witness the results of his work first hand.

Richard climbed to his feet, wobbling a little as his co-ordination returned, a fuzzy feeling in his head from the high doses of tranquiliser he had been fed. Despite the grogginess, he noticed that he actually felt quite good, strong and powerful. His shirt had been removed and he could see the vast difference in his normally flabby physique. He was actually about four inches taller, and the fat had entirely gone from his body, revealing new enlarged muscles.

He smiled to himself appreciatively and flexed his now enormous arms, the biceps rising into solid humps. It appeared that Dr Simmons' formula was everything they thought it would be and more. He had never felt so strong and fit in his entire life having never had the inclination to exercise, preferring the pursuit of money instead.

Across the room, he noticed Gwen staring at him through the bars of her cage with a murderous look on her face, her lips turned up in a feral snarl. Her body had changed too. The soft, welcoming curves he had lusted after had been replaced by a muscular physique, and it appeared she had grown an inch or two as well.

Apart from her facial expression, she seemed to be relatively calm, but Richard could not tell if she was entirely in control of her actions. He knew there was a good chance the affliction could have taken hold by now, and she would be a powerful adversary. He tested the bars and felt how solid they were; even with the enhanced strength he now possessed there was no way he was getting through them. The lock, however, looked a little more fragile, but before he tested it, he decided to assess her mental condition. He was not going near her if she was going to try to kill him.

"Gwen, I am going to try and get us both out, are you hurt in any way?" he shouted across to her.

Her reaction to his voice was instantaneous; she leapt onto the bars, placing her feet against them and shaking the enclosure violently with her whole body, snarling and screaming like an animal.

"It looks like I am on my own then, doesn't it?" Richard shouted at her, wondering if she even knew what he was saying.

He stepped back into the cage and faced the door. He rushed forward and kicked the lock plate with as much force as he could muster and was surprised to hear something crack inside the lock. He repeated the action again, and his enhanced strength added so much more force than a human being could normally manage. The mechanism in the lock shattered, and the door swung violently open, clanging against the cage bars. Free, Richard ran over to Gwen's cage. Standing just out of reach he began mocking her, pulling faces and dancing, watching her violent reaction as she tried to reach him from within her enclosure.

"When I get out of here, you crazy bitch, I am going to find a tranquiliser gun and come back and give you what I promised," he said, grabbing his groin and thrusting himself at her, laughing cruelly.

Gwen raged, throwing herself at the bars physically and reaching between them to try to grab any part of him, her hands just falling short of his dancing form. At that moment, Richard with his improved hearing heard one of the cameras above the cage whirring as it turned to follow him.

Distracted for a split second as he looked up at the ceiling, he lost concentration.

Gwen, taking advantage of his mistake, crammed as much of her body as possible through the gap in the bars, extending her reach just enough to be able to grab his arm. Richard looked in fear as her fingers closed around his wrist, and she dragged it through the bars using both arms.

Richard could not believe her strength; she was not as large as he was, but she had pressed him into an awkward angle against the bars and he couldn't get the required advantage to free himself, so he began to scream. He felt her twisting his arm back until there was a sickening pop as his shoulder dislocated.

Now in a lot of pain, he was even less able to move and watched in horror as she sank her teeth into the exposed part of his neck that she had squeezed between the bars and drank deeply.

He could feel his strength waning as the life giving fluid flowed into her mouth as she sucked noisily. He felt her grip loosen slightly as she drank, but it was enough and he yanked forward with all his strength, pulling himself free.

She sensed his escape and dug her teeth hard into his neck, the momentum of his body tearing a huge strip of flesh free.

Richard dropped to the floor screaming and tried to stem the flow of blood that, to his amazement, began to stop quickly as his advanced healing kicked into action. Angrily, he grabbed his dislocated arm by the wrist and pulled his joint back into the socket. He felt it pop and a sharp pain shot down one side of his body. The heavy clotting his body produced had almost stopped the flow of blood to his neck, and he felt the pain subside in his damaged shoulder joint. He turned to her cage, this time standing well back for his own safety; he was not going to make the same mistake twice.

"You bitch; you're going to pay for that. When I get back, I'm not just going to have my fun; I'm going to kill you, slowly and painfully," he shrieked at her.

Having received the blood it needed, Gwen's body was already absorbing the required nutrients and her coherence was returning. She wiped the back of her hand across her blood soaked lips and smiled at him sweetly.

"I told you if you ever touched me again I was going to kill you," she told him coldly, still smiling, the blood making her look slightly insane.

Now in control of her faculties she too had spotted the weakness in the construction of her enclosure.

Richard watched as Gwen began to pound on the door, each blow shaking the door violently. Having fed, her strength was much improved and Richard knew that despite her smaller size, she would soon break free. He did not want to be present in his weakened state when she did. He ran to the main door leading out of the room and noticed the lock was the same type as that on the cages. He kicked it with all his strength, buckling the metal with the first strike; a second blow snapped the retaining mechanism and the door swung out into the corridor.

Bidding for time, he forced the door shut behind him and grabbed a stainless steel trolley, forcing it against the door and wedging it beneath the handle. He grabbed anything he could get his hands on and soon had a pile of furniture spanning the entire corridor, utilising the structural strength of the wall opposite to block the doorway.

Once he was free, he glanced around him until he found the camera he knew would be watching his escape.

"Now old man, I am coming for you!" he threatened, shaking his fist at the camera before jumping up and tearing it from the ceiling.

Hidden away in the surveillance room everyone was staring, shocked by the display of strength from the pair of them and the gruesome attack. The old man's face was white with fear as he realised it would be almost impossible to stop the monster he had created.

"How could he do that? Those cage doors were designed to hold a four-hundred pound silver back gorilla, it just isn't possible," stammered one of the technicians, pushing away from the screen as if Richard could climb out of the image.

George Simmons turned to his bodyguards and pointed to the door.

"I've seen enough. Get out there and put him down, do you understand? No tranquilisers this time, just kill him!" he ordered, almost frightened out of his wits.

Jonas and Ben un-holstered their handguns and nodded, smiling. Dave and Dan kept a tight grip on John's arms as he looked at the screen and began to laugh at their predicament. They too drew their weapons, just in case.

"We need to get into the lab; the doors are specially reinforced. That room used to be the main food storage when this facility was a fallout shelter during the cold war," George ordered, pushing the controls on his wheelchair and grabbing his oxygen mask at the same time.

He vanished through the open door with the others hot on his heels, and John was forced to follow by the remaining two bodyguards. In the corridor, the booming sound of Gwen beating against the door where she was trapped could be heard reverberating through the entire facility. They rushed into the lab and Dan immediately shoved the long metal latch beam into place across the doors and through the pre-fitted rungs. He began to drag anything he could get his hands on in front of them to barricade the doors further.

John watched with amusement and laughed at their efforts to protect themselves; as far as he was concerned, they were all about to get what they deserved after what they had done to Gwen. The woman he knew would never have been capable of performing the heinous attack he had just witnessed without their intervention. He just hoped she was not beyond saving when all this was over.

Richard glanced up and down the corridor and listened. His hearing was hypersensitive, and he quickly detected two sets of footsteps approaching his position. He flattened himself against the wall and sidled along, remaining just out of sight until an arm appeared around the corner carrying a gun. He grabbed the arm and forced it down with so much force that the ulna and radius bones in the forearm shattered, and the gun dropped harmlessly to the floor.

As Jonas screamed out in pain, Ben spun around the corner, pointing his weapon directly at Richard's head and pulled the trigger. Richard was no longer there; in a burst of inhuman speed he ducked under the man's arm then grabbed Ben by the scruff of his shirt. He ran at the wall, carrying Ben's substantial weight as if he were a child, and rammed his body hard into the reinforced concrete.

Richard felt the sickening crunch as the bones in the man's ribcage cracked inwards, spearing his internal organs and killing him instantly. He released him and Ben's body slumped forward, falling heavily to the floor, the life crushed out of him.

Jonas, now cradling his injured arm, was attempting to climb to his feet when Richard spotted him and kicked him hard in the face. The force of the kick snapped his head back violently, shattering four of the vertebrae in his neck and severing the spinal cord. Just like his friend, he slumped to the floor dead.

Amazed, Richard held his hands in front of him, examining them carefully, barely able to comprehend what he was capable of doing with his new found strength.

"I'm unstoppable," he muttered arrogantly to himself, still staring at his outstretched hands.

Remembering where he was, his focus returned and he glanced round the corner to check for further pursuers. When he realised the corridor was clear, he headed in the direction the men had come from. He knew who had sent them and had his own score to settle with the man.

***

The helicopter was almost at the abandoned church when the pilot saw something below them pushed into the foliage in an attempt to conceal its presence.

"Inspector, we've spotted Dr Taylor's car abandoned about half a mile away from the church," the pilot told Michael.

"I can't see anything," Michael shouted into the headset as he tried to peer through the side window, "Can you see any sign of Dr Simmons?"

"Negative. There's no indication of anyone down there other than the car itself," the pilot answered.

They drifted over to the church itself and there was still no sign of anybody anywhere.

"Do you have thermal imaging on this bird?" Michael asked.

"Yes sir, switching over now," the pilot replied, operating several switches at the side of the glowing screen on the dashboard.

The picture of the scene below vanished and a myriad of reds, yellows, blues and greens appeared on the screen.

The dark surface of the church was clearly visible being the coldest structure around, but there were no telltale red signatures to suggest there was a human down there. The pilot drifted slightly, changing the view on the screen and the picture changed as well. There was a large, faint yellow trace about fifty metres behind the church in the graveyard.

"Inspector, we have something unusual, but it's not a person," said the pilot, pointing at the screen.

"What is it?" asked the inspector, peering over his chair to see the image.

"It looks to me like there is something below the mausoleum that is generating quite a lot of heat for us to be able to detect it through the ground. Either the South Downs have suddenly become volcanically active, or there is some sort of manmade structure below the ground. It looks like Dr Simmons' hunch was correct," the pilot declared.

"Okay, take us down; let's have a proper look around," suggested the inspector confidently.

The helicopter began its descent and the soldiers immediately began releasing their restraints. As soon as the helicopter touched down, they piled out and formed a perimeter, weapons trained in all directions.

"Right guys, I want you in two squads; one to protect the civilians and the other to protect the chopper. We have no reports of the afflicted at this location, but there is still the possibility there may be enemy personnel below ground. Remain vigilant!" one of them shouted, the commanding officer Michael presumed, but he could not see which one it had been.

***

The dying screams of the two men could be heard in the lab as Richard easily despatched them.

"It looks like you've done it this time, haven't you, Dad? It looks like Richard Jennings is not too happy with you. I'm sure he will understand that you only did it for money when he finally finds you," John taunted his father, who was sucking noisily on his oxygen supply.

"Shut up!" George suddenly snapped at him, "he may be strong but he can still be killed. My men have guns, and if he gets through that door he's a dead man."

Almost on cue, the doors began to bow inwards as Richard pushed against them from the outside.

Everything went quiet for a few seconds until, unable to shift them, Richard must have found something heavy as he began to pound on the solidly built steel doors.

Every blow shook the doors and dust began to rain down from the ceiling, the barricade sliding back a little each time.

Dave gave his gun to one of the lab technicians, instructing him to keep it pointed at John and went to help Dan who was now putting his entire weight against the slipping furniture.

By now, everyone's attention was on the doors and they were all trembling with fear, except John. While they were not paying attention to him, he slowly slid his feet across the floor, edging himself over to the bench where he could see the two weapons he had brought with him.

It was obvious by now as the doors buckled that they were not going to hold for much longer; even the furniture had been almost entirely shoved to one side. A couple more blows and the raving mad man outside would be through and free to rain terror on those inside.

"You two, get ready to take a clean shot as he comes through," George ordered, wheeling backward as far away as possible from the entrance.

Totally ignorant of the fact that John had moved several feet away, Dan and Dave grabbed their weapons and took aim, waiting patiently for a clean shot.

In the specially prepared room, Gwen had finally managed to shatter the lock to her enclosure and was now banging against the outer door, her strength returning bit by bit as her body absorbed the blood she had just drank. Thanks to the improvements Methuselah had imparted, Richard's blood was four times as dense. Filled with modified blood cells capable of carrying much greater quantities of oxygen in each cell, part of the reason for his improved physical abilities, it had the benefit of giving Gwen a lot of energy and the materials she required to replenish her failing circulation. She banged harder and faster on the door and realised Richard must have barricaded it from the other side. She could hear him ranting and raving further away in the facility and she began to worry about John; John, who had risked his own life to come and save her. She mentally crossed her fingers and hoped that he had not seen anything of her actions. How could he ever look at her the same way again if he had? Even now, she was saturated with blood and realised that she would be a frightening sight to anyone she met.

Finally, the laboratory doors buckled inwards. All they saw was a flash of motion as Richard grabbed first one door then the other, throwing the huge steel structures into the corridor. They each weighed over three hundred kilograms and Richard tossed them aside as if they were tissue paper. The two bodyguards opened fire immediately but could not get an accurate shot as Richard criss-crossed the entrance. Out of nowhere, the dead body of Jonas came flying through the air, striking both armed men simultaneously and knocking them to the ground. Without a second's hesitation, Richard rushed in like a steam train and snapped their necks like twigs, kicking the handguns to the back of the lab.

The lab technicians tried to run, but he was too quick for them. He had not forgotten the way they had spoken to him while he was secured to the table. He literally tore them limb from limb where they stood.

George operated the wheelchair's controls and headed for the corridor in an attempt to make it to the relative safety of his office and the secret escape route he had constructed, unknown to all the other staff at the facility.

Richard stepped in front of him and stopped him dead in his tracks, holding the chair in place with his huge muscular arms.

"You're not so tough now without your armed guards, are you old man?" he said, bending down and peering at the him with an evil, self-satisfied grin on his face, relishing the fact that the tables had turned so dramatically from only a few hours ago.

John stood nearby and, despite the fact that he hated both men, he could not stand by idly and watch his father get hurt.

"Richard, you need to calm down and think about what you are doing. Let's hand him over to the authorities, I will explain that you were forcefully experimented on," John pleaded as Richard taunted his father.

He did, however, continue to sneak slowly towards the two weapons.

"Ahhh, Dr Simmons, you must think I'm stupid if you expect me to hand myself over to the authorities. I am sure they are aware of my part in all of this thanks to you. But don't worry, I haven't forgotten the part you and your slutty little girlfriend have played in my predicament, and I will deal with you both when I'm finished with this piece of detritus," he hissed back at him without looking round.

As Richard focussed his attention on his father, John began to move a little quicker, although still cautiously, towards the weapons. He knew the lightning fast Richard would be on him in a second if he sensed any danger.

"Dr Jennings! Richard! Look, we got off to a rather confusing start. I'm an exceptionally wealthy man with a great deal of powerful contacts. If you choose to forget what has happened here then we can still come to some sort of arrangement. Just name your price and I will make sure you get it," George pleaded as Richard grabbed hold of both arms of the wheelchair and began to lift it from the floor.

"Problem is old man: I don't need a single thing from you any longer. I also have a full set of John's notes and am perfectly capable of manufacturing the serum myself, which means I will not have to share the profits with you or your organisation. I also know that you have my money here, and I would guess a little more of your own stashed away for a rainy day, so I will be adequately compensated for my time here," he said, laughing in the face of his terrified foe.

Richard lifted up the wheelchair in front of him without an ounce of effort and held the old man out at arm's length. He began to spin round and round as if he was preparing to throw the hammer at the Olympic Games. The old man screamed, his voice making weird echoes in the lab as he spun faster and faster.

Without warning, Richard let go of him.

George and the wheelchair went flying at great speed, landing against the far wall with a sickening crash. The old man dropped to the floor amidst the wreckage of his wheelchair, still coughing and gagging. Richard was about to turn his attention to John when the old man, crushed but still alive, raised his body up using his arms and tried to drag himself forward.

"Son, you have to help me, please John!" he pleaded pathetically, blood pouring from a deep laceration above his eye.

The man was already dead; his body just had not accepted the fact yet.

"Son? You mean you're John Simmons' father! That's perfect, I'm going to take a lot more pleasure from this than I thought," said Richard as he walked over to the dying man.

Richard raised his foot above the man's head and brought it down with such force that his victim's skull exploded, splashing brain tissue and blood several feet in all directions. He then threw his head back and started to laugh. The Methuselah may have amplified his speed and strength, but it had also enhanced his capacity for cruelty.

"Now that was an interesting sensation, you ought to give it a try," Richard said, turning to face John.

John had reached the weapons and his hand was well within reach of the pistol grip of the SA80. He felt as if everything was in slow motion when he lunged for the weapon as Richard simultaneously began running towards him. He pulled the trigger as he raised the barrel, hoping the safety catch was still off and, luckily, bullets began to fly towards the approaching monster. The weapon struck the floor a few times before finding its target and ten of the rounds ploughed into Richard's legs and midriff before the firing pin stopped on an empty chamber. The force of the impacts knocked Richard's legs from under him, splattering the floor behind with his blood. His body slid forward with momentum, but it did not stop him. As if he did not feel the pain, Richard began to climb to his feet and John dropped the rifle, reaching for the tranquiliser gun. Richard screamed like an animal and rushed forward yet again, slowed only slightly by the bullet wounds.

Enraged by the pain, he held his hands out in front of him at the same height as John's throat, meaning to throttle the life out of him.

His hands closed on John's throat so hard it felt like someone had clamped his neck in a bench vice and his eyes began to bulge in their sockets.

Richard pushed his face right up to John's and snarled.

"Now that wasn't very nice, was it?" he asked sarcastically.

Richard did not see that John already had his hand behind his back or that he had drawn the tranquiliser gun slowly round until it was pointing directly at his groin.

John prodded Richard with the barrel to alert him, his finger firmly on the trigger.

"Let me go, or you can say goodbye to the boys," John coughed, tapping him between the legs as a reminder.

Richard released the pressure and a concerned look spread over his face. He did not know the limits of Methuselah, but he doubted that it could grow him a new set of genitals.

"Come on John, I was only joking. You and me are friends, we go way back," he pleaded nervously, his eyes transfixed on the barrel hovering around his nether regions.

These were only tranquiliser darts but they were projected using ultra high-pressure compressed air. At that proximity, the force would shred any soft tissue near the barrel. Richard began to back off slowly and John followed, keeping the gun pressed tightly against its target.

"I heard what you said to Gwen in the other room," John said, smiling menacingly.

He had not forgotten the threat Richard had made, and he was going to make sure that he was not capable of carrying it out. Richard saw the expression on John's face and, realising what the man was planning, he began to reach for the gun. John was too quick for him and pulled the trigger hard, firing several darts in quick succession. The force at that distance threw Richard backwards onto the floor, but not before turning his reproductive organs to a pile of mush and injecting him with an exceptionally strong dose of tranquiliser. Unfortunately for John, the chemical took time to work and Richard was back on his feet immediately. He grabbed John by the throat and by his belt before lifting him high above his head. He threw him with every ounce of effort his tranquilised muscles could muster, sending John's helpless body flying through the air and out through the doorway of the lab. John landed heavily on top of one of the broken doors, and a fragment of twisted metal pierced his back, sticking straight into his left lung and causing him to start coughing blood. He watched satisfied as the blood dripped from Richard's groin as he approached. Methuselah was good, but not that good; even Richard would not manage to grow those back, he thought, gloating.

"See if you can abuse Gwen now, you sick bastard. You will never know the pleasure of another woman for as long as you live," John said, laughing, the pain causing him to cough up more blood.

Richard, fighting the effect of the drugs, reached towards him and bent over his prone form, pulling back his fist to land the killing blow. John closed his eyes in anticipation and waited, satisfied that he had at least messed up the one thing that made Richard a man.

"I'll teach you not to steal my girlfriend, you whining piece of shit," said Richard as he punched down with all his force.

John, with his eyes still closed, felt the man's weight disappear from his body and opened his eyes to see what had happened. In front of him stood an infuriated woman, above her head the struggling form of Richard Jennings held at arm's length. Using all of her strength, she bent his body in half, the cracking sound as the vertebrae shattered clearly audible, echoing gruesomely around the walls of the corridor. She tossed his body to the floor, and John could see the surprised expression still frozen on his face where he landed.

"I told you before, you piece of scum, I'm not your girlfriend!" she hissed aggressively at him and kicked his crumpled body clear across the corridor.

Gwen's eyes were manic, and for a moment John wondered what she was about to do. He was not worried; he had done what he had intended to do, and if nothing else, she would survive. She dropped to her knees beside him and her eyes softened, instantly filling with tears.

"John, please don't die. You have to stay with me; I love you," she begged, tears rolling down her cheeks as she examined his body.

She leant forward and kissed him on the lips, holding his hand delicately in hers and sobbing.

"Don't worry about me. I have done what I came here to do. Look in my pocket; there is a bottle with a strong dose of acyclovir and tranquiliser. Inject yourself with it and you'll be fine," John told her and then collapsed back, beginning to fade.

"No! Come on, you can do it," Gwen screeched, searching for a pulse and finding a fading beat.

She reckoned without hospital care he would be dead within ten minutes, and she looked about frantically. Knowing that there was nothing she could do,

Gwen reached into his pocket and pulled out the drugs he had brought especially for her.

He had known she was infected and given his life to save her, she thought, staring at the vial.

She took one of the needles, injected the whole contents of it into her leg and then threw the bottle angrily at Richard, who had used her as a guinea pig.

Gwen closed her eyes, then realisation dawned on her.

"Oh my God, I'm so stupid. Methuselah!" she suddenly screeched, jumping to her feet and fighting the effect of the tranquiliser.

She rushed back into the lab and over to the fridges, pulling the doors open one by one until she found the right one. She snatched the bottle with the remaining uncontaminated Methuselah and ran back to John. By now, she was starting to feel very lethargic as the tranquiliser took effect, but she forced her eyes to stay open and drew the sample into the needle.

"Hold on John, this is what you need," she said, sobbing desperately.

She carefully found a vein on the side of his neck and, still struggling to stay awake, she injected the clear liquid into him.

Twenty-Three

It hadn't taken the special forces long to blow the front door and even less time to work out how to get to the elevator room behind the wall. There were six of them with Michael and the MPA doctor, and they were in full attack mode.

"Sir, I suggest we use the stairs; the elevator will give up our element of surprise," suggested one of the soldiers. Michael knew it was not the commander as he recognised his accent was Welsh.

"Agreed, what do you think, Inspector?" the commander asked.

"You're the expert. You and your men lead, the doctor and I will bring up the rear." Michael answered, his heart racing as adrenaline pumped into his bloodstream. "Move out!" the commander ordered, directing them with a wave of his hand down the stairs.

Without another word, the soldiers began running down the steps, each of them taking them two at a time, and although he kept himself in shape, Michael soon found himself out of breath. He managed, however, to keep up and he was right behind them when they reached the doors leading into the facility.

"Remember, we need Dr Simmons alive at all costs, and I would like the same for Dr Taylor if at all possible, so use your tranquiliser guns," Michael iterated.

The commander nodded and each of them slung their submachine guns around their backs and grabbed the hand pistols containing the darts. These were not as accurate as the rifle form but were easier to use in an enclosed space, and after all, these were SAS. Each of them reached into their belt holsters and grabbed handguns loaded with live ammunition as well. They were willing to try sedating the victims, but if things went wrong they wanted the reassurance of a proper weapon. Using a series of hand signals, the commander gave his men orders and they rushed into the corridor beyond.

As they stepped into the corridor, they saw the blood soaked, semi-naked form of Gwen leaning over John's immobile form, and all of them recognised her from the photos they had been shown. When she spotted them, she tried to rise to her feet to speak but the soldiers hit her simultaneously in the stomach and chest with six tranquiliser darts. On top of the tranquiliser she had already taken it was too much for her body, and she crashed face forward to the floor.

As the soldiers spread out to check for survivors, Michael rushed over and felt for her pulse, wondering if she would survive with enough tranquilisers to knock out a fully-grown rhinoceros running through her body. She opened her eyes for a second and squeezed his hand.

"Save him, please," she said, before sinking into deep unconsciousness.

***

Bob Newing was driving along the A336 when he saw a strange sight by the edge of the road. The girl looked like she was completely naked except for a long camouflaged jacket. She had no shoes on, her matted hair looked horrible and it appeared as if she had been sleeping rough. He pulled the lorry over to the side of the road and got out to speak to her, cautious in case she was one of the afflicted they had been talking about all over the news.

"Are you alight, my love?" he asked nervously as she approached.

"I'm not sure; can you tell me where I am?" Helen asked timidly, "I don't remember how I got here."

"You're just outside Southampton, love. Where are you from?" he asked, pretty sure that she could not be one of the afflicted by her nervous disposition.

One of the first things they said to look for was the inability to speak and aggressiveness and this girl was showing neither symptom.

"I'm from Brighton, but I must have been in an accident because I've just woken up in the back of an army Land Rover. I don't know how I got there or what I was doing because I can't seem to remember anything. Can you help me, please?" she pleaded pitifully.

"Of course I can love! Come on, I'm going into Southampton now and I can drop you off at the police station. I'm sure someone will have reported a pretty young thing like you missing," he said kindly, placing his arm round her shoulder and leading her to his lorry.

He helped her climb inside and then walked round the front of the vehicle, staring at the towering column of smoke and flames from the forest.

"Poor little bugger," he muttered under his breath.

***

John opened his eyes slowly, the illumination in the room seeming a little too intense despite the drawn blinds. He wondered where he was, and then he heard a sound and a sigh escaped his throat.

"Hello, sleeping beauty," said a familiar voice beside the bed.

He turned his head and there she was; Dr Guinevere Taylor, the woman he had risked his life to save. She was beautiful, her face no longer drawn and haggard, her perfect blue eyes twinkling. He tried to sit up in bed, but his head began to spin and he flopped back down against the pillow.

"You stay where you are. I'm not letting you move a muscle until the doctors tell me that you are one-hundred percent well," she threatened, pressing down gently on his shoulders and holding him on the bed.

She leant forward and kissed him passionately, stopping only to whisper in his ear.

"They told me what you did and what happened to you by coming for me. I'm so sorry for putting you through all that just for me. I cannot express how much I love you, John," she said ever so quietly, making sure the others nearby could not hear.

He smiled at her and nodded, realising that at no point during the last few days had it occurred to him that giving up on her was even an option.

"Where am I?" he asked, finally breaking from her gaze and peering around the room, noticing the walls were actually made of fabric, tent fabric to be exact.

"It's alright, you're safe at a decontamination unit just outside the quarantine zone," she assured him.

He struggled and tried to sit up, looking frightened.

"My God Gwen, you can't be out here. If they find out you're afflicted they will shoot you on sight," he said, panicking and trying to get out of bed.

Gwen pushed him firmly back onto the bed and another person appeared in his peripheral vision.

"Not any more, thanks to you," said another familiar voice moving closer.

Michael walked over and grabbed John's hand, shaking it enthusiastically, but John just looked at him confused.

"John, you took the Acyclovir to her. She took it immediately, and she's now alright," he explained, but John still looked confused.

"That may well be, but the antiviral takes several days to work properly, and she could be contagious for longer than that," he warned.

"John, she was; in fact, we kept her quarantined at her own insistence for a week. You have been unconscious for over a fortnight, and you were lucky to survive. Thanks to Gwen's quick thinking, however, you did; you both owe each other your lives," Michael told him.

John began to relax and looked curiously at them.

"How did I pull through? I seem to remember having a large chunk of my father's facility jutting through my rib cage" he asked, intrigued.

"Simple," said Gwen, "you saved yourself, really. I gave you the uncontaminated Methuselah remnants from the lab, and when they got you back to Swiftgene, I instructed them to dose you up with five times the amount Richard used on me. They gave you the Acyclovir a couple of hours later to counter the virus, by which time your body's healing processes were in overdrive," she told him, smiling.

"What about the quarantine zone, how is it going there?" he asked curiously. The last he had heard they were exterminating almost everything that moved.

Gwen and Michael shared a knowing glance wondering whether he was strong enough to hear the news.

"I am afraid it was a total loss. The government stepped in and levelled everything. They have poisoned all the wildlife and everyone infected has been exterminated," Gwen replied, the sadness apparent in her eyes.

"There is, however, one bit of good news I'm sure you will be happy about. Brian Travis's girlfriend, Helen, was found wandering around just outside the New Forest over a week ago. It seems from her recollection that a kindly soldier took pity on her and gave her the anti-viral. She is now one hundred percent recovered, and the two of them were reunited," said Gwen, knowing the trouble John had gone through to treat Brian after he was infected.

Andy Strutt

The inspector and Gwen sat with John and discussed the situation for a couple of hours before finally
leaving him to get some rest. He lay picturing the destruction in his head and made a decision; there was no
way he would be able to continue with his line of work
ever again. The risks of genetic manipulation were just
too great a price to pay.

***

The manor house looked dark and menacing as the
black Rolls Royce drove up the tree lined drive. A small
figure sat in the back, her face obscured from view by
the darkened privacy glass fitted around the passenger
compartment and the hooded cloak she wore. She felt
nervous because she would be meeting an important
person from The Establishment. To her, they were a
series of electronic voices on the end of a telephone
line. When the car pulled to a stop, the door opened
and she was ushered through the imposing entrance of
the mansion by a group of dark suited men wearing
earpieces. They hurried her past the centuries-old por-
traits strewn across the walls and led her to a pair of
antique double doors. As they approached, both doors
opened to reveal a huge library, lit only by the flickering of a log fire in a grand Victorian fireplace. In the
centre of the room was a collection of large, luxurious

leather chairs arranged in a semi-circle. An important looking man or woman sat in each, all staring expectantly at her. She approached them nervously and stood surrounded by rows and rows of ancient books worth millions in today's market.

"Have all copies of Dr Simmons' work been secured or destroyed?" asked a large framed man in the centre of the group, his voice deep and authoritative.

"Yes, we've confiscated all his work from Swiftgene, his flat and the copies placed in the safe by Richard Jennings. Any records taken as evidence by the police have 'mysteriously' vanished. The only place where the research exists that we do not control is in the head of Dr Simmons. He, however, has made it perfectly clear that he refuses to continue with his work following the outbreak. I think we can rest assured that he's not a threat," she assured them.

She waited patiently as the group discussed the situation quietly amongst themselves, occasionally glancing in her direction. She gazed around the room curiously while she waited, amazed by the grandeur and impressed by what she had heard: that the library contained the greatest collection of rare books in the world.

"Is there any evidence other than rumour and supposition that could link 'The Affliction' back to The Establishment?" the large framed man asked.

"No sir, we're safe. I have dealt with it personally. All leads point to Dr Jennings and Dr Simmons senior. The police believe they were simply committing industrial espionage and neither of them will be talking," the woman replied ironically, as both of them were dead.

"What about the serum, did we manage to salvage any of it?" he asked optimistically.

"No, I am afraid that because of the contagion Dr Taylor insisted all the remaining samples were destroyed. Dr Simmons senior used the pure sample, originally intended for you, for his own personal experimentation. I think his intent was to produce more so that the theft was never discovered," the hooded woman assured them.

She had personally witnessed the destruction of the material at Swiftgene but had been unable to secure a sample.

"Thank you. I think it's time my friends and colleagues were made aware of your identity. I think you have a bountiful future ahead of you," the large framed man instructed.

She pulled back the hood and Dr Roberts, the head of the MPA emergency response team, nodded to each of them in turn.

"Dr Roberts here has been an invaluable asset to me over the years and will continue to be for a long time to come. Here we have a small token of our appreciation;

I'm sorry that we can't talk longer, but we have some rather urgent business to discuss, please excuse us," the large framed man said, handing an aluminium briefcase to one of the bodyguards, who took it over to Dr Roberts.

Realising she had been dismissed, she turned and followed her escort back through the house. Now they had introduced her to the inner sanctum, she knew that she would be all right. They admitted few into their ranks; after all, that group of people controlled more money than many medium sized countries.

In the library, the inner sanctum of The Establishment continued their discussion on Methuselah.

"Dr Simmons is correct; Methuselah must never be made available to the masses. The world would not be the same if it were full of super-humans; I mean, how would we, the elite, stand out as special?" the large framed man told his colleagues.

"Has the new facility been built to produce Methuselah in small amounts for us and our wealthier clients?" an elderly woman asked, her body ravaged by the rigours of age.

"Yes, the facility is almost complete; we will soon be able to approach our clients. At a price of one billion dollars, I think the returns should be healthy, but we have to make sure new identities are used. After all, we cannot have the richest men and women in the world suddenly growing younger overnight, can we?" the large framed man laughed.

"What about Dr Roberts? Was it wise to reveal ourselves to her, especially as she has knowledge of Methuselah?" the old woman queried.

"Oh, don't worry about her my dear; I've taken care of that little problem already," the large framed man said, holding up a little black remote control.

He pressed the button and outside they all heard the unmistakable sound of an explosion. All of them burst out laughing.

***

Over two weeks had passed and Brighton was a changed landscape. Where period buildings and seaside attractions once stood, blackened rubble lay for miles in every direction. Khaki clad men worked in shifts, sifting through the rubble and disposing of the thousands of dead bodies in trucks piled seven or eight high with layers of corpses.

These ferried back and forth twenty-four hours a day, moving their gruesome cargos to the dozens of portable incinerators around the city.

Occasionally, they found one of the afflicted hiding in some darkened crevice, but the orders were simple: destroy on sight. Those that did crawl out were already weak from starvation and did not put up much of a fight.

The government hastily built a huge permanent wall around the entire circumference of the quarantine zone, with animal traps and guard towers positioned regularly along its entire length. Here, they were a little bit more understanding of the afflicted as they could be tranquilised with the Acyclovir-tranquiliser mix without risk to anyone else.

They moved survivors to decontamination camps, and they treated every one of them with the anti-viral just in case, as well as inoculated.

In the rest of the country, people were inoculated as a precaution. Despite the efforts to destroy the virus, the government realised that even one stray creature could start a new outbreak, and they could ill afford to extend the international quarantine. Treatment centres were in every town, immunisations were used faster than they could be produced and riots were commonplace. Slowly but surely, the country was getting back on its feet, but there was still a long way to go.

But Great Britain remained under international quarantine. Diplomatic relationships with the rest of the world had been severely damaged and would remain so for years to come. For the first time in centuries, humanity had pooled their resources against a common enemy, a wonderful achievement for humanity. That was unless you lived on a small island just across the English Channel from France!

The End

During the preceding two weeks rat Number 20 had stayed hidden, venturing out only at night and then only long enough to hunt. Her hunger was so great now with the pregnancy that she did not just drink her victims' blood, but consumed the entire body; bones, flesh, skin and all. This in itself helped her to stay alive as she was not spreading the infection and drawing attention to herself. Her body was huge, her abdomen distended and swollen, her pups almost ready to be born.

When the fires came, she had run with all the others, but her large body hampered her movements and she found a dark, warm hole to curl up in and die. During a particularly powerful explosion, her hiding place had collapsed around her, dumping her into an old forgotten drainage tunnel. She had followed it for miles underneath the destruction above until it exited into an abandoned mine shaft deep in the South Downs. Exhausted and hungry, she had found somewhere to hide. Prey was scarce there, but enough to keep her going for the time being.

When the time came, she found herself a nice warm, dry shelf in the tunnel and settled down to give birth. When the pups came they were enormous; two males and a female, all three times larger than a normal baby rat and unusually well developed, almost self-sufficient from the womb.

As soon as they exited, they nuzzled her and found her waiting nipples to suckle. Her instincts told her she would need to hunt soon if she was to sustain three such as these. A pain wracked her chest as they drank, followed by another, then another. She looked down in dismay as the blood ran from the holes where here teats had been. Her brood had certainly inherited her thirst and, already exhausted, she felt her strength slip away as her bloodthirsty spawn devoured her alive.

When they finished, the three of them began the long, slow climb out of the ancient shaft, and a new smell assailed their nostrils as they breached the daylight.

A field of white fluffy creatures spread out for what appeared to be miles. Young and small, they settled back into the shaft to wait for the night. They would emerge when the creatures were asleep, instinctively

The Afflicted

knowing the creatures would resist less when they were asleep.

***

John and Gwen sat in the garden of her luxury house in Worthing, the sun beaming down on a wonderful autumn day.

"Can you believe how nice the weather has been lately?" she asked, reaching over and grasping his hand.

He turned over on his side and rested his weight on his elbow, smiling down at her.

"And I intend to make the most of it," he said, leaning over and kissing her tenderly.

She pushed him off playfully, "Steady on tiger, we have neighbours; and besides, I'm hungry."

She climbed to her feet and walked into the kitchen. Grabbing a jar from the fridge, she fished out a gherkin and munched it thoughtfully. Watching John through the window, she smiled; it was good to see him finally happy. She put down the jar and thought how much of a taste she had developed for the tiny pickled cucumbers in the past few days, wondering if it was a possible side effect of the antiviral.

Inside her body, a tiny embryo throbbed as the beginnings of a strong heartbeat pulsated through it.

The unformed embryo had attached itself firmly to the uterine wall and happily absorbed nutrients. Deep inside its body, tiny alien particles floated through its system, destroying blood cells almost as fast as they were absorbed through the placental connection with its mother. Its mother's treatment with the antiviral had not penetrated the protection afforded by the placental wall. Its enhanced DNA had already adsorbed some of the intruder's DNA into its own genetic code. It slept peacefully, unaware of the changes currently underway within its tiny body.

"Do you ever worry that those men your father worked for are out there as we speak, manufacturing more of the Methuselah serum?" she asked, lying down beside him on the picnic blanket.

John stared at her lustfully; she was on a new low protein diet and her subcutaneous fat had started to reappear, returning her feminine curves. Add that to the fact that Methuselah had increased his libido tenfold, and he found himself unable to keep his hands off her.

"No, I know they aren't," he said with some conviction, running his finger down her exposed back, pausing at her bikini fastening.

"How can you be so sure? Those men were ruthless" she challenged, wriggling around as she tried to shake his hand free, giggling manically.

"Because the formulae and the gene locations were never written into my notes. They were in my private notebook, and no one else knows that it even exists except you!" he told her confidently, finally managing to untie her bikini and pulling it from under her.

"John, don't you dare," she screamed playfully, getting up and attempting to cover her ample breasts with one hand and grab at the dangling bikini top just out of her reach.

He ran off through the patio doors with her hot on his heels, the pair of them laughing hysterically as they ran. Not paying attention, John slipped in the front room and fell, splayed on the floor allowing her to catch up. She jumped astride him as he turned over and attempted to liberate her bikini top. Failing, she held his hands to the floor and stared sternly at him.

"Say you're sorry and give me back my clothes, you rogue," she teased.

The sight of her unfettered breasts and the feel of her sitting on top of him were too much, and he began to get excited once again. She felt the growing pressure underneath her as he flipped her onto her back and removed her bikini bottoms.

"You really don't need any encouragement, do you?" she said, leaning forward to kiss him, succumbing to her own growing excitement.

Within seconds, they were making love for the fourth time that day, both of them having developed the sex drive of a nymphomaniac rabbit thanks to Methuselah.

Across the adjoining yard at the back of the house, the upstairs curtains twitched as they withdrew the lens of a telescope. The two people inside watched with interest as the couple frolicked on the floor of the living room.

"Can you believe that they're at it again?" one of the men asked the other.

"Oh, let them enjoy themselves; after all, they haven't got long. We're going in tonight," the other one answered, opening his suitcase on the bed.

Inside, a collection of high-powered rifles and ammunition were spread in smaller connectable parts. He began removing various items and clicked them together to form the body of a high-powered submachine gun. The Establishment scientists had failed to reproduce the serum correctly, and the authorities were not happy that they had been deceived.

John Simmons was about to find out that nobody escapes The Establishment!

THE AUTHOR

Andy Strutt was a former scientist whose love of the written word propelled him towards writing 'The Afflicted' within twenty-six days. He entered the novel in a competition and was shortlisted and that encouraged him to take writing as a full time profession.

Andy lives in Worthing, West Sussex with his wife and children.

Acknowledgements

I am indebted to the staff at Arrow Gate Publishing Ltd for their patience in going through my novel. I am grateful to my editors, Erika Sanger and Chloe Pilsbury - whose professional attitude shone through as they read my massive manuscript and their constructive comments.

I am immensely grateful to my family and friends, especially my wife Narissa for her love and patience as I wrote this novel.